ETERNAL SOUL MATES

A Paranormal Love Story

By

Vini de Pristi

PublishAmerica
Baltimore

First printing

At the specific preference of the author, PublishAmerica allowed this work to remain exactly as the author intended, verbatim, without editorial input.

ISBN: 1-4241-1252-4
PUBLISHED BY PUBLISHAMERICA, LLLP
www.publishamerica.com
Baltimore

Printed in the United States of America

Acknowledgments

I should like to thank my husband George, my daughters Saskia, Aida and Tosca as well as my friends Kat and Les, Vickie and Dave for their believe in me and their constant encouragement.

Vickie and Dave, I hope and pray that you are happy in the world you have entered not too long ago. I shall see you again. Godspeed…

WHAT IS DEATH?

Death is nothing at all. I have only slipped away into the next room. I am I and you are you. Whatever we were to each other, that we are still. Call me by my old familiar name. Speak to me in the easy way which you always used. Put no difference in your tone. Wear no forced air of solemnity or sorrow. Laugh as we always laughed at the little jokes we enjoyed together.

Play, smile, think of me, pray for me. Let my name be ever the household word that it always was. Let it be spoken without effect, without the trace of a shadow on it. Life means all that it ever meant. It is the same that it ever was. There is absolutely unbroken continuity. Why should I be out of mind because I am out of site?

I am waiting for you, for an interval, somewhere very near, just around the corner. All is well.

Harry Scott Holland
1847-1918
Canon of St. Paul's Cathedral

FOREWORD

As uncomfortable as the thought of our death might be to us, we all will face our last moment in our physical surroundings at one point. As comforting as reading the bible and practicing their faith may be to some; In a world that is constantly changing and progressing, many more want real answers and facts about the realm that is considered 'The Unknown'. Knowledge is being vastly increased today in science and technology in all fields as medicine, physics, chemistry, biology, astronomy, communications, mathematics and countless others.

Merely religion singularly is trying to maintain the stationary position, which was established two thousand years ago and earlier yet. Any change in these concepts is considered sacrilegious or even blasphemous. Surrender of these doctrines and views long held as the word of God is therefore taken as an admission to loss of faith and punishable by loss of salvation in the hereafter. Faith, has been stressed as all that is needed for salvation. There is no doubt to the existence of the higher power and spirit of creative force we call God.

However, in a world, where weapons of mass destruction and even technology are threatening the very existence of mankind and are used against us by misguided individuals, we have to strengthen faith with undeniable facts and assure ourselves and the generations to come, to the reality and far reaching consequences of justice, punishment and reward for our deeds in the life to come.

1. What is the other side like?
2. Is it really possible to communicate with the other side?
3. Are you not afraid if spirits?
4. Is there really life after death? How can you be so sure?
5. Are you not just delusional and make it all up in your mind?
6. Why can't *I* hear any voices?
7. Is it really true, that physical contact between a 'living' person and a 'spirit' person is possible? If so, how is it done?
8. I can hear my grandmother, but how can I be sure it is really *she*?
9. I did have an out-of-body experience and it scared me. Why was I so scared?
10. I would love to communicate with the other world, but I am afraid of it. How can I get over my fear?
11. Are there really devils and demons?
12. What happens to babies and children that die and go to the other side?
13. I saw my aunt and she was much younger then when she died. Why is that?
14. Does anybody work over there or do they all just sit around like on a long vacation?
15. If they have music, do they have concerts and such?
16. I enjoy cooking. Will I still be able to cook when I die and go to the other side?
17. My step dad abused me, when I was younger. Will I have to see him again?
18. I always wanted to travel and see the world. Can I still see the world when I am on the other side?
19. My adopted son is terribly deformed and mentally retarded. Will he be normal and in a different body when he dies?
20. My husband was my life and my joy. I feel he is my soul mate. Will he wait for me on the other side?
21. Do people get married on the other side?
22. Can people have children on the other side?
23. My baby died at birth. Will he recognize me later on as his mother?

24. We took dad off life support. Is he ok and did he forgive us?

25. When I was a kid, I used to kick our cat a lot. He was vicious and used to bite people. Will I get punished for it?

26. I love animals and I had a beautiful dog, named Dracula. Will I see him again in the other life?

27. Are there insects on the other side? The reason I am asking is because I hate spiders.

28. Do people hit and be nasty still in the after-life? And how do they get punished?

29. Do people have houses or apartments over there?

30. If people still have sex over there, do they still have the same feelings?

31. If the people over on the other side have a body of energy, where do the saliva and other body secretions come from? I can't imagine myself with a dry mouth for eternity.

32. Where do the little kids go when they die and their parents are still alive?

33. My son got killed in a shooting. Is he a restless spirit or is he ok?

34. I work in a lab and do a lot of research. Is research still going on, on the other side?

35. If the other side is so perfect and all knowing, what is the sense of existing there?

36. I used to think that life after death is all a bunch of crap. After my heart attack I changed my mind. I saw the other side and didn't want to come back. Why was I sent back?

37. I was in an accident and was dead. Then I came back and told my wife and doctor, what I experienced. They don't believe me and my wife thinks a have gone nuts. It changed me and I am a whole different person. How can I make my wife believe me?

38. My son almost drowned and told me a story, which I had a hard time believing. That was many years ago and after reading your book, I asked him more questions. I was surprised that he told me many things, which you wrote and he told me that it's true. He also told me, that his sister, whom he never knew, saved him. She died before he was born. Is his sister his guide or are there others with my son also?

7

40. The Ouija board scares me. Is there another way to communicate with the dead?

41. I do like to swim and dive. Is this still possible in the after-life?

42. Are there really Angels and what are they made off?

43. What do all the doctors and nurses do in the dead world? If there is no sickness anymore are they not bored out off their minds?

44. I love to paint. Can I still do that then and sell my work? How will I get paid for my work?

45. What is to become of all the sex-offenders? What if they go near the little kids over there?

46. Are there prostitutes in this other life?

47. I didn't believe in any of this life after death bull until my wife had a coronary. She told me what I was wearing while sitting in the hospital room. My shirt had a stain from the coffee and she saw it. How is that possible?

48. My brother is blind and had to have surgery. He died for a few minutes and then was resuscitated. I was astonished to hear him say, that I might look better with my beard. I had shaved it off, the morning he was to be operated on and he could not have known. How could he see me?

49. Do the people over on the other side wear the same clothes for all eternity?

50. Can I meet some famous people over there, like Elvis and Caesar or Cleopatra etc. and are they still dressed like in their time and days?

These are merely a fraction of the questions, which have come to my office and landed on my desk via the Internet. As I said before, to believe or not to believe is entirely up to the reader's discretion.

INTRODUCTION

A second chance was all I wanted. However, I never would have thought in my wildest dreams, that there is indeed something to the old saying, 'be careful what you are asking for, you might get it.'

Ever since my trusted friend Robert, who is one of the elders in our community approached me with the matter, I was excited. Anxiously I waited as the time drew near to the day, on which the little girl was to be born. What an honor it would be, to guide and guard a new life to adulthood, so she would become a valuable member of human society.

I was prepared for it and was carefully trained for five long years, to become her guide. It was made clear to me to never interfere in her life and to stay out of sight, no matter if she made errors in judgment or not. I found out right then, she certainly would have a mind of her own.

She was supposed to be arriving on April 21. She didn't wait that long. Her rather noisy entrance into the world was made on April 14th. After a short warning sign, which we might call labor for nature's sake, she had sent her mother running for the bed. I, on the other hand, experienced something I thought might never happened to me again. I broke out in a cold sweat.

Watching her being born is something I shall never forget, as long as I exist. I was moved and strangely touched by this new and wonderful miracle of life. Nevertheless, she seemed not at all impressed by being slapped on her little bottom and it was obvious, what she thought about it? Evidently outraged and protesting loudly, she made it clear to the doctor that she was not to be treated in such fashion. The expression on the doctor's face was priceless and he almost dropped her in total surprise.

Not even a minute old and she made me and a few other people laugh. However, the doctor was not amused and cussing under his breath he left to change his soaked clothes.

With big eyes she gazed around as if she wanted to ask, what all the fuss was about. Not long thereafter she was sleeping like a little angel her tiny fists pressed against her rosy cheeks and making soft 'baby noises.'

Where had all this time gone? As if it was just yesterday, I remember her first steps, her first day of school. How is it possible, that this little girl is so grown up and for the 999th time is trying to get herself into trouble?

Once again, her immeasurable inquisitiveness is getting the better of her and I must interfere to save her from harm. I know I am not supposed to do this, but...! This is how it all began...

CHAPTER 1

Some Toys Are Just Too Much

"Mother, what are you doing?" asked Ruby.

"I am talking to someone," Martha answered with a smile.

Disbelieving, Ruby stared at her mother Martha. 'How can this be?' Ruby asked herself, 'Has mother suddenly gone crazy?' She couldn't see anybody else in the room, besides Martha. The phone was on the other side of the night table—untouched—.

Before entering her mother's bedroom, Ruby had heard her mother talking and laughing. Now, there was nobody else in the room.

"Who exactly are you talking too, mother?" Ruby asked again.

Smiling, Martha answered,

"To a spirit."

"Oh, good heavens, mother," Ruby exclaimed, throwing her arms up in exasperation. "just tell me one thing, how do you talk to spirits and how do you expect me to believe such nonsense?" Ruby asked shocked and looking at her own mother as if she doubted her senses.

"Come over here and I will show you," Martha said chuckling and shaking her head at her daughter's obvious doubts.

It was then that Ruby saw what looked like an ordinary thin wooden cutting board lying on her mother's bed. However, printed on this board were the letters of the alphabet from A to M, and from N to Z, in two rows in a slightly circular pattern. Beneath the alphabet were the numbers from 1 to 0. The top left corner of the board showed a smiling face of the sun and the word "yes," printed next to it. At the right top corner was a waxing moon, a star and the word "no" next to it. Below the row of numbers were the words "good bye".

Not even trying to hide the biting sarcasm in her voice Ruby drawled,

"Oh, great, and this piece of wood is indeed talking back to you?"

Ignoring the acid in Ruby's tone, and chuckling softly, Martha responded, "Why don't you try and find out for yourself. I'll show you how to do it; it's really very easy. Here, you take this and hold it over the board."

With that, Martha handed Ruby a ring pendent on a small gold chain.

"Hold the ring very still over the board and ask a question," Martha instructed her skeptical daughter, "you will see the ring move from one letter to another, forming words and words will become sentences. Try it, you might like it." Getting up from the bed, Martha looked over he shoulder,

"In the meantime I'll go downstairs and make us some coffee. I have the special feeling that this will be a long and revealing afternoon for you my dear."

Martha left the room still chuckling and humming a happy tune. Flabbergasted, Ruby sat on her mother's big bed. There was no expression or remotely any explanation for the feelings, which were surging through Ruby at that moment. She knew that her mother had not had a contented life, particularly with a husband who was alcoholic. But the thought that Martha would allow her own senses to be corrupted so completely was somewhat unsettling.

Perhaps she could prove Martha wrong and convince her that there was no such thing as talking to ghosts in reality. No, she had to convince her mother that there was no such thing as talking to ghosts. The little hobgoblins were only in her mind and of her own making.

'My gosh', Ruby thought, 'mother was always a down to earth person and now she has lost it completely. What am I supposed to do now? Should I indulge her and play along for a while? If she can see, that nothing is going to happen when I pick up this stupid ring, she might realize that she was wrong. I just don't know, how long this is going to take. However long it will take, I have to try.' Ruby decided. Eventually, her mother would come back down to earth and just be normal again.

After all, Ruby knew that there were no ghosts and spirits. Though she had heard stories from the old people even in the country she grew up in. She remembered when she was a child and her aunt Hilde told her a particular story, which happened during World War II. Aunt Hilde's husband Karl Weiser had been drafted and was a navigator on a German submarine. For several long weeks, she heard nothing from him.

Then one night she went to sleep and suddenly awoke with a start. There had been a strange light in her bedroom and a figure stood by the foot of her bed. The figure was somehow illuminated by this light and looked lovingly and smiling at her. She recognized her husband and thought she was dreaming. Then the figure seemed to be receding while the light around him seemed to go dimmer. The figure grew smaller and smaller until he had vanished into the darkness. Aunt Hilde had jumped out of bed and turned on the light. By now she had realized, that she had not been dreaming at all and she knew in that moment, that her husband had been killed, which the telegram she received the next morning confirmed.

However, this had been only a story, her aunt had told. As a child, Ruby had been fascinated and had believed every word of it. Well, she had also believed, that the stork brought the babies to the mothers and that Santa brought the gifts on Christmas. Her sixth grade classes in biology enlightened her way of thinking at the age of twelve.

Catching her grandmother wrapping a Christmas present disillusioned her at the tender age of nine. Still, she had been told, that Santa was getting too busy and had agreements with mothers and grandmothers to help his elves. Another two years had passed, as Ruby became aware of the stores selling the presents. Grudgingly, grandma had admitted, that there was not really a Santa.

The idea had been taken over from a very rich Nobel in Turkey. His name had been Nicholas and at Christmas time he had bought gifts for the little children in his village to place them in secret at the doorsteps of the houses or drop little bags with money down the chimneys. Sometimes he snug into the houses and stuck little gifts into the stockings, which were hung by the fireplaces to dry.

At that time Turkey was known as 'Myra' and Nicholas was the child of a wealthy family. Unfortunately, his parents had died when he was very young and orphaned; he was raised in a monastery. He must have been a very smart fellow, for he became a priest by the age of seventeen. He had been a kind man and enjoyed bringing a little happiness to the needy, especially little children. He became a bishop and that's why our Santa Claus is wearing a bishop's hat and a staff. Over the years, the red cape was replaced by some cultures with a red suit. Only after his death was he elevated to Sainthood. Since the Germans celebrate Saint Nicholas day on the sixth of December, it was assumed that he had been born around this day many centuries ago in around 300 AD.

Ruby had finally accepted this explanation as a logical one and from then on had realized, that everything in this life must have a logical explanation.

If her mother believed in ghosts, there must be some reasonable explanation also. The ring in her mother's hand had moved and had swung over the board seemingly on his own accord. Ruby knew also, that wishful thinking and fooling one self into believing certain things might be the simplest explanation for her mother's thinking. Though fascinated as a child by ghost stories, Ruby knew for certain that she was not a child any longer and things like that did not exist.

One lives ones life and dies and everything is dark and over with and that's the end of it. 'All right', Ruby thought, 'I will show mother that this is only in her mind and a figment of her imagination. I will hold this ring over the board, just like she did and nothing will happen.'

Hearing her mother coming up the stairs, Ruby braced herself. Martha entered the room with the freshly brewed coffee she had promised and filled the two cups on the tray with the hot aromatic liquid. She put two lumps of sugar and one teaspoon of cream in one cup, which she handed to Ruby. Ruby thanked her mother with a nod and took a sip.

"Now mother, for your sake I'll try this once to show you that this is really nonsense. Here look, I am holding the ring right over the board and there will be no answer at all." Ruby had picked up the ring and trying to hold it very still over the 'magical board', asked out loud,

"Is there anybody, who wishes to speak to me?"

The ring kept hanging very straight and motionless suspended on the thin gold chain, and just as Ruby was starting to say,

"You see mother it's not moving," suddenly…as if this ring on the gold chain had taken on life of it's own, it started swinging. Ruby followed it with her eyes to the letter -y-.

Swinging in a different direction, the ring motioned to the letter -e-. Changing ever so slightly, the ring came to a stop over the letter -s-.

'Now this is curious', Ruby thought. My own mind is playing tricks on me. I just might have to do the whole thing one more time to demonstrate that it was perhaps the movement of my own hand, which let the ring swing to these letters and spelling out -yes-.

Changing her posture and supporting her arm with her other hand to hamper any movements; she smugly smiled while she was asking,

"Who is talking?"

—There!—. The ring was moving again. The first letter was -M-.

The second letter the ring swung over was -I-. Letters -C- and -H- were next. Then -A- and -E-, stopping on -L-.

Peculiar, this was strange, but how on earth did she come up with the name M-I-C-H-A-E-L-. Ruby now started to get worried about her own sanity. Incredulous she looked at Martha, who was leaning with an amused smile on her lips against the headboard of the bed.

"No, this is just not possible," Ruby uttered. Her mind was reeling.

"I don't even know a Michael except from long ago a little schoolmate. How on earth did I come up with that name?"

"Ha ha, sweetheart, I think in time you'll understand that there is a lot more then hot and cold air in between heaven and earth. Right now I have to get going to pick up James from work. So, why don't you have some more coffee and try not to analyze everything so scientifically.

17

You are a real doubting Thomas my girl.—Believe—! I'll be back in a little while, see you later."

Taking her empty cup, Martha got up from the bed, and left the room. For a moment Ruby sat very still. She heard her mother noisily closing the front door. She heard the engine from the station wagon, as well as the sound from the tires rolling over the gravel in the driveway as Martha pulled out. All those familiar sounds seemed comforting to Ruby and yet deep inside she was afraid that this daily routine would change somehow.

If she would pick up this ring again, who would know what would happen next. She realized suddenly, without really knowing why, that nothing would be the same. In a last desperate effort to prove her mother, and now also herself wrong, she slowly picked up the gold chain with the ring on it. Then not believing herself and her own stupidity, she jumped up from the bed and threw the ring on the board.

"This is absolutely ridiculous," She shouted angry, "no intelligent human being would ever believe such nonsense." Her face turned from a mask of anger into a sudden surprised realization and as a mischievous little smile formed around her lips, she giggled,

"I almost fell for the little prank mother tried to play on me."

Her mother's room was very hot, since the knob on the heater was stuck and she was not able to turn the heater down, the small table fan had been going.

Thinking and trying to figure out a way of how she would pay her mother back in kind, Ruby sat back on the bed again. Almost without thinking, and the smile still on her lips, Ruby's hand playfully picked up the ring and held it over the board. It moved rapidly rushing from one letter to another. Ruby could only stare in astonishment, viewing this board and the swinging ring. When the ring came to a halt, she let out the air that had accumulated in her lungs. She was not aware that she had held her breath. There it was.—A whole sentence in her mind.

"Are you afraid of me?"

Even the little fan could never spell out a whole sentence, which would make sense. Ruby knew that she was certainly not talking to herself. So what in all the Saints name was going on here? How was it possible that there was someone speaking to her? Shaking her head in the negative, she answered out loud:

"No I am not afraid. But where are you? Who are you? What the hell are you?" Still holding the ring, Ruby's eyes followed its motions to spell out an answer she had not expected.

"Please, one question at the time."

"Okay," Ruby said, lifting her eyebrow skeptically: "Where are you?"

"In another dimension." Ruby swallowed and asked,

"How did you get there?"

"I died."

'All right, that does it', Ruby thought, 'not enough, that mother is totally of her rocker, now some damn screwball ghost or whatever it was, is talking to me from the grave. How did I get myself into that!' Out loud however she asked,

"When did you die?"

"A long time ago." Not stopping in his movements, the ring spelled out,

"Please rest for a while. We will talk later." It took a few seconds to sink into Ruby's brain, as to what had just happened. But when it did, she felt an ice-cold shiver run up and down her spine. It couldn't be…and yet. Could her mother be normal after all? Could she be right about those things?

Things which never were mentioned or even taken into serious consideration to be a fact, and existed outside the 'normal' physical world. Ruby, having been born and raised in the eastern part of Europe, knew only facts. Spiritual and other beliefs, not in agreement with the communist regime were ridiculed, and waved up as crazy. Over there in her former country it was taught not to believe in things other than life on this planet. It was utter nonsense even to consider, believing in things that were not perceived by the five senses.

Smelling, touching, seeing, hearing and tasting were to be the only real and true and real experiences that Ruby had ever known.

Having followed her mother only recently to the USA, she never knew anything but reality. The harsh reality of a tyrannical government

19

that kept about seventeen million people trapped behind a wall of concrete, barbed wire and patrolled by armed men and vicious dogs. The politicians in command knew, that, by taking away hope and faith, the people of this nation would be easy subjects to control. This same tactic was used over centuries by many governments and was nothing new. However, Ruby was not a person to be controlled. After more than three years of insistently renewing every rejected application to lawfully move and live in the US, Ruby finally succeeded and was given a passport to freedom.

And now Ruby was free. Free to think and say, and to do whatever she chose. This was a new beginning. A new beginning in the USA. And now this. 'Then something like this happens to me', Ruby thought.

Ruby heard her mother's car pull into the driveway. Martha had returned with James. Slowly, Ruby went downstairs to help her mother prepare dinner. Martha took only one look at Ruby's face and at once knew that her dear daughter apparently just had a first glance of a world far beyond human senses. A world she might have thought, never existed, and yet was a nevertheless immensely beautiful truth to the continuum of life in a realm of its own.

Very joyful, with what she noticed in Ruby's face, Martha started to cook dinner. She could accept that Ruby was deep in thought and after peeling the potatoes, was absent-minded setting the table. James didn't notice. He was on his third shot of booze, drank it and poured another.

Dinner was ready and Martha served her own creation of delicious pot roast onto Ruby's plate. And provided Martha had put straw on the plates, Ruby would not have noticed that the meal she was eating was unconventional at the moment and more a bovine nourishment. Her mind was still trying to figure out a way to cope this new situation. Again and again, like a broken record the sentence repeated in her mind,

"Please rest for a while. We will talk later."

She had to find out and investigate further, if this was true. She had to find out if it was likely for a dead person to communicate with her by means of that guileless, and innocent looking board.

Dinner was over, the dishes were done. Martha sat in the living room to watch her favorite TV-show. James had gone to the corner pub—his second home. Ruby had only one thing in mind. If she still had one. It wouldn't take very long to figure it out. Ruby took a can of soda from the fridge and nodding satisfied, she closed the fridge purposeful and bid her mother a good night. In a few days, she would have cleared it all up and could go on with her 'normal' life as she always had. She had no idea, how long it would really take…

CHAPTER 2

New Discoveries and Startling Revelations

Ruby had noticed the hard line around her mother's mouth, as James had walked out the door to go and get 'pickled' as she called it. Martha's face had softened as Ruby had kissed her cheek good night. She felt bad for her mother and also knew that there was nothing she could do about the situation.

Ruby couldn't think of James or Martha. All she could think of was this being who was answering her through a piece of wood, which Martha had called an 'Ouija Board'. Her curiosity piqued her mind intrigued; Ruby did go to her mother's room upstairs. Taking the board and the ring, Ruby walked to her own room. She closed the door behind her and opened the can of soda, which she had taken earlier from the fridge in the kitchen downstairs. Instantly she undressed herself and put her warm robe on.

Slipping under the blanket on her bed, she leaned back and put the board on her lap. Somehow she knew in that same instant that if she picked up the ring, her whole life would change. Her beliefs and philosophy of life would have to undergo a total makeover. Her whole way of thinking must reverse to exactly the opposite from the past thirty years. Nothing would ever be the same. Her heart was beating rapidly. She was exited, but fearful of the discoveries to come. Afraid that her mind was not playing tricks on her and taking another sip from her soda and a few more deep breaths than soda-sips, she picked up the ring and asked:

"Michael, are you here?"

"Yes, I am here," came the answer.

"I really don't understand how it's possible for you to talk to me like this. How is it done, to motion this ring and establish communication? Please, I never would have thought of anything like this to be possible, not even in a dream. Tell me how you do it." Ruby was rattling.

"G O S L O W!" he answered. And moving very fast now, from one letter to another the ring began to swing, Ruby watched in fascination and 'Michael' began to -talk-.

"In time, you my dear Ruby, will be able to 'hear' me in your mind. You will understand every word, as if you were talking to another person. This is not nonsense. Your dear mother is not 'off her rocker' and no one has any sort corruption of senses around here. Neither did you!"

'Now wait a minute here', Ruby thought. 'This is what I was thinking a few hours ago. How can he know what I was thinking?' This was getting kind of spooky, but was likewise getting more fascinating by the minute. Eager and curious to find out more, and unravel this mystery, she held up the ring once more. M-i-c-h-a-e-l began to 'talk' again.

"Ruby, I know you have never heard about m-e-n-t-a-l t-e-l-e-p-a-t-h-y, that is what mind to mind communication is called. Soon you will catch on and conceive how it works and why it works. For now, you should rest and go to sleep. I shall talk to you tomorrow. Good night Ruby."

Stunned, Ruby sat on her bed. She had not been conscious of how much time had passed, since she came up to her room. It took quite some time, to spell out all the words, write them down and to form sentences from 'Michael's talk. Remembering that she had come to her room before eight-o-clock, she was astonished as she took a glance at her alarm clock to see, that it was now past midnight. She suddenly felt drained and totally exhausted. Taking another sip from her Pepsi, she turned off the light and fell asleep almost immediately.

23

How she fell asleep so fast and without fear was puzzling to her only until the next day. Certainly, the former day had been full of new discoveries and startling revelations. But, if this 'Michael' beyond doubt existed and was not only a figment of her imagination, why then was she not afraid. Why was she not spooked by the possibility that there might be spirits after all? More questions that needed answers, and more puzzles to piece together. A truth to be revealed.

Ruby could hardly wait for Martha to pick up James from work the next day. It would give her time, to 'talk' to 'Michael'. Putting the board on her knee and positioning the ring, she intended to ask 'Michael' if he was in the room, as the ring began its swinging dance.

"Hello, Ruby, I am glad that you want to talk to me once again." Curiously Ruby felt in that instant as if she was talking to a friend and strangely enough she was glad also. Almost bursting with questions, she set out on an incredible and strange journey. A journey into a world far beyond any human conception. A world, which truly existed and held all the answers to questions humankind has been asking ever since time began.

With the simplemindedness and wonderment of a child Ruby began to submerge into this world. Patiently and cautiously led by a being unseen and whom she called 'Michael'. It would become a nightly ritual for her, to rush up to her room and l-i-s-t-e-n and record every word what Michael had to say. But even during the daytime, she had the particular feeling that she was not alone. She felt a presence, and great anguish coming from this presence but also an almost overpowering sense of devotion toward her.

A few months had passed. There was one day, as Ruby started to clean the carpet, when through all the racket the vacuum made, she heard a man's voice. She almost dropped the carpet cleaner. She listened to the voice, and stood frozen to the spot. 'What was that?'

"Ruby?" there it was again. Turning off the vacuum, Ruby held her breath.

"Don't be afraid, Ruby, I know you can hear me."

Very clearly now she could hear the man's voice, but it didn't come from outside, nor from another room. It came from, or rather t h r o u g h, her own mind. It felt like someone had spoken into her inner ear. Except, the outside world would never hear. Ruby, marveling at this new event, had to sit down. And bluntly without forewarning, the hard realization overcame her. She realized that the presence she felt was truly a man. A man who at some period in time had been alive as she was now. Only he was theoretically assumed to be dead by now. He was without a form or body so it seemed to her, but somehow he was still present. Tears were unbidden running down Ruby's face upon the immensity of this powerful, and yet beautiful discovery. At that same moment, she began to understand that her mind was able as it was in good working order. Nothing, and no one could change that ever again.

"I can see that you are shocked to hear my voice," he spoke to her mind.

"Ruby, many very normal people throughout history have had the same experience you are having right now. They likewise said to hear voices. Not too many of them however, were able to 'affirm' their claims. Only a very few who could hear, could also predict impending events of historical proportion. Where do you think their insight and wisdom came from? It was without a doubt their own spirit guide to let them know about coming events. Benightedness and denial of the unknown marked those enlightened souls in malicious attempts to silence them, witches and warlocks. The works of the devil was the excuse of the church to mercilessly hunt, prosecute and slaughter those unfortunate souls."

After a moment of silence he continued, "Don't worry, I wasn't one of them. I was really only an ordinary man, with an extraordinary life. Some day perhaps, I will tell you. Right now is not the appropriate time for it. You should finish your chores now. We will talk more later. "

There was only silence, and Ruby sat as if she had just swallowed a stick. Visibly shaken, she thought about what had occurred a few short seconds ago. Slowly she got up from her seat and mechanically completed her cleaning. She heard her mother's car pulling into the driveway, and as soon as Martha opened the front door, Ruby excitedly ran toward her.

"Mother, you'll never guess what just happened. I am still in shock, but I heard a voice, and it was a man's voice."

"Would you have believed me, if I would have told you this only a few months ago?" Martha asked. "I hate to tell you this, Ruby, but right now it gives me great pleasure to say, I told you so." Martha was laughing softly.

"Well, you could be a bit nicer about it," Ruby said, "it is after all my first encounter with something as eccentric as that. How on earth should I have known and understood," she pouted while winding the cord onto the vacuum.

"You could have kept an open mind, even to things that cannot be seen or touched or scientifically proven as a fact. Not everything in this world can be seen or heard nevertheless it is there. Making jokes of other peoples beliefs and ridiculing them still doesn't make things in the other world go away. I suppose you'll think before you'll ever sneer at different beliefs and just close your skeptical mind again. C'mon now tell me, what did he say?" Martha asked while brewing another pot of coffee.

Ruby told Martha about the little lessons she had learned from ' Michael'.

"True enough," Martha replied, "you found out on your own that ignorance is no excuse for stupidity. Most people are afraid of the things they can't explain and therefore they deny and ridicule it."

Right after dinner Ruby rushed up to her room. She took the board out and placed it on her lap, as very obviously and clearly the voice in her mind spoke,

"I don't think you will have need of that anymore. You can hear me just fine without it. Put it away Ruby, it takes to much time. I do have the very funny feeling you want to ask me something."

"Yes, oh yes, yes, yes, I have so many questions, and I don't even know, where to start. Don't you understand, how surprising and new all of this is for me. Today, in a flash I realized it and for the first time I understood that I am actually talking to a person. How this is humanly possible is still a great and unsolved riddle to me. Even though I cannot see you, I must learn to trust you and accept the things you are telling

26

me as truth. How can I ever know if you are in fact, telling me the truth? I can't see your face. I don't even know, what you look like. I would like to make myself some picture as to whom I am talking to. I don't know the first thing about you," Ruby finished with a flustered tone in her voice.

"Okay, alright, enough already, Ruby. My dear, remember that I told you not too long ago, I was an ordinary man. To answer all of your questions as to my physical appearance, let me tell you that I am tall. I measured from head to stocking feet about six feet and two inches. My hair is shoulder long and dark brown, and I wore it in what you might call ponytail at the nape of my neck, bound with a velvet ribbon. The color of my eyes is brown and I did have a mustache and beard. I was never obese and my weight might have been about 215 to 225 pounds or so. I died when I was forty years old. That should answer some of your questions. However, you will have to be patient until I shall unveil to you my whole life story. There is plenty of time for that."

Ruby listened, but nothing else was said.

"Please, I'd like to acquaint myself with you a little more. You don't mind telling me, do you?" she said into the quiet questioningly.

"Ruby, as I just now told you, I lived my life and died and I am here with you as your guardian. Is it not plenty enough for you to know for now?"

"Definitely not, Michael." Ruby answered, shaking her head vehemently, "how did you get here in the first place? Please tell me please, I am really beginning to enjoy this."

"Yes, Ruby, I know you do, but right now it seems to me, you only want to satisfy your own curiosity. That might not do for me. Let me tell you what you must learn first. If another person is to give their trust entirely, they must feel that you are not only curious about them, but also kindness, care, and compassion are of extreme importance. Things I hardly encountered in my lifetime. Only in the sphere in which I now exist, did I get to learn what the meaning of those words is. I did acquire a rethinking and readjusting to my perception of mankind. In my lifetime unfortunately I never learned to trust another person. Only here in the afterlife, after a long time of solitude and reflection, was it possible for me to forgive others and myself. Do you know that you, yourself are your own most merciless judge?"

After a few moments of repose, his voice continued anew, "What I really would like from you, is to please accept me for what I am now."

"How can I do that?" Ruby asked.

"Ruby, if you could only look deep into my soul right this moment, you could see that I rejoice in the fact that I can speak to you. I am happy like never before that you can hear and understand me. But please also understand that I should like to trust you. Ruby, trust is earned, you do understand that too, don't you?"

"Yes Michael, I understand," Ruby said, "I really hope that in time you will see that you can trust me. I apologize for being insensitive, I did not mean to upset you."

"Apology accepted, Ruby. I know it is hard for you to think of me as still being a person, but you must also understand that is what I still am. Feelings do not die together with the physical body, Ruby. Feelings are stored in the soul. A soul is everlasting and never dies. You see, only because my physical body has ceased to function, that does not mean my feelings have ceased or vanished as well. Even or rather especially here we do know how someone is feeling about us. I could give an account of many people who crossed suddenly, and without warning, into this world where I am now. You have no idea how heartbreaking it is for them to see and to feel that members of their own family are angry because their loved one left them behind. In their own sorrow, as well as self-pity, the relations left behind are not aware that they keep the soul over here trapped in between. In between dimensions that is. Now, it may sound insignificant to you, but prayer and good wishes, and foremost loving thoughts help a lot. Love, being the most potent travel insurance, will guide many lost souls into the light."

"What light are you talking about, Michael?" Ruby interrupted quickly.

"A light that one feels. A light that is Love itself. You will understand some day, only not now," he said.

"Oh, Michael, it is all so new and fascinating for me. I really don't know if I am just dreaming a very extensive daydream or if I am making this all up in my own mind. I wonder…"

It was then, that Ruby heard laughter. A voice in a world far beyond human physical senses.—And yet—she could hear him, laughing.

"Believe me, Ruby, this is even more wonderful than a dream could ever be. No dream could last forever, but I assure you, this will." Herself now laughing, Ruby said,

"As long as our relationship is not going to be a nightmare. Now please, my knight in shining armor, tell me one thing, how long have you actually known me. Did you come to me as I started talking on the Ouija Board, or were you in this house before I came into the USA?" To her amazement he asked,

"Ruby, do you remember when you were a little girl and you were leaning much too far out of the window at your grandmother's apartment. You were loosing your balance and you would have fallen four stories down,—head first—to your death. There was nobody with you to pull you back, and yet you were pulled. Do you remember?"

Chills were running up and down Ruby's spine, and she could only stare. One event from her childhood long forgotten. Now she did remember. She was no more than nine years old at that time. She had watched some children play a game of hopscotch, and the children had drawn the game onto the sidewalk that was partially hidden from her view. In order to see the children playing the game, she leaned much to far out of the window on the fourth floor, and suddenly lost her balance. At the same moment it felt to her as if a big hand had pulled her back into the room.

Slightly scared, she thought that her grandmother had come to her aid, and now she would get her well-deserved thrashing. She turned around and found she was alone in the room. Considering herself very lucky and without giving her frightening experience a second thought she shrugged her shoulders, not giving this event any significance at all. However, she decided not to tell anyone about it.

Knowing that grandmother would get upset and punish her, she kept this episode to herself. A shocked expression on her face and clapping her hands over her mouth, she whispered.

"Oh my goodness, how did you know?" Only someone who had been there at the time would know.

"That's unbelievable!" Ruby cried, "you must have been there, weren't you?"

"Yes, Ruby, I was always there. From the day you were born I have been with you. I was there with you on your first day of school. I was there as you got your first kiss from the boy Hans. I was also there when you went to your first dance. I felt your pain and joy, each and every day of your life. And I will always be with you 'til the day you join me here in my world."

"Oh heavens," she was totally awestruck, "then you know everything about me! And I mean e v e r y t h i n g !" And for the second time, she heard him laugh. Sounding genuinely amused he answered,

"Yes, I know it all, but remember that I am not your judge. I am here to guide you. I could have used more of this in my lifetime. I just did not listen well enough and follow the tiny little voice we call conscience."

Now this was getting more interesting by the hour, and Ruby wanted to hear more, but all she could hear was,

"It is time for you to go to sleep. We will talk again tomorrow. Goodnight Ruby, my little Love." Still his soft voice was echoing inside her head as she pulled her covers over herself and turned off the light. He had called her,—what—!? 'My Love'?! Well, she thought, he is just trying to be friendly. But there are still so many questions I have to ask. Ruby said into the dark, "Good night, Michael," and she closed her eyes.

The next morning she barely had her eyes open when she heard his voice,

"Good morning, Ruby, happy birthday." He sounded very chipper. It had never happened to her, that she forgot her own birthday. Seemingly there was a certain truth to the old saying, 'there is a first time for everything'.

"Thank you, but what makes you so cheerful, that I am getting older?" Ruby grumbled.

"First of all, everybody is getting older. And I mean that exactly as it sounds, every b o d y is getting older. Your soul, however, remains the same. It only grows and matures. Since it is only your physical body, which is designed to undergo the aging process, you are always beautiful where it counts. Now come and let me have a smiling face. I think I smell coffee."

Finishing her morning ritual of hygiene, Ruby went down to the kitchen.

"Good morning, Ruby, happy birthday," she was greeted by Martha.

"How would you like to go to the mall today, Ruby? I want you to choose your own birthday present. I thought of a nice blouse or a pretty dress. I really think you could use something new for a change. But, let's have my creation of cake and some coffee first. Then we'll have ourselves a nice day out."

"Thanks, the cake looks very delicious. Ah, chocolate cake is my favorite." The cake Martha had made for Ruby's birthday stood on the table, with three pinks and one white candle on top.

"I thought, it might make you feel better, about getting over thirty, so I took pink candles for the decades and the white one for the single years," Martha chuckled, "now, make a wish."

There is something to the old saying 'Be careful what you wish for, you might get your wish when you least expect it'. How true this was going to be, she had no idea at the moment. There was only one in the room who knew what she had wished for. He wasn't talking.

After having her coffee and a big piece of the chocolate cake, Ruby and Martha drove to the mall. 'I wonder if all the people here have a guardian like I do?' Ruby thought, while browsing through the colorful display of the many dresses.

"Of course they do, Ruby, but unfortunately, many people are not even aware of it. That's a big problem. You have heard of the tiny little voice inside, right? Yes, you have guessed it. That tiny little voice inside is actually the guide or guardian who is with them since the day they were born. Ignorant and arrogant as the people are, they do think solving problems is accomplished by elbowing their way through life and not considering the consequences and feelings of others. Even as the little voice inside warns them not to do what is wrong for others, they choose to ignore it. Afterward is not the time to be sorry. People

31

should think before a loved one gets hurt. So you see, nobody is ever totally alone or forgotten," he finished.

"Is this the dress you would like?" Martha asked Ruby slightly annoyed, "you have been looking at it for the past ten minutes now. Go try it on, I'll wait here." Ruby had not been aware that she had gazed at a dress on the rack in front of her for so long. She had listened again to 'Michael'.

"Oh, yes, this is pretty and my size. I'll go and try it on," Ruby snapped out of her daze and answered her mother quickly. She took the dress and walked to the dressing room.

"This look's really fetching on you, Ruby." It was 'Michael's voice.

"Oh, you are not going to tell me that you see me and are watching me, when I get undressed, do you?" Ruby whispered somewhat furious.

"Oh yes I do, my dear. Remember that I have been with you for the past thirty o n e years now," he was putting a special emphasis on the o n e, "you really didn't grow anything new for me to be curious about. Besides, the human body is absolutely nothing to be ashamed of. Everybody has got one. Big or small, tall or short, fat or thin. It makes no difference to us over here. Our values over here are measured a tiny fraction deeper. Never forget that it is the characteristic of the soul, which shapes the real person my dear. Furthermore we are discrete and do turn when necessary. You forgot the zipper!"

'How am I going to live that down', Ruby thought. 'Not only is it enough to realize, that he knows everything concerning me, he also sees everything! This is something, that takes some getting used to.'

Martha was waiting outside the dressing rooms and impatiently pacing holes into the floor. But, upon seeing her daughter she said,

"Wow, it look's gorgeous on you. Red is really your color. After all, you should persist on wearing red, you are an Aries. Really, really nice."

"Yeah, but the soul is more important," Ruby voiced dryly to Martha's chagrin. Not at all surprised at her daughter's poignant remark however, Martha uttered,

"Yeah tell me about it, but even a soul needs a little pick-me-up, once in a while. There's really nothing' wrong with it. Now get changed, "Miss Freud," and let's go and have some lunch. I'm really hungry."

'Well, so much for trying to impress mother with my newfound wisdom,' Ruby thought, and went to change again.

Arriving back home several hours later Ruby felt tired and exhausted. Walking through the mall for hours in high heels was a mistake she vowed to make only once. Her abused feet felt like they were on fire. Considering a nice nap, she told Martha that she would like to rest for a little while. It was time that James would have to picked up from work and Martha got ready to leave.

Ruby walked up to the second floor and after hanging her new dress in the closet, she let herself flop on the bed and closed her eyes. Before dozing off she could hear Martha's car pulling out of the driveway to pick up James from work. After his accident while still a soldier, stationed in Munich his arm got crushed as his jeep turned over, James didn't drive a car anymore. Martha had told Ruby, that James had been a fine soldier and she had showed her daughter newspaper clippings and medals, he had accredited to his name.

He had been in the Korean War and made Sergeant major. After the War, he was stationed in Munich, where Martha had met him. They fell in love and planned to get married soon. Then the terrible accident happened and he was in the hospital until he was well enough to be transported. He had been transferred from the hospital in Munich to a hospital in the USA to his home state Pennsylvania, where he had to stay for six months. His arm had nearly been severed and after many operations, the arm was crippled but he could still use his fingers to work.

He had become the finest smelter of precious metals in the state of New Jersey, where they had moved to later on. He could however never console himself with the idea of not being a soldier any longer and started to drown his sorrow with booze. Though she resented the consumption of alcohol, but also still loved her husband, Martha routed him to work every morning and picked him up every afternoon. Ruby slept.

Chapter 3

Daring Experiments

Waking up what seemed merely minutes later, Ruby sat up in her bed. Swinging her legs about, she put both of her feet on the floor. She took a glance around the room and saw the little orange light bulb aglow on her desk. Somehow, she had never gotten around to putting the small and cheerful looking candelabra away with all the other Christmas decorations. She liked that velvety light and therefore kept it standing on her desk.

At this moment however, it seemed as if the light was a bit brighter. Or was it that the room was somewhat darker, as if the sun had gone behind a big dark cloud. It couldn't be that late yet. Strange, but why was it so gloomy in the room? What time was it anyway? Ruby couldn't make any sense of it. If it was so late that the sun was setting, then her mother and James should be home by now. There were no noises from downstairs.

Puzzled, Ruby still sitting on the bed, and wondering about the time, had turned her head to check her alarm clock. 'That's funny', she thought, 'its only 3:15 PM. So I was asleep for no more then about ten minutes. But why is it so strangely dark right now'? Wanting to make sure she had not misread the time, she took another peek at the clock. Out of the corner of her eye she noticed something dark on her pillow. What was it? It looked like…No, it can't be…!

'How did this woman get into my bed? She look's like…! Heavens, it is a woman, that look's like me. Oh, dear, i t—i s—m e—!'

Seeing herself for the first time three-dimensionally was not at all what she had expected. She looked somewhat like a complete stranger to her own self. Suddenly realizing that it was herself, a wave of panic went through her. In that instant she felt like a snap had gone through her and terrified, she opened her eyes and sat up in her bed. Her heart was pounding like a jackhammer and she was trembling. She was back in her own body again.

The room was bright and sunny. The orange light bulb on the little Christmas candelabra was alight, illuminating nothing at all. Ruby looked at her clock, the time was 3:16 PM.

Shaken, and more puzzled than ever, she tried to make some sense of what just now had happened to her. She knew that she had not been dreaming. That she had been totally aware of her surroundings. Then, how was it even possible that she could observe herself sleeping when she was awake and in what felt like her normal body?

"This is crazy," she said out loud, "how can I leave my own body without dying? Maybe I was dead for a minute and by some piece of good luck I came back to life once again?" More spooked than before, she got up from her bed and with unsteady knees, walked to her writing desk. It had been a long while since she had lit up a cigarette, but right at this very moment she felt the need for one. She reached still shaking into the drawer to take out a pack of her cigarettes, but she couldn't find any matches. Surely in mother's room there is a lighter she remembered and went to Martha's room to get it.

Crossing the hallway she heard the sound of water running. Forgetting the cigarettes and lighter, Ruby, taking two steps at once, rushed downstairs to see where the noise was coming from. The kitchen sink was not even dripping, the bathroom sink was okay. Where did the noise come from? Ruby opened the door to the basement and cried out:

"Oh no, what a mess." It looked like a pipe had broken and the whole basement was about three inches flooded with water. She didn't know, what to do first.

'Okay, calm yourself', she thought and taking a very deep breath, she stepped into the water to follow the piping on the ceiling with her eyes, trying to detect the pipe with the damaged part. The pipes were all in one piece, so it must be the water heater that had to be broken. She tried to turn the little knob on the heater, to cut off of the water supply. It didn't budge. Making her way back her shoes made watery squashing noises as she was climbing up the stairs.

She had completely forgotten to take off her shoes and now they were saturated with the filthy murky water. She knew that James kept a few tools in one of the drawers, in the kitchen. Finally she found a pair of pliers and reaching for it, she heard a key turning in the front door.

"Oh, mother, I am happy to see you. We have water all over the basement, and I can't twist the knob on the heater." Glancing behind her mother, Ruby asked, "Where's James?"

"I drove him to the doctor. He had an appointment today," Martha answered, "now let's see, what's going on down in the dungeon." Martha put her purse on the chair, and went down to the basement. Only a moment later, she came back smiling as she said to Ruby, seemingly doubting her senses:

"You had me going there for a moment girl, and I almost believed you." Ruby couldn't understand, what was going on. She turned to the door into the basement again, and with a cry of total surprise eased herself down onto the steps. The entire basement was dry as a bone, not one single drop of water in sight. This was certainly not Ruby's day, and by no means the birthday she had always been dreaming of. To top it all off, now her mother would not believe a word she said. Crushed, and nearly in tears, she fussed with her skirt, as her eyes suddenly got wide.

'Of course, that's it', her mind screamed. Running back up to the big kitchen again, where Martha was just pouring a cup of coffee for herself. Ruby excitedly pointed to her shoes,

"Look Mother, I wasn't kidding, I only would like for you to give me a good explanation right about now, to what in all the devils name is going on here. Maybe you could be so kind and enlighten me just a little bit." Martha looked at Ruby's shoes and shook her head, she was saying nothing. The shoes were soaked and around Ruby's ankles a dirty brown ring, like she had been wading in dirty water about three inches deep. Martha suddenly was very still. After a while, she broke the silence by saying:

"When James gets home, don't say anything. He is afraid of things he can't explain." Ruby, throwing up her arms in exasperation snorted,

"Humph." She couldn't understand any of this, and stomped to her room, to change her stockings and shoes.

"Anything can be taken from one dimension to another, my dear Ruby." It was Michael's voice, "don't you understand now? Let me try and explain to you, what happened to you earlier, and the water in the basement...well we will get to that at a later point. I know, you left your body for a few short moments. But you were fully aware, of being alive and well. What you saw in your bed was merely the physical body that is nothing but an empty shell, made out of all sorts of chemical substances neatly set together continually cell by cell, to become the vessel for you to conduct yourself and manifest in the physical world. Try to think of it as a car, which wouldn't run without the motor. If you turn on your television, it will not work unless the electric cord is plugged into the outlet." After a brief pause, he continued, "you see, nothing in this world or in any other, functions without energy. And that energy always comes from the source without, never from within. It is the same with your body as it is with the car or the TV. Only the spare parts are a little more difficult to come by," he added with a chuckle.

Ruby, while she was listening, had changed her shoes a bit irritated she grumbled,

"I still don't get it, why this is happening to me. Never in my whole life would I have thought such things possible and here I am experiencing things ripe for the books of Fairy tales, Saga's and Myths. I wouldn't be a bit surprised, if the fairy godmother showed up, and put a pair of new shoes and stockings on my feet. A brand new coat would be nice too."

"Sorry, our cobbler is on vacation and the seamstress is on star shine duty today." Michael teased humorously. "oh, my precious, I have so many things to tell you and more yet to show you. Close your eyes, and don't be afraid. You'll like what you are about to see. I promise."

Thinking, that after what happened to her on this day not much else would scare or even surprise her, Ruby closed her eyes. Momentarily she saw a man's face appearing in front of her still closed eyes. A man's face smiling at her. Ruby held her breath. This was not possible, it couldn't be...

Breathless and her heart pounding she whispered,

"Michael, is it your face?" Only nodding his head, his face somehow seemed to move backwards, until to her amazement she saw a whole form. A face and form not unpleasing and come to think of it, very handsome indeed. Certainly nothing to be frightened about. His dress code however, was quite different.

His dark brown hair was shoulder long and openly laying on his broad and strong looking shoulders. His dark beard and mustache with tiny streaks of gray in it, was cropped short. His whole form was completely covered by a long brown robe. On his chest was a cross, which seemingly was somehow a part of the robe. Somehow, his full attire reminded her of a very handsome Franciscan Monk. But only for a moment.

Concentrating on his face once more, she looked into his eyes. She saw a tiny twinkle and a smile developing. Her heart almost stopped. How can this be that she could see him like in a dream? Her eyes were still closed tightly.

"This is my present to you, Ruby. I know that this was the wish you made. I hope that you are not frightened. Here I am, you wanted to see me."

"I really don't know if I was wishing for it to happen today. But thanks for the thought. I usually get cake and flowers and other useful things." She remarked dryly with her eyes still closed tightly. Curiosity was paramount however and she couldn't help asking:

"How is it possible for me to see you like a vision or something?"

"This is something that will take some time to explain. Don't forget your notes. You will need all this later. Let me ask you a question first. Do you have any idea, how the human brain works?" he asked.

"Oh gosh, I am not a scientist," she snorted. "I only know that I am doing the thinking and depending on my surroundings and other people I feel happy, sad, scared, mad and a whole bunch of other emotions."

"Now you will have to be patient Ruby, and listen to me. I am not a scientist either. I will try and explain to you as easy to understand as possible. Even if it sounds a little childish. So hang in there. Ruby, think about what scientists are saying about the human brain. It is the mass of gray cells, connected to a network of nerves throughout your whole body. Every nerve ending is like a small twig connected to a branch, which again is attached to one big trunk just like a tree. In the human body, in that case, the trunk is its spine. A bony structure is surrounding and safely protecting the big string of nerve that has its base in the back of your neck. There it's connected to your brain in your scull. Now in order to let you walk and talk and touch things, a proper command must come from your brain to all your body parts, which you must use to walk and talk and touch.

Remember now, Ruby, I had explained to you that nothing in this world functions without energy and your body requires it just the same. Minute electromagnetic impulses are send from your brain to the nerve in your spine and from there they travel to the tiny nerve endings in your feet, hands and tongue and all other body parts. Just as the TV or any other device in your house does get the energy from the Electric Company through a cable to your home where it is branched off to outlets. A plug from your TV or the coffee machine into the outlet will supply the appliance with the needed energy. Do you see, what I am getting at?"

Ruby thought for a moment and scratched her head,

"The Electric Company is far away from here."

"Exactly, the energy comes from outside the appliance. Not from within. So where does your brain get the energy from, to give the body parts the commands to function properly? Right, from Y O U. The real Y O U ! You realize now, that your brain is the messenger from YOU to your physical human body, to conduct your self and manifest in the physical world.

Ever since birth, your five physical senses make a supreme effort to fool you into believing that, at the moment of your death, you also will cease to exist. Not quite so Ruby. The real YOU is this very source of energy, which is indestructible. Since no one in the past ever found the appropriate name for it, what is actually the existent being, it is called soul or spirit." He paused.

"That was easy enough to understand." Ruby thoughtfully nodded, "I still don't get it, where the energy comes from, which sustains this real ME. I can explain to myself the energy in my fridge or coffee maker. That comes from huge turbines at the Electric Company. Now where is my turbine which gives my soul or spirit the energy to direct my body through my brain?" she asked.

"Let me explain to you what a soul or spirit is. It is a miniature personification of a whole supreme super intelligence, which is host to all existing life throughout the universe. All right let's do it the easy way again.

Try and visualize in your mind a tremendous globe of any given material. You know, that everything in this world is nothing but a bunch of molecules and atoms. Different chemical components forming or being formed or built into a certain structure. Like a table, a chair, a vase and so forth. Assume now, so is your globe in your mind. Now isolate and disconnect all the miniature miscellaneous chemical components in your mind, and try to see them, one by one. Now imagine, that the big globe in your mind is one super intelligent being, and only that one tiny atom of this globe is you. The atom next to you is James and next to him is Rosemarie, your friend from New Jersey. Each one of you as well as every intelligent being is a separate atom of this big globe and yet put together and connected you all are a part of this big globe. Now that every one of your little atoms has a name, let us go a little further. You also know from your school studies that one atom consists of a positively charged nucleus surrounded by negatively charged electrons. The electrons are attracted by the nucleus. However, the electrons repel each other. A nucleus alone would not be an atom without the electrons. The electrons would have nothing to orbit about if the nucleus was missing. They can be split into several parts and yet they need each other to be a whole atom. You also might recall that electricity or energy must be connected to any appliance by a pair of wires of negative and positive polarity. Just like the batteries in your little radio have a plus and a minus polarity on the top and bottom. As the infinite wisdom of our host, the Lord God provides (the big globe in you mind), we are divided into male and female souls. Like the atom is made of nucleus and electrons, we are not much without the other part. Therefore we are only one half of an atom, and all the time is searching for the absent part, to become the whole being again. And that is why every man and woman in this world and also in mine is ceaselessly instinctively searching for the other half. Until the exact other half is found there are separations and even fights due to the fact that we are a nucleus or electron of a different atom so to speak. This accounts for the imbalances in both spirits because in truth, they are not suited to be together. They were not 'made' for each other. But once the genuine other half is found they will never be separated again and will function as one.

They are **SOUL MATES**. Once the two parts like nucleus and electrons become one again, they also become the whole atom which was missing from the big globe. This might shock you a bit what I am about to say. You are my other half Ruby. That's why you never had any fear of me. You subconsciously were already accustomed to me before you knew that I was indeed, what I am. I am a part of you and you are a part of me. When people do get married, at some point during the ceremony the clergy says, 'what God hath' put together, let no man put asunder.' How truthful this phrase is, becomes clear to you now, doesn't it."

Michael had stopped talking and Ruby sat stunned on her bed. Now it all made sense to her. The method in which he had explained it was accommodating and easy enough to understand. What made her angry at this point was the fact that he had claimed to be her true soul mate. What kind of joke was that? Almost burning with her question she asked,

"You are joking right? Did anybody ever tell you that you have a lousy sense of humor? Here I am, stupid little me, dreaming about the perfect man for me and living happily ever after. Now I find out that my other half is a damn ghost. You wouldn't by any chance know of a minister who could marry us without asking too many funny questions?" she finished sarcastically.

"Life is eternal and many people find each other only in the here-after. Still, they find each other. Meeting the wrong people is not necessarily a bad thing. Each person you meet in your life contributes to your own soul growth. Either by helping you or by being a challenge to you. People who are helpful are teaching you love and compassion and understanding. People who are a challenge to you, which you would consider mean and nasty, will teach you to be a loving soul compassionate and understanding. Now here is the good news. People, who are not meeting their soul mate in life, are strong enough to do without him or her. Furthermore, they have something to look forward too in the after life. So you see, there is plenty of time to be happy in both worlds. You and many others should be grateful for every opportunity to grow and mature in spirit without having to depend on your other half." he advised.

"Darn, now I feel like I'm cheating. I already know you and the surprise of meeting you is somehow not a surprise any more. Why the hell did I ever listen to my mother with this crazy piece of wood?" she cussed in mock anger.

"Because you are curious by nature and you will not except things that have no apparent reason. You always have to see for yourself and sometimes even then you'll doubt your own senses," he laughed.

"Well, you didn't have to answer me on the darn board and perhaps should have left me to my doubts. Why on earth did you answer me to begin with?" Ruby asked.

"I answered for one reason only. That was to protect you. Let me explain that to you. As soon as someone is playing around with an Ouija Board, they are opening their mind automatic to the spirit world. That can be dangerous indeed. Especially to people who are 'just' playing around to prove a point. It is likely and not uncommon to draw a spirit toward you, which is earthbound confused and unfortunately sometimes even nasty. If you make contact, you'll never be able to get rid of them and slowly but surely they take over your life to make it their own. Some of the spirit people don't even know that they are out of the physical vessel and they get very angry and frustrated, that nobody can see and talk to them anymore. Do you remember when you read the Bible just a few weeks ago that the Lord said, 'where you store up treasure, there, your heart will be also'. So true Ruby, some of them can't let go and there they remain trapped and earthbound. Those souls will stubbornly hold on to things, which in their own mind and soul are considered imperative for happiness. It could be anything, like a house or money or alcohol, to even become obsessed with sex. You understand that a person who has lived for a long time in a house which he or she has bought, loved furnished and repaired and taken care of it, could also become obsessed with it.

Sometimes and unfortunately, a person gets killed by accident or at the hand of another person in a house or any other location. This unfortunate soul does not realize that he or she has died and will stay and search for loved ones. The same with all the other things I have mentioned. Anything that takes presidency over a person's life will further rule their mind. And the mind my dear Ruby is a curious thing. I will get to the power of the mind another time. I realized only in the last few months, what you are and who you are. For now you should get some rest, Ruby."

"I never thought of it that way. Well, thank you anyway. I think you are trying to tell me that you saved my butt just like when I was a kid." she yawned. "Well good night then." She undressed and slipping into her bed she snuggled under the covers. She felt safe, loved and protected.

Several days had passed and Ruby luckily had found a job and an apartment of her own. Since it was not a very demanding job, Ruby was mostly left to herself and had time to work on her apartment, which was above the small store she minded during the daytime. In the evening she was free, to talk to 'him' and got to learn more about the things she had never thought even would be in existence. One night she asked him,

"Please tell me how can you talk to me without anybody else hearing you? How is this form of communication accomplished? Does it require some kind of special training or cultivation on your side over there, or can it be done by anybody?"

"No, Ruby, no special training is needed to do that. And you are correct that anybody could do that. Do you recall when you started talking to me on the Ouija Board? You did not realize then, that you while you were holding the ring over the board to spell out the words, in an instant, but not realized by you, the whole answer was already in your mind. I had given you the answer, and you were the one, swinging the ring to the correct letters. So you see, Ruby, you could hear me then, as you hear me now. In your own mind. Only it took for you a while to realize it and to catch on that you could hear me clearly speaking through your own mind. But I had to be patient and wait for you to understand."

"Yes, but I still don't understand, how it is done!" she interrupted.

He had yet to explain how he could talk to her or rather 'through' her own mind and was able to communicate with her.

"I was just trying to get to that, Ruby," he fell into her thoughts. "Think back a few days, as I told you that your brain is sending out electromagnetic impulses, which in turn are miniature sparks from the source of energy, the real YOU. You are a small 'bundle of energy' which is constantly broadcasting it's own sense of being intelligently on a particular frequency into the endless stratosphere. This is what you call thinking. Every single 'bundle of energy' has his or her own frequency and is like a radio station broadcasting on it. Remember that you could not hear your choice station, if others would broadcast on the same frequency. Since you are not only beaming, but are also the receiver of signals, you can and must converse with others, physically by using your body. With the body parts, designed for communication like your hands your eyes your tongue and your voice, you are able to signal to others, what is in your mind, and what you desire. But that is not where it ends, because the thoughts you are having are broadcasted into the dimension, where I am right now. Since our bodies here in my dimension are existing on a higher level of frequencies which equals the frequency of subconscious thought in your world we are able, to 'hear' and feel your thoughts loud and clear. The frequency, which your core of intellect is broadcasting on, is your subconscious mind at first that develops an idea, and realization of the idea is brought forward to the conscious mind to act upon it. That could be a new recipe for example. At first you'll buy a piece of meat. However, you feel that you really don't want to cook this meat as a pot roast. You already know that you wish to change things. Your conscious mind has given your subconscious mind something to work on. The desire for betterment or change was there. Now your subconscious complies with the desire in form of an idea sent to your conscious, which you will act upon. You will cut the meat and season it with different herbs and spices to create a whole new dish. Before you knew for certain what kind of dish you would cook, I knew your thought process. I heard and actually felt what you were about to do, before it reached you conscious mind. The subconscious is the thriving force to comply with desire and other outside stimuli which is never to change it's waves or broadcasting station in all eternity.

However your conscious mind is broadcasting on a much lower frequency in order for you to make the intelligent conduct and manifestation possible, which is life on earth. To hear and understand word for word exactly what I am speaking, I have to 'tune' my own frequency consciously into yours and there you have it. You can 'hear' me through your own 'radio station', which is your conscious mind. If I would be speaking and make my presents known to your subconscious, you would only have a 'feeling' about what I am trying to tell you. Sometimes it happens by coincidence that even in the physical world two people can communicate like we do every day now.

Think about it, Ruby, how many times has it happened to you that someone says to you,' I was just thinking the same thing,' or, even does say the same thing, at precisely the moment you are beginning to speak. You know why? Because for only a short coincidental moment you were both sending as well as receiving on the same frequency. It's that simple. If all the fine scientists who are to this day, trying to figure out how the human mind works and have not found a thing except a mass of gray cell's, only would look outside the brain. They could discover the energy field that is sending and receiving as the true source of intelligence, which is actually the real person. The human brain is merely the intermediate between the intelligent spirit and the body, which the entity temporarily inhabits to manifest and conduct itself in the physical realm of life. Our world over here could be accepted as a wonderful fact and would no longer be feared and shrouded in mystery and superstition. Ever since time began, mankind fancied themselves as an immortal and hoped to live forever. The only problem is that most of them forget that this is not going to happen in the physical world. The world as you know it, is only a playground for the human soul to grow and learn how to get along with the other playmates. When a soul separates from the big globe our wonderful host, which is the spirit of the Lord our God, to be born into this world and experience physical existence, it has to undergo as any other soul in this world, the up's and down's which are common in the physical world. They grow and mature, to reach a principal level of understanding and by reaching that goal, it can now return to its origin. In order to give the soul a head start, it is born into a human body and must first get it's 'feet wet'. And that is the world you are living in right now Ruby. You have to recognize every circumstance in the physical life as a learning experience to develop and increase your spiritual growth. Learn how to love and accept others for what they are not for what they have. After all, we all originate from one big globe. But there's a lot more, so much more what I must tell you. I only hope you understand how happy you made me feel over the past few months. Give me time and I will tell and teach you all that I know."

CHAPTER 4

The Lie and the Greatest Love

Time was all that Ruby had. Patience was another story. She had never been a patient person. Everything in her life had to be done right away, or supposed to be finished yesterday. But she also knew, that he would not be a being to be rushed. And whoever he was in his lifetime, and whatever had happened in his life, she sensed 'he' had an aura of sadness around him and probably only now, was opening himself up to another person. She felt indeed how happy and enthusiastic he was talking to her, and liked to share with her everything he had learned on the "other side". She only wondered how long it took his own mind to understand it all that he could explain so well. She would find that out too.

There was one hot day in the summer, as Ruby recalled the cross on Michael's chest and she asked,

"Michael, why do you wear the cross? Have you been a religious man in the physical life?" At first, there was a long moment of silence, and then she did hear his voice.

"Ruby, everyone has to carry their own cross. I am no exception. I realize now that I have a confession to make. Since I am wearing this cross, which represents not only suffering but also truth I must tell you now, that my real name is J U S T U S. It is not 'Michael'. Please forgive me for my deception."

Stunned into silence, Ruby sat in her chair. What reason did he have to lie to her? What had his name to do with it? What other things had he kept from her? Not knowing what to think, Ruby got angry.

"So, you had me call you 'Michael' all this time and now you have a change of heart and you 'confess' to me, it is JUSTUS. Name me one good reason, why I should believe you now," she spat into the seemingly empty room.

"First of all, my dear Ruby, I must tell you, that a name is only a vibration of sounds. It is given to an individual at the start of life to be identified and also recognized in the physical world. My given name was JUSTUS. Over here in the world where I am now however, we are recognized not only by a name but also by our soul. Names mean not that much over here in my part of existence. Some day, you will understand this also. Please, Ruby, you must believe me that this is indeed the truth. Furthermore I had to see at first if I could trust you with my feelings. And then there is another silly reason really. I was a little afraid you would not understand my ancient name. If I would have spelled this name out at first on the Ouija board you might have thought this is a mistake. I know for a fact that you have never heard this name before. That is why I choose a more current and effortless pronounced name. And then I was also afraid you would tease me about it. Please don't be angry, Ruby."

In spite of herself, Ruby just had to laugh. How could a supposedly grown adult being be so complex? Here he was on one side teaching and telling her about secrets of the spirit world and the universe and on the other side he was insecure, afraid of revealing to her his true name for fear she would tease him about it.

"You great fool," she exploded, "did you really think that I would mock you or make fun of a lousy name. Someone should take the time over there and loosen up your halo my little elf because I believe it's screwed a bit to damn tight onto your ego. All this time you have been with me, you have not become aware of, that I care for you also. I have learned only in the past few months what it means, to care and to understand many things I had not understood before. You have shown me a side of life, which I would not have even suspected to be in

48

existence. I hade to discover a strange being existing in another world caring for my feelings and me. I've learned, to like this being and to like very much what I recognized. No, wait correction; I learned to love this person very much. Like I would love my best friend. Why do you believe that I am not capable to loving you and excepting you for what you are now? Teachers like you just don't come a dime a dozen. I also have learned, to recognize you by your soul. I know exactly what you are. I don't consider you a ghost and I know, who you are."

Angrily she wiped the unbidden tears from her face that had overflowed her eyes. She blew her nose noisily and with a furious gesture, showing her temper, she threw the tissue in the trashcan under the little round table next to her chair, she sniffed, "I wish, you would still be alive and I could give you a well deserved punch in the nose or I could put my arms around you right now and show you how much I care for you. Maybe you don't remember, but there are way's in this physical world, how to bestow affection and appreciation toward a person, one care's for. Wayward children get punished. Good people get a hug." Ruby was angry.

"I do have a request, Ruby. Would you please get a very large glass of water and put it on the table. Perhaps with some ice in it." Justus had spoken.

"What strange thing are you trying to explain now with a glass of ice water?" Ruby asked.

Assuming that he would possibly explain another strange phenomena, she went to the kitchen without waiting for an answer. She filled a tall glass with ice water and coming back to the room, she placed it on the little table as he had requested. Sitting back down on her recliner, she grumbled,

"Do you want to make a flood now here in my house. I think I had enough of it the first time around."

Her tears had abruptly stopped flowing and she stared wide eyed and with her mouth agape, at the tall figure that had, seemingly out of the thin air, somehow materialized right in front of her. It felt, as if her heart would stop beating at any second now. Motionless, holding her breath, she sat. Her fingernails digging deep into the armrests of her chair. She closed her eyes trying to blink the vision away. But the figure would remain where it was, try as she might. Slowly, very slowly, he bend down and like the wing of a butterfly, gently touched her hand. His dark brown eyes never leaving hers, which were as wide as saucers. His mouth did not move, yet she could hear his voice as he relayed to her mind,

"I had to lower my astral vibrations to your physical level," and with a twinkle in his dark eyes and his lips curling into a flashing smile, he added, "maybe I should have called first."

"Oh, God, I must be dreaming," she whispered, "what magic is this that I can see you, like I would see a real person. How is it possible that I can feel a hand on mine and that feels real too?" Her heart seemed to skip a few beats and felt like it was about to jump out of her chest. Not to frighten her more he slowly eased his big form down to kneel down in front of her. His hand softly remaining on hers he smiled openly and trying to put her more at ease, spoke to her mind telepathically,

"Was there a phenomenon in the physical world which I am supposed to remember? And you wanted to show me? And I don't mean the punch in the nose."

She tried to force her eyes away from his. To no avail. A million questions seemed to bombard her mind at this moment. Yet she couldn't think of a single thing to say. No,—it was simply unfeasible, she must wake up at any second now and he would not be there at all.

—His dark brown eyes,—his sensual lips,—his smile, and even his touch,—his touch, would be all a figment of her overactive imagination. She would wake up just like the other time, as she saw her own body lying on her bed. Well if it was a dream she suddenly realized, that she would not like to wake up so soon. The only items that did not quite fit into her vivid dream, was her pounding heart and her trembling knees. Patiently he had remained kneeling in front of her, and softly increasing the pressure of his hand, intended to let her frantically working mind adapt to his presence he asked,

"Did you hear me, Ruby?"

Of course she had, and seeing that the twinkle in his eyes had been replaced be genuine concern, something strange inside her, a force, gave her the courage to take a deep breath, as she answered him,

"Yes, I did hear you, but I can't believe what I am seeing. I am not sure if I am ever going to be capable to stand up again from this chair. Please tell me, my legs will stop shaking some day. Maybe even my heart will resume his usual beat in the year two thousand and twenty. I can't believe it that I can really see you, and that I can feel your touch. How is that possible?" she asked with a quivering voice and after a slight pause, "may I touch your face?"

Instantly, the warm smile and the twinkle in his eyes returned to his face as he answered her in his usual way of communication,

"What do you suppose would happen to me if you do? I know that I am not going to change into a frog. I realize, that I have frightened you a bit and I humbly beg you pardon but please, Ruby, do feel free to explore."

"You just about scared the living daylights out of me. I am still shaking like a leaf. And you just say you scared me a bit. I'd like to know what your definition of a lot is?" She said with a slight hint of sarcasm in her voice. Nevertheless her curiosity was raised and very shy, slowly, and trembling she raised her hand to his face and with her index finger gently touched his cheek. She was doing the unthinkable—she touched a ghost!

"I think, that I am still pretty lively for a ghost," he fell into her thought, "I'm pleased that you are not afraid of me."

She should be. Perhaps she was afraid.—Anybody she knew would be frightened to death if suddenly out of nowhere a spirit appeared in his or her house. Then why wasn't she just fainting dead away? She had to be mad to do what she did. But she knew the answer to her question, as she looked into his face. What she felt under her touch was alive and real. What she felt inside, was love.—The love for a being whose trust she had gained. A soul, which seemed strangely familiar to her as if it was somehow a part of herself. Now, she understood what it was, that he had told her about soul mates. Unthinkable and fantastic as it may seem to her senses, right in front of her was this other half to make her feel and be complete. Overwhelmed and awestruck at the discovery and moved by the sudden feeling of piece inside of herself, she gently put the whole palm of her hand on his face. His beard softly tickled her wrist as if to verify the reality of it. She didn't move and was hardly breathing. By lifting her other hand from the armrest, she gently still somewhat shakily touched his hair. Seemingly quivering under her hand, and with his eyes closed, he whispered,

"From the pits of hell you lifted me,
Like a giant beam of sunlight you walk before me.
Following you I can see myself now,
Casting the dark shadows behind that follow me.
I shall not look back,
For I see only the light of your love.
Ruby, my love, my life, now and forever."

Unable to speak and with tears running down her face, Ruby had listened to this lyric, which seemed to be the most beautiful poem she had ever heard. But it was not the beauty of the words that made her cry. It was—his voice.

For the first time audible to her ears, she had heard his voice. And with slow unbelievable tenderness as if moving in slow motion, she took his face in both of her hands. He opened his eyes to look straight into her tearstained face. Raising his hand, he put the tips of his fingers on her lips as if to silence her, saying softly,

"Hush, my love, don't cry. I am here with you. Please don't cry, Ruby, or are you frightened?"

Still holding his face she shook her head and said under tears,

"I am scared to death. Somehow I wish to wake up from this dream and yet I am curious. Which unmerciful and cruel circumstance is it that has kept us apart? We can never be together as other couples can. How can I not be sorry and feel sad to know, that you are living in one dimension, and I in the other."

Again he put his finger over her lips and smiling, he said,

"I am here now, Ruby, and I will always be with you. I have not left your side even for one second in the past thirty-one years and I will never do so, I promise you. I love you more than I can say and other dimensions are only different states of being and awareness. It can never impair, how a person feels. No matter where I am or where you are, we will always feel loved by one another, as if we had spent a lifetime together. And however strange the circumstance may be, in a way we are together. How many people out there have the feeling and this strange yearning, to some day meet and find their true soul mate. They love this other person subconsciously deep inside, even though they have never seen them before. Instinctively they know that this perfect other half is out there somewhere and won't feel whole, until they are reunited. Some of them are lucky and they can find each other in life. Many others unfortunately do not. Separations and divorces are the results of it. Marriages lasting a lifetime where mutual trust love and respect is given are evidence that what I am telling you, is true. Sometimes in your world, for certain in mine, people do eventually find the perfect mate and will stay together forever. I can give an account of many couples, which refuse to be separated by dimensions. A loved one makes their presents known and their spirit can be felt very distinct. In many cases they can be seen or heard. They will find a way to let their mate know that they are all right and that they will be together again some day. That's how powerful love can be, Ruby."

While he spoke, Ruby's hands slowly moved from his face to his shoulders. Even the cloth of his robe felt real and somewhat like rough linen.

"Oh, Justus," she whispered, "if we really belong together, how is it, that you were born in another time and had to die before I was even born? I can't make any sense of it. How can you explain that to me?" she asked. Her knees were shaking uncontrollably as was her whole body.

"I am not able to explain that to you my dear. Even I don't have all the answers. Life is a mysterious thing in both worlds. I can only guess that as we mature in soul and spirit, the answers will reveal themselves throughout eternities." he answered truthfully.

Lifting her face to look at him, she smiled and said,

"It feels wonderful to see you and touch you." Her whole body was still shaking. The immensity of the situation was still far to enormous for her to comprehend. However, it started to sink in. Her mouth felt dry.

"Poor dear, I know it is indeed hard to understand that I can stand here in front of you. However it can also be explained. We will get to that at a later point. I think you should have some of the water now. You are still in shock and indeed a bit pale."

Unable to resist in body or spirit, Ruby sank deeper into the chair. With shaking hands she reached for the water and drank obediently in big gulps. Only a few seconds later she felt better and started to relax somewhat. Only her mind wouldn't stop reeling. Justus sat down right in front of her on the carpet. Ruby began to speak:

"Believe me, I still have a hard time understanding and believing what is happening. I am still shocked because my own eyes and ears are now telling me, that there is truth to this other existence beyond human senses. Ask any other person in this world. They believe and hope for a continuation of a life after and I never thought that much about it. Up until this moment it was still such far out thing to comprehend. Now I feel like the doubting Thomas, which is awestruck but finally confronted with undeniable proof. However, I am not that much afraid any longer."

"But how so, Ruby? I would like to hear it from you, why you feel that you have nothing to fear from me. You know, what I am!" he emphasized placing his hands gently on her knees.

"Why, Justus, of course I know what you are. You are not afraid of me, are you?" she teased him with a sweet mischievous smile. In mock resignation he let his arms drop to his sides and little devils and demons dancing merrily in his eyes, belying the tone in his voice, he said,

"I am at your mercy, do feel free to do with me as you wish."

'Oh, the little demon' she thought, 'wants to play, now I will play just as nicely'. Immediately realizing, that a response to her thoughts was not forthcoming, Ruby put her hands on his shoulder, and questioningly looked into his face,

"Justus, you are not able to read my thoughts right now, why is that?"

Quietly applauding her sharp sense of observation, he answered truthfully,

"You are correct, Ruby, I am not capable to see or hear any of your thoughts, because I'm totally and entirely in your dimension right now. I was not joking before as I told you that I had to reduce or rather decrease my own astral vibrations, to come to your level. You see, what you feel is actually my astral body. Once a soul leaves the physical body, it slips without interlude into the other dimension, clothed and inhabiting a precise replica of the human form, to live and exist in the next dimension beyond normal human senses. It looks and feels altogether identical to the mortal body, with only a few differences. The astral is not constrained by time and space. The earth's gravity has no effect on it, nor do molecular structures like walls of stone or wood or even another human body. We can walk right through it and we can do it without getting hurt or hurting someone. I know you will ask how that is possible. Let me give you an example. You remember a few days ago as you bumped your shin on the coffee table. Your mind was telling you, that you hurt yourself on a seemingly solid object. But now look upon the table's real solidity from a microscopic view. You would see that the table's polished and smooth surface is actually very rough and looks like little mountains and valleys. Take a much more powerful microscope and look once more. There you detect the many atoms of every molecule. Each atom looks like a little miniature universe with one big planet in the middle and several smaller ones are orbiting around. In between those atoms is a tremendous space just like in the universe in between the stars is a lot of empty space. Now remember what I told you about vibration in and throughout the universe. Since the atoms of the table and any other solid object in the physical world vibrate at a lower rate than in the next dimension, you can see and feel and relate to it as real in your world. Since the vibration level of our bodies and objects are vibrating at a much higher rate as the physical, you cannot detect any of it with you five physical senses. And that also means, that our bodies can pass through any solid object in the physical world because our atoms vibrate at such high rate as not to *bump* together with the atoms in the physical world. To make yourself a picture of what I mean, think for example of a piece of cloth. Pour water over it and the water seeps right through it. Only our body is not liquid, it is merely consistent of a higher energy structure, but identical to the one of the physical world in appearance. The impression you are having of the next level of existence is therefore still unreal and untrue. You might like to think, that if the spirit is the *'bundle of energy'* and if we can go through walls, then the astral is nothing but air. Not so, Ruby. Look very closely into my face. There you can see, that not one single hair from my beard is missing and even my eyelashes are still there.

In his infinite wisdom, the creator of all life did not only design a physical body for a soul to live in, but he also designed a body of higher energy, to so-to-speak photocopy the physical body cell by cell. At the moment of physical death, your bundle of energy, the core of your intellect and self awareness which you call soul propels the body of higher vibration into the next dimension of life and you have the feeling of rushing through a long tunnel. That is actually the period and time, which is needed to adjust to the astral body. If people would be able to remember their own birth, they also would instantly recognize, that it feels almost the same as slipping through the birth canal. Only it is not quite as painful. At first it feels tight and warm and at the end is a bright light. I know you want to ask me now that if we have this astral body, why can't you see it with the physical eyes even though it is present already in the physical life within the body. Let me give you another example.

Visualize a swan in flight, and you can clearly see his wings slowly go up and down as he goes. But now try and follow with your eyes the wings of a hummingbird. Right, it's impossible. All you are able to detect is a blur and the wings of the little hummingbird are nearly invisible to your eyes. Aha,—You see, what I am getting at now. The higher the vibrations, the less visual it becomes to the human eye. And that is actually all there is to say, to this mystery. The other dimension is all around you in just a much superior and to human senses undetectable vibration level as the lower physical.

Our Lord JESUS, knew all of these things two thousand years ago.

You know that there are no records and accounts of him for a long period of time. In all this unaccounted time he studied in various countries of the orient. He studied physics, chemistry and many other subjects. He became a wise and a supremely intelligent human being who through his diligent studies and understanding also came to realize and recognize within himself the ultimate power of the creative and life sustaining spiritual being, we call God. At that time, he recognized this absolute universal force as the father of all and eternal creation. It was prophesied by several wise and spiritually advanced men, that some day there would be a Messiah, who would come and free humankind from the bondage of sin. They knew that for certain, that every event and happening of historical proportion would come in it's own time. Just when the time and the need for it were right and had arrived. As many wise men also know and realize, every occurrence of tremendous and historical outcome and eternally lasting effect would have its counterpart in nature. In this singular case, it was the alignment and conjunction of several planets in our solar system. Precise mathematical calculations of several learned astrologers, among them the famous kings of the Orient, pointed to the little town of Bethlehem.

Even as I can materialize in front of you, so could at that time any other spiritual being appear in front of Mary, Joseph and the shepherds in the field. I know this is difficult to understand but even though we do know on our side what is supposed to happen in the next hour, we also do know what is to come in the world where you live in. That is why Mary received a message that she would bear a son. That is why Joseph was told to call his son Jesus and the shepherds in the field also saw the man, telling them that a child is to be born who would some day be a king. Knowing and understanding human nature, the spiritual beings knew, that King Herod would not take too kindly to the much feared toppling of his throne, he had indeed all the newborn male children slaughtered. And again Joseph was warned beforehand to take his wife and child out of the country. Now you see, that many things that were written down in the Bible were actually true and totally accurate. There was no doubt in Mary's or Joseph's mind, that their son Jesus would some day be the one prophesied to teach the truth and the laws of the spiritual existence of mankind. Every time he spoke to the people of his time, he tried to make those laws of spiritual nature easy to understand. He also knew then that through meditation and prayer he could draw from the spirit of the creative force God and by following the law of this universal spirit rather then oppose it he gained such power of mind, that he actually advanced spiritually to the high awareness and truth of the Christ spirit. Even though he had attained this awareness, he was still a man in a human body and he would prove to mankind once and for all, that life is everlasting. But how could he make it clear to the people, other then to die and appear in front of them in his seemingly physical body. To make you understand, how it was actually done, I must remind you now of the water in your mothers basement. You had the wet shoes and the dirty ring around you ankles as evidence and yet when you entered the basement a second time, there was not one drop of water in sight. Here is the explanation to this. The vibration structure of the water simply had to be raised to such a degree that it became invisible to your physical senses. That is the whole secret. And the same was done with the physical body of Jesus. He had promised to his men that he would rise again, and rise he did. However, he did not rise in his poor battered physical body. He rose and appeared to his apostles and others in the spiritual astral body. Now you know, that even the resurrection of Jesus is true. But, tell me my love, how could he have come along, and spread his wisdom by telling people at that time about vibrations and mind frequencies of the astral? Nobody would have understood that it is the three-dimensional image of the physical, which is the body in the next dimension to conduct oneself and manifest and just as real as in the physical world. He had to find a different approach to tell the truth. Many things he said, do make now sense to you, correct? And now you also know, that he is as real as you and I. Mind over matter, that's the whole secret. Yes, yes, I know you will say, that doing things like that with his own body, does not explain, how he healed the sick. How could he make a lame person walk? Simple, he knew at that time, what I had told you not to long ago. That the *bundle of energy* or *core of intellect* gives charges to the brain and makes body parts work in the proper order to let a person walk. Now, if a person is not able to walk, and there is no apparent damage to muscles the or nerve tissue, then he knew also, that it was this part of the brain that was not able to receive the command of the real person, the core of intellect where the thought process originates. With his powerful mind, Jesus *'taught'* the spirit of the man, how to put a seemingly dormant part of the brain to work, and give commands to the leg's or any other body part to function. Today scientists call this powerful transfer of electro magnetic impulses *'PSYCHO KENESES'*. It can be directed from the brain toward objects as well as another brain. Medical scientists found out, that only a small part of the human brain is in operation and for the love of God they can't figure out, what the other ninety or so percent is supposed to do in the skull. Well doctor, consider it a different file in the hard drive. All they should do, in some cases mind you, learn how to redirect the stimulating electromagnetic impulses from the real person, the spirit *'bundle of energy'* (the core of intellect). Until some of the scientists come off their high horse and except the fact that the brain is not at all doing the thinking, but is rather the mediator in between the intelligent bundle of energy, and the physical body, they'll just tap in the darkness and never figure out, where the thinking process originates. I could also tell you right now, that researchers could develop a particular instrument to actually capture the astral world over there on my side. Yes, my darling, it also has to do a lot with high frequencies. Perhaps some day we'll share all our secrets. Only not now, because the elders on my side believe it may not be the right time just yet. I will tell you much more in the future but now you must tell me if you understand why you can see me and feel me just like you would another person in the physical world."

Ruby had listened intently to him, and said,

"I think I do understand that everything existing is submissive, to a certain amount of energy coming from the life force, you call *'bundle of energy'* or rather *'core of intellect'*. I also think, that I am seeing and touching a three-dimensional image of you, which is the way you looked in your lifetime on this earth.

You are telling me now in other words, that your own self subconsciously projects into this dimension where you are the exact

59

form of your former human body, because the memory of yourself down to the minutest cell is imprinted likewise a three-dimensional photograph into this 'bundle of energy' which is the real you.

This very same subconscious, which is rooted deeply within the human soul, is then also responsible for life and existence everlasting. Therefore this *'core of intellect'* does make conduct and social interaction with other humans and various other life forms possible in my dimension, as well as yours."

"Correct, Ruby," Justus said, lovingly giving her knees a little squeeze, "I can see that you basically understand, how important the subconscious is. It is a piece of the whole *'bundle of energy'*, which so to speak works from behind the scenes. So to speak in the 'background'.

But yet another part of your subconscious is rooted even deeper in your own being which is a secret super subconscious mind in the center of every living organism. This center of the core is the actual life sustaining force in the physical and later the astral body.

You know, that you do not have to remind any organ of the body to work. Your heart and lungs your stomach and liver, and all the other organs do their job evidently on their own. You do not have to tell yourself to breathe in and breathe out. This very same core of super subconscious is responsible for giving your whole *'bundle of energy'* the sense of being in existence as a unique and individual component of creation which is indeed capable of intelligent conduct, as well as to interact in human society."

"Would you explain to me then, if all men are created equal, why do we have different races in the world? I do understand well, that to all people is given the same potential for spiritual development. But I like to know, why was it essential for the creator to make differences in skin color, and other variations of peoples appearances?" Ruby asked.

"That's the beauty of creation, Ruby," Justus smiled and nodded slightly.

"You did not forget about the big globe which I mentioned to you as example once before. And you know very well, that H_2O is not only one chemical substance but it contains different components to be exactly what it is, water. If only one group of molecules was missing in the ball, it would not be what it was supposed to be. And that is also, what makes our existence challenging, and beautiful at the same time. To learn to accept and get along with another. You do not question the existence of flowers or trees. Nevertheless they are a part of this world as well as mine. You except them as a part of creation and you would not want to have a world without them."

"Oh boy, that'll take another few eons or so before some members of the human race learn that," Ruby chuckled but without much humor," unfortunately there are always people who think that they have the right to dictate other lives and in reality spread nothing but misery and suffering in this world. Look what some so-called chief's are doing to his or her own countries. For the sake of financial and territorial gains they make war, and send young men into battle to fight for them and their demented causes. Oh Justus, is that insanity never going to stop. Why couldn't we just have God as the only ruler in this crazy world."

"Ruby, God is our spiritual leader. In the physical world leadership is just as necessary. Think what kind of disorder there would be, if factories would be without the leader and his staff in the office to oversee the production of cars for example. Nobody on the assembly line would know what to do, if there would not be the people in the office, to take the responsibility for design and management and distribution of the products.

The same is to be said about leading a country. It takes a wise and understanding counselor to assure their constituents that their human rights are upheld and their welfare assured. Unfortunately, some of the leaders get chosen because they make long and loud speeches and promises not kept. They just bribe their way into leadership, only without having the qualification for it. They are powerful in their finances, but not in wisdom. This has been done ever since time began and there is not much that could be changed, my dear Ruby. Only if people them selves change within, will there be a change without. Now it does make sense to you, what John the Baptist said. 'Before kingdoms can change, man must change'."

"How did you ever get so wise, Justus? I do have another question that is bothering me and possibly millions of other people also. It's about sex. Is it still going on in the afterlife or does it stop with death?" Ruby asked.

"Nothing gets taken away. Didn't I tell you, that our astral body is the exact duplicate of the physical body? How cruel and irrational would our creator be if he gives us these natural urges and the sex organs, if they only function and be of certain use in the physical world. Lovemaking as the finest expression between two people would be suddenly taken away, rendering these parts of the human body useless and dysfunctional. Could you imagine spending eternity with your soul mate and not being able to physically worship and adore him or her? Touching caressing and kissing and lovemaking is a part of existence in your world as well as mine. If you would move to another country to live, would you leave all acquired wisdom and knowledge of your previous experiences behind? Of course not. The same goes for the change or transition we call physical death. Our memories and all our experiences are still a part of our being and are not suddenly forgotten. You see now what I am getting at? As you will see very soon, if love is given and felt even in between dimensions, there shall be hope. Even for the most wretched. Now, I must tell you all and truthfully what occurred in my life. Then you will understand everything."

Ruby noticed that, despite the little squeeze earlier, the pressure of his hands on her knees had not changed at all. Still light as the wing of a butterfly his hands were resting. He did not want to frighten her any further. Feeling better now and seeing that there was nothing to fear from him, Ruby gently placed her hands on his. This was something she would have never dreamed of doing in all her life. Yet she was touching him once more. Willingly and not only out of curiosity but in a gesture of friendship and love for this being in front of her. Well pleased with this show of courage on her part, Justus smiled at her.

"It is getting late Ruby and you must get up early. I will return to you after work tomorrow. Then I will tell you more. Get some rest now and sleep well. Don't worry, I will not just disappear right here in front of your eyes. I'll wait until you are in the other room."

Indeed, Ruby suddenly felt tired. It was getting close to midnight and six-o-clock came early. She did not argue and said:

"Yes it is getting late and my boss will not understand when I fall asleep on the job." Slowly she got up from the chair and walked toward the door to her bedroom. Suddenly she realized what he had said only a few moments earlier. He would return to her after work. Would he return as he was now or would she never see him again? Fearful that the latter was the case she turned and asked Justus, who was still sitting on the carpet.

"Will I see you tomorrow or will I just be able to hear you as always?"

Smiling and obviously glad to see this kind of fear in her face, he answered,

"You'll see me."

Strange as it may seem but she let out a sigh of relief. He blew her a kiss and her heart skipped a beat. Her knees began shaking again and quickly she closed the door behind her. However, curiosity got the better of her and slowly she opened the door once more to see if he was gone. Almost like a child on Christmas Eve taking a peek at Santa, Ruby stuck her head into the room again. As if he had anticipated what she would do, Justus still sat as he had only a moment ago. His mirth visible. With laughter in his voice he ordered,

"To bed, Ruby."

And like a child on Christmas Eve who got caught peeking Ruby's face turned red and impish she smiled back at him,

"I just wanted to say good night."

He knew she was lying. And she knew that he knew that as well. Quickly she closed the door again, undressed and jumped into her bed. Soon she was asleep.

CHAPTER 5

Cold Hard Facts

The next day was gone by fast. Ruby had to do some inventory at the store and was kept busy.

Finishing her work, Ruby closed the inventory book and locked up the store. Thinking that she would make herself just a quick TV dinner, she went to her apartment upstairs. Time was precious as she was looking forward to see Justus later. Just thinking about it made her heart beat faster. But dinner would have to come first. Suddenly she realized that this was another question she had to ask him. What kind of nourishment does the astral body require if any at all. She could not imagine, to have to go through eternity without having at least a taste of her favorite foods. To her surprise she heard him say telepathically,

"Yes, Ruby, we do eat and drink just like in the physical world. However we do it when we feel like it or just have an appetite for a certain dish. Like a bowl of fruit or a glass of wine."

"Great, that should make my mother's husband happy when he gets there. He can get pickled even when he's dead." Ruby said laughing. She took her dinner out of the microwave oven and placed it on the small kitchen table.

"Not so, Ruby, we can drink all we want but we do not get drunk. He and any other alcoholics will have to get used to the fact that there is no drinking to forget or solve problems. Furthermore as I found out drinking creates problems, not solve them."

"So, you did like to drink also while still in this world?" Ruby asked in between bites.

"Yes, I did very much. And that was a part of my life I am not proud of. But one thing at the time. Finish your dinner first. I will see you in the living room."

Ruby almost dropped her fork. That's it. She would actually see him. Oh boy, that would take some getting used to. Once again her heart began to beat faster. Would he just appear out of thin air? Would he walk through the door like a living human being? As these thoughts went through her mind, she finished eating and cleared the table. It was strange that there was no answer forthcoming. She poured herself a large glass of soda. Ruby with the soda in her hand went to her bedroom to change her shoes and clothes. She pulled on her comfortable sweats and slippers took the soda from her night table where she had placed it to change clothes and walked down the small hallway to her living room. As she opened the door, she found the answer to her questions earlier. She stopped in her track. Justus was sitting on her couch. He smiled. A beautiful open friendly smile. Ruby's knees almost buckled. The soda started shaking slightly.

"I thought it might be better that way. I figured it might be silly to ring your doorbell. If your boss saw me, he might want to know who your gentleman caller is."

Instantly Ruby saw the humor in the situation and she began to laugh until her sides ached. She could only imagine her bosses face if she would have to explain as to who this man was. She walked over to the couch and sat on the other end placing the glass with soda on the coffee table in front of her.

"You could sit a little closer, Ruby. I am not in the habit of biting, you know." Justus said with a chuckle. Ruby fussed with her pants and took a small peace of lint off. Shyly, she moved a few inches closer to the middle of the couch. Her bravery was rewarded with another warm smile and softly, he placed his hand on top of her hands, which were folded in her lap. Her eyes lowered she said quietly,

"I suddenly don't know what to do or how to behave. Here is a man sitting in my living room who is actually dead for a long time already.

65

It just hit me that the man is not dead but very much alive, jumping from one world to another. I really don't know what to be afraid off more. The fact that you are supposedly dead or the undeniable fact that you are a man."

"Let me ask you a question, Ruby. How do you think the apostles felt, when they saw Jesus after the resurrection? Do you think they were afraid of him?" Justus asked.

"I have no idea what could have possibly gone through their mind. I would think they were astonished and happy to see him. But that is a little different. They all knew him and they knew what he looked like in life. I however have never seen you before," Ruby answered. and taking a deep breath she continued, "don't you understand how strange and crazy this is? Until last night you were still something not really real. Now I am confronted with the cold hard fact that there really is life after death. Something I never much thought about. Certainly not in the country I grew up in. There, people that prayed and believed in God were laughed at and considered pitiful self-delusional idiots. I myself was one of the laughing, as it comes out now, fools."

"Now, Ruby, this is not true," Justus interrupted, "no way are you to be considered a fool. You just didn't know any better. Like you said, you grew up where religion was not a great part of people's lives. Now you live in a great country where even the money says 'In God we trust.' What a tremendous and wonderful change."

"Ha that's a laugh. Can you imagine me telling someone about you? They would stick me in the loony bin and throw the key away. They all want to believe in something but confronted with it they just call anyone like me crazy and send them to a shrink. It doesn't get any more two-faced then that. Until they have a experience like I am having and see a ghost or hear a voice which is not their own they would never believe it."

"I can tell you right now, that most of those people are just afraid of the unknown. Since there is no scientific evidence to the existence of my world, they just deny it or in some other cases only hope for it to be true. Their believe is based on hope and faith alone."

"That still doesn't give me a clue how to convince anybody about the truth of the existence of your world. In case the subject should ever come up among my friends or co-workers. What am I supposed to say then?" Ruby pouted.

"Let me just tell you in a very few words something a wise man once said. To a believer no explanation is necessary. To a non-believer no explanation is possible. So very true. There are many people all around the world who changed their mind after having experiences similar to yours. Some people do leave their body involuntarily just as you did at your mother's house. Or after having an accident being brought back to life by doctors. Some of them cannot recall anything. Many however do recall seeing their own bodies just like you did that one time. They will go through a tunnel with a light at the end. They see and meet long dead relatives. If you could ask any one of them, they could tell you that they have a whole new outlook on life. So, Charles Dickens 'Christmas Carol' doesn't seem so far fetched anymore. Wouldn't you agree?"

"You mean to tell me that Dickens died and came back and then wrote a nice story about it? To me it was just that; a nice story. Now I have to look forward to seeing my whole life flash before me, when I die. There are some things I'm trying very hard to forget. Like the beatings I got from my grandmother. Like my failed marriages. My children being taken away from me by a damn communist regime because I spoke out against it. Why am I telling you all this. If what you say is true, and you have been with me from the day of my birth, then you really know what I don't want to re-live again." Ruby shuddered.

"I know very well the whole story and to put your mind at ease you will only be an observer and see most of it without much emotion. Emotions are only very strong if you hurt somebody. Physical and emotional abuse both hurt as you found out. But it will not be you who is doing the suffering for it. The ones who have done the hurting will feel your emotions and your pain at their own life replay. Nobody can get out of that. No matter how poor or rich one is. Even if some people think they can buy their way out of situations in life, they cannot buy their way out of judgment. They will do the paying later on. And God doesn't take money. Just remember that the last shirt on earth doesn't have any pockets."

"Oh now wait here, I remember you telling me that you can eat and drink anything you like. How do you pay for it? You are not telling me, that you grow a little vegetable garden or some fruit trees in your world to satisfy your appetites, do you? And what about the wine you spoke of? Is there a vineyard right behind your house?" Ruby asked humorously.

"You are going to like this very much, Ruby. Anything you want and require, is free in my world. No mortgage to pay; Even though, everybody has a home here. We don't need any electric or gas or telephone. If we want to talk to someone, we call telepathically and meet at a point of our choosing. Well, of course we cannot call a complete stranger though. You will have to know a person first, before you can call. So, there are also no annoying calls." he laughed.

"I don't understand, Justus, how this is possible. If you can call someone in your mind, does that not also mean, that everyone in your world can read your thoughts as you can read and hear mine right now?" Ruby worried.

"Remember, that I told you that everybody has his or her own frequency. I don't think, I have to tell you that it would be impossible to exist here in my world, if everybody could read and hear each other's thoughts. The other frequencies are blocked out by your own mind, until you choose to get in touch with someone you know. And then you tune in only for a brief time, to call for a meeting with loved ones and friends."

"Ah, now I get it. The call frequency is something similar to the Internet. Besides that, everybody still can retain his or her privacy. But what about the homes Justus? Don't they have to be furnished? Where do you get the furniture from?"

"You forgot, that everything created or built, has a exact replica in our world. Physical molecules, no matter if they be natural or man-made, like plastic, have energy, which is created by the atoms of the object in question. In my world, this energy shows up as a dense and solid object, which we may use if we choose to do so."

"Goodness, then your world must be cluttered with chunk from many centuries," Ruby laughed.

"Not so, Ruby, this energy is without life force and can be destroyed. A chair or table or bed does not have a soul or intelligence," he chuckled.

"Since you speak of a bed, Justus, there is another question I am curious about. You said, that it is always bright in your world. Your body must get tired some time. Don't you ever go to sleep?"

"Yes of course we sleep also. It is not our body, which needs the rest. It is our mind that needs it. Can you imagine to expose your poor mind to constant stimuli without taking a nap? Our naps are just as refreshing and rejuvenating as in your world. They can take from a few minutes to a few days however."

"Hi hi, I would like to do that sometimes. Especially as a kid. Then I would have loved to take a long nap until Christmas. The time seemed to stand still then. Now it goes like a flash. Before you know it, another year has passed. Tell me, Justus, do you have any awareness of time passing?"

"We know, what year it is. Since new people arrive here every day, we know the date also. We don't count however, if that is what you mean. In the physical world there are four seasons, which we don't have. The weather is constant here and always nice. We have no storms or natural catastrophes to deal with."

"Well Justus, I don't know if I would like that so much. Once in a while a little rain is quite pleasant. What if you feel like taking a walk in the rain? Or see a nice rainbow. Where do you go then?"

"If we want to see that, we just lower our vibration to the earth level and we can experience all the rain we want."

"Ah, so that is why some people see ghosts huh? Just out for a little stroll in the world." Ruby giggled.

"No, no, Ruby, they are not out for a stroll. There is a big difference between a ghost and a spirit person." He had to laugh at her humor.

"I'm sure you are going to tell me about the difference. I thought you people over there are all ghosts." Ruby cocked her head in question.

"People like me are aware of their surroundings and know, what happened to them. Others don't know, that they have gone through the transition we call death. These are ghosts. Sometimes, as a matter of fact in most cases, his or her dying experience was so traumatic, that their own mind is blocking the experience out to protect them. You have heard of people having a terrible experience in life and cannot remember anything. Their mind is blocking the terrible and frightening happenstance out also. You call this amnesia. In most cases in your world, these people will have little flashes at a time and they will finally remember what happened. But that will take time. Over in my world, it takes time also. Now remember, an accident can happen to a person a few times. However, dying is something you do only once. So, however long it takes to let the soul adjust and remember what happened to them, they will be in a dream-like state for just that period of time. They have no concept of time passing and some of them are around for centuries already. To interfere, could send them into shock and it would be cruel to say the least. They are watched and well taken care of by either relatives or guides. Sometimes these ghosts, as you call them, venture out into your world, because they are looking for something or someone. They feel that they have some unfinished business."

"Oh, but what about the nasty ones, that spook around in old castles and houses? They frighten innocent people half out of their wits and seem to enjoy it. You can't tell me that they don't know what happened to them. Some of them do even talk and tell that they have died. They go as far as to tell their own name." Ruby shot back.

"Ruby, I told you that people do not change when they come into my world. Their characteristics and demeanor is still the same as it always was. It does not take a genius to figure out, that they enjoy scaring people. That's just it. If people would come up to them and say something, instead of running, they would soon realize, that the fun is over. They would stop this nonsense soon, because they could get no more satisfaction and fun. These are mostly people, that had no courage in life and were always scared of others. Now they enjoy their power of scaring people in the world, which might also not have been too kind to them. Others, which introduce themselves by name, might just look for a nice person to talk too. They are mostly friendly, which the introduction with their name suggests."

"Oh, well excuse me, do you really expect people to just say, 'oh hello, it's nice to see you'?" Ruby asked somewhat sarcastically.

"Why not? You remember your uncle Robert, right? Would you think that he could hurt you just because he is in my world? He would no more hurt you, as he never had done in all your life. He loved you and he still does. What keeps most loving relatives in my world from making contact, is the fear of the unknown from the people in your world. We know and we can feel, when someone is afraid and that is why we stay away and have to wait until you can join us in my world. It is because of love, that relatives keep away from the so-called living. Even though there are thousands, who would rejoice in a word or loving thought. It is sad to think, that people are considered something dangerous, just because they have died and crossed over into my world. Even people that have loved you all their lives. If you let them, they might even help you with a little advice here and there. Especially when it is a parent or grandparent that has made the transition. Let me tell you Ruby, it's some of the living you have to be afraid of. They can hurt you."

"I know that, Justus, we decent people have to put iron bars on our windows to keep burglars and home invaders out these days. But there are other criminals as well Justus. Some of them are just plain mad and seem to have no idea, of what they are doing. They can mislead a whole country and bring it into uproar with their damn craziness. Don't they get punished for their crimes?"

"Oh yes, Ruby, if I tell you, you might shudder. They get punished severely and no one gets around it. They all get, what's coming to them."

"Wonderful, now I can sleep better knowing that Hitler and his ilk are burning in hell for all eternity." Ruby was slapping her knee. Only for an instant did Justus wrinkle his brow. Only for an instant did his look become dark and sad. Nevertheless Ruby had noticed it.

"What is it, Justus? Did I say something wrong?" Ruby asked, concerned that he could hear her thoughts at this moment. That's all she needed. A ghost from the netherworld, pissed off at her.

Justus bit his lower lip and chuckled. Ruby face turned red.

"Actually, it was quite correct what you said. People like Hitler and other criminals burn in a hell you could never imagine. If you cut a life short, you are made to see what you have cheated this poor soul out of. Six million Jewish people were killed alone in concentration camps. Among them countless children who never had the chance of growing up in the physical world. They could have been mothers, fathers, doctors, teachers, artists and the list goes on and on. Each could have been contributing to the human race in their own way. Not to mention all the other innocent people thrown into a war by a madman's idea. Now imagine that he and all the other war criminals have to feel and see each person's pain and anguish they inflicted on their victims.

They'll feel the fear and the unspeakable terror of the children being ripped away from their parents. They'll feel the horrendous heartbreak each parent went through as they heard their children screaming ripped for them. Not stopping there, they'll feel the horror and the fright of each victim who was tortured, beaten or gassed to death. All in all not counting the six million Jews, there were fifty five million people killed in this war. It's going to take indeed a hell of a long time to let them see and feel every life they have destroyed." Justus finished his speech.

"You can't be serious;" Ruby exclaimed, "every one of them? How long will that take?"

"Let's put it that way, Ruby, Napoleon is still watching his victim's lives. But that is only part of it. Just think about it, how much can human souls endures. Remember a few months back as I told you that the soul couldn't be destroyed. It cannot be destroyed from without. But it can be destroyed from within. Evil as such will eventually become demonic and annihilate itself until there is no sense of being and awareness left," Justus explained.

"O boy, I better behave. Otherwise I might blow myself right back out of heaven. That's actually the place I would like to go and stay for a while," Ruby said after a brief pause.

"Whatever you want to call it, we don't pay any bills and the air is not polluted. As much as I would like to romanticize our existence in the after life. It is not so much different from earth life. I had no idea about this existence in the after life myself and was quite surprised to find out that it is true. We have everything that you can think of. Except things we do not need over here in my dimension, which is cars and trains and airplanes. We do totally nicely without, since we journey just a little faster. We do, what many people sometimes would love, to be capable of doing. We travel by the speed of thought. As daft as it may sound to you, but we transport our bodies of sheer compressed energy with one thought to a distant destination in the fraction of a second. Sound's fun right? But it's true.

Tomorrow I shall tell you more. It is late and you should get some sleep. I will be here tomorrow," Justus promised.

"Yes you are right," Ruby agreed, "it is late and I feel tired. I almost forgot, tomorrow is Saturday and I don't have to work. My bosses' wife is minding the store on weekends. That will give us a lot of time to talk. What time can I expect you to be here?" Ruby asked.

"I will be here after you had your breakfast. Go to bed now. Good night, Ruby." Justus smiled.

"Good night, Justus." Ruby smiled back at him. Drinking the last of her soda, she took the glass and walked with it to the kitchen. She rinsed the glass and went to bed.

Ruby woke up around nine-o-clock. Looking at her alarm clock she mumbled and cussed under her breath,

"Damn, what a lazy ass I am. So many things to do and write and here I'm still in bed. Well, first things first." She jumped out of bed and took a shower. She slipped into a light comfortable day robe and went to the kitchen to eat breakfast. Pouring herself another big cup of coffee into a mug, she walked to the living room. Not surprised at all by Justus, who was sitting on the couch at the same spot he had been the previous day, she put the mug on the table and sat down on the other end of the couch. Giggling she said,

"Sorry I'm late. I am starting to feel like the Ghost and Misses Muir. Boy, if my boss knew what is going on here, he would charge me double the rent."

"I have the feeling that he would tell you to find yourself a different place to live. I don't think he would be too keen on having a ghost appearing in his employee's apartments." Justus laughed. Ruby sipped on her coffee and reached for her notebook, as she noticed his attire. He was wearing a dark green shirt and black pants. Why wasn't he wearing the ugly brown robe?

"Justus, where is your robe and where is the cross you wore yesterday?" Ruby asked.

"It all has to do with the story I am about to tell you. Now listen and write it all down. You will see what I mean by that, when I tell you about my life and what I had done. It will shock you and make you angry and sad. Nevertheless, it's all true," Justus answered. Ruby took her pen as he started to tell his tale…

"It was a cold October morning, when I came in to this world. Born in Manchester England on October 14th in the year of our Lord 1772, when my mother was only a young girl of fifteen. Upon finding out, that my mother was expecting a child, she was left by her lover. Since he was much older, and already in his late twenties or early thirty's, he took advantage of her innocence and destitute situation shamelessly. Now that I was to be born, mother was as piteously poor as the day, when she had met my father. She tried her best, to keep the both of us alive. My father's servant had befriended my mother and helped her after, as best as he could. A disaster struck and we found ourselves without a home. Then through a stroke of good luck, she was coincidentally brought together, with people helping us with tremendous generosity and charity out of our dire situation. A wealthy couple, which had bought my fathers house, just had returned from America. They suggested to their friend, who also knew my father, to take mother and me to this new land. With the help of this good friend, who owned the ship that had brought this rich family back to England, we sailed for the new land America. So, we ended up in Virginia in the spring of 1774, when I was nearly two years of age. Only for a brief time of two years, our lives were better then ever before. Mother had succeeded to deceive a lot of people with her display of naive, which had precisely the effect she had hoped for. Mother had introduced herself as a widow and with the aid of her friend, whom she later married, her secret seemed safe. Then another disaster struck and we ended up back in Europe in 1776. With substantial assets from the sale of jewels and overtaking her husband's business, she bought a new life for us. I was four years old at the time and began to show at this budding age already the effects of having been spoiled. I was a very strong willed tike and mother did not know, how to properly discipline me. She feared that she would wreck the only precious reminder of the love of her life. The man, who was my father, became an obsession to her. A dangerous passion, which she was not able to curb. Even though he had abandoned her, when she would have need of him most, she considered herself still in love with him. By a strange coincidence, mother had found my father in Spain a few months after we had moved there. She knew even before we went to America, where he had taken residence. I was in my teens as I was introduced to him. My true identity however, was kept from him, as well as him being my parent, was kept from me. I can only suspect, that my fathers refusal to marry my mother, even though she had been living in his house before I was born, addled her wits to such an extend, that she somehow subconsciously, sought revenge on my father, by hurting the very thing, he had to come to love. Even to this day, I do not understand, what state of mind would lead a person over the edge to go that far? That was merely a very short version, of what really happened. There is so much more and I will tell you everything in detail. So, let me start at the beginning.

Many years ago there was a young innocent girl..."

Chapter 6

England 1772 The Birth

Margaret was screaming. She was frightened and in pain and once more she was screaming at the top of her lungs. She had been in labor for nearly eighteen hours now and the pains became increasingly worse. She felt like pushing. Pushing this life, which had grown inside her for the past nine months from her body. Sweat was pouring down her young face in little rivulets and yet another pain which was seemingly trying to split her apart, went through her again. Grunting, sweating and screaming she bore down and pushed, as she felt a light slap on her face.

"Shut up and do not push yet. You will tear yourself, dumb girl," the midwife was shouting at her. The older woman who was a usually kind and gentle person was showing her anger and frustration. Altogether appalled and much disgusted by the conditions, this tiny room was in, she was more so depressed by her own predicament she had to do her work under. This girl, whom she guessed, was no more than a wee bit of a child being around fourteen or fifteen years of age, was actually living in this filth.

A small room with one big bed and a square wooden table in the corner,—she wrinkled her nose in disgust—weeks-old rotting food and moldy bread on the grimy surface. Two wobbly three-legged wooden stools standing in front of the table, they also could use a good scrubbing. To the side next to the huge bed was a plain small candle stand with one single, dripping, smoking candle in its holder. In the right corner of the apartment stood what looked like a hope chest, which unquestionably had seen better days. In between the candle stand and the chest was a tiny window, it's glass broken. Shreds of fabrics had been stuffed in the hole, to keep out the cold air. The night was cold and there was no wood in the small fireplace. The midwife felt the ice-cold draft and the dampness from the foggy night air seeping through the rags in the window. Looking around, she noticed behind the hope chest, a pile of filthy rags that turned out upon closer inspection, to be the meager clothing the girl possessed. Sloppy and unwashed stuffed into the corner. Seeping through the pile that emanated a rancid moldy odor, she saw little silverfish, rushing over the floor. Finally she found, what she was looking for. One of the girl's skirts was large enough to function as a window hanging as she had noticed before, that two rusty hooks above the window were still in the wall. A sign that long ago there might have been curtains, but there were none now. The midwife fastened the skirt over the hooks, which would keep the cold night air out, but would also keep the stink and stale air inside the little room. The stink from the un-emptied chamber pot and the pile of moldy clothing in the corner, as well as the spoiling food on the grimy table. The only implication that at least the girl kept her own self reasonably clean, was a water pitcher and a matching cracked porcelain basin on the little vanity table, standing near the foot end of the big bed. Examining her young patient ones again she found, that the squirming and frightened girl was almost fully dilated and making matters worse, her water had broken soaking the filthy moldy straw mattress. Worried that the girl was sinking to far into the straw mattress and thus could prolong and complicate the birth, the midwife yanked the blankets from the bed. She quickly ran to the other tiny room across the hallway and logged the smaller mattress into the bigger room where she placed it on the floor. Opening the chest, to her relive she found some reasonably taintless bed linen. She grabbed one of the linens spreading it over the mattress on the floor. She went back to the girl and helping her up, after she had just finished with another contraction she supported the girl under her arms.

"Come girl, lie down on the mattress over here. It shall be much easier that way." Having eased the girl carefully onto the small mattress on the floor, the midwife who had introduced herself earlier as Misses Bowman went back to the bed and took the big feather pillow to place it under the girl's head. Right as she was doing that, the door opened and a man stood in the doorway. The same man, who had introduced himself as Hammed, humble servant and steward of Master Viego's household. He came to her many hours before to tell her that his Master's mistress was in labor and was in need of her services. The young Lady would be found in her tiny apartment above the laundry kitchen. Misses Bowman knew this neighborhood well. Besides this tiny filthy room was another room across the hall, which was not in any better shape then this one, where Margaret was laboring. The girl told her that it had once belonged to her late mother. The other smaller room across the hall with only a small bed and a wobbly chair was her own small living space.

Awestruck, as pale as his dark features would allow he stared at the scene in front of him and he asked,

"Is the child about to be born?"

Angrily and not in the least intimidated by this dark looking fellow, Misses Bowman retorted,

"I need plenty of hot water, and yes the child is about to be born. Make yourself useful Sir, and fetch me some."

Hammed's nose slightly put out of joint by the older women's commanding voice, turned on his heels and left without another word, quietly closing the door behind him. Convulsing and squirming, Margaret clutched the bed linen and mattress she was laying on, huffing and puffing through another contraction. Kneeling in front of Margaret at the end of the small mattress, Misses Bowman pushed up Margaret's legs. She could see, that the baby's head was crowning. The door opened again and the shoemaker's wife Misses Tippins from down the street came in, accompanied by Hammed who was logging two huge buckets of hot steaming water. He put the buckets on the floor with a thud.

"Here is your water Madam," he said. Out of breath and feeling the need to rest Misses Tippins sat heavily on one of the wobbly little stools and shaking her graying head said to the midwife,

"The poor dear, what will happened to her now. I know Margaret, ever since she was a wee girl. Her mother,—God rest her soul," she was making the sign of the cross, "died only this Christmas past. She was such lonely woman, ever since her beloved husband had passed on. To support Margaret and herself, she nearly worked her fingers to the bone down in the laundry kitchen. And there was not any money, to give the poor soul a decent burial." Misses Bowman and Hammed had listened to the kind elderly woman, who sat heavily sighing on the little unsteady stool. But she had not taken her eyes from her patient. Due to her occupation as a Midwife, Misses Bowman had been in this neighborhood on several occasions. She was fairly well acquainted with Misses Tippins and said to her sadly,

"It is a great tragedy, my dear Misses Tippins, so many people without any means. I know too many of them,—push now, girl, come on push hard, take a deep breath and push,—there—, very good, child, now—stop pushing,—blow,—blow, like blowing out a candle, yes good, very good the baby is almost out, one more time,—come, give me a good long push."

Margaret pushed, and felt the baby's body slither from her birth canal. With a steady and firm grip Misses Bowman caught the child in her hands. Binding and cutting the cord, the midwife began cleaning the child's mouth and nose with a little sanitary piece of linen, she carried in her bag and turning the child, she softly slapped the small bottom, which resulted in a howl of outraged disapproval and insult from the baby. Having witnessed just now the miracle of life, Hammed feeling queasy and somewhat light headed sank on the other chair. His face however beamed radiantly and flashing a bright smile he said,

"Allah be praised, what a big beautiful child."

Misses Tippins stood up and silently walked to the vanity to get the basin and placed it next to Misses Bowman on the floor. Carefully,

Misses Tippins poured some of the hot water in the basin and handed the pitcher with cold water to the midwife. Misses Bowman then adding some cold water to the basin checked the temperature with her elbow. Kneeling on the floor, she took the baby and another small piece of linen from her bag and placing the soft little bottom into the water, she started to cleanse the child of every evidence bespeaking it's birth.

While the Midwife was still busy with bathing the child, Misses Tippins looked around the in the room, as if she was trying to find something and said,

"Earlier this day I gave Margaret some nappies and wrappings for the child. It was worn, but neatly washed. It was from one of my little grandson's things. I wonder where I can find it."

Nodding her head and motioning in the direction of the chest Misses Bowman answered,

"I noticed a bundle in this chest over there earlier, Misses Tippins. Is this perhaps what you are looking for?"

Misses Tippins opened the chest, as it's rusty hinges screeched annoyingly, there she found indeed the bundle she had been searching for and unwrapping it quickly, she handed the nappies and a warm soft little blanket to Misses Bowman. Appreciative Misses Bowman smiled at Misses Tippins:

"Much obliged, Misses Tippins, I merely pray that there would be more good hearted people like yourself in this wretched world." At once she wrapped the baby into the woolen blanket. Smiling now, she picked the baby up and handed it to Margaret, who had watched her every move in amazement.

"Here is your big son, my girl. It is the day of October the 14th in the year of our Lord 1772. He is a healthy and beautiful child. Take good care of him."

Faint and exhausted, Margaret cradled her son in her arm. While the midwife carefully and thoroughly examined the just now expelled afterbirth and began to cleanse her patient, Margaret looked at her tiny son. His dark hair clinging damp to his little forehead. A pair of tiny fists pressed against rosy and rounded little cheeks. Astonishingly, he was very quiet now and making soft baby noises he seemed to muster his mother with his big dark eyes. She cautiously touched his face with her finger and was surprised, at the forceful grip as he grabbed her thumb, holding on with a strong clasp. As if he wanted to stake his claim once and for all indisputable, he hungrily suckled on her finger, as she carefully touched his soft little mouth. In that instant, Margaret smiled and mother and child formed a bond between them, which could never be broken. Hammed still slightly dazed stood up and kneeling next to Margaret on the floor, gently touched the baby's cheek with one finger.

"I shall go and inform my master of the birth of his beautiful healthy son. Perhaps now he is going to soften his heart." With tears in her eyes, Margaret put her hand on his arm,

"Oh, Hammed, he is going to get angry at you my dear friend. I do not think that...," her words were trailing off, as he put a silencing finger over her lips.

"Please, Miss Margaret, do not exhaust yourself any further. I shall return tomorrow. Get some rest, and may Allah protect you and the child." He stood up and quickly left the tiny room.

Margaret, not much than a child herself, was a radiant beautiful girl, with big hazel green eyes, surrounded by long dark lashes. Her mass of auburn hair cascading down to just below her tiny waist in soft waves. Natural reddish golden highlights fetchingly catching the sunlight framing the milk-and-blood-skin of her silky cheeks. Her forehead and her stubborn little chin bespeaking intelligence and determination. Showing a row of taintless pearly-white teeth and her straight little nose wrinkled charmingly, as soon as her generously full lips turned into a smile. Petite in stature her full breast of promising proportion contrasting her tiny waist. Her long skirts and dresses however hid her wide hips over short but shapely legs.

Born and raised in Manchester she had never known her dear father, who had died in 1759, as she was only two years old at the time. Her mother had told her, that her beloved husband had suffered a severe seizure of falling sickness and never regaining consciousness, had passed on. After that Margaret's mother, destitute and without a husband and provider, was forced to vacate the comfortable little four-room flat above the shoemaker's store. She rented this small two-room apartment over the laundry kitchen. Since her mother worked in the laundry kitchen, Margaret was left to her self most times. She would run errands for the shoemaker Mister Tippins. Every coin Margaret received from Mister Tippins, was proudly handed to her mother, who would purchase bread and fish and occasionally a piece of cheese, which didn't last for very long. Nevertheless it was enough for a humble meal. Then disaster struck as her mother suddenly fell ill. There was no money to pay the doctor. Coughing and laboring heavily for every breath, she lay feverish and delirious in bed and within one week died, never recovering from her inflamed lungs.

It was nearly two weeks after her mother's death that Margaret, returning from church where she had prayed for her mother's soul, met this man leaving the shoemaker's store. Intending to visit with Misses Tippins, Margaret collided with this man.

"Ho, little Lady, I beg your pardon. You must be thinking some very deep thoughts that you did not notice, I was walking here. A gentleman perhaps is occupying the young Lady's mind? You almost ran me over," he chided with a twinkle in his eyes.

"Pardon me, Sir, but I do not think of gentlemen. I am returning from church, where I prayed for my beloved mother's soul," and crossing herself she continued her apology, "she died but two weeks past. Please, Sir, do forgive my absent-mindedness," she finished sadly and unbidden tears welled up in her beautiful eyes.

"Except my sincerest condolences, young Lady. It is I, who must beg your pardon. Hopefully I did not hurt you. But please can I be of assistance in any way? I should like to help, if I may." Seeing that her destination was the shoemaker's shop he assumed she wanted to pick up some shoes.

"Perchance you are having some shoe's repaired. I should like to offer escorting you home in my master's carriage, once your business is conducted."

Margaret lowering her eyes, quietly answered,

"That will not be necessary, Sir, I am not here to shop. I merely intended to visit Misses Tippins and perhaps run an errand for Mister Tippins." She sighed heavily.

"A young lady should not have to run errands for a cobbler," the strange looking man said. He had noticed her poor and shabby attire, which was desperately in need of mending, and her worn out gloves were torn in a few spots. To keep out the cold air, Margaret clutched her cape tightly around herself and holding her hood under her chin. However the face of this girl was stunningly lovely and very familiar. Catching himself as he smiled revealing his snow-white teeth which was contrasting his dark black beard and mustache.

"Do forgive me I did not mean to violate your private affairs, my dear young lady. Have you no one to care for you then? A brother or sister perhaps or your father?" he questioned.

"My father died when I was a little child and I do not have any brothers or sisters, Sir," Margaret said, "I do need to buy food and therefore I have to do what I must to survive."

"Perhaps I am able to help, but let me consult my master first," the mysterious man mused, and catching himself, he continued, "oh, pardon me, I should like to introduce myself. My name is Hammed. I serve a wealthy man in the upper part of the city. His name in Master Giaccomo Viego. However, all his friends and servants call him 'Jack' or 'Master'. Perhaps you have heard of him?" Politely curtseying Margaret replied,

"I am pleased to make your acquaintance, Sir. My name is Margaret Katarina Ziegler," she said with a shy smile, "to answer your question, no, Sir Hammed, I have not heard the name of your master before."

"Please do not call me Sir. I am merely a humble servant. Just call me Hammed," he said with another flashing smile.

"It is an unusual name and stranger yet your attire, Hammed, particularly your hat." Margaret was shivering and pulling her cape tighter around herself.

"I grew up in Istanbul which is far from here and the climate much warmer then this place," he explained squinting to avoid the cold wind blowing dirt in his eyes, "I am wearing garments which are traditional in my homeland, Miss Ziegler. This is not a hat I am wearing on my head. It is called a turban. It is a long cloth which men in my country wrap around their head. Perhaps some day you shall see for yourself." and noticing how uncomfortable she was, he suggested, " it might be better if you go inside and out of this dreadful wind. I shall talk to my master this very night and will give you the answer in a few days time. I will come and meat you here at the cobblers shop the day after tomorrow. Wait for me here at noontime. I am sure that my master can help you." With that he turned and jumped into the waiting carriage before Margaret could say another word. Stunned, she looked on as the carriage slowly rumbled up the narrow street. Hesitantly she turned and went to the cobblers shop.

Once inside she took off her gloves and cape, to stand by the merrily crackling fireplace in Misses Tippins kitchen. Rubbing her cold hands together and holding them out towards the fire to warm herself she said to the older woman,

"Misses Tippins, you would never believe what just now happened to me."

Taking the wooden spoon out of the soup she had just stirred and seeing the look upon Margaret's face, Misses Tippins tilted her head in question and curiously asked,

"What happened my child, that you are so ecstatic? I have not seen you like this in a long time. Did you perchance find a fat purse with gold in it?" she chuckled. Ignoring Misses Tippins good-natured humor, Margaret lowered her voice to almost a whisper and she said meaningfully and with great importance,

"Misses Tippins, I shall not be running errands for Mister Tippins. I also will not do laundry any longer. I believe my fortune is about to change for the better."

"What are you getting yourself into my child? Ever since your poor mother, God Bless her soul, died, I have looked out for you. Now tell me this instant, what is this nonsense about your fortune?" Misses Tippins asked with rising alarm in her voice.

"Oh, my dear Misses. Tippins, calm yourself. I shall tell you what occurred only a few moments past right outside this very shop." And pulling the older woman by her hands to the chair, Margaret sat down herself on the other chair and she began to tell her tale,

"I collided with a strange looking man in front of the door to the shop. Apparently he conducted some business with Mister Tippins for he held a pair of boots under his arm."

"You are speaking of the dark looking fellow in the colorful coat and the strange head-dress?" Misses Tippins interrupted.

"Yes, Misses Tippins, the very same man spoke to me about taking a position in his masters house after hearing my story. As I tendered my apologies for almost running him over I had explained to him, that I was merely returning from church to pray for my mothers soul and was not thinking about gentlemen, as he jestingly suggested. He gave me his word and promised to be back in two days time to tell me his master's answer," Margaret said with an air of great importance.

"Do you have any idea, who this man's master is my child?" Misses Tippins asked in an agitated tone of voice. Despite her great girth she jumped up from her seat and was pacing back and fro wringing her hands in dismay.

"No, I do not know who this man's master is Misses Tippins. I have never seen this man before and I hardly ever go to the upper side of the city where all the wealthy people live. Tell me, Misses Tippins, do you know his master then?" Margaret asked with an uneasy feeling in her stomach.

"His master is a Spanish Nobleman and he is living in the wealthy section uptown since a few years past. He inherited a great big manor house and he is frightfully wealthy. He has become famous and notorious for his services to the local nobility. He is a whoremonger. Need I say more, Margaret?" Misses Tippins asked with a flustered tone in her voice.

"Good heavens, I had no idea!" Margaret exclaimed, "but I do not think that this nobleman from Spain will show any interest in my person. I was offered the position as a maid servant," Margaret lied quickly, "but whatever I have to do, Misses Tippins, I shall do. You know that I am a hard worker and I am not shying from scrubbing my hands raw. Since I do not have any skill other then doing laundry I can only aspire to be a maidservant or laundress. But I must work to support myself. You can see now that I do not have many choices available and I am not very knowledgeable about other matters since mother herself educated me in reading, writing and only simple adding and subtracting numbers. She did not have any means to pay a tutor for any higher education. However she believed that I should know how to read and write and also add, so I would not be cheated by a merchant or any other person conduction a business transaction with me. Think on it Misses Tippins that I am not in possession of fine and elegant attire or jewels to be noticeable to this master of the manor." Margaret finished her speech with a satisfied nod.

"God have mercy and forbid you, child. Have you looked at your own reflection in the mirror of late? You are asking for disaster if you should get a position in this man's house. This man is neither blind nor is he daft in his mind. How did you think, he acquired all his wealth? His servant Hammed, whom you met outside, is notorious for selecting the fairest maidens, to enter into his master's service. He most certainly noticed your beauty and chaste demeanor. Your own virtue and not to mention your chaste reputation is in great danger my child. I cannot begin to think what your poor mother would say. My own soul and conscience would not give me a moments rest, if I not try to talk you out of this foolish notion," Misses Tippins said resolutely.

"What am I to do then, Misses Tippins? I cannot live in the tiny rooms above the laundry kitchen forever. And I will not wash other peoples dirty laundry for the rest of my life. I do dream about a decent life, having a good husband and children some day and enough food on my table. Do you have any idea how many times I have gone to bed with an hungry stomach since my mother's death?" Margaret asked, her voice quivering while she was trying to hold back the tears which were threateningly close to overflow her eyes. But try as she may, she could not stop the sob escaping from her chest. Burying her face in her hands, she gave her sorrow free reign. She felt Misses Tippins arm around her shaking shoulders. The older woman had rushed to her side and now was making soft crooning noises, padding and motherly caressing the grieving girls arms gently. She felt powerless in sight of the young girls great sorrow and was asking herself silently, why fate was showing his cruel face to this innocent young life in front of her. After a few moments Margaret lifted her tearstained face and with an impatient gesture wiped the evidence of her grieve from her cheeks with the back of her hands. Misses Tippins reached into the pocket of her enormous apron and handed Margaret a clean square of linen. Noisily Margaret blew her nose and mopped up the rest of the dampness beneath her eyes. Facing Misses Tippins once more, a strangely mature expression in her eyes and full soft lips drawn into a hard line, she said:

"Misses Tippins, I cannot expect you or any other kind soul in this city to feed me and take care of me, until my knight in shining armor comes along to rescue me. Dreams and foolish fantasies do not feed or clothe me. I have only myself to rely on this very moment and work I must," she finished bitterly. Seeing the determination in Margaret's face, Misses Tippins reluctantly acquiesced,

"Very well then, Margaret. I can give you no other advice as to stay out of this 'Noble' Spaniards sight. Perhaps you are right and you work in the kitchen or any other position where he would not even notice you. Only promise me to visit here now and then so I may know that you are well."

"It is settled then," Margaret said to the somewhat mollified older woman. "I will work until I have enough coins to stand on my own two feet."

Misses Tippins had set the table for three and called out to the workshop,

"Argyle, my dear, put your work down, we can have supper now."

Meanwhile, Hammed who was standing in front of the huge fireplace warming his hands, said to his master:

"Master, I saw a beautiful young lady as I came out of the cobbler's shop. She did not notice me and I arranged for her to seemingly by accident bump into me. Even from afar I could see, that her features were exquisite. After she recovered from her initial shock of my appearance she told me that she was an orphan with no family left. She is petite and stands about as high as this," he pointed to the onset of his shoulder on his arm, "and as I mentioned before, she is young and

87

extremely beautiful master. Her demure demeanor suggests, that she is still innocent and chaste."

"And you want me to give her a position in this house, Hammed?" his handsome master queried while he reached for the wineglass on the small table next to his chair with his elegant manicured hand. He knew, that Hammed had a soft heart but also a very keen eye as far as beautiful women were concerned. Sipping his wine he placed the glass back on the little table. Rising he put his hand on Hammed's shoulder and said with a smile,

"Very well then old friend, I permit you to talk to Misses Potter. She could use help in the kitchen." he was teasing his loyal servant and friend he knew since childhood.

"I am not amused, Master," Hammed pouted. "Miss Margaret is exquisite in face and form. Even though I could not see her full beauty under the dreadful gray cape she was wearing, I know that her beauty will rival any of the other ladies in this house. The only thing I could not see was her hair. She had the hood of her cape clutched tightly under her chin. Please, Master Jack, judge for yourself the day after tomorrow. I shall bring her to you."

"How can I resist, you old softhearted fool. Bring her to me. Now, please go and tell Misses Potter that I am quite famished." With that he dismissed his servant, who gave him a flashing smile and replied with an unusual familiarity toward his master,

"Thank you, Master Jack, I shall go to Misses Potter at once." He hurried through the door before his master could have a change of heart. Knowing how much he could rely on Hammed's sense for business, Jack sat back on the chair and took another sip of wine.

CHAPTER 7

Hammed, the Urchin

Smiling satisfied to himself, Jack thought of the past as he met Hammed. Born in Bursa, which is on the southeast route toward Istanbul, Hammed grew up in the poorest section of town. Never knowing from where his next meal would come from, he ran away from his mother's house after she had died and he was left with three older brothers and two younger sisters. At age eleven he was running the streets of the city like so many other street urchins. Stealing food from the farmers at the market and at night sleeping at the outskirts of the city under the sky. It was on such occasion then, that Jack, who had gone with his father on a business trip to Bursa, met the boy Hammed.

The urchin had stolen bread from one of the street vendors and clutching the precious treasure to his chest he was pursued by the vendors wife with a broom. Running as fast as his young legs could pump, he sharply sprinted around the next corner of the narrow street, as he glancing back at the woman who was still hard on his heels, ran straight into the arms of Jack's father. The piece of bread he had stolen fell to the ground in the dirt. Kicking and screaming at the older gentleman he tried to get away from the iron grip around his thin arm.

"Ho, what have we here," the old man laughed, not in the least disturbed by the filthy boy's protest, who was desperately trying to squirm away from his grip.

"Let me go, Sir," he cried, "the old hag is going to kill me."

"Why would she kill you, boy, what have you done?" he asked in a stern voice.

"I am very hungry and I took a piece of her bread," he said defiantly. Meanwhile the merchant's wife had caught up and swinging her broom she was threatening to hit the boy. Seeing however the richly dressed gentleman holding the boy with an iron grip, she lowered the broom and pointing an accusing finger at Hammed, she shrieked in a shrill voice,

"He stole from me the little thief. He must pay. I am a poor woman, getting up in the middle of the night to bake bread and he steals from me. He must pay," she repeated.

"How much does he owe you woman?" the gentleman asked with obvious annoyance in his voice at the insult to his ears. The woman named a price and her greedy eyes flashed as she saw this man pulling out a fat purse.

"Here, this should more than compensate. Now leave the boy to me and be about your business woman." He tossed the woman a coin, which she eagerly caught and bit it to verify its validity; she stuck it satisfied in the little pouch on her waist. Casting the boy another venomous look, she turned and clutching the broom under her arm she waddled down the street back to her husbands cart full of freshly baked bread.

"Now as for you boy, what do you think will become of you, if you are going around stealing other peoples wares. Some day, the soldiers shall catch you and you're loose your hand. Is that, what you want?" the man asked.

"Sir, I have no home, I was hungry." he wined. Under all the filth, one could see intelligent eyes and cleaned up, this boy would be a handsome child. Perhaps he was taking a risk, but Enrico Viego decided, to take the boy with him and showing him Christian charity, as Father Paulus time and time again stressed in his sermons. A soul would be saved and the boy would not starve to death in the streets of Bursa. Feeling jovial and his business with the merchant of silk conducted to his great satisfaction; he spoke to the boy who was quiet and looking questioningly at him.

"If you are willing to mend your ways and give me your word not to steal any longer, you may come with me. I do have a son, who is about your age. He would welcome a male companion since his sisters are older and his big brothers are not interested in boy's games any longer, he feels lonely. Now do you wish to come with me?"

"Sir, I wish to eat every day and sleep under a blanket at night. My mother died last winter. My brothers and sisters are living with different relatives all over the city. I did not wish to live with any of my relations. My uncles as well as my aunts are quick with the stick. Too many times have I seen the black and blue marks on my cousins. I have no desire to be beaten with a stick and not being able to sit for a week," the boy said with a small grin. "I vow by Allah and on my mother's soul, not to touch any of your possessions, Sir," wisely he added," I do not bite the hand that will feed me. Hammed ben Hassan at your service my Master." He attempted something like a small formal bow, which made Enrico laugh out loud.

"Then come with me, you little jester. My carriage is waiting over there." He pointed up the street, were an elegant carriage with two well fed horses was waiting for its master.

Jack had been instructed by his father, to wait for him at the little tavern and read the 'good book', as he called the Bible. His father should be back shortly. Suddenly there were loud voices coming from downstairs. Curious to what the commotion was all about, the boy put the bible on the little table. Crossing the dark and musty smelling hallway, he leaned over the rail to look down into the main room of the tavern. There he saw his father standing with a filthy little boy by his side and arguing with the tavern keeper.

"Sir, you cannot bring this filth into my house. I have a good reputation to uphold. Do you not know that this wretch is nothing but a shifty little thief? " the owner of the establishment cried.

"My good man," Enrico tried to appease the flustered tavern keeper, "I am well aware of what the boy is and I shall see to it that he is behaving himself. From this day on he is my liability. The first thing he needs is a bath and something to eat. In that order." The shocked little man who's dirty fingernails and yellow teeth were merely the obvious tell-tail signs of his 'good reputation', whined,

"Sir, it is none of my affair, but are you certain that this is a good idea? After all, you know nothing of his background."

"You are absolutely correct, innkeeper, it is not your affair!" Enrico's stern voice left no room for argument, "however, give the boy what I ordered and there shall be another coin in your purse." he finished with a winning smile. He did not have to say any more.

"Leila, Leilaaa, bring some cheese and ham and bread out here this instant," the innkeeper shouted toward the huge kitchen. Leila, his daughter stuck her head around the corner of the door leading to the kitchen and taking one look at the filthy thin boy, she said absently as if not really believing her father,

"Y-y-yes father, should I also bring some w-w-water?" she asked.

"Certainly, and plenty of it!" Enrico forestalled the fat little man who was opening his mouth to speak.

Jack had followed the exchange with astonishment and fascination. Out of the corner of his eyes, Enrico had noticed some movement and looking up, he saw his son standing upstairs. Waiving and motioning him to come downstairs he said,

"Come to me, son, I want you to meet someone." Obediently, Jack hurried downstairs and standing before his tall father, he bowed respectfully. His father put a heavy hand on Jack's shoulder and turning him toward the filthy boy, who was openly grinning at him, Enrico introduced,

"This is Hammed ben Hassan my son. Your Christian duty shall be to help him to learn how to read and write as well as all your other studies. He will be living with us from this day on and you must be an example to good behavior and obedience as well as to follow your studying diligently."

"Yes, Father, as you wish," Jack bowed obediently to his father. Turning to Hammed, he said faintly smiling, "I am young Master Giaccomo Emanuel Viego. You may address me 'young Master'. You have heard my father, we shall study together." Admiringly and somewhat in awe the boy Hammed attempted a bow and still smiling he said,

"Pleased to make your acquaintance, young Master Giaccomo."

"Now, this is settled and we must be on our way by the morrow. See to it, that Hammed is cleaned up and well fed, innkeeper. Meanwhile send for the vendors at the market. The boy must have new clothes and shoes. My son and I shall wait upstairs." Enrico commanded.

"Yes, Sir, it shall be as you wish." the innkeeper bowed, showing his yellow teeth. Leila, who had prepared the food for Hammed, came with the heavily laden tray out of the kitchen and placing the tray on the table, she took Hammed by the hand and pulling him with her she said,

"You must bathe first before you can eat. I have hot water in the kitchen."

Ogling the delicious smelling food, and having a small protest on his lips Hammed saw the stern look on Enrico's face. Not daring to disobey however, the protest died on his lips and with a sinking feeling is his stomach he followed Leila who was resolutely pulling him into the big kitchen. Seeing the big steaming tub full of water though, his stomach lurched and he motioned to run. Leila grabbed him by his arm and putting her hand over his mouth she hissed,

"Do not think of screaming, you silly boy. Do you not realize, that Allah—may his name be praised—is sending you this good fortune. Do not be foolish now and defy your kind master. He ordered you to clean up and clean up you will. Take these rags off and step into the tub so I may wash you properly, you ungrateful little wretch. Another dark look from you and I might drown you." she threatened as he glowered at her from beneath his dark eyelashes. Grumbling that this was indecent to submerge his whole person into the water, he caught Leila's severe look at him. Standing with her hands on her hips, she tapped her foot impatiently on the floor. Nude and red faced, Hammed gingerly stuck his big toe into the tub and whined,

"This is too hot, am I to be boiled like a cabbage?"

"Cease your wining, little one, or you'll feel my big spoon on your backside. Now get in the tub." Leila had taken the big spoon from the table and stood, waiving the instrument of impending torture at him.

Without another word, Hammed jumped into the tub and a stone faced Leila began to scrub his grimy little body. Washing his hair nonetheless was another matter. As some of the sweet smelling soap got into his eyes, he wailed and screamed as if being put on a spiked. The sounds he made were as horrifying to behold as some foreign animal being put to the slaughter to say the least. It could be heard throughout the inn and young Master Jack's hair stood straight in the back of his neck. There was something so familiar about this noise.

"Father, what was that sound? Our pigs never scream this awful, when they get to be slaughtered," the young master whispered with icy cold shivers running up his spine. Hard pressed not to laugh, Enrico suggested,

"Perhaps you should investigate my son. I think the sound came more out of the direction of the kitchen. The slaughter house is next to the stables,"

Cautiously, Jack crept down the stairs and with a pounding heart, he tiptoed inch by inch nearer the door, which separated the kitchen from the dining room. The door was slightly ajar. There it was again. This unearthly awful sound. But how was it, that he could hear Leila's voice and the sound of waves? Puzzled and with shaking hands, young Master Jack pushed on the door. The sight that greeted him was indeed incredible to behold. Leila was soaked to the bone. Her hair was sticking to her head and dripping wet. There was more water on the floor, than in the big tub and sitting in the tub, was something big and fluffy with thin arms and legs flailing and making this inconceivable noise. Taking a bucket full of water, Leila poured it over the white fluffy creature in one quick motion. And lo and behold there was Hammed sitting in the tub all clean and fresh. Jack started to laugh that his sides ached. Hearing the sound of Jack's undisguised hilarity, the boy in the tub turned and looked straight into his young master's tearstained face. Turning beet red Hammed pouted,

"Young Master, I do find no humor in being tortured and scrubbed within an inch of my life. Please tell this female to stop this nonsense. I can bear no more of her ministrations. She is killing me." He squealed.

"Very well, Hammed," Jack said under laughter and desperately

94

trying to gain his composure, "rinse him one last time and get him dressed, Leila," he ordered the young woman. Pulling the door shut, he heard another splash and something like a 'meee ouch". Shaking his head at Hammed's obvious dislike for cleanness, he laughed once more. Just as he was raising his foot to climb up the stairs to the room, the fat innkeeper returned with the merchants, who were both carrying heavy bundles with clothes and shoes.

"Make certain that my servant has five changes of clothing, shoes and undergarments, innkeeper. He is presently being bathed in the kitchen." Jack said with an air of great importance and authority. Knowing, how wealthy this young man's father was and anticipating silver in his pouch, the innkeeper ushered the two merchants into the kitchen. There they were told to put their wares on the table, so the young master's servant could choose a selection of clothes. The boy, clad only in a big towel unerringly made his choice of sturdy yet elegant clothes and shoes. He firmly insisted on a small white cloth for his first real turban. Shortly there after the transformation was astonishing. Garbed finely and shoed, he looked every bit the young man he was approaching to be. Satisfied and with a smile, Leila pointed to the dining room and said,

"Now you may eat your meal boy." She did not have to tell him twice and seconds later, he was stuffing himself with generous helpings of ham, cheese and the freshly baked bread. Washing it all down with orange flavored water. Sitting back after he had finished his meal, he took a deep breath. It was wonderful to have a full stomach and savoring the feeling he got up from his chair. Dignified and aware of his good fortune, he climbed up the stairs, to knock politely on his new master's door.

Looking at the boy standing shyly in the doorway, Enrico was delighted by what he saw and he nodded satisfied. Motioning him to sit on the chair, he said,

"We shall begin our first lesson at once. Now, Hammed, can you count?" Shaking his head in the negative, Hammed said truthfully,

"No, Sir, I do not know anything about this." He was looking helplessly and suspicious at the big fat book on the table. He felt an almost panicky feeling sweep over him. He was never going to learn the meaning of all of the strange looking scribbles in this book.

"Do not worry, Hammed," the older master was saying, "first you must learn the letters of the Alphabet before you can read this book. We are going to start with some simple counting for today. Tell me, how many chairs do you see in this room?" Shrugging his thin shoulders, Hammed answered with a shy smile,

"There are chairs for you and the young Master in this room."

"Correct, Hammed, which means there are t wo chairs. How many chairs will we need, for all of us to sit down?" Enrico asked.

"We do not need any more chairs, Master, I can sit on the floor," was his sly reply. This was getting hard.

Hiding a smile and sending his son a disapproving look at the sound of a boyish giggle, Enrico said,

"No, Hammed, you must not sit on the floor. Your new clothes will get dirty. Now answer me, otherwise tell me you do not know the answer."

"I do not know the answer, Master." was Hammed's quiet reply.

"The answer is three, Hammed. Three chairs should be in this room for all of us to sit down."

So had begun the education of the boy Hammed. He proved to be quick with his mind. Quicker yet with his little silver tongue, Father and son were laughing tears at times. The teachers, who were hired to educate both boys, agreed. Both children were highly intelligent and a pleasure to teach. Never forgetting their station though, the boys became close friends and confidants. Hammed saw in Jack always and foremost his young Master. Faith would have it, that Jack who never traveled without his faithful Hammed, was one day bathing in the sea. He got caught in the strong undercurrent. Realizing too late, that he had not the strength to swim back to the beach, he panicked. Gasping for air and desperately coughing the water out of his lungs, his head went under water. Hammed, who had been standing in shallow water up to his knees, realized instantly that his beloved young Master was in grave danger. Screaming and waiving frantic and desperately at the small fisher boots who were fishing some distance from his Master, he pointed toward the young man who was bobbing in the water. Realizing that they could not understand what he was shouting, he dove into the water and with powerful strokes swam toward Jack. At that moment, one fisherman realized the situation and jumping to his ores he rowed his small boat with powerful strokes. The fisherman arrived at the point of distress the very same instant as Hammed. Together they pulled and pushed the exhausted young man into the boat. Turning his pale and unconscious Master on his stomach, Hammed forcefully pushed his knee with a few quick and strong motions between Jack's shoulder blades, to pump the water out of his Masters lungs. Coughing and gagging Jack slowly opened his eyes.

"Master, you have frightened me half to death," Hammed said with a quivering voice. "Praise Allah, you are alive," he added.

"Hammed, my dear friend, you have saved my life." Jack stated weakly, "I am eternally grateful for my father's wise choice to bring you home. I shall not forget this."

CHAPTER 8

New Beginnings

Jack had not forgotten and once again amazed by his loyal servants faithfulness, he smiled and poured himself another glass of wine. He knew that he could trust Hammed's taste were women were concerned. He had seen the sparkle in Hammed's eyes as he described this young lady as beautiful and virtuous. And hoping that he may never regret his decision to let this young lady accept employ in his house, he gulped down the rest of his wine and went to the dining room to eat his supper.

Two days later, it was still early in the morning, as Hammed cheerfully entered his master's bedchamber.

"Good morning, Master, I gather you had a pleasant night." Walking over to the huge window, he pulled the heavy velvet drapes open. At that moment, the little under maid Elizabeth entered the room with fresh lavender scented linens in her arms. Curtseying and blushing, she put the linens on the magnificently carved oak dresser and turned to leave the room again. Hammed called after her and said,

"Elizabeth, see that the Master's breakfast is served in half an hour and then finish preparing Miss Margaret's room so she may feel welcome and comfortable. Do not forget the flowers and a bowl with fruit." He smiled at her. Once again blushing and bobbing another curtsey, she hurried from the room. Stretching himself leisurely and rubbing his eyes, Jack threw the satin clad down coverlets from his nude body. Rising from his bed, he grumbled his mock annoyance,

"Why is it that you never enter my chamber with a sour face, my old friend? What is the secret to your cheerful disposition?"

Flashing his master another brilliant smile, Hammed answered,

"I praise Allah for every day that I am in your service, my Master. It makes me wake up with a smile and with gratitude in my heart I go to sleep at night. Now we best hurry and get you into your bath." However, Hammed had kept his real concern from his master. He knew the reason that Jack was sometimes irritable and would wake up with a hurting head.

Ever since his beloved parents and his two brothers has died in 1755, Jack indulged too much in drink and because of that he found himself having slight problems as to where his sexual prowess was effected. Opening another door in the room, he motioned his young master to enter the bath. The bath was built in Turkish fashion. After his uncles' death, which left Jack this big mansion in his will, Jack himself had overseen and designed the complete reconstruction of the mansion. With the wealth he has inherited from his father, Jack had hired a Turkish architect to build in two baths and pools on the ground floor.

The bath on his side of the house was tiled in light blue color except for the wall with the huge window, which was framed with cobalt blue tiles. The bath and pool on the other side of the house were built to accommodate the Ladies who were living in his house. Tiled in feminine lavender and purple, the pool was larger then Jack's by five feet in length. Having lived in Istanbul for many years, he could not fathom anybody not enjoying a daily bath and freeing themselves from body odors.

Luxuriating in the big tub of steaming water, he let Hammed wash him with sandalwood scented soap. After he had lathered and scrubbed his master, Hammed rinsed his body with a bucket of cool water. Shaking himself, Jack jumped out of the tub to dive into the pool. Submerging and swimming to the other end and back, he came up and ascending the steps was wrapped in a large soft towel which Hammed held open for him. Jack sat on a small tile bench and Hammed reaching for a smaller towel rubbed his master's hair. Jack reached for the small cup and a small brush that Hammed had placed on the bench while Jack took his swim. He took the brush and dipping it into a porcelain tray filled with a powder smelling of mint, he began to brush his teeth and rinsing his mouth, spat into a sink on the floor that was formed like a little seashell. Hearing footsteps and turning around, Hammed saw the young maid bobbing another curtsey and she announced,

"Breakfast is served in the dining room and the young lady's room is ready, Hammed." Handing her the used towels, Hammed said,

"Here, Elizabeth, take these to the laundress. Then you may go to the kitchen and have your meal."

She grabbed the towels and blushing she smiled and turning she almost ran from the room. Secretly she chided herself for having fallen in love with this tall man. He must never find out how she felt. Her mother would box her ears for being such a silly chit if she found out about this. After all, Hammed was the master's body servant and was considered his friend and confidant. She could not hope any time soon, to be more then a little maid in this house. Unless there was a new lady in need of a tiring woman, her station would not improve for quite a while yet. Hammed however had suspected for some time, that the young girl had feelings for him. It had not escaped his sharp senses and every time she looked into his dark eyes, she would blush becomingly. He was a man of great patience and he would find the right moment to approach Elizabeth. Now was not the time. He would make sure that the little maid would become Miss Margaret's tiring woman and then he would see how she would react to his suit. Smiling to himself, Hammed helped his master dress and said,

"Master Jack, I think it would be necessary to appoint a tiring woman to Miss Margaret's service. May I suggest young Elizabeth? She is good-natured and a hard worker. I was also thinking, that she may be about the same age as Miss Margaret and the young lady might feel more comfortable with someone her own age. Furthermore, Elizabeth is loyal to this household and will report only to me. If Miss

Margaret is taking Elizabeth into her confidence about girlish secrets, I would be the first to know about it."

"I see, that you have thought of all the necessary arrangements concerning this young lady. Very well, you may give Elizabeth the position as a tiring woman to this wonder of feminine charms. I leave the servants and their positions in this house in your most trusted and capable hands." Jack laughed and putting his soft leather boots on with Hammed's help. He stood up and cuffed his servant's arm playfully, "Come Hammed, let us break our fast first, I am famished."

Unheard of, Hammed, though considered a servant and steward of the mansion, ate with his young master at the same table. Jack's father had always stretched the importance of kindness and fairness to develop ones spirit and soul, rather than seeking only worldly wealth. Both Jack and Hammed strove to honor and cherish this wise and wonderful old man's memory. Living by Enrico's example, both young men were kind and generous to those less fortunate.

That his business was considered scandalous in the city was more to blame on the twisted morality and ethical values in people's minds. Most married women and men among the nobility had lovers and mistresses. Yet they were acting shocked and outraged, as the nature of Jack's business became known. Nobody in the Orient would think to hide his or her natural urges and desires of sexual nature. And many times, Jack had silenced waging tongues and accusingly pointing fingers by quoting the Bible, 'thou shalt not judge' and 'he among you, who is without sin, let him cast the first stone'. On more then one occasion he said to vicious gossips, that he himself was not the one who is married and commits adultery. However, as the elegance and grace of his selected ladies became known to many of the noble men, Jack's business began to flourish and greatly increased his wealth. He had hired a moor doctor, to check his ladies regularly for disease and soon the cleanness and delicious freshness of these ladies became legendary. Much to the consternation of the local gentle women, who tried to hide and disguise body odors with creams and powders and plenty of strong smelling perfume. A few of the noble ladies however, who did not want to loose their lovers or husbands, were smart enough and quickly, almost overnight the barrel maker's craft became a sought after and successful enterprise. Many tubs were ordered and became a prized addition to households. Suddenly, soap was in high demand and many poor housewives were able to add a few coins to their husband's meager income, by making deliciously scented soaps and selling it to the gentry.

Both men were eating. There were poached eggs and thin slices of ham and cheese. There were small bowls of hot porridge with bits of dried apples in it. There was a platter with slices of cold pork and beef and a basket of freshly baked bread. There was a pot with honey and another container with sweet butter. The coffee was served steaming hot in thin cups, hand painted with Asian motifs and dainty flowers. Satisfied, Jack leaned back and padded his stomach,

"I can't eat another bite. It is getting to be almost nine o'clock and after I finish my second cup of coffee, I shall go to my study to do some accounting. Hammed, did you make the entrance of the profit into the blue book last night?"

"Yes, and I also added up some the expenses for this week, Master Jack. I shall finish the rest of the accounting after our meal. I thought to do it right away. We might be a bit busy, with training and educating Miss Margaret in the next few days. I also took the liberty to hire the old dance master to teach Miss Margaret how to walk and move around gracefully and learn the proper ways of a lady. He will come and give his first lesson to the young lady tomorrow in the afternoon." Hammed answered.

"Once again I am very pleased with you, my dear Hammed, and not at all surprised about your efficiency to all matters in my house." The Master beamed radiantly. Sipping the last of his coffee, Hammed dabbed his lips with the fine linen napkin of a light peach color, which matched the spotless tablecloth. Folding the napkin he stood up,

"I had told Miss Margaret, that I would be there around the noon hour. So, I best be on my way to take care of the books. Once I am done with this I will see to her moving arrangements. She may not expect me early, but I know you are curious about this young lady, and it looks like a storm is brewing. I have no intensions of getting stuck in the snow.

Earlier this morning, I had instructed Alfred, to have the blue carriage ready. If there is nothing else, Master Jack, I shall go now."

"Very well, Hammed, take the blue carriage, in case this young lady should decide to bring some of her possessions with her. The black carriage might be too small and is not quite as comfortable. I also need the black carriage to go to the warehouse. I shall be in my study when you return."

Hammed bowed slightly and walking across the room, he entered the study with many books on the shelves, which reached up to the ceiling. He finished all the accounting in the books. As he was done, he checked the little clock on the mantle from the fireplace. It was ten minutes before eleven. Quickly he closed the books and left the library. He walked through the opposite exit of the dining room and made his way to the kitchen, to find the coachman Alfred. Almost all the servants of the house were gathered around the huge table in the kitchen and were having their second morning meal. At his entrance into the enormous kitchen, Hammed said with a friendly smile,

"A good morrow to all of you." He was greeted with nods and a respectful, "Good morrow to you also, Hammed." by everybody sitting around the table. Alfred, a elderly man rose from his seat and said with a small bow,

"The carriage is ready, Hammed, I shall wait for you outside."

"Thank you, Alfred, I must talk with Elizabeth for a moment in private. I shall be with you in a short while." Hammed dismissed the older man. Upon hearing her name, Elizabeth almost spilled her milk from the glass in her hand. Putting the glass of milk with shaking hands on the table, she rose slowly from her chair.

"I should like to talk to you in the hall, Elizabeth." Hammed said with a serious face. The girl's heart was thumping hard against her chest, and for a moment, Hammed felt sorry for her. He was also enjoying himself tremendously. Frightened and with shaking knees, Elizabeth followed the big man into the hall. Away from prying eyes and ears of the other servants, Hammed turned toward her and asked, even though he knew the answer,

"Elizabeth, please tell me the amount of you current wages." The girl named the figure of her payment and she asked with a quivering voice,

"Hammed, I hope that nothing is amiss. My mother is dependent on my wages and my family would be destitute, if I should loose my position. Am I to be let go then?"

Hammed saw, how fearful and frightened the girl was looking at him and now feeling a pang of guilt for having her frightened thusly, he put an reassuring hand on her arm.

"No, my dear girl, do not fret. It is nothing like that at all. Elizabeth, I do have some exiting and wonderful news for you. You are to be made tiring woman to the young lady, who will move into this house this afternoon. What say you?" Hammed smiled. Elizabeth went pale and nearly fainted. She was swaying precariously and Hammed caught her in his arms to steady her. For just an instant, he felt her luscious youthful form and her generous full breasts against his chest. Catching herself, she blushed crimson and pushing herself gently away from him, she stammered,

"Ha-hammed, you are a wicked jester. You have frightened me half to death. I thought that…"

"Please do forgive me, Elizabeth. I humbly beg your pardon for having fun at your expense. But I thought to pleasantly surprise you with such great news. I did not mean any harm." Chagrined he looked at her and lowering his eyes he picked an imaginary speck of lint from his sleeve. Her heart was still hammering, but Elizabeth smiled and said,

"I am still in shock, Hammed, but I feel better now." and suddenly she gasped, "oh, Hammed, I must prepare a bath for my lady and which gown should I choose for her to wear?"

"Do not think on it right this moment, Elizabeth. I have not seen the color of the young lady's hair yet, but I do know that she has beautiful hazel green eyes. We shall then choose a gown, when I get back with Miss Margaret."

"As you wish, Hammed," Elizabeth answered, "I should also like to know, which fragrance I must use in her bath. Should it be the rose or may bell fragrance or perhaps the gardenia?"

Hammed had turned to leave through the front door.

"Oh, no, my dear girl, Miss Margaret is petite and all of those fragrances are too heavy for her. You must use the lilac fragrance, for it will suit her." Hammed answered and turning once again, he left the hall. Climbing into the luxurious carriage with real glass windows and soft leather cushions, he knocked twice on the wall where the coachman was sitting to signal their departure. Wisely, Alfred saw to it that several hot bricks wrapped in flannel were placed on the floor boards of the carriage and over the leather seats he had draped some rabbit furs to sit on. Taking one of the heavy knee covers of silver fox fur, Hammed wrapped it around his lap and legs. Leaning back into the soft cushions, he took a deep breath and closed his eyes. It would take the carriage about a full hour to rumble through the narrow streets of Manchester, to reach the other side of town.

Margaret woke up with a start. This would be the day she would leave this dreadful little room. She would also leave the poor neighborhood and never return again, so she thought. Jumping out of the big bed, she shivered as her feet made contact with the icy floor. Splashing some cold water on her face, she quickly dressed and put her little boots on, which had belonged to her mother once. She took a bed linen out of the chest and folding her meager belongings she put the two skirts and three dresses which also had belonged to her late mother on top of the linen. Knotting the four corners of the linen together, she took the bundle and glancing around the room once more she left, closing the door behind her firmly and with a satisfied nod. Carrying her little bundle, Margaret briskly walked up the narrow street to the cobbler's house, sidestepping the puddles of muddy water and small thatches of ice. Her boots were in desperate need of repair and the soles had holes in them. Entering the cobblers shop, Margaret greeted the older man with a friendly,

"Good morrow, Mister Tippins." Looking up and glancing at the girl over the rim of his spectacles. A fine invention that had been manufactured by the guilt of spectacle makers in England since 1629.

"Hello Girl, the Misses is in the kitchen. Go and have yourself a bowl of hot porridge. I have to finish these boots, before noon." Mister

Tippins returned Margaret's greeting. Margaret lifted the heavy curtain, which divided the shop from the kitchen and seeing Misses Tippins, she exclaimed,

"What a wonderful day it is, Misses.Tippins. I shall be only too glad, to leave my cold little rooms and move to a nice warm house. The first things I shall purchase with my wages are some new boots. Look, it took only those few steps up the street and my feet are cold and soaked." Holding up the hem of her plain gray skirt, Margaret looked at her boots with distaste and pulled them from her feet to place them in front of the fireplace. She took her heavy dark gray cape off and flung it over one of the chairs in Misses Tippins's kitchen.

"I sure hope that everything will go well with you and your position in this big house, Margaret. Now sit and have something to eat. It is still hot." Ladling a big spoon of the steaming oat porridge into the wooden bowl, she pushed it in front of Margaret, who began eating with gusto. Misses Tippins cut a fat slice of bread, which had just come from her oven and spreading butter and some honey on it with a spoon, she handed it to Margaret.

"Here, eat and have some hot milk. That should warm you up." Misses Tippins said motherly and poured some hot milk in an earthenware cup. Washing the last bite of bread down with the milk, Margaret leaned back on the chair, padding her full stomach. There was still time to run a few errands for the old man. While Margaret had eaten her meal, Mister Tippins had taken Margaret's boots to nail new soles on them. It was the least he could do for the poor girl. It was shortly before noon when Margaret returned from delivering repaired shoes to costumers. Shivering and cold she pulled a chair in front of the fireplace and stretched her icy hands toward the flames. She heard the noise of a carriage rumbling down the street. Exited she jumped up from her seat and ran toward the door in the shop. Her heart leapt in her chest, as she saw the big blue carriage stop in front of the shop and as the coachman opened the door to the carriage, Hammed emerged from within. He pulled his elegant cape, which was lined with fur from the silver fox closer around him to keep the icy wind at bay. Almost beside herself with excitement, Margaret went back into the kitchen, were Misses Tippins was wiping the table clean.

Margaret said with burning cheeks,

"Misses. Tippins, the big dark man kept his word. He is here and he is taking me away this day. I cannot thank you enough for all you kindness. Wish me luck and pray, that all goes well."

Margaret had hugged the older woman and quickly threw her cape over her shoulders. Just as she was lifting the curtain to step into the shop, the door opened and Hammed entered. Margaret had not put her hood on over her head and stunned, Hammed looked at her. Her glorious auburn hair fell in soft waves over her shoulders down to just below her waist. 'Magnificent' was all he could think for an instant. Catching himself, he smiled warmly at Margaret and said,

"Greetings on this glorious but cold day, my dear Miss Margaret. I trust, you are ready for our departure. I must beg your pardon that I am earlier to arrive here, but it looks like a storm is coming and I do not want to take a chance of getting stuck on the road. We best hurry, before the snow begins to cover the streets and makes the horses slip." Glancing out of the tiny window toward the sky, he looked indeed concerned. The sky was gray and heavy leaden with snow. Pulling the hood over her head, Margaret said,

"Yes I am ready to leave, Hammed. I am only taking my clothing with me. There is nothing else that I would wish to bring into your master's home." Taking her bundle, she moved toward the door.

"Take good care of yourself, child, and remember to send word to us." Misses Tippins said with tears in her eyes, as Hammed opened the door to let Margaret pass. Wiping her face with the edge of her big apron, Misses Tippins turned and went back to her kitchen with a heavy sigh.

CHAPTER 9

The Position

Outside the shop the coachman was waiting and opening the door, he helped Margaret into the carriage, where she shyly sat down onto the fine leather seat lined with fur. Sitting across from her, Hammed once again signaled to the coachman with the knob of his cane to move on. Margaret was still shivering and rubbing her hands together, to warm them, she snuggled deeper into the seat. Hammed took one of the heavy fur lined coverlets and put it over Margaret's knees.

"Put your feet onto the hot bricks, Miss Margaret. That should keep you comfortable until we reach our destination." She had not seen the flannel wrapped bricks on the floor as she had entered the carriage; she put her bundle on the floor and had been glad to be out of the icy wind. Now she noticed the carefully wrapped stones and thankful for the warmth on her feet, she smiled at Hammed.

"Oh heavens, it is such elegant carriage, that I hardly dare to move. I have never been in a carriage before and never have I seen one so beautiful as this one. Your master must be very wealthy indeed, to afford all this."

"Yes, Miss Margaret, my master is wealthy. But he is also kind and generous to everybody around him. You shall see for yourself this day that I am speaking the truth. I took the liberty and appointed one of the maids in my master's house to the position of your tiring woman. I hope

108

you are comfortable with my decision. Her name is Elizabeth and she is a pleasant young girl of about the same age as you, Miss Margaret. If I may be so bold to ask, but how old are you my dear?" Hammed asked.

Margaret had stared wide eyed at Hammed while he spoke and whispered,

"I am going to have a birthday by the end of this month. I shall be fifteen years old. I was born in the year of our Lord 1757 on January thirty first. But, Hammed, there must be some mistake as to my position in your master's house. I was under the impression to take up work in the kitchen or the laundry. How can I have a tiring woman, if I am to work in your master's house?" she asked.

As much as she had told herself that she would do anything to make money, she was suddenly fearful of this new development of the situation. Hammed had anticipated this and said with a soothing voice,

"Do not be frightened, Miss Margaret, for your position shall be no hard work and you will be trained at first to learn all there is to know. If you are still not comfortable about it at the end of your training, you may tell me so and I will find a more suitable work for you within my master's household. For now, you should concentrate on your cultivation of elegant etiquette. You shall be instructed in reading and writing and also counting, subtracting and dividing numbers. Your first dance lesson will be tomorrow afternoon and I will take over the instructions of proper table manners. This all will take some time and you never have to be afraid of speaking your mind. If someone in my master's household should treat you with anything other than kindness or respect, please let me know this at once and I shall be the one to set things straight again."

Margaret could hardly believe her ears,

"I do know, how to read and I also write a passable hand. Numbers however are still giving me problems. As to dancing, I shall do my best not to appear unfit for the position you are suggesting."

'So, Misses Tippins had been right all along' Margaret thought and it suddenly dawned on her, which position she should take in this master' house. But if other girls her own age could do it, so could she. With that, Margaret had made up her mind not to fight against her obviously good fortune. She would do whatever she had to, to earn money and live in a warm comfortable house. She would save her money carefully for a few years and then later she would buy a little house somewhere far away from this city. Hammed had noticed, how her mind was working franticly,

"We should reach the mansion in a short while, Miss Margaret. Look, the snow is already falling. We are indeed fortunate, to have come this far. The bricks at our feet are getting cold and you shall have a nice hot bath, when we arrive at the mansion. Please do not be shy and ask for anything you need. Your room is ready and after your bath you should rest for a while. Later this afternoon, I shall introduce you to the master. I am certain, he will be as pleasantly surprised as I was, when I saw you for the first time." He smiled at her.

"Thank you, Hammed, you are very kind." Margaret said, shivering again, for the carriage was getting colder with every passing minute without the comforting warmth of the bricks. She was actually looking forward to a nice hot bath and she hoped, that her new room would have at least a small fireplace and a warm blanket on her bed. Remembering, how she had taken a bath whenever the small tub in the laundry kitchen was available at night and nobody was there to see her, Margaret smiled to herself and looked out the window of the carriage. The landscape was unfamiliar and wide-eyed she stared at the huge mansion coming into her view at some distance. Surrounded by park like gardens and walkways the main drive went straight for about half a mile to widen in front of the mansion and leading up to the steps where the huge main entrance door was. Never in her whole life would Margaret have expected such glory. The gardens seemed to expand from the back of the mansion into a forest with huge trees of all sorts. Now however the landscape seemed to change in front of her eyes and large wet snowflakes were covering everything in white. Shivering, Margaret thought that it must be wonderful to take a stroll in the garden when the sun would shine and the flowers and trees would bloom. At this moment she could almost imagine herself walking on the carefully manicured lawns and feeling the sunshine and a warm breeze in her face. The big blue traveling coach had come to a halt and momentarily the door was opened by a young boy, who had been at the stables to the left of the huge mansion. Hammed got up from his seat and jumping out of the carriage, he helped Margaret to climb out. Since she had been looking out of the window on the right side of the carriage, she had not seen the stables and a few small cottages where as she found out from Hammed, some of the servants lived. Each one of the small houses seemed to be in good repair and each parcel was divided from the other by a thick hedge.

Overawed, Margaret stood for a moment to let the entire situation sink in to her mind. It seemed to her, that even the servants in this house had more than the people in her old poor neighborhood. Hammed had not let go of her hand and he was leading her gently and carefully up the now partially icy and slippery steps to the colossal entrance door. As if by magic, the huge door opened and an elderly man bowed to her and Hammed beaming a friendly smile.

"Welcome back, Hammed. Quickly, come into the house and warm yourself. It is such nasty unpleasant weather to be outside today."

"Thank you, Mister Potter, it is truly freezing and I should like a nice hot cup of tea. Oh I beg you pardon, this is Miss Margaret, Mister Potter. She will be living here from this day on. Please call Elizabeth and tell her, that Miss Margaret has arrived." Hammed ordered Mister Potter. Bowing once more toward Margaret, the old man said,

"Welcome, Miss Margaret, I hope your stay in this house shall be a pleasant one."

"Thank you, Mister Potter, I am delighted to make your acquaintance and I am sure it will be lovely to live here." Margaret curtsied politely. Nodding, Mister Potter hurried from the great hall to fetch Elizabeth and the tea from the kitchen for Hammed. Only a few moments later, a fresh faced young girl emerged quickly from one of the many doors in the big hall. Coming to stand in front of Margaret, she bobbed a curtsey,

"I am Elizabeth, and you must be Miss Margaret. Let me take you to your room and make you comfortable." With that, she was reaching for the little bundle, Margaret was still holding in her hand. Margaret looked at Hammed and he nodded encouragingly at her to go and follow Elizabeth. The young maid lead Margaret up the marble stairs, which swung up to the second floor toward a landing with several doors to her left and a carved oak balustrade on the right side to allow a view down into the big hall. The long hallway was flooded with light coming from the big glass doors at both ends, which were leading to a enormous balcony reaching from one side of the mansion to the other side all around the second floor and allowing a magnificent view of the forest in the back of the house. Margaret had counted the doors in the long hallway and found that there were six all together at a distance of about thirty feet in between them. There were also six small windows a few feet to the left of each door. Arriving at the last door of the long hall, she found, that there was a small set of stairs to her right leading down. Another set of stairs lead up to the third floor.

"These stairs lead down to the kitchen and to the lady's baths, Miss Margaret. Up on the third floor are the guestrooms," Elizabeth explained as she noticed Margaret's curious glance. Opening the last door, the maid bade her young mistress entrance. Gasping, Margaret could only but stare at the luxurious room she had entered. The fireplace at the left corner in the large room was blazing merrily spreading its cozy warmth throughout the room. On the right side stood an enormous richly carved oak cabinet and a big table with four chairs was set in the middle of the dining area. A few feet further on the right side of the wall stood an enormous couch with several colorful pillows and in front of the couch was a low table its top made out of glass, were a bowl of fruit had been placed. To the left of the couch was a big chair its material the same as the couch, which was rich burgundy velvet. Another matching chair was placed on the left wall a few feet away from the marble fireplace. Next to this chair, Margaret saw a smaller door. Almost the entire left wall beyond the door was covered with a colorful tapestry depicting a hunting scene. Standing still at the entrance door to the room, Margaret also saw a small table with a glass lamp standing on it to her left and a small bowl of flowers. Never in her whole life had Margaret seen anything like this. A mansion as such must make a king envious and she let out her breath with a sudden sigh. She had not been aware, that she had held her breath.

Elizabeth had opened the other door in the room and slowly following the maid; Margaret had to gasp once more. The smaller room she was entering had another small fireplace backing in the right corner into the bigger one in the sitting room. Next to the window on the right far corner stood a lovely vanity table with a little stool in front of it and looking straight ahead from the door where she stood, was a gigantic bed. The heavy oak masterfully carved posts of the bed were reaching nearly up to the ceiling where a large ring was fastened, draping the burgundy bed hangings elegantly down over the bed. On the big bed was a thick down coverlet made out of a dark rose-colored shimmering silky material as were the matching big fluffy goose down pillows, leaning at the headboard. To the left of the bed was a small candle stand with another oil lamp standing on it, spreading its aromatic fragrance of sandalwood. On the left wall of the bedchamber was yet another chair with a lovely tiny table next to it. On top of this table stood a hand carved wooden box, which would hold jewelry.

Turning to her left, Margaret saw Elizabeth open a small door, which lead into a closet where her dresses and coats would be hung and some shelves for her shoes and under garments would be placed. Amazed she found, that there was another small door, leading out of the other side of the closet and into a lovely little room, where Elizabeth's tings had been moved to, since she was to serve Margaret. Shaking her head in disbelieve, Margaret could see, that there was a smaller bed for the girl with a candle stand next to it. On the other wall at the foot of the bed was a big trunk, which held the girls private things and on the third wall in the tiny room was a small table with two small chairs. Margaret noticed the small window at the wall across from the closet wall. A soft light was streaming into the room and she found, that this window had been on the side of the long hall, which she had walked down and noticed earlier. At the reconstruction of the mansion, the master of this mansion had enormous windows build in above the main entrance, so that there was enough light flooding even the tiny cubicles inhabited by each tiring woman of the ladies.

Slowly, Margaret was unfastening the clasps on her cape and taking the cape of she handed it to Elizabeth, who was standing behind her with a knowing little smile on her lips. She could understand, that the young lady was somewhat astonished about the clever construction of the mansion. But now she bustled back to the closet to hang up Margaret's cape and seeing the shabby dress, her Mistress was wearing, she said.

"We best take that dress of and hurry to your bath, Miss Margaret. I believe that Hammed will come for you later to introduce you to the master. Here, let me help you." And taking the still awestruck young lady by the hand, she pulled her into the bedchamber, where she quickly unfastened the buttons to the dark dress. Margaret was wearing some worn out old under garments, which had belonged to her late mother and indeed had seen better days. Elizabeth went back into the closet and only a few moments later she came back with a lovely flannel padded silk robe of a light green color over her arm. The rim of the sleeves and the hem of the robe were embroidered with tiny roses of silver thread. In her other hand she was carrying a large soft towel. Helping her new Mistress into the robe and fastening it with a matching sash, which was also embroidered with tiny silver roses, she picked up the towel from the bed, where she had laid it before and gently pushed Margaret out of the bedchamber. Walking ahead, the maid opened the door leading to the long hall,

"Follow me please. Your bath is ready and I must wash your hair. No other lady in this house has such long and beautiful hair as you, Miss Margaret, and I shall take very good care of you." The girl smiled and leading Margaret down the smaller set of stairs, she opened a door. Margaret could hardly believe her eyes, at the sight that greeted her. To the right stood an enormous big oak tub, where two people could easily sit in and bathe with water up to their chin. I the middle of the bathing room stood two padded long tables, where the ladies would be massaged and creamed. On the left wall were several shelves with little bottles and jars with sweet smelling soaps and lotions. The lower shelves held individually small trays with a mint powder, various brushes and sponges. Hanging over a rod were little squares of soft material that was the same as the towel, Elizabeth had placed on one of the long tables. In both corners of the room were huge fireplaces crackling merrily and spreading a comfortable heat.

Turning, she helped Margaret to take the soft robe off,

"Please take off your undergarments, Miss Margaret, and your boots and stockings, I shall be with you in a moment." Leaving the mortified young lady to wonder, why she should take her undergarments off in front of a total stranger. She had never even taken her clothes of in front of her own mother, who always had stressed, that it would be indecent and immodest to flaunt one's body. And here she was, being told to do the very same, her mother had told her never to do. Hesitantly, she started to unlace her boots and to roll her woolen stockings that had been darned many times in various places, down her shapely legs. Slowly, she pulled down the lower of her under things and stood in the room helpless and embarrassed in her shift.

"That must come off also, Miss Margaret, if I am to wash you properly." Elizabeth said in a friendly but stern and motherly tone of voice, and before Margaret could voice a protest, the little maid had quickly yanked the shift off her young Mistress. Taking Margaret's hand, she lead her to the four steps by the huge tub and helping her in, she reached for one of the little jars she had placed on the upper step. With her other hand she gently bend Margaret's head back and ordered.

"Let me wet your hair like this, Miss Margaret. You can soak a while, while I wash your hair first." And helping her mistress to straighten herself up again, she scooped a generous helping of the fragrant soft soap out of from one of the jars. She began working up lather and rubbing vigorously, she washed Margaret's hair, repeating the process three times. After she had wrung out the excess water from the hair, she pinned it on top of Margaret's head and taking one of the new sponges, she took a small cake of soap to lather the sponge and started to wash her young lady's back and neck. As her hands moved to the front however, Margaret blushed crimson and she softly protested,

"I can do the rest myself, Elizabeth. Forgive me, but I am not used to someone seeing me like this, let alone touching my person."

"Now, now, Miss Margaret. I know it is all very strange right now. But you must not be ashamed or embarrassed. The human body is something natural and a wonderful invention of the Lord God. Hammed has been teaching us maids all about the human body and he said, that no one should feel ashamed of something that comes directly from God. I do think that he is correct, for I too felt just like you, when I started working in this house and so did all the other lady's maids. Believe me, you'll get used to it and you will not think anything of it in a few days time." While she had chattered on, she had continued washing Margaret, who could not find any words of argument and so she kept quiet. Elizabeth had gently pulled her up, to wash her lower backside and legs. Here however, she handed Margaret one of the little squares from the rod,

"Please take this and cleanse your private part with it. All the other ladies have to do the same. Hammed insists on it, to cleanse every part of the body daily. I must admit, that it feels wonderful and all the ladies in the house do smell sweet and fresh. You might want to squat down a bit. That works best." And turning to leave Margaret some privacy, she fussed with the little jars and trays to put them back on their place on the shelves and reached for the towel on the table. Doing as she was told, Margaret finished her ritual of hygiene as fast as she could and rinsing out the little wash rag, she handed it back to the maid, who hung it back over the rod next to the shelves. Holding the huge towel open, she wrapped it around Margaret and lead her to a little stool where Margaret sat, so the girl could dry her feet and taking another small towel, she took the pins out of Margaret's hair to rub it dry. She took one of the brushes from the shelve and began brushing Margaret's hair until it was dry and shone with golden highlights. Dry and clean now, Margaret was helped once more into her robe and picking up the despicable old undergarments from the floor, Elizabeth flung them into one of the big fireplaces. She was leading her Mistress up the stairs to her own rooms. There she went into the closet and coming back, she had some lovely silk undergarments and silk stockings with a pair of charming lacy garters, which she bade her Mistress to change in to. Knowing better already, that protest of any kind would be futile, Margaret wordlessly took of her robe and let Elizabeth help her to put on the new things. All of it fit her, as if it was made for her and Margaret wondered out loud,

"I do not know, how Hammed could know my size and I still am in shock. I hope I am not dreaming all of this." She smiled ruefully.

"Oh, it is easy for Hammed to know ones size. We do have a seamstress working exclusively for this house and if Hammed tells her, how high you stand and if he would be able to span your waist with his hands, the seamstress will know, what size gown to make. And then all the ladies here are just about your size. Only your breasts are a more generous than Miss Fiona's. For the past two days, the seamstress and her four helpers have been working hard on your wardrobe and you will be getting more gowns yet. So far there are three gowns in your closet and also new under garments and three pair of stockings for you Miss Margaret." Elizabeth said with great air of importance.

"How is it possible to afford all this for the master. I cannot imagine all this only coming from the services he is providing for the gentlemen?" Margaret asked the girl.

"Master Jack is still in the merchant trading business as his late father and his uncle were before him. Not too many people know about this and they think, that he is only making his fortune by providing the certain services you have in mind Miss Margaret. Master Jack is a clever and kind man and I am happy to work in this house. When I first started working here, my mother was mortified and wanted to forbid me, but then she found out, that the Ladies are all getting a high education and actually making enough monies in a few years time to be wealthy in their own right. Just a few months ago, Miss Dorothy moved out of the room you are occupying right now and she took her tiring woman with her. Miss Dorothy had met a wealthy Scottish merchant and she married him. Now she is living in a big mansion out somewhere in the highlands and is already with her first child. Perhaps in a few years time, you will be just as fortunate as Miss Dorothy and meet a wealthy man and have a beautiful house of your own." The little maid was bustling back and forth between the closet and the bedchamber, while chattering. She had selected a pair of stockings and fresh under garments for her mistress and pulling the silk stockings over Margaret's legs, she fastened them with the pair of fetching green garters with a tiny pink rose in it's center. The light green stockings were embroidered with climbing vines of silver thread and black roses on the outside of her legs.

Just as Margaret was admiring the silkiness and beauty of the embroidery on her new stockings, there was a soft rapping on the door. Elizabeth hurried to answer the door and Mister Potter entered with a small tray in his hands. On the tray was a steaming cup of tea and some fresh bread. There were also a few slices of thinly sliced ham and small wedges of cheese. Smelling the bread and seeing the bounty in front of her, Margaret's stomach softly rumbled, as if it would agree that it was indeed time for a meal. In all the excitement she had completely ignored her hunger. Mister Potter had placed the tray on the dining table,

"Hammed said to serve you some hot tea and something to eat, once you were finished with your bath, Miss Margaret. It still is early afternoon and supper will not be served until later. You might want to eat and then rest for a while until Hammed will call you to meet the master. Oh, Elizabeth, Hammed also suggested, that Miss Margaret should wear the apple green gown later." he said and turning, he left the room with a slight bow. Margaret felt like a little queen at this moment. Never had she been treated like in this big mansion and letting Elizabeth help her to put her chamber robe on, she shyly sat on one of the chairs by the table and began to eat her meal. Savoring every bite of the fresh bread and the ham, she washed it down with the aromatic hot tea, which had been sweetened with honey. Sated, she leaned back and suddenly felt very tired. Elizabeth had pulled back the covers of the bed and coming back to the room, she said,

"Now into bed with you, Miss Margaret. With all the new and exiting events of today, you must rest for a few hours. I shall be back, when you are rested and help you dress." With that, she tucked Margaret into the big bed. She put another log of sweet smelling apple wood into the fireplace and quietly left the bedchamber, where Margaret had followed her without so much as a word. Her mind was still trying to comprehend all of the day's events so far and now she was so very tired, that she hardly could keep her eyes open. Hammed had ordered to lace her tea with a mild sleeping drought, to give the young girl some rest and let her overcome her fear of all the unknown new happenings. He had great experience with young girls like Margaret and he also knew; that most of them were somewhat frightened the first few days. But he also knew, that each one of the girls had lost her fear and apprehensions and adjusted well and fast to their new life style. So would young Miss Margaret, who was sleeping peacefully and warm in her bed at the moment. Her last thought before she fell asleep had been, that she would have to bend the truth somewhat, to put Misses Tippins mind at ease and not let her worry that she would be actually one of Master Jack's 'ladies'. She knew now with certainty, what was expected of her and she would do everything to make lots of money. Some day, all her dreams would come true and she would have everything she had dreamed of. With that, she had closed her eyes and now she slept with a small smile still around her soft lips.

Meanwhile, Hammed had entered the library, where Jack was sitting with his head over some books on the highly polished surface of his huge oak desk. Looking up, he smiled satisfied at Hammed and asked,

"Did everything go well with our new young lady? I suppose, she is adjusting to her new surroundings and not too frightened?"

"She will be fine, Master Jack, and is getting her bath as we speak. I also ordered to have a light meal and some herb tea brought to her room. She will be resting for a few hours." Hammed said with a wink and Jack understood his faithful servant. Pouring his master some of the light fruity wine, and himself some coffee, he pulled a chair next to the big desk and together, the two men finished making the entries into the several books.

Jack expected his friend and business partner Thomas Crandall from America any day soon and he knew, that he would get a full shipload of new fabrics and herbs and exotic spices as well as precious stones. With any luck, he could introduce this new lady to Thomas, who was enjoying the female company without erotic encounter to follow. It would put the girl at ease to male company and also would once again be a pleasant interlude for the big captain. His friend Thomas would stay in Manchester for a few weeks and would be a welcome guest in his house.

Jack had met Thomas in Istanbul. Both families had been in the merchant trading business for several generations and Jack's father Enrico Viego, who had overtaken the business in 1724 after his father's death had befriended Thomas Crandall's father.

Jack's grandfather Marcello Viego had been killed in a severe storm at sea and two of his merchant ships sank to the bottom of the ocean. The remaining four ships of his merchant fleet made their way home to take the sad news of his father's death Marcello to the 28-year-old Enrico who was residing at the time in Madrid. Enrico Viego had married the daughter of his father's friend, who was at that time expecting their first child. Two months after his father's death, Enrico's wife Lucrezia gave birth to a healthy son, Jack's oldest brother Roberto. Almost two years later another son, Giuseppe, had been born in 1726 and the girls, Victoria who was born in 1729, was followed by Veronica in 1732. And six years later, to his parent's great joy, Jack had entered the world on December the 28th in 1738 in Madrid. Many times Jack's father Enrico had taken his two older sons on his trips to teach the boys the business of trade to become merchants them self. Only when his father Enrico deemed his son old enough, was Jack allowed to accompany his father. Seeing a great opportunity, to increase and expand his business further, Jack's father bought a home in Istanbul and moved his entire family to live there in 1740, when Jack was only two years old. So it was, that Jack grew up in Istanbul and he traveled with his father and occasionally with his older brothers. Having heard of the fine quality of fabrics and other goods, Thomas and his father Paul Crandall had made a trip to the Turkish cities of Bursa and Istanbul, where he met Enrico. Thomas's mother had died in childbirth and having loved his wife deeply, his father Paul had not remarried. Paul did have no other choice, as to take his son Thomas with him on his business ventures. Being aware of the financial gains he could amass due to a suggested merging of trading fleets with Jack's father, the two men became close friends and partners. While his father

Paul had ordered a house build in Istanbul, Thomas was living in Enrico's home and the two boys became inseparable. Unfortunately only a few years later, Paul's own mother send word from America, that she was ill. She never had recovered from her husband's untimely death. Paul's Father had been kicked in the head by one of his horses and died a few days later, never regaining consciousness. And now Paul's mother was dying also. So, Paul sold his house in Istanbul and moved back to America. Nevertheless, Enrico and Paul stayed in constant contact with each other and also the two boys Jack and Thomas corresponded through letters regularly. After his mother's death, Paul visited Enrico quite often and Thomas got to stay with his friend Jack, while both of the men set off on their business ventures together for months at the time. Feeling lonely and with all her older children grown, Jack's mother Lucrezia begged her husband to take her on his voyages. It was arranged on one of these occasions, that Enrico and his wife Lucrezia would meet with both of their older sons to set out for a long voyage to the Far East. Jack and his sisters, as well as Thomas were left behind in Istanbul. Since his frightening encounter with the powerful sea, Jack was not enthusiastic to join his parents and brothers for any length of time on a ship. The meeting place was to be in Lisbon Portugal, where the cargo would be awaiting to be shipped out by the end of September in 1755. However, one of the merchandises deliveries to the port was late and so Enrico and his wife had to wait together with their two sons Roberto and Giuseppe in one of the city's finer inns. Paul, his friend was furious and had ordered six of the trading vessels loaded with the cargo, to move ahead to Algiers. There he would wait for his friend while overseeing the unloading of part of the cargo and trading. The remaining two ships would then come a few days later, when the rest of the cargo of fabrics arrived from Paris. Not having anything to do but to wait, Enrico, Lucrecia and their two sons stayed at the inn in Lisbon. It was September the 28th as Paul left for Algiers. And then a few days later, the great disaster struck.

Suddenly the earth was moving so violently and all of Lisbon was leveled and destroyed. One of histories most severe recorded earthquakes killed about 60,000 people including Jack's parents and brothers on November the 1st. It was felt as far as southern France and North Africa. Upon hearing the news of this great earthquake, Paul traveled straight from Algiers back to Istanbul to give Jack the sad news. The young man was devastated and he realized, that a considerable responsibility was placed on his shoulders. He would have to take over the business and also take the devastating news to his two older sisters. Both women were married and the older one, Victoria settled with her family in Oldham England. While she was visiting her uncle Adolpho, who was Enrico's brother and lived in Manchester, she madly fell in love with a young man got married only a few months later and moved to his house in Oldham northeast of Manchester.

Veronica was married to a Spanish nobleman and was now living once more in Spain in the city of Granada, which was far south of Madrid. Taking his faithful Hammed with him, Jack set off to travel to Spain on one of his father's ships and then to England. Paul and Thomas traveled with him on the other remaining vessels and would wait for him in Liverpool. While visiting with his sister for a few weeks, Jack also went to see his uncle Adolpho in Manchester. The older man was delighted to see his nephew and invited him to stay at his house for a few months. Realizing, that the young man had a good sense of business and would do the family proud, he made out his will to leave all he owned to young Jack at his death. Adolpho had never been married and had no children of his own. Once more, Jack went back to Istanbul and he sold his parents estate. The great warehouses however were kept open for himself and Paul, who had taken Thomas on his voyages to the Far East and back to America. Meanwhile it was the year 1758, when Jack left for England and moved in with his uncle Adolpho in Manchester. It was the year of 1763 that uncle Adolpho suddenly died. Having inherited his uncle's estate and worldly possessions, Jack sent for the architect from Turkey, who also had designed and build his parents and Paul's house, to reconstruct the great mansion Jack inherited from his dear uncle. At the beginning of the following year in 1764 he had the mansion completely remodeled to his own taste and being a healthy young man, he visited the finest brothel in town with great regularity. He became fairly acquainted with the Madam in charge of the house of ill repute and at her untimely death; all six of her young charges had no place to go. At Hammed's suggestion, he had all six girls move into the mansion, after once more remodeling part of the first and the entire second floor and now the section for the female baths and pool was added and the rooms on the second floor were build to house the six ladies, who were in Jack's employ from that time on.

Over the period of the next few years four of the ladies had left and got either married or moved away to different locations around Europe. Merely Miss Fiona and Miss Sarah were left in the house and so it had been Hammed's task to find new and young girls to be trained as high prized and willing escorts for the noble men of the city and it's surrounding locations. However, at the suggestion of the doctor in Jack's service, no girl was allowed to engage in sexual relations until she had reached the age of sixteen. Up until then, all girls were trained and educated in other matters, such as reading, writing, languages and forms of art like music and dancing as well as painting and poetry. Wise beyond his years, Hammed advised his Master, that he should keep the young Ladies no more then ten years in his services, so they may have a good chance to lead a normal life once they would move away from the city. All of the young ladies had done just that. At their own free will, Miss Fiona and Miss Sarah had volunteered to stay in Jack's house and help train the new girls to master the tasks of not only the arts of Eros, but also housewifely duties, which included embroidery, soap and perfume making, preparing meals and preserving food. If a girl had a nice voice or was talented with a musical instrument, she would get lessons from the music teacher. The house was run, like a Turkish harem and each girl had to learn certain chores to perform.

All the gentlemen in and around Manchester agreed, that each one of the Ladies was well educated, tastefully dressed, graceful and highly accomplished, to be also worth the high price one had to pay for a night of extreme pleasure and amusement. So it had been for the past eight years an indeed very profitable enterprise in addition to the trading business.

CHAPTER 10

New Friends

Margaret woke up from a deep and dreamless sleep. Only for a moment did she have to look around the room, to realize where she was and how she got here. She heard a noise and knew instantly that Elizabeth was in the next room.

Leisurely, Margaret stretched in the big bed and let her hands slide down over her body to savor the feel of the silky nightgown she wore. Swinging her legs over to the side on the floor, she noticed a pair of green slippers. They matched the robe she had worn earlier which was now carefully folded over the chair. At the same moment the door opened and Elizabeth entered the bedroom with a small tray. On the tray was a glass of milk and a dainty cup with hot steaming coffee. Alternately arranged on a small plate were slices of apple and halve of an orange. Placing the tray on the small table, Elizabeth smiled at her mistress,

"I trust you had a nice nap, Miss Margaret. Here is some milk and coffee to refresh you and some fruit. Please eat and drink. I will lie out the gown you are to wear this evening. Here, let me help you with your robe." She took the robe from the chair and helped Margaret into it. Margaret slipped her small feet into the lovely green slippers and sat on the chair next to the little table. Obediently she drank the milk and ate a few slices of apple. The hot aromatic drink was something she had never tasted. Sniffing carefully, she took a sip and wrinkled her nose at the bitter taste. Gently, she put the cup back on the tray and took a slice of orange. She bit into it and was pleasantly surprised by the sweetness of the fruit. Quickly she reached for the napkin that lay on the tray, to wipe away the juice that ran down her chin. Holding the napkin under her chin she ate the rest of the orange slices, savoring every bite of the delicious tasting fruit.

Elizabeth returned with an apple green gown draped over her arms.

Margaret gasped as she saw the richly embroidered hem of the skirt and the neckline of the bodice. Little pink roses and purple lilacs were finely stitched randomly with silk thread along the hem and the neckline.

"Oh what a beautiful gown," she exclaimed, " I cannot believe that I am supposed to wear anything as wonderful as this. All my life I wore my mother's worn dresses. When I was still a little girl, she used to sew me clothes out of her old skirts."

"We must hurry, Miss Margaret. Master Jack is not fond of tardiness." Elizabeth quickly changed the subject. She had seen the unbidden tears well up in Margaret's eyes.

While Margaret slept, Hammed had informed Elizabeth and the rest of the staff that the young lady's mother just recently passed away. Wisely he intended to forestall any unnecessary pain for the girl. Rudeness and callousness was not tolerated in the master's household. Therefore it was to be avoided to speak of anything that would remind the young lady of the past.

Quickly, Elizabeth took the robe from Margaret's shoulders and flung it on top of the bed. She helped Margaret into the three silken crème colored underskirts and the gown. Wide-eyed and in astonishment Margaret watched Elizabeth open the jewelry case were she pulled out a small strand of pearls. The little maid bade her mistress to sit on the stool in front of the vanity to fix her hair. After fastening the necklace around Margaret's neck, Elizabeth took a brush from one of the drawers and dipped it into a lovely scented liquid. She began to brush Margaret's hair free of tangles and taking a few strands of hair from the top of Margaret's head, she curled them around her fingers.

125

She fastened the curls with pins on top of the head. Stepping back, she admired her work and satisfied nodded her head in approval. The top portion of hair was shaped like a small crown. The remainder of Margaret's glorious hair cascaded in soft waves over her shoulders down to below her waist. It gave the young girl a sophisticated but still youthful look.

"How beautiful you are, Miss Margaret. I believe you to be the fairest lady in the house. Miss Fiona is fair, but her hair is not nearly as wonderful as yours. Let us keep this to be our secret she must not know I said that. It would hurt her and the master would be angry with me," the maid finished with a hushed voice.

"Oh, Elizabeth, your secret is safe with me. I will not repeat what you said. However I do not believe that I am more beautiful than the other ladies in this house." Margaret finished with a little girlish giggle.

"Very well then, see for yourself, Miss Margaret. I will get the pier glass." Her nose slightly put out by Margaret's disbelief and humor, she went to the big closet to come back only a few moments later. The maid pulled a long mirror out of the closet and leaned it onto the wall across from the big bed.

"That is where this should be fastened, the other pier glass had broken and was right here on this wall. Hammed will tell Mr. Potter to have this fastened by tomorrow." The little maid spoke with an air of importance. Margaret had never seen herself in a mirror as large as this and stared in shock and disbelief at her own reflection. This beautiful creature could not be her. The gown fit like a glove and complimented her auburn hair with golden high lights. The tight bodice of the gown had a deep neckline to show the top of her generous breasts and her flawless skin. The strand of pearls circled around her soft neck as a lovely edition to her whole outfit.

"Dear me, I cannot believe this. Elizabeth, how right you are. I do look very grown up and beautiful. I never saw my own self in a wonderful mirror as this one," Margaret cried out.

"Now you know that I spoke the truth, Miss Margaret. It is time for you to go down to the big dining hall to meet the master. He will like very much what he is going to see." Elizabeth smiled and gave her mistress a meaningful little wink with her eye. The maid walked to the door and opening it she let Margaret pass into the other room, who's heart was starting to hammer in her chest from excitement, anticipation and fear. Lifting the hem of her dress, Margaret started to pace the room. She was thinking what kind of impression she would make on this master. Would he like her, or would he send her back to her old home? Her mind was working frantically. Everyone in this house had told her that the master was kind and generous. However, she was not certain that the young master would find her interesting and grown up enough to personally involve himself with her.

Elizabeth had returned to the bedroom to clean up and Margaret was alone with her thoughts. It took only a little while and the maid who had finished her chores came back to the sitting room. She saw how distressed her young mistress was, and as if she could read her thoughts she said,

"Miss Margaret, please calm yourself. The master will like you. Hammed should be here at any moment. You must not show him a frowning face."

"I know you are right, Elizabeth, and I shall try to behave myself. I am as nervous as a bride on her wedding night. Tell me; is the master fair in face? No one has told me anything about him except that he is kind and wealthy and I do not know what to expect." She was nervously rubbing her hands together.

"Yes, Miss Margaret, the master is very fair in face indeed. He is still a young man who celebrated his thirty-fourth birthday this December past on the twenty-eighth day."

Suddenly, there was a soft knock on the door. Elizabeth hurried to answer the door and opening it she let Hammed into the room. For a moment, there was a dead silence and Hammed sucked his breath in sharply. The lovely young woman in front of him astounded him. The transformation from the shabby dressed orphan he found virtually on the street, to the outrageously beautiful maiden was incredible. Hammed seldom bowed to any other than his master, but here he made the exception. Bowing elegantly and deeply, he took Margaret's hand and kissed it gallantly.

127

"Miss Margaret, you are indeed beautiful. My master will be pleased. Shall we go downstairs?"

By taking her hand, he had noticed that they were slightly sweaty. To ease the situation he quickly took Margaret's arm and motioned to go. He felt that she was trembling and gave her an encouraging little squeeze.

"Do not fret, my dear, the master does not bite. Only occasionally does he bark, and then mostly at me," he said with a chuckle.

Despite her nervousness, Margaret had to giggle at Hammed's jest. She imagined the unseen master barking. Feeling a little better, she let Hammed escort her along the long corridor to the stairs and down into the dining hall where a young woman was sitting in a comfortable chair by the huge fireplace, which was crackling merrily. The young woman was embroidering a little piece of linen with some lovely yellow roses and vines in green. A man occupied another big chair by the fireplace opposite the woman facing away from the door. An enormous couch stood facing the fireplace and a long coffee table in front. Margaret could not see his features, upon her and Hammed's entering the room however the man rose from the chair and turned to greet them. Clutching Hammed's arm, Margaret felt her knees buckle. She was looking into the most handsome face and the darkest eyes she had ever seen. For all purpose and intention, he could be her father by age. However she did not feel that she could see him as a fatherly figure in her mind. Jack had heard the door open and with a meaningful look toward Fiona had risen from his chair. Turning and facing Hammed and the girl, who entered on his arm he stopped in his tracks. The girl was outrageously lovely and he felt his heart skip a beat. He looked straight into her big hazel green eyes as she shyly smiled and curtsied still clutching Hammed's arm. Hammed amused by this development of the situation began to speak.

"Master, may I introduce Miss Margaret Ziegler, the young lady I was telling you about." Hammed beamed openly at his speechless master. Catching himself he crossed the room with a grin on his face, which was meant for only Hammed to see. Margaret having her eyes lowered did not notice anything but her pounding heart and weak knees. She had hoped not to make a complete fool of herself by falling on her face at the very moment.

Mouthing, "You devil" toward Hammed he stood in front of Margaret. Her eyes were lowered, and taking her cold little hand into his powerful hand he greeted her politely,

"I am pleased to meet you, Miss Margaret. I do hope that your stay with us is going to be a long and happy one." He had noticed how pale she suddenly was and concerned he put his arm around her trembling shoulders. His touch was like a fire that had burned her. She suddenly felt faint and the room started to whirl around her. The last thing she remembered, were his strong arms around her as she fell into darkness. Lifting her up, Jack carried Margaret's seemingly lifeless and limp form to the big chair and carefully eased her into the soft cushions. Flinging her embroidery aside, Fiona had jumped up from her chair with a little cry of compassion.

"Oh the poor little dear. She must be frightened to death! Here, step aside Jack, let me help her." With that she gently pushed Jack aside and reaching into her little pouch she took a small vile of smelling salt. Waving it under Margaret's nose a few times, while her other hand gently patted and stroked Margaret's pale and clammy cheek. Standing beside the chair, Jack felt helpless. He took Margaret's small hand in his, and began caressing it in a comforting manner. Slowly, Margaret opened her eyes and was greeted by three concerned looking faces. As Margaret motioned to jump up, the young woman gently pushed her back,

"Hush now little one. Sit back, relax and take a deep breath. You gave us a start. Now, now there is nothing to be frightened about, here drink this." She took a small glass from Hammed's hand, which he had filled with brandy. Fiona was holding the glass filled with brandy now to Margaret's lips and made her drink a small sip. It burned her throat and Margaret began to cough. Almost instantly, the color returned to Margaret's cheeks and she felt better. The liquid made her feel warm inside. The concerned look on Jack's face however had made her feel foolish. Embarrassed she gently pulled her hand from his,

"Oh, dear Sir, I beg your pardon. I do not know what came over me

I never fainted in my whole life. You must think me a fool, please forgive me."

"There is nothing to forgive, Miss Margaret. Like a wise man once said, 'There is a first time for all things', you just experienced the truth to the matter. Do you feel better now? Perhaps we should wait for dinner a little while longer. You sit and rest and drink the rest of the brandy."

Turning to his faithful servant, Jack ordered,

"Hammed, go to the kitchen and tell Misses Potter to wait with dinner until Miss Margaret has regained her strength, she must rest for a while."

Fiona picked up her embroidery from the floor,

"Please excuse me, I shall return when dinner is served. Meanwhile I will write a letter to Dorothy." Lifting the hem of her skirt, she curtsied toward Jack and walked gracefully out of the room. Hammed had followed Fiona's slight nod with her head toward the door and understood instantly. He followed Fiona out into the hall. There she smiled knowingly at Hammed,

"Have you noticed the exchange? I will eat my embroidery if Jack is not already in love with the lovely girl. She reminds me so much of…"

Of course Hammed's sharp eyes had noticed the resemblance at his first meeting with the girl and quickly put a silencing finger to his own lips.

"Shhhhhh, I know exactly what you are trying to say. I noticed the resemblance at the first instance, I saw Miss Margaret. My only concern is her youth. She is much younger than the late Miss Sibylla."

"How old is the girl then, Hammed?" Fiona looked questioningly at Hammed.

"She is going to be fifteen years old by the end of this month."

"Oh, Hammed, you know that many girls her age already have a husband and children to care for. So her age should not be a problem," Fiona pointed out.

"This is correct Miss Fiona, however our good doctor stresses to abstain from any sexual relations until a girl has reached the age of sixteen. He might be right, many girls at twenty look worn out and old when they start having children too early."

"Hammed, my dear," Fiona interrupted, "although Miss Margaret is petite in stature she seems to be a healthy and strong young lady. Let the doctor have a look at her and then we shall see." Fiona put her hand soothingly on Hammed's arm.

"Perhaps you're right Miss Fiona. Master Jack should have a family of his own soon. He is not getting any younger and he needs an heir."

Turning, Hammed left for the kitchen while Fiona climbed up the stairs to her own room. Meanwhile, Margaret and Jack were left alone in the dining room. Jack was still in shock over the resemblance between Margaret and his late fiancé Sybilla. He stood by the little table to pour himself a brandy. Sybilla had been about two or three inches taller than Margaret. However the facial features were shockingly similar. Memories started to flood back into Jack's mind. Sybilla had been the love of his life. He seldom spoke of her and still seemed to blame himself for her tragic death so many years ago. Jack and Sybilla had been on holiday in Egypt. They went riding into the country, and were picnicking under a big tree. Suddenly, out of nowhere there was some movement in the grass near the blanket she was sitting on. Before he knew what was happening Sybilla screamed in pain. A snake had bitten her in the wrist. He rode like the wind back to the estate of Sybilla's father, with Sybilla on his horse. As the doctor arrived, Sybilla was unconscious and hardly breathing. The doctor was helpless, given the fact that Sybilla had been bitten by an asp. A few hours later, and only a few weeks before the wedding she was dead. His heart contracted painfully as he looked at Margaret. She was sitting in the big chair, carefully and obediently sipping the brandy from the glass in her hand. Her eyes were lowered as if she were trying to avoid his. What was the matter with her? She had never felt like this. This big man was so much older, and yet she felt like she was drawn to him in some strange way. Was it because of the way he had looked at her at the first moment? She could not explain it.

He turned his head to pour another drink; she watched him fill his glass a second time beneath her lashes and noticed his elegant yet strong hands. Only a few moments ago, these hands had held hers and she had felt the warmth and tenderness coming from those hands seemingly seeping through her whole body.

Jack turned away from the little table with the glass in his hands, and was facing her. He knew that she was watching his every move. Confused by his own feelings, he sat down in the other chair and took a sip from the brandy. He looked straight at her and lightly shook his head as if in disbelief. To his amazement Margaret began to speak.

"Sir, please forgive my forwardness, but you are looking at me like you are seeing a ghost. Why is that?"

Catching himself Jack answered truthfully:

"No, Miss Margaret, you must forgive me. You are correct that I am seemingly seeing a ghost. I knew a lovely young lady a long time ago. You are her spitting image."

"What happened to this Lady, Sir?" Margaret queried, "if I may ask."

Swirling the brandy in his glass, he lowered his eyes sadly and quietly answered,

"She died."

Assuming that it might have been one of his ladies, Margaret said,

"I am truly sorry, Sir. I did not mean to be insensitive." Seeing the sudden sadness in his face, Margaret quickly changed the subject and asked with a shy smile,

"Please, Sir, would it be possible to have some water? This drink burns my throat, and I feel my cheeks burning from it."

"Oh I am sorry, Miss Margaret. I am the one who is being insensitive. I should know that you are not used to drinking alcohol." He jumped up from his chair and taking a different glass from the table, he filled it with some water from the pitcher that was standing next to the brandy. He handed her the glass and she reached for it. Once more his hand touched hers and she blushed becomingly.

"There is your water, Miss Margaret, drink slowly now."

"Thank you, Sir, you are kind…Oh no," She exclaimed, the glass slipped from her hand and fell to the floor onto the thick carpet.

Immediately Margaret's eyes filled with tears and she stammered, "I am so very sorry sir. I ruined this beautiful carpet."

"Not to worry, my dear Miss Margaret, it is only water and will dry up again." He tried to comfort her smiling. Nevertheless, the tears spilled down her cheeks and he felt truly sorry for her. There she was sitting with her face in her hands and her shoulders shaking from crying. Gently he took her hands from her face,

"Look at me, my dear, it was no great tragedy. You see, the water is almost absorbed and one can hardly see anything. Now dry your tears." He was kneeling in front of her, with her hands in his. Margaret lifted her tear stained face, and with quivering lips she started to say,

"I feel like such a fool..."

"Hush now," he interrupted. "you are not a fool, I told you it was an accident. It could happen to anybody. Now let me dry your tears, and stop crying." With that he reached into his pocket and pulled out a spotless handkerchief. Gently he padded her cheeks with it and was trying hard not to show his mirth. As he started to wipe her little nose however, a soft chuckle escaped his lips. She snatched the handkerchief from his hand blushing,

"I am glad that you at least find the situation amusing, Sir. I can wipe my own nose, thank you." He could not help himself and he laughed. She was upset with herself and with an angry gesture wiped her nose, which made him laugh even more. She dared not to look into his face. Suddenly, she hiccupped and a small giggle built up in her throat. The whole situation seemed ridiculous. He realized that she was slightly tipsy from the brandy, and was laughing until his sides ached. Margaret had no idea why she felt this way. Here this big man was kneeling in front of her and was laughing, while she wanted to sink into the floor together with the water. On the other hand, she felt giddy and now was laughing herself. Jack got up from the floor and filled another glass with water. He sat on the armrest of the chair Margaret was sitting in, put his arm around her shoulders and held the glass to her lips. Thankfully she drank a few sips and raised her face to look at him. Before she knew what was happening, his face came dangerously close to her own. She inhaled the scent of his fragrance. She felt his arm around her and her heart seemed to stop beating. Their eyes met and locked. Slowly he was bending over further. She was holding her breath. His lips touched her forehead. Feathery and lightly, her first kiss from a strange man.

Suddenly, there was a noise coming from the big hall outside. Footsteps were nearing the door to the dining hall. Jack got up from the armrest and still holding the glass in his hand walked to the table to place the glass on it. At the same moment the door opened and Hammed walked into the room.

"Misses Potter is awaiting instructions to serve dinner. How is Miss Margaret?" Hammed was facing his master.

"I believe Miss Margaret is feeling better now, Hammed. You may ring the bell so we can eat."

It took Hammed only a short glance at the girl to know that something had happened while he was gone from the room. She sat motionless in the big chair and her face was flushed. Around her lips was the hint of a dreamy smile, as she watched every one of Jack's moves. Hammed could not help himself and a knowing smile curled his own lips at that moment. He had to find out what the master had said to Margaret that she had changed in only an hour from a helpless trembling girl, to a radiant young woman. For now however, he had to make sure that the girl felt safe and protected. Any lack of tact might scare her and Jack would be very angry indeed. Hammed walked over to the side of the fireplace, and pulled on a cord which signaled to Misses Potter in the kitchen that dinner should be served. Only a few moments later, the door to the dining hall opened and Fiona entered followed by yet another young girl. Both females walked over to Margaret's chair, and Fiona said, smiling at the girl

"Miss Margaret, I did not have a chance to introduce myself earlier. I am Miss Fiona Pauli. This here is my friend, Miss Christine Hatley." Fiona took Christine's arm and gently pulled her toward the chair to meet Margaret. Margaret stood up from the chair and curtsied to both women.

"I am pleased to make your acquaintance, Miss Pauli and Miss

Hatley. May I thank you for your kindness earlier, Miss Pauli, I do feel better now."

"I am glad to hear that Miss Margaret, are you sure it is nothing serious? I heard that influenza is going around," Fiona asked worried.

"Oh, no, Miss Pauli, it is nothing like that. I believe it was just all the excitement. I am not used to be in such elegant company. I admit, I was scared and everything is indeed new," Margaret assured Fiona.

"I can understand that well, Miss Margaret. I also was somewhat scared and did not know what I should do or what was expected. I assure you that we are all going to try our best to make you feel comfortable and welcome in our home," Christine said and smiled friendly.

"Let us go dining, Misses Potter served dinner," Jack commanded.

Still a little shy, Margaret slowly walked behind the two young women toward the huge table covered with a spotless white linen tablecloth. Obviously, each girl knew exactly where to sit. Before she could ask where to sit, Jack took her hand. Pulling her toward the table, he pointed with an elegant gesture to a chair. He had placed her on the chair to his left on the long side of the table next to his own at the head of the table.

"This is from now on your chair, when we have our meals together. Since we all have a place in life, we should keep a certain order within the small things in our life also," he remarked.

On the table was a bounty, such as Margaret had never seen. There was a side of beef, roasted crispy brown and seasoned with salt and peppercorns cut into thin slices. A big bowl with boiled potatoes was placed next to the beef. Their skin had been removed. Another bowl with small green peas and carrots garnished with chives and tiny onions were placed on the other end of the platter with beef. There was a small platter with sweet butter and a basket with freshly baked bread.

Margaret sat motionless. She looked fascinated at the silverware and the elegant hand painted plates and bowls. She decided to wait and see, how the other Ladies would eat with the forks and knives. Hammed had noticed that Margaret hesitated to take any of the food. He stood up from the chair on the other small end of the table. He took

Margaret's plate and loaded it up with slices of meat, potatoes, and vegetables a slice of bread and some of the sweet butter.

"Here, Miss Margaret, you must eat something. Misses Potter is an excellent cook. Her meat will melt on your tongue. So enjoy…" he said with a flashing smile. He placed the full plate in front of her on the table.

"I am sorry, I did not mean to be disrespectful. I am sure that all this food is delicious. It is merely that I had never seen such bounty. Not even at the shoemaker's house. It was only Misses Tippins who would have a knife to cut little pieces of meat in the soup, if any. I only know how to eat with a spoon. This is new to me to have a knife and a fork next to my plate. Please forgive my ignorance," Margaret explained shyly.

"There is nothing to forgive, Miss Margaret. Take the fork in your left hand and the knife in your right. Yes, just like this. Very good, Miss Margaret. Now you cut a small piece of meat from the slice and spike it with your fork like this," Hammed demonstrated.

Margaret followed every move Hammed made on his plate with her utensils on her own plate.

"There now you have it. Very nicely done indeed, Miss Margaret. I can see you are a fine student. Tomorrow we shall start with your first dance lesson." Hammed smiled.

So, Margaret's schooling and training had begun in this great mansion.

CHAPTER 11

A Birthday with Consequences

A few weeks had passed and Margaret had indeed adjusted well to her new life. She had learned to dance gracefully. No one would suspect that she grew up in the poorest section of town if she was seen at the dinner table in her rooms or embroidering. It seemed that she had always been in elegant

surroundings. Every one of the servants seemed to have a special interest to make her feel comfortable and at home. Especially Hammed, who sang high praises of the girl's accomplishments to his master. Nevertheless, Hammed was worried. He noticed that Jack indulged in drink more and more on a daily basis. At times Jack didn't seem to remember what went on the night before. Hammed wisely informed Jack every morning about little events that seemed to have escaped Jacks mind, while bathing and helping his master dress. The last day of January had arrived. Hammed helped Jack to pull his boots on and said

"Master Jack, today is Miss Margaret's birthday. I took the liberty to buy her a lovely necklace with matching earbobs and a matching ring. However, if the gift does not suit your taste, there is still time to exchange it. I thought that you might want to give it to Miss Margaret at dinner." He handed the three little boxes to Jack.

"Ah, my dear Hammed, what would I do without you? I totally

forgot the girl's birthday. I think she would have been hurt if we did not remember this special day." Jack opened the first little box. On tiny velvet cushion was a gold ring with fifteen small diamonds surrounding a sparkling emerald that was shaped like a teardrop. The second box contained a pair of earbobs, shaped the same as the ring. Fifteen small diamonds each set in gold surrounded two teardrop emeralds. The third box's content was a breathtaking necklace. Fifteen emeralds had been set like a teardrop hanging from the gold chain. The widest part was five stones. Underneath were four stones. Below that were three, then two and the biggest single stone was also set in gold surrounded by fifteen small diamonds. It was a magnificent present for a girl that age.

"I see you have not spared any expense, my dear Hammed. Your taste as well as your heart is flawless. I hope the girl is happy with her present. Tell me, is she still progressing well in her studies?" Jack asked absent-minded.

"Miss Margaret is smart and eager to learn Master. As I told you yesterday and all the days before that, she is making a tremendous effort to please her teachers. She does not want to disappoint you and the faith you have shown her. As I had suspected, Elizabeth is her confidant. Our little maid told me only last night that Miss Margaret has in mind to work hard and save her money. Some day she plans to pay you back for all her wardrobe and even for the lessons." Hammed chuckled amused.

"So, the little lady has plans already. Hopefully she also knows that she is supposed to be trained later in the arts of Eros," Jack said dryly handing the three little boxes back to his servant.

"Yes, Master Jack, she knows what is expected of her. Which brings me to the next subject. Your friend Thomas Crandall arrived late last night. He is eager to see you," Hammed changed the subject quickly. He let the jewelry boxes slide into his big pocket in his pantaloons.

Hammed knew, how much Jack wanted to see his dear friend. Unfortunately, Jack was as too often lately, too drunk to receive any guests. Forestalling an embarrassing encounter with the big captain, Hammed had told Thomas, that Jack was suffering from a terrible headache and had been given medication to sleep. Thomas had understood and said that he would greet his friend Jack in the morning. After having been served a late dinner, Thomas was shown to one of the guest rooms on the third floor.

"Hammed, why didn't you tell me this before? You know how much I am longing to see my dear friend. I wonder, why it took so long for him to arrive this time. He should have been here weeks ago," Jack mused.

"Well then, Master Jack, let's hurry. Here, let me help you. I just have to brush a little lint from your jacket." Quickly, Hammed brushed over Jack's shoulders and beamed a radiant smile.

"There, all done. I will finish cleaning up here. I shall meet you at the library later, Master."

"Thank you, Hammed. But I wish you to come with me now. Tell Mister Potter to clean up the bath. I need you by my side," Jack said to his servant.

"As you wish Master Jack," Hammed replied and opened the door for Jack. Just as both men were walking across the big hall to enter the dining room, Thomas Crandall came walking down the stairs. Seeing his old friend Jack, he took two steps at once and shouted joyfully embracing Jack,

"Jack, dear old boy. I have not seen you in ages. How are you? Let me look at you. Hey, what have we here? Do I see some silver already?" Thomas laughed teasingly while holding his friend at arms length.

"I am so glad to see you again, Thomas. You might be right. I feel like I am getting older by the minute." Jack laughed back squeezing his friends arm.

"Let us have the morning meal. You must tell me why it took you so long to get here." Jack said while he took his friends arm to lead him into the dining room. Misses Potter had the table set for the three men only.

"Jack, I was detained for several reasons," Thomas started to explain, while spooning honey on his bread. "some of the cargo had been stolen from the warehouse in Hong Kong. So, I had to wait for another delivery of silk from the inland. Once in France I had to wait for the weather to change for the better. I did not want to risk loosing all my precious cargo in a storm. You will be well pleased with the wares I brought this time." Thomas took a big bite from his bread.

"Wonderful, I can't wait to see it all and take inventory." Jack responded exited.

After they had finished their meal, all three men took the big carriage to Jack's warehouse where the ships cargo had been stored. It took several hours for all the wares to be documented. As many times before, Jack was astounded and indeed well pleased with the profit he would make from the sale of the fabrics, leather, herbs and spices as well as the gemstones.

"I am famished. Let us return to the house. Misses Potter will be upset if we are late for dinner. Especially today," Jack chuckled.

"Oh, Jack, I told you not to make a big fuss on my account. I am almost considering you like a brother and I don't want any special treatment. So please tell Misses Potter not to cook up a storm every night," Thomas said while he pulled on his fur-lined gloves.

"I forgot to tell you, my old friend. We do have a new addition to our other little enterprise. Hammed found her in the poorest section of town. She is a charming sweet girl. As my good Hammed will swear too, she is Sibylla reborn," he laughingly teased his faithful servant.

"I am not amused, Master. Miss Margaret could be a younger sister to the late Miss Sibylla." Hammed turned to Thomas and continued; "You will see for yourself, Captain. The resemblance is astounding. Today is the young lady's birthday. Misses Potter is preparing a special feast to honor Miss Margaret."

"Oh I see," Thomas laughed. He knew Hammed almost as long as Jack did and was very fond of the big man from Bursa. He also knew, that Hammed would never forget how poor he once was and that only the kindness of a stranger had saved him from a terrible fate. He would always try to help the less fortunate in return.

Arriving back at the mansion, the three men were greeted by Mister Potter.

"Quickly come and warm yourself by the fire gentlemen. Dinner will be served in a few moments."

In the dining hall, Jack poured brandy for himself and another for

Thomas. He handed the glass to Thomas and raising his own he toasted,

"Here is to good friends and a good business."

"Hear, hear. I second that." Thomas raised his glass.

"So, when do I meet this lovely little lady? I am getting curious. She must be special indeed, to deserve all these gifts and flowers," Thomas remarked while pointing with a nod toward a table, which had been moved into the dining hall and decorated with boxes and flowers.

Instead of answering his friend, Jack poured himself another brandy. Quickly Hammed answered Thomas,

"Yes, Sir, the young lady is special. She is bright, amusing and accomplished in embroidering and she also wrote a poem all by herself." He seemed proud as if Margaret was his own child.

"How old is the girl then, Hammed?" Thomas asked with an amused smile on his lips. It had become obvious that Hammed had taken a special interest in the girl.

"She is fifteen years old today, Captain. Tragedy is no stranger to her. Only this Christmas past she lost her dearly beloved mother. She is all alone in the world with no family left. Her father died when she was still a small child and she does not have any other relations. I met her by coincidence and she is living and being trained here since nearly the beginning of this month."

Ah, now it made sense to Thomas. It seemed that the girl reminded Hammed of his own childhood in Bursa as he was starving and had to steal his food. Furthermore, the servant had a soft spot where beautiful girls were concerned. So, here was the secret to Hammed's devotion.

"You know our softhearted Hammed, Thomas," Jack said after swallowing his drink and poured another. Concerned, Thomas sent Hammed a meaningful questioning look. Hammed lowered his glance.

"Don't you think it would be best to have something to eat first, old friend? We have not been eating since this morning. I feel light headed from one drink alone. You are already on your third." Thomas put a heavy hand on Jack's shoulder.

"Oh, I was just frozen to the bones. I needed to warm up, Thomas. Do not worry. I am fine," Jack assured his friend.

141

Meanwhile, after finishing her dance lesson and bathing, Margaret was getting ready for dinner. Elizabeth was satisfied with her work. She had fixed Margaret's hair into two braids and wound them around her hands, she had pinned them on top of Margaret's head. To the front of the braids she had fastened a small tiara made from thin gold with tiny diamonds in it.

Margaret's gown was burgundy velvet with small seed pearls sewn to the hem of the skirt. Elizabeth had been instructed not to adorn Margaraet with any other jewelry, besides the tiara. To Margaret the gown was incredibly lovely as she spied herself in the large mirror, which was now fastened securely on the wall. Could this beautiful creature really be her? With her hair up, she looked grown up and very mature. If only her dear mother could see her now. If only Misses Tippins could see her. She wished that all the people who had looked down on her before could see her like this. She would show them all, that she would be rich and a fine lady some day. Right now she had to concentrate on pleasing Jack. She had to learn how to be like the late Miss Sibylla.

Margaret had learned in a very short amount of time to ask the unsuspecting Elizabeth many questions. Thinking that Margaret was only trying to satisfy her girlish curiosity, Elizabeth chattered about anything and everything she knew went on in the mansion. Margaret found out, that Jack liked the drink very much. She knew from the poor section that people who drink a lot do try to forget problems and also forget what they are doing at times. She did not want to be poor again. She wanted to stay in this big mansion with servants and enough to eat for the rest of her life. However, she did not want to become one of Jack's 'Ladies'. Her mind was made up. She had to find a way to bind him to her. If he would get very drunk, she would seduce him. If she would carry his child, he would have to marry her and her fortune would be made. She would never have to do other peoples dirty laundry again. Today was her birthday. She would be old enough to be a wife and mother. Other girls her age had husbands and children already. She had no time to waste. She would ask Fiona, what a man expects from a girl in the bedchamber. She had to be careful however, not to tip her off. Perhaps Fiona had her eye on Jack. A sudden wave of panic and jealousy swept through her and she felt herself getting angry. She could not let anybody stand in her way and spoil her plan. She wanted it and she wanted it all to herself. She would get it. Satisfied she turned once more in front of the mirror. The low cut bodice gave a delicious view of her full breasts whose nipples were barely covered. She knew from her chats with Elizabeth, that all men liked breasts and to squeeze and suckle on them. It made them exited and then the men want to couple with a woman. That much she knew. Whatever else was there to be found out, she would learn from Fiona. Elizabeth came from the closet with a pair of red high-heeled velvet slippers. Bidding her mistress to sit, she pushed the slippers onto Margaret's feet.

"There, now it is time for you to go to dinner Miss Margaret. Felicitations on your birthday again. I hope you get many wonderful gifts," the little maid said cheerfully.

"Thank you, Elizabeth, I have all I ever hoped for. A wonderful apartment, breathtaking gowns, enough to eat and what could be worth more than a loyal maid like you. I am so glad to be able to talk to you about those certain things. We should let that remain our little secret. Perhaps the master or Hammed would get upset with us if we seem too curious. The other young women might laugh about my girlish worries," Margaret said slyly.

"Of course, Miss Margaret. My lips are sealed. Now go and have a pleasant evening." Elizabeth opened the door for Margaret. Just as the maid was about to close the door from the inside, Margaret turned and called back over her shoulder,

"Don't wait up, Elizabeth. It might be late when I return to my rooms."

Waiving and nodding understanding, Elizabeth pulled the door shut.

Arriving down in the big hall, Margaret stopped in front of the door to the dining hall. Smoothening her skirt she lifted the hem of her gown slightly with her left hand. Slowly she reached for the doorknob with her right. Her heart pounded. She knew she would not make a fool out of herself this time. She had learned how to curtsy gracefully. She had learned how to eat properly and how to hold a glass with only three fingers. She also knew how to make a graceful entrance. What she didn't know was how Jack would react this time. She had not seen him since her first night here in this huge mansion. She had been kept busy with lessons and her meals were served in the comfort of her own rooms. Slowly she turned the doorknob. Standing in the dining hall were Hammed, Jack and a strange man by the fire. Miss Fiona, Miss Christine and two other young women, whom Margaret had met during her dance lessons and had introduced them self as Miss Sarah and Miss Ann were standing next to the men listening to the strange man's stories. Ann and Margaret had developed a friendship, since Ann was closest to Margaret's age. She had turned seventeen this past October. Just as Margaret entered, the whole group exploded in laughter at a jest that Jack had told. Quietly Margaret pulled the door shut behind her. Hammed was the first to notice her standing there. He could hardly believe his eyes. By the door stood a radiantly beaming young woman. There was not much left of the shy little orphan from just a few weeks ago. Hammed put his big hand on Jack's arm. Turning his head, he followed Hammed's glance with his eyes. So did the rest of the group, as both men got quiet. Thomas could only but stare for a moment. Hammed had been right all along. This girl looked very much like the late Sibylla. She was beautiful. Now that she had every ones attention, Margaret softly smiled and walking gracefully toward the group to stand in front of Jack. She lifted the hem of her gown slightly and curtsied deeply, bowing her head.

"Good evening Master Jack," Margaret extended her soft greeting. Curtsying once more toward the rest of the group she said politely, "good evening Ladies, good evening Gentlemen."

Fiona was the first to speak, "Good evening, Miss Margaret. How lovely you look. My best wishes on your birthday."

"We all wish you the very best, Miss Margaret," Hammed said smiling.

"I can only add my own best wishes to everyone else's, Miss Margaret. Let us all drink a toast to many happy returns." Jack had found his speech and was pouring wine for all. Jack handed Margaret a glass of wine. Gently she took the glass from his hand.

"Oh, where are my manners. Miss Margaret, this here is my oldest friend and business partner, Captain Thomas Crandall." He pointed with an elegant gesture toward Thomas. Thomas took Margaret's hand in his and kissing it gallantly he smiled friendly and openly:

"I am pleased to finally meet you little Miss. I have heard a lot about you all day. I was beginning to have the impression that Hammed had found a princess from a far away land." He chuckled, still holding her hand.

"Oh, our dear Hammed is too kind. It is a pleasure to meet you, Captain Crandall. I assure you, I am a poor girl who is grateful to live in this fine mansion and I am merely trying to please our wonderful Master. Without him I would still be washing laundry and run errands for the shoemaker," Margaret admitted with a rueful smile.

"You are here now, dear girl, and hopefully for a long time," Thomas said almost fatherly. It seemed to give him pain as she gently withdrew her hand from his.

Everyone drank to Margaret's health and happiness. Dinner was served and the ladies and men were seating them self around the table. At first a tasty broth with tiny dumplings swimming in it was served. The table was heavy laden with a whole ham, a goose roasted brown and crispy. There were trout on a big platter garnished with thin slices of lemon and dill. There was a big bowl with steaming potatoes and another bowl with red cabbage cooked in white wine with apples, tiny bits of bacon and chopped walnuts. There was another bowl with green beans and tiny sliced mushrooms. There was a basket with freshly baked bread and a platter with sweet butter.

Everyone ate heartily. After dinner, wine was served to drink another toast. Margaret barely sipped from her glass. She knew that she needed her wits to make a good impression. She could not afford to get tipsy. Jack called for more wine and filled his glass again. Thomas exchanged a concerned glance with Fiona. She took the initiative and said cheerfully,

"Miss Margaret, you must open your gifts. I am certain that you like your presents very much."

"Ah, yes, Miss Margaret, we all want to see. Please open your presents now." Sarah stood up from her chair and walking around the table, she took Margaret's hand. Excitedly, Ann clapped her hands and had also jumped up from her chair.

"Wonderful, I can't wait to see your face, Margaret. Come, come."

She took Margaret's other hand and together, both girls pulled her toward the table with the presents on it. Handing Margaret a small package wrapped in a colorful piece of silk and bound with a gold ribbon, "Here, open mine first. I made it for you. I hope you like it," the girl giggled.

All eyes were on Margaret, as she slowly and carefully unbound the ribbon. Undoing the piece of silk, she found a pair of black velvet gloves lined with fur.

"Oh they are wonderful Ann, thank you. I shall never have cold hands again." Margaret smiled and hugged her friend.

"Now this one. I also made it for you, Miss Margaret." Fiona handed her a small package wrapped in a piece of white paper and bound with a purple ribbon. Margaret found three beautifully embroidered handkerchiefs in it.

"Thank you, Miss Fiona, I shall treasure this." Margaret curtsied toward the smiling woman.

"Please, call me by my first name only. We are all living in this house like a family and we should not be so formal. I should like to call you Margaret."

"I agree, Margaret, call me Sarah." The other girls had joined the little group by the table.

"I second that. I'm Christine and this one is from me." Christine laughed and handed Margaret a bigger package. Margaret unwrapped it and she held a beautiful fur lined muff in her hands.

"Oh you are all so kind. How can I ever thank you all for these lovely gifts? Not once in my life did I ever receive so much." Margaret was genuinely touched.

"You have not opened mine yet Margaret. The fun is only starting,"

Sarah said with a giggle in her voice. She handed Margaret a square box. As Margaret opened the lid, she blushed. Inside the box was a book whose covers showed couples in various positions of passionate embrace. Speechless, Margaret quickly closed the lid of the box again. Hammed knew which present Margaret had received from Sarah. After all, he had suggested it. Smiling amused, he stood up from the chair and poured himself a glass of water. He drank a few sips and put the glass back onto the little table by the fireplace. Slowly he walked over to the group of young women who were still standing by the birthday table chattering and laughing. He reached into his big pantaloons and pulled out the smallest box of the three.

"This is one gift from Master Jack, Miss Margaret. Happy birthday and many joyous returns." Hammed beamed.

Margaret had not expected this. Slowly she took the little box from Hammed's hand and opened the lid. Gasping she stared at the ring on the small velvet cushion. The four girls had moved close to see the content of the box. With little cries of delight and genuine tears of joy they watched Margaret's face. She could not believe her eyes. Only staring, shaking her head and her mouth slightly agape she searched for words.

"Here, let me put it on your finger. Let me see if it is the correct fit." Hammed took the ring from the cushion and taking Margaret's hand, he slipped the ring on her left ring finger. He knew it would be the correct size.

"Oh it is magnificent." Margaret had found her voice and held her hand away from her body. The ring sparkled on her finger, reflecting the light from the oil lamps on the walls. Thomas and Jack had moved from the table to the big chairs by the fireplace to continue their conversation. Jack sipped on another brandy. Thomas had told Jack about some of his adventures. Amused he now watched Margaret's reaction to his gift. The girls were chattering and giggling. Fiona had taken the book from the box and was obviously explaining the blushing Margaret some of its contents. The girl had no idea, that there was more to come. He was starting to feel the effect of the alcohol he had consumed. Thomas had ordered some coffee from Mister Potter who was clearing the big table.

"Right away Sir. It will only be a moment." Mister Potter went to the kitchen to unload the little service wagon with the used dishes. Moments later he returned with a big pot of freshly brewed coffee and about a dozen dainty cups and saucers. He placed the service wagon next to Thomas and motioned to fill a cup with the hot aromatic drink.

"Thanks, Mister Potter. I can help myself. You know me, I am not used to be waited on hand and foot," Thomas laughed and gently took the big pot from the older man.

"As you wish Captain." Turning toward Jack, Mister Potter asked, "will that be all, Sir?"

"Yes, Mister Potter, that will be all for tonight. You may retire." Jack dismissed his servant. Bowing, Mister Potter wished the men a good night and glad to have some time to himself, he quickly walked across the lawn outside the mansion to go home to his lovely little cottage, where he and his wife lived.

Margaret knew she had to thank Jack for the magnificent gift. Slowly and somehow still a little shy she walked over to his chair. Curtsying deeply, her voice was slightly shaking,

"I do not know what to say, Master Jack. Somehow 'thank you' does not seem enough. This ring is such wonderful gift."

"You are welcome, Margaret. Since the other Ladies have told you that we are quite informal, please call me Jack. Master makes me sound so terribly old. Only my faithful Hammed will never get used to it. He claims it is not befitting his station to address me by my first name." Jack winked laughingly at his big servant who stood by the Ladies shaking his head and grinned.

"It is getting late and I must take inventory in the morning with the laundress. Please excuse me Jack." Fiona curtsied.

"I am learning to prepare a new dish tomorrow with Misses Potter. May I be excused also?" Sarah followed Fiona and curtsied.

"I don't know about you, Christine, but I am simply tired. I think the wine got to me. I wish to retire." Ann giggled.

"Yes I am tired also, Ann. I have a date tomorrow with this big Swede. I need my beauty sleep." Christine chuckled and curtsied.

"Good night then Ladies. You are excused," Jack nodded. It was strange that all four girls suddenly had excused them self and walked giggling and exchanging knowing looks out the door.

"I think it is time for another small present Margaret," Jack said quickly as Margaret was about to speak. He suspected that she also wanted to make her excuses and go to her rooms. Hammed, sitting on the big couch, reached in his pantaloons again to retrieve the remaining two boxes. He leaned toward Jack and handed him the items. Jack took them and held the smaller one out to Margaret. With shaking hands she opened the little box and another cry of surprise escaped her lips.

"Oh, Jack, this is too much. I do not deserve this," she cried. Once more Hammed came to her aid as her eyes seemed to fill with tears.

"You most certainly do, Miss Margaret. You are a diligent student and we are proud of you wonderful progress. Here, let me help you put them on."

He took the ear bobs from their cushion and expertly fastened them on Margaret's ear lobs before she could even protest.

"Ah, now let me look at you, Margaret. Yes, yes, very nice. Hammed, do you think that there is still something missing?" Jack teased. Rubbing his chin as if he was thinking, Hammed responded, "Hm, I am sure Miss Margaret is not missing anything. Now I see, her neck is looking a bit bare. What can we do?" The big man grinned.

"I have an idea," Jack said, barely able to contain his mirth. He had seen Margaret helplessly looking from one man to the other. Thomas sipped his coffee and chuckled softly.

"Margaret, turn around and close your eyes," Jack commanded laughing.

Not daring to disobey, she turned to face Thomas and squeezed her eyes shut. She felt something being placed around her neck. It was cold. The hands, which did however, were warm and gentle. She assumed it was Hammed's hands. Gently those hands turned her on her shoulders to turn again. Her eyes were still closed.

"You may open your eyes Margaret. Happy birthday again." The hands holding her and the eyes she looked in were Jacks. Her knees almost buckled. Gingerly she touched the object around her neck. Somehow Hammed had produced a small mirror from his pantaloons and held it out to Margaret. Slowly and with a shaking hand she reached for it.

"There now the outfit is complete." Jack was holding her by her upper arms now away from him to take a good look. The necklace looked stunning on her milky white flesh. The biggest green stone nestling in between the onset of her generous breasts. Margaret looked at her own reflection and suddenly felt faint. It was just not possible. Jacks suddenly concerned face was all she could remember. Suddenly everything went dark and she was falling.

Catching the girl in his arms, Jack said to Thomas who had jumped up to help,

"She said she didn't know what to say. Well, this is the best 'thank you' I had in a long time."

Hammed had also jumped from the couch so the two men could lay the unconscious girl down. Again he reached into his big pantaloons and pulled out a small veil with smelling salts. He pulled the tiny cork from the veil and waved it a few times under Margaret's nose. Slowly she opened her eyes and looked straight into the dark eyes of the big captain. He found the situation humorous and laughed until his sides ached. Jack sat in the chair again and gulped down another brandy.

"Oh dear, I did it again. I swore to myself not to act that foolish and here I am on the couch," Margaret said distressed. Suddenly she remembered why she had fainted in the first place. She tried to sit up and touched her neck. It was still there. This beautiful necklace that Jack had fastened around her neck with his own hands. Hammed gently pushed her back on the cushion and ordered,

"No, Miss Margaret, you must lie still for a little while. You are still pale. Let the blood return to your face first. Here, take this, drink this." He handed her a tiny round pill and a glass with cool water in it. Obediently Margaret leaned back on the cushion. She swallowed the pill and took a few sips of water. She did not dare look at any of the men at this moment. Like her life depended on it she clutched the glass with both hands and her eyes lowered she sipped and sipped until the glass was empty. Gently Hammed took the glass from her and chuckled,

"There now, I can see the color returning to your cheeks. Just lie back and relax." Margaret could feel her whole body relaxing and her mind seemed to relax as well. Whatever this tiny pill was, it worked wonders. Hammed saw that the girl was feeling the effects of the pill. He only wished that his Master would stop drinking hard spirits. At the risk that his Master would be slightly annoyed, Hammed rose from the couch and seemingly by accident swept the crystal carafe with brandy from the small table. It fell to the ground, spilling almost all it's contents. The crystal had not broken since it landed on the heavy carpet.

"Oh dear, I am truly sorry, MasterJack, what a shame. No more brandy left in the house. I'll send Alfred the coachman to the warehouse tomorrow. May I pour you some more wine or would you prefer some coffee?" Hammed asked slyly.

"Oh well, I will have some wine then," Jack said with a sour face.

As if he was looking at something distasteful, Hammed said with the full glass in his hand about to hand it to Jack,

"I thought I had told Mister Potter to lay out some traps. I think I just saw a mouse run under the door."

"What? Where?" Jack turned to see for himself. He couldn't see anything.

Hammed took the moment to empty the content of his big ring, who's stone flipped over, into the glass of wine. It was only a few drops nearly tasteless and odorless liquid. It would have its effect in a short while. Hammed hoped for the best. Margaret had not noticed. She was looking dreamy eyed at her own reflection in the little mirror, admiring her jewels. Thomas had followed this event however with rising interest. Questioningly he looked at Hammed, who pointed with his eyes meaningful toward the door while he handed Jack the glass with wine. Thomas understood. He would make his excuses also.

"Jack, I am dead tired. I am going to seek out my bed. I'll see you in the morning, good night." Thomas rose from his chair and walked slowly toward the door.

"If there is nothing else, I wish to retire also Master." Hammed yawned.

"Very well, Hammed. I'll just finish my wine. Go seek you bed. I am able to manage." Hammed was not to be told twice. Flashing Jack a big smile, he hurried toward the door, exiting with,

"Good night, Master Jack. Good night, Miss Margaret."

Only upon hearing her name did Margaret suddenly realize, that she was left alone with Jack who sipped his wine while he openly smiled at her.

Thomas had waited outside the door and wanted some answers from Hammed. Impatiently he paced until finally the door opened and Hammed stood with his finger on his lips to silence the big captain. He whispered,

"Come to the kitchen Sir, I shall explain." Thomas had not much of a choice. He followed Hammed to the kitchen. Both men took a seat by the big table and Hammed poured two cups of herbal tea.

"Now tell me, my big fellow, what is going on here. Jack is drinking himself into oblivion. As I suspect, he is doing this on a regular basis. Then there is this new little girl. If you are asking me, she is not quite as innocent as she seems. Something is on her mind. I will not have Jack hurt Hammed. I saw you putting something in his drink. What was it?" Thomas demanded.

"Captain, put your mind at ease. It is true that my master is drinking very much spirit. I am worried sick about it. However, he is a grown man. There is nothing I can do to stop him. Which brings me to the next problem. He needs and heir. Miss Margaret is young and as the doctor assured me, very healthy. She would be perfect for Jack. Since she is still young, her mind can still be bent to his will. She will not give him as many problems as a grown woman who already had other relations to compare him with. Which is another problem. Master Jack's drinking has greatly affected his sexual performance. The drops I slipped in his wine will only temporarily correct this shortcoming. However if it is given to often, the body develops a dependency and the drops will lose their effectiveness. I know from Miss Margaret's maid, that she is in the middle of her monthly cycle right now. Which means she is able to conceive a child. The little pill I gave her will make her relaxed and stimulate and excite her sexually. In a short while her body will yearn for passionate embraces. In other words she will lose her fear and inhabitations. We all hoped, that tonight would be a special night," Hammed finished his speech.

"You mean to tell me, that even the other girls are in on this little deception?" Thomas asked somewhat dumbfounded.

"We all agree, that some day the master needs a son to take over the business. His nephews have their own father's estates to care for. His sisters do not correspond with my master any longer. So, there are no other heirs. We all want what is best for Jack." Hammed sipped his tea.

"I understand, Hammed. I only hope it is not going to bite you all in the ass. As far as I know things like that have far reaching consequences. Not always good I might add. Well, I'm off to bed now. Good night, Hammed." Thomas finished his tea and rose to walk from the kitchen.

"Good night, Captain Crandall. Pleasant dreams," Hammed wished the big captain and sought his own bed.

Chapter 12

Rude Awakenings

Margaret tried to remember her first night with Jack. She had felt him lift her up from the couch and carried her into his bed. Over and over, he had whispered; 'I can't believe you are here. I can't believe I am holding you in my arms.' She had felt as if her young body was on fire. All her shyness seemed to have vanished and she gave her body in wild abandon. Somehow she woke up in her own bed. It was almost noon. A noise, which sounded like crying, woke her. What was the reason for some ones obvious sorrow? Margaret jumped out of her bed and rushed to her sitting room. She found Elizabeth sitting on the chair. It was her maid who was crying. Upon Margaret entering the room, the girl jumped up from the chair and quickly wiped her tears with the back of her hands. Margaret demanded an explanation.

"Elizabeth, what is wrong? Why are you crying? Tell me this instant."

"Oh Miss Margaret, something terrible has happened. Master Jack is angry with all of us," the girl cried.

"Why is he angry, Elizabeth? What has happened?" Margaret asked with an alarming rise in her voice. She suddenly had a sick feeling in her stomach. She somehow knew, that Jack's anger had something to do with what happened last night. Unfortunately, she could not recall any details.

"Hammed told the Master, that he and all the others are only trying to help. Now Master Jack is furious. I have never seen him that angry." The girl looked scared.

"Elizabeth, you are not making any sense. Start from the beginning. How is everybody trying to help Master Jack?" Margaret demanded.

"They all wanted him to be happy and have an heir soon. So Hammed gave him and you a secret drug last night. They were hoping you would conceive a child. The Master is angry, because he does not want any children by you. He said that you are only a child yourself and much too young for him. He also said that he would choose a wife and mother to his children when the time is right. He does not need his servants to interfere in his life," the maid explained with a quivering voice.

"Oh dear, that does not sound good, Elizabeth. What am I going to do? What if I indeed conceived a child? What will become of me?" Margaret said suddenly frightened.

"I do not know the answer, Miss Margaret. I merely know that all the other ladies were asked to leave this house. Their maids are packing their belongings as we speak. Hammed said that only you and I can stay. I had no idea what all the others were planning. Neither did Mister and Misses Potter. I feel bad for all the other ladies and their maids. They are all scared," the little maid said under tears.

"This is terrible, Elizabeth. What is going to happen to Hammed? Is he leaving also?" Margaret asked concerned.

"No, Miss Margaret, he is not leaving. The Master's own father made Master Jack promise long before he died, that he would never have any other personal servant but Hammed. I heard that the old man was very fond of Hammed. However the young Master is angry at Hammed right now. In time he hopes the Master will forgive him."

"That does make me feel better. Hammed will know what I should do. I must talk to him. Go and ask him to come to me, Elizabeth." Margaret ordered her maid.

"As you wish, Miss Margaret." The girl quickly curtsied and rushed out the door to find Hammed. She had seen him last in the kitchen as she picked up the tray with Margaret's noon meal.

It was incredible. Without her knowledge Margaret had been aided in her plan to bind Jack to her. She hoped that she was carrying his child. She doubted that there would be another night like the last. He would have to do the honorable thing and marry her after all. A soft knocking on the door startled her out of her thoughts.

"Enter," Margaret called and Hammed opened the door. His face was sad. Margaret had seated herself on the big couch and Hammed sat beside her. He took Margaret's hand in his big brown one,

"I am so terribly sorry, Miss Margaret. We all hoped it would be the right thing to do. Now I have to do another terrible deed. The Master told me to make sure that you would not carry his child. I must ask you to eat this little pill here. It will help to continue your regular monthly cycle. Please forgive me, Miss Margaret, and may Allah forgive me also." He handed Margaret a little green pill and went to fill a glass with water from the pitcher on the table. While Hammed had turned his back, Margaret quickly stuck the little pill under the cushion where she sat. She would not loose the child to a dumb little pill that Hammed gave her. If she were pregnant, she would have this child at all costs. Jack must marry her. Hammed handed her the glass and said sadly;

"Please eat the pill and drink some water with it, Miss Margaret. Believe me, never have I been asked to do such cruel a deed."

Margaret said nothing. Pretending to stick the little pill in her mouth, though her hands were empty, she took the water and drank some of it. Hammed had not noticed. He must never know. He started to speak again:

"I must give you a pill like this every day until your monthly cycle returns. Please, Miss Margaret, do not be angry with me."

"I am not angry with you, Hammed. I am angry with Jack. How can he ask you to do such thing? He held me in his arms last night and now he is asking you to kill his child if I am indeed carrying one," Margaret said furious. She would show him, that she was not to be pushed around. The deed was done.

"I cannot answer that, Miss Margaret. I do not know what is in the Master's mind any more. I only thought he would be able to find happiness again with you. I see now, how wrong I was to use your resemblance to the late Miss Sibylla. The Master told me this morning about a strange dream he had last night about making love to his late Miss Sibylla. Then he found the stains of your virgin blood in his bed and on his person. I told him, that I arranged this night of passion and it was not a dream. He got very angry and told me to dismiss all the other people who were in on the plan," he said with hanging shoulders.

He raised his hands in a gesture of despair and slowly walked out of the room. Margaret was left to her own thoughts. All she could think was, that she would make Jack love her and the child if there was one inside her. She would need help. She must win him over. She knew that she could not count on Hammed any longer. He would not betray his master again. Elizabeth was scared of loosing her position. She could not be taken into her confidence. Margaret had to do it all on her own. Deep in her thoughts she ate the meal on the tray. She had a plan.

Almost two weeks had passed. Hammed had given her a little green pill every day. Every time she stuck the pill quickly under the cushions. If Hammed was looking, she put the pill in her mouth and spat it back out as soon as he left her room. Margaret knew, that he asked Elizabeth every day, if there was a show of blood in her laundry. She went to the kitchen. Misses Potter was busy cooking. Alfred the coachman sat by the table drinking some hot tea.

"Alfred, I have need of your service. Take me to the jeweler. I noticed that one of the little stones in my ring is somewhat loose. I must have this repaired so I will not lose this stone," Margaret said sweetly.

"Right away, Miss, I shall be waiting with the black carriage. Please dress warm. I will have the hot stones ready in a little while." It was not his place to ask any questions. Alfred took some stones from next to the fireplace and stuck them into the flames on a big shovel. Margaret hurried back to her rooms and got dressed. Elizabeth was with the laundress. Quickly Margaret put on her new burgundy red warm cape that was lined with fur. She grabbed the new gloves and the muff after pulling her new warm boots on her feet. She took her little purse from the drawer in her vanity with the coins that Hammed had given her as allowance. She hurried down to meet Alfred by the carriage. He helped her into the carriage and placed a big fur over Margaret's lap. She set her feet onto the hot stones that were carefully wrapped in pieces of flannel. Alfred closed the door and moments later the carriage rumbled down the driveway.

The carriage came to a halt after about thirty minutes ride. Margaret knew this section of town well. Many times had she been there to deliver shoes and boots to Mister Tippins costumers. The door to the carriage opened and Alfred helped her out. Smiling sweetly, Margaret suggested,

"It might take a while, Alfred. It is starting to snow again. Go to the tavern at the end of the street and have some hot punch. I shall meet you there once I am done with the jeweler."

"As you wish, Miss. The tavern keeper is my sister's husband. We might have a nice chat while I wait. There is no hurry." Alfred chuckled.

"Oh, I had no idea. I know the tavern keeper also. Not long ago I delivered some boots, which Mister Tippins repaired. I shall see you there later, Alfred." Margaret smiled and watched as the carriage rumbled down the narrow street toward the tavern. From the niche at the entrance to the jeweler she watched as Alfred entered the tavern. She made her way quickly in the opposite direction toward the other end of the street. Around the corner was the butcher. The young Lady's request was not strange to the fat little man. Many housewives bought pigs bladders filled with blood. Seasoned with certain herbs and spices and boiled it hardened to a solid loaf and it made an inexpensive addition to bread or lonely potatoes on many poor tables. This young lady was dressed in expensive clothes. Perhaps she just liked the taste of the dish. It was not his place to ask any questions. He took the coin from her and handed her the bladder with blood. The young lady's face was partially hidden by her big hood with the fur around.

The butcher wished her a good day and she left the shop. Outside the shop, Margaret checked the string on the bladder. It was tight. She stuffed the bladder carefully in her big muff and walked toward the jeweler. Once inside she handed the thin man the ring:

"Please, could you check this ring, I believe a small stone is coming loose. Can you fix this for me while I wait."

"Of course I can, Miss. Let me have a look." The Jeweler inspected the ring, "I remember this ring. A big strange looking fellow had ordered it to be made by me."

"Yes, I know him. His name is Hammed. He is my betrothed's servant," Margaret lied.

"Ah, I see. One of the little settings to hold the stone is bent slightly. It is no big problem. The stone would not have fallen out. There, all done." The little man handed the ring back to Margaret.

"What do I owe you, my good man?"

"No charge, Lady." The thin man bowed. He obviously thought Margaret a wealthy young lady, who had been gifted by her betrothed with this expensive jewelry. It could not hurt his business, if she spoke highly of his prompt service. The jeweler thought.

"Thank you and good day," Margaret said while she slipped the ring back on her finger. She pulled on her glove again and left the store. Slowly she walked up the street toward the tavern. Alfred had just finished his big earthenware mug filled with hot rum punch as Margaret entered.

It was late afternoon as Margaret returned to her rooms. Luck was with her. Elizabeth was obviously still busy folding laundry. She was the only maid left in the house to help the laundress. Quickly Margaret untied the string on the bladder with the blood. She took a fresh pair of undergarments and soiled it with some of the blood. She opened the closet door and flung the soiled garments into the basket with dirty laundry. Fastening and binding the string tightly, she opened the window and stuck it in the niche under the window. It was the fourteenth day of February. It would keep fresh for a few days and would not be found. Margaret repeated the procedure with the folded pieces of linen, which were used to catch her monthly flow for five days. She diligently followed her studies and a few days later, a new girl had moved into the house. She was a pretty slender girl with curly long dark hair and dark brown eyes. She was about two inches taller than Margaret and about two years older. Her name was Gretchen Hofmeier. She spoke with a heavy accent. Margaret and Gretchen became friends quickly. Fascinated by this strange language, Margaret started to learn more of it every day. Soon the girls conversed in German and many times could be seen together in either rooms giggling. The girls seemed to be having a little girlish secret. No one paid much attention to it. On March the 14th Margaret asked Alfred once again to take her to town. She wished to show Gretchen some shops. Once again she told him to wait at the little tavern. It was Gretchen this time who bought a bladder filled with blood. Gretchen knew only part of the secret. Margaret told her, that the Master did not know she was carrying his child and would be ecstatic, once he found out. It must be their secret for a while longer. In a few months time she would tell him. Both girls knew, that Hammed kept precise records of their monthly flow. Since there was no reason for the doctor to check Margaret, she was able to keep her secret. Luck would be with Margaret once again. There was no morning sickness in her first trimester. She had deceived the whole household for nearly four months. However, that all changed at the end of May.

Elizabeth woke up to a strange sound. She jumped out of her bed and quickly threw her robe on. She had left the doors to her Mistress' bedroom slightly ajar. As she entered Margaret's bedroom, the window was open and Margaret vomited out onto the huge balcony.

"Oh dear, my poor Miss Margaret. Why are you so ill? What can I get you to make you feel better?" the maid asked concerned.

"It is nothing, Elizabeth. I shall be fine in a minute. Perhaps I ate too much of Misses Potter's clotted cream last night," Margaret said.

"Very well, I will get you a light meal Miss, Margaret. I will return shortly." The maid hurried out the door. This was not good. She had to make sure that she could keep her secret a while longer. She had to make sure that Elizabeth was not able to help her into her dress, which seemed to get tighter every day. Margaret sat on the floor and hit her ankle as hard as she could against the carved leg of the big bed. The pain was intense and her eyes filled with tears. Moments later her ankle was swollen and a big bruise began to build. Angry, she wiped the tears and limped into the sitting room where she sat on the floor again. She slipped her high-heeled slippers on her feet. Elizabeth returned and found her Mistress sitting on the floor crying. Elizabeth almost dropped the tray. As fast as she could, the maid placed the tray on the table and cried out,

"What happened, Miss Margaret? Are you hurt?" Reaching under her arms, she tried to pull Margaret up from the floor. Margaret cried out in pain.

"Oh it hurts. I do not think I can stand. I twisted my ankle in those cursed slippers." Elizabeth noticed the big bruise and helped her to hobble to the big couch. She carefully lifted Margaret's legs up and covered her with a light blanket.

"Thank you, Elizabeth. I think I will not be able to take any dance lessons for a while. Please inform Hammed, that there is no need to send for the dance master for a while and have Gretchen send to me at once."

"Right away, Miss Margaret. Please lay still and do not walk. I will talk to Hammed at once. Here, drink some of the freshly squeezed orange juice." She handed Margaret a glass with the juice. The maid left.

Slowly Margaret sipped the juice, as a soft knock came from the door. Her German friend Gretchen rushed to her side.

"Ach du liebe, what is it Margaret. What is kaputt?" she asked.

"Nothing is broken, Gretchen. I had to do it. Elizabeth told me just yesterday that my dress has to be altered. I am getting too fat," she giggled.

"Why did you have to do what, Margaret? You are speaking in riddles. I do not understand." The German girl looked at her and seating herself at the edge of the couch where Margaret was laying.

"I am starting to show, Gretchen. My stomach is getting bigger now and I will not fit in my gowns any longer. I hit my foot on the bed on purpose so I can stay for a few days in my wide robe. No one will ask any questions just yet. I need a little more time to tell Jack," Margaret whispered.

"I see, how much more time do you need, Margaret. Shouldn't he know soon, that he is to become a father?" the girl asked suspiciously.

"I am so afraid, Gretchen. He does not want any girls. What if I am carrying a girl child?" Margaret lied, trying to sound convincingly enough.

"What a bloedsinn, Margaret. All papa's love little girls. He will get used to it. My papa in Germany has eight girls and he told us he could not wish for better children. He has not one son and is happy. So what is true?" the dark haired girl pressed. Somehow for the past few days she had become aware that Margaret was not telling her the whole truth.

"Very well, Gretchen, I will tell you the truth. You must promise me not to tell anyone. I cannot tell Jack, because he does not want any children at all. I was used like a pawn. Hammed and the others thought he would be happy with me and needed an heir. On my birthday Hammed gave Jack and me a drug. I do not remember much about that night. I merely know, that I was in Jack's arms and he was gentle and passionate. He thought that he was dreaming and was making love to his late Sibylla whom he was engaged too. Everyone told me, that I resemble her very much. Jack found out the next day, that he had not been dreaming at all. He had made love to me. He spilled his seed inside my womb and Hammed gave me a pill every day until he was sure, that I was not carrying Jack's child. Jack demanded from Hammed to do this to me. I will not have my child killed by either one of them. That is how I came up with my plan and the bladder with blood. I had to convince Hammed, that there was no child. I somehow knew from the first day, that I would have a child. Jack must marry me, once the child is born. So, you see that is the reason I could not tell anyone. My child must live and some day will be the heir to everything Jack owns. I will have my revenge. Imagine Gretchen, he wanted to kill my unborn child to shy away from the responsibility of marrying me. I will not have it." Margaret hit her little fist on the cushion. Gretchen sat stunned. She didn't know what to say.

The door opened and Elizabeth came into the room followed by Hammed.

"Miss Margaret, what do I hear from Elizabeth? You hurt your foot? Let me have a look." He lifted the blanket and carefully touched Margaret's ankle. It was swollen and bruised badly.

"I am not sure if it is broken. We best have the doctor take a closer look. I will send for him at once. Lay still and do not move the foot. Elizabeth, bring some pieces of linen and very cold water. We must cool the ankle and get the swelling down." Hammed ordered. Elizabeth ran out the door again and went to fetch the required items.

"Miss Margaret, you have not eaten anything this morning. Are you sure there is nothing else wrong?" Hammed asked concerned.

"Oh not to worry, Hammed, I was not very hungry. I think I ate a little too much last night. Misses Potter's clotted cream is delightfully delicious and I had a big portion of it," Margaret explained. She had no idea, if Elizabeth had told Hammed that she had vomited. Forestalling any suspicious questions, she better spoke up now.

Elizabeth returned with the cold water and a few pieces of linen. She soaked the linen in the cold water and wringing the excess water out, she carefully placed the cold compress around Margaret's ankle. Margaret winced. Hammed left the room to call for the doctor. He would send Alfred to bring the doctor to the house. Gretchen sat in one of the chairs and said:

"Elizabeth, I will help Miss Margaret. You may go to the kitchen and have a nice chat with Misses Potter. I wish to speak to Miss Margaret alone."

"Very well, Miss Gretchen. Do you wish any tea or perhaps some coffee?"

"I can serve myself and Miss Margaret, thank you, Elizabeth," she dismissed the maid. She had to speak with Margaret. The maid curtsied and left the room. Gretchen pulled the chair next to the couch and sat down again. She took Margaret's hand in hers and asked:

"How can I help you now, Margaret? You will be discovered in a very short time and what will happen then? You will not be able to hide this from Hammed for the next five months." She smiled softly and squeezed Margaret's hand.

"Gretchen, I have an idea. I must go away for a few months. My mother had a sister somewhere up north. Mother never spoke much about her. As soon as my foot is healed, I will go and visit her for a while. I will come back when my child is born. You must not tell anyone that I am enceinte. I will think about telling Hammed once I am in safety at my relations. Please, Gretchen, you must help me with this," Margaret begged.

"Of course I will help you, my dear friend. We must make certain, that you are welcome at you aunt's house. You must write her a letter this day. You do not have much time. I will go with you. You must not be alone on a long voyage in your delicate condition. I will tell Hammed, that I must return to Germany for a few months because my mother took ill and my papa needs me to look after all my younger sisters. I am the oldest one. He will not question that. You shall see, it will work," the girl said resolutely.

"Oh, Gretchen, what would I do without you. You are truly a wonderful friend. In the little desk over there is some paper and quill. Please bring it to me. I shall write a letter to my aunt this minute." Gretchen quickly fetched the paper and quill and the little bottle with ink. She handed the items to Margaret, who began to write the letter at once. Soon she signed it and folding it, she wrote the address. She sealed the letter with a few drops of wax and handed it to Gretchen.

"See to it, that the letter is going to reach the mail coach in town today. You are correct. We do not have much time," Margaret whispered. She had heard voices from the hall. Quickly Gretchen stuck the letter in the pocket of her skirt. The door opened and Hammed entered with the doctor. The big dark man smiled friendly and asked:

"Let me take a look at the foot, Miss." He removed the cold compress and examined the swollen ankle. Margaret sucked the air in through her teeth. It hurt indeed much, as the doctor bent her foot from side to side. He asked, if Margaret could make little circles with her foot and she did.

"I see nothing is broken. This big bruise puzzles me however. How did that come to pass, little Miss?" The doctor rubbed his chin and looked at Margaret over his spectacles. Gretchen held her breath.

"As I stumbled, I hit the foot on the table doctor. I was wearing my high heeled slippers at the time," Margaret explained without flinching.

"Ah, that would explain it. You must stay off this foot for a few days. It is going to heal fine. Continue the cold compresses. You will be as good as new shortly." The big doctor smiled and grabbed his big black bag, which he had placed on the dining table. The doctor left again.

Hammed followed. He promised before leaving to look in on Margaret later in the evening. Gretchen wiped imaginary sweat from her brow.

"Phew, that was close. I thought this big fellow would examine you further. That would have been a disaster. My knees are still weak," the girl giggled nervously.

"Hurry and get the letter on it's way Gretchen and come back to me soon. I need you. We must plan everything carefully," Margaret said in a low voice. Gretchen did not have to be told twice. She hurried to the kitchen to find Alfred. She handed him the letter and told him it was of great importance that the letter would reach the mail coach this very day. Alfred took the letter and went on his way into town. This was done. Gretchen rushed back to her friend's room and placed another cold compress on Margaret's foot. The two girls plotted and thought out a battle plan...

CHAPTER 13

Greedy Relatives

"Margaret, a letter has arrived for you. It is from you aunt in Scarborough. Open it, quickly." Gretchen entered the room and handing Margaret the letter. Margaret held the letter and saw that the return address was indeed her aunt's, Delia Grisham. She opened the letter and began to read out loud,

"My dearest niece Margaret!

It is a pleasure hearing from you. I am saddened that my sister Dorothea has passed away. I had not heard from her in several years. After your dear father died we lost contact. She had moved with you to a different location and my letter was returned. I am not sure if you will remember this. You were at my house as a little child. You were fascinated with the pigs and sheep. This brings me to your request. My husband and I could certainly use some help around the house. We have plenty of room and would welcome you and your friend for a little while. Please inform me, when we are to expect your visit. I am looking forward to seeing you again. My best regards, your aunt Delia." Margaret folded the letter and stuck it in the pocket of her robe.

"This is wonderful, Margaret. We can go at once. I have given the letter that I wrote to myself to Hammed. He has no idea that it was not from my mother. I wrote it with my left hand, so it looks different than my own hand writing and it was in German," Gretchen giggled.

"Hammed is clever, Gretchen. He speaks several languages, including German. What exactly did you write in your letter?" Margaret worried.

"I merely wrote, that I was needed at home. Pretending to be mother, I wrote that I took ill and need help with the girls. Papa is working all day and is too tired to take care of them," Gretchen answered.

"Good, we cannot afford to make any mistakes. As long as Elizabeth is with the laundress, you must help me with my gown. She must not see, that it is getting too tight," Margaret said and flung the little blanket from her legs. Quickly she jumped from the couch and pulled Gretchen with her into her bedroom. She selected a light blue gown with dainty flowers embroidered at the hem and sleeves. Pulling and pushing, the girls finally succeeded to fasten all the little buttons at the back of the gown. Both of her huge trunks had been packed for several days now and with a heavy sigh she took a glance around the room. She did not know, if she would see all those wonderful things ever again. She could only hope that everything worked out for the best and Jack would marry her as soon as she returned with his child. She reached for a light cape and threw it around her shoulders. The wide cape would hide her figure and she could say her farewell to Hammed, without his sharp eyes discovering her secret. She grabbed the bag with her personal things like brush and hairpins from the vanity. Quickly the girls walked out of the room and made their way to the room on the other end of the hallway, where Gretchen slipped into her own cape. Alfred and one of the stable boys would carry her trunks as well as Margaret's down to the coach. Both girls hurried down the marble stairs and crossing the big hall, went through the dining hall into the library. Hammed sat by the desk and wrote into the books. Hearing the girls knock on the door, he looked up from his work.

"Ah, I see you are ready for your departure. I hope your mother is feeling better soon, Miss Gretchen. Please give her my best wishes for a speedy recovery." Turning to Margaret, he smiled and said, "I am so happy for you Miss Margaret, that you finally found your long lost relatives. I wish you a pleasant voyage and hope you will return to us soon. Master Jack wishes you both well and will inform the teachers to continue with your training at our return."

Margaret had hoped to see Jack once more. Why was he not here?

"I wanted to say my farewells to Jack in person Hammed. Is he in the house?" Margaret asked wrinkling her brow.

"Master Jack accompanied his friend Master Crandall to his ship early this morning. Master Crandall is returning to America. He received a disturbing letter from his wife and had to leave at once. He also wishes both of you well and extends his best regards to you Miss Gretchen. He enjoyed your company very much," Hammed winked and kissed her hand farewell. He took Margaret's hand and kissed it as well. Both girls curtsied and left the library, where Hammed once again bent over his books. Gretchen had convinced Hammed that it would be best to travel to town together with Margaret. From there they would travel with the public coaches in different directions to reach their destination. Since he knew that the girls had become close friends, he figured they wanted to spend the time together while traveling into town. Obviously he did not suspect anything. Gretchen couldn't help it and a little giggle escaped her throat as she hurried through the dining hall with Margaret in her wake. The bigger blue coach stood outside in the driveway and Alfred together with the stable boy lifted the big trunks onto the coach. Fastening them securely, he climbed back down and helped Margaret and Gretchen into the coach. He had been told to take both young Ladies to the inn where the public coaches would stop and take the passengers from there to their destinations. Margaret and Gretchen leaned back into the seat with a sigh of relieve. So far so good. They were on their way to town. Margaret could hardly believe her luck. Her purse would be filled with coins. Each one of the dismissed Ladies five months ago had given her a farewell present. Most of it had been jewelry. Opening her bag, she took out a little pouch and pulled on the drawstring. Sadly she looked at the rings, bracelets, broaches and ear bobs in her hand. She would sell all of it to the jeweler in town. The coach rumbled slowly through the narrow streets and came to a halt. Both girls climbed out with Alfred's help. The Innkeeper had the trunks brought to the rooms the girls would occupy until the public coach would arrive. They were informed, that it would be early in the morning the next day. It was still early afternoon and Margaret and Gretchen had taken their midday meal at the inn. Slowly they strolled down the narrow street toward the jeweler. The man inspected the jewels and named a price. It was much more than Margaret had expected. She stuffed the money into the little pouch and the girls left to walk back to the inn. She would have enough money to travel and eat for many months. The rest she would hide by sewing it into her winter cape. She had done so with her own jewels as soon as her plans to travel had become reality. Gretchen had plenty of money on her own. She was seventeen and had worked for several weeks as one of Jack's escords. Her wages were generous and she had saved most of it. She had sent a small amount of money home to her family. It would help her mother to have some new dresses made for the older girls. Anneliese the second oldest was going to be fifteen. She had a suitor and would marry soon. Then there were Elfriede thirteen, Rosalinde ten, Margot eight, Marie five, Dagmar three and the baby Ellen eleven months by now. Anneliese needed a few things for her mitgift. Gretchen had explained to Margaret a few weeks ago, that this was which dowry was called in Germany. It was expected of a girl to bring furniture like a table, chairs, bed and linen trunk into the marriage. There would also have to be dishes and utensils and linens to be made and purchased. This money would help her parents to give Anneliese a good mitgift. She would not have to marry a pauper.

Margaret and Gretchen rested in their rooms until the evening meal was served. The Girls went to bed early. It was still dark, as the innkeeper's daughter knocked on the door to call for the morning meal. The coach would arrive soon and after changing horses and the coachman had eaten, they would be on their way. After many days of travel, Margaret and Gretchen had reached the last inn near Scarborough. Margaret sent word to her aunt's house. She would be waiting for her aunt's carriage at the 'Raven'. It was the next day as an older man arrived to pick up the girls. One horse pulled the wagon, where hay was transported with at harvest time. The old man's knees almost buckled, as he lifted the four heavy trunks onto the wagon. The girls took their seat next to the old man on the wooden bench in front. It took several hours over dusty roads and rocky paths to reach the house. Margaret gasped as she saw the estate. The big house was obviously in dire need of repair as was the big barn and stalls where the animals were kept. Gretchen and Margaret looked at each other in shock. This was not at all what they had expected. Chickens and pigs were running lose in between several scrawny looking dogs and cats. An older woman was pumping water from a well it's rusty handle screeching loudly. This was not going well. The wagon came to a halt and the woman looked up. Her worn face was wrinkled and strands of her gray hair had come loose from the bun at the nape of her neck and were fluttering in the wind. She put the bucket with water on the ground and came slowly toward the wagon. The two girls had jumped down from the bench and waited. The old woman wiped her hands on her big dirty apron and took Margaret's hands in her own. She held her at distance remarked,

"You have the look of your mother, Margaret. Welcome to my house. I see you have become a fine lady. Is this your friend Gretchen then?" she asked. Both girls curtsied.

"Yes, aunt Delia, this is my friend Gretchen. Thank you for inviting us. Where is my uncle?" Margaret asked the old woman looking toward the door. The stink from the pigs almost made her gag and she wanted to go into the house as quickly as possible. Her back hurt from the uncomfortable ride on the hard wooden bench and she felt tired.

"Your uncle Jester is out with the boat fishing. I hope he will come home with a big catch. We need the money from the sale of the fish. There has been not much lately. Giles," she hollered at the old man, "take the trunks up to the rooms I have prepared for my niece and her friend. Let young Arthur help you. He is in the barn." she ordered. Margaret felt sorry for the thin old man. He said nothing and walked to the barn to get the boy Arthur. Together they carried the heavy trunks into the house. Pushing and pulling they made their way up the narrow wooden stairs, which seemed to creek and moan under the heavy load. Margaret and Gretchen had followed the old woman and the men into the house. The windows in the house were tiny and didn't let much light into the room. It took a moment to get used to the dark smoky room, which was obviously the big kitchen. To her right on the far end of the wall was a big fireplace, which had a big black kettle hanging over the fire. In the middle of the kitchen was a big wooden table with long benches on both sides. The table needed a good scrubbing as well as the benches. Next to the fireplace on the wall were shelves with earthenware plates and cups. On the lower shelve were wooden spoons and forks. There were no knives. Inside the kettle boiled a fish soup that was stirred by a young girl. The smell made Margaret's stomach turn.

"This is Charlotte. She helps me in the kitchen. She is the daughter of the pharmacist. Her mother died a long time ago," Aunt Delia explained.

"Charlotte, this is my niece Margaret and her friend Gretchen."

The young girl turned and smiling she curtsied.

"Pleased to meet you both," Charlotte said friendly. She had noticed the elegant attire on both young ladies. Her eyes followed the big trunks that were lugged up the stairs by old Giles and young Arthur.

The old woman walked by the table to the other side of the room. She opened the door and waived the girls in.

"Come into the parlor and rest. You must be tired from your long trip." She had noticed, that Margaret was getting a bit pale. Only to glad did both girls follow the invitation. They sat down on the big comfortable couch whose fabric had seen better days. Aunt Delia sat in one of the big chairs next to a small table with an oil lamp on top. The cylinder from the lamp was black from sod and smoke. The parlor smelled musty. The wooden floor was cracked and dried up from lack of polish and oil. There was a small carpet in frond of the couch. The holes the moths had eaten into it were repaired roughly with heavy twain. Aunt Delia called for Charlotte to make some tea.

"Tell me, Margaret, when did my sister die? You merely wrote that she passed. Was she ill?" the old woman asked.

"Yes, aunt Delia, mother was very ill indeed. She died this Christmas past. Her lungs were inflamed and she was delirious for days before she died. I had no money to give her a decent burial. She was laid to rest in a paupers grave with many others," Margaret said sadly.

"Good thing she does not know about it. It would break her heart not to be buried next to her dear husband. You however seem to be doing well my dear. I see you have fine clothes and shoes. How is that

171

possible?' the old woman asked suspiciously. Perhaps her niece was married to a wealthy man and could give her some money. Why didn't she mention it in her letter? Why had she still her maiden name on the letter? She must find out and she must be careful.

"We both work for a wealthy merchant in Manchester, aunt Delia. He has many big warehouses and we keep records of all the merchandise that arrives by ship and by land. It is a lot of work and we are paid generous wages," Margaret explained quickly before Gretchen could say anything. She had noticed the greedy look on her aunt's face as she mustered her fine cape and her high-heeled satin slippers. She felt uncomfortable and took the cup with tea that Charlotte had brought to her. Slowly she sipped the aromatic drink. She put the empty cup onto the little table and said,

"Dear aunt, I am quite worn from the long voyage. So is my friend. I wish to rest for a while. Please have Charlotte show me to our rooms." She could hardly sit any longer. Her back ached terribly and her aunt's prying eyes made her nervous. She was suddenly not sure that this trip was the right thing she had done.

"Oh of course, Margaret. Go with Charlotte and rest a while. I will call for you at dinnertime. Your uncle should be back by then," Aunt Delia agreed.

Both Girls followed Charlotte up to the second floor. Charlotte opened the first door to the right,

"This is your room, Miss Margaret. The next door is you friends room." She smiled and let Margaret pass into the small room. On the right wall stood a small bed with a straw mattress and a heavy woolen blanket on it. Next to the bed under a small window stood a small table with a candle on top. Next to the table was a wooden chair. The second chair was placed by the foot end of the bed. Her trunks had been moved on the wall opposite the bed. Margaret knew at the instant she had entered this small room that she would not stay here for more than a few days. She believed that Gretchen felt the same. However, she needed a few days rest. She would make her excuses to her aunt later this week. She took her cape off and flung it over the chair by the bed. Disappointed she sank onto the bed and put her feet up. Soon she was asleep. A knock on the door startled her out of her sweet slumber. Gretchen stuck her head around the door. She sat on the bed next to Margaret and said in a low voice and giggling,

"Margaret, I do not know what you have in mind. We must get away from this stinking house as quickly as possible. I will eat my slippers your aunt is thinking about putting us to work in the stalls."

"I have the same feeling, Gretchen. However, I have no intentions milking cows and feeding pigs and chickens. Can you imagine Hammed's face if he knew where we are?" she laughed. Both girls laughed until their sides ached. They could only imagine Hammed's horror at the prospect of having their finely manicured hands stuck in dirt and cow dung. It was getting dark outside and a knock on the door startled the girls. Charlotte called from outside, that dinner would be ready shortly. Margaret got up from the bed and opened the door.

"Tell my aunt, that we will be down in a few moments. I wish to change into some comfortable clothes," Margaret said to the girl and closed the door again.

"Gretchen, help me out of this gown. It is better not to let my aunt suspect my condition. I will wear my big day robe. We will go from this place in a few days. I will not give birth to my child here in between pigs and dogs. We must return to Manchester. I will stay at my old place above the laundry kitchen until my child is born. I still have enough money for the trip back and a few months to live on. Then I shall see what is going to happen," she whispered while she took her gown off with Gretchen's help. She opened one of the trunks and pulled out her pink day robe. She loosely bound the sash under her breasts. Her slightly expanding abdomen was not noticeable.

Satisfied she nodded at her friend and motioned to go.

It had worked once and it had worked again. After two days of rest, Gretchen had written a letter, explaining that both young women were to come back to Manchester at once. There has been a huge new shipment of merchandise and they were needed urgently. Aunt Delia had not much choice as to let Giles take them back to the inn to catch the public coach once again. Margaret had counted her aunt a few coins on the grimy kitchen table. Greedily the old woman had snatched the coins from the table and said, "I wish you would not have to live so far from here. I sure could use some more help. Perhaps you could send some more money. After all, I let you and your friend stay here in my house. Food is expensive and does not fall from trees," she finished bitterly, ogling Margaret's little pouch.

"Unfortunately this is all I can spare, aunt Delia. I merely have enough for the return voyage," Margaret lied and motioned her friend to depart. Her stingy aunt was beginning to tear on her fragile nerves. For the past two days Margaret had heard nothing but complaints. New candles would have to be bought. She let them burn too long in the evening. The linens would have to be washed. The soap costs money. The milk Margaret and Gretchen drank could have been sold. It went on and on like this. They had met uncle Jester only briefly at dinner the first night. He was a grumpy old man and after greeting Margaret and Gretchen at the table, he wordlessly ate his soup and went to bed. The fishing had not been good.

Both girls waited a few days at the inn. Margaret needed some more rest. She felt tired and her back had started to hurt from the long trip back on the hay wagon's wooden bench. The rooms at the inn were far more comfortable, bigger and cleaner than aunt Delia's house. The girls would take their time to get back to Manchester. After a days ride in the coaches they would stay a few days in each inn on the way. Finally they arrived once again in the little inn in Manchester. The decided to stay a few days and develop another plan. Since Gretchen was supposed to be in Germany for a few months, she could not return to the mansion so soon. She would go to London for a few months and then return to Manchester. Margaret would ask Misses Tippins for her old rooms back. She would have to convince the kind older woman to not tell anyone about her return to the old neighborhood. Hammed and Jack must not find out where she was hiding. This plan would work. Gretchen promised Margaret to stay in contact and let her know when she had returned to the mansion. She would find a way to notify her. After a tearful farewell the girls parted. Gretchen gave Margaret the address of her parent's house in Germany in case she had need of it.

Some day she would return to Germany. As soon as she had like Margaret enough money for a rich dowry.

Margaret had stayed at the comfortable little inn for a few more months. She had visited Misses Tippins often and the older woman had promised not to tell anyone about it. Margaret had told Misses Tippins the whole truth. The kind old woman was shocked at Jacks request to have Hammed try and get rid of the child by giving Margaret the pills. She got very angry with this rich snob who would ask his servant to do such dirty deed.

Margaret woke up and noticed a slight pain in her stomach and back. Quickly she dressed and walked from the little inn slowly through the streets to reach Misses Tippins. Upon seeing Margaret, the older woman said resolutely,

"Margaret, I will send for Hammed. He must know, what is going on. You are about to have your child. I will send for him at once."

"Oh, Misses Tippins, I am not sure that this is the right thing to do. What if he gets angry? I have deceived him and Jack for the past nine months. What if he is still trying to kill my child?" she asked fearfully.

"No one is killing anyone, Margaret. Unless he wants to end up at the hangman's noose," Misses Tippins said and handed Margaret a glass with warm milk. She drank the milk and rubbed her back:

"I will go to my old rooms now and lay down, Misses Tippins. The pains in my back are getting a little stronger."

"Very well, Margaret, I will look in on you later. Here, take this bundle. I have wrapped some nappies and little blankets in there. My grandson does not need them any more. Where are all your things?" Misses Tippins worried.

"I left them in my room at the inn. Please make certain, that the innkeeper is informed that I will return in a few days time. Here are a few coins for the rent at the inn. Make certain that my room at the inn is locked and no one will steal anything. Here is the key. Thank you for these baby things." Margaret handed Misses Tippins some money and the key to her room at the inn. She took the little bundle from the kitchen table. Luck would have it that at this moment a young boy came

175

into the little store. He was running errands for Mister Tippins now as Margaret had done many months ago.

"I am glad you returned early, Patrick, I have something to do for you," the older woman said. She send the young boy to the inn and pay the innkeeper and then he would have to go to the big mansion and ask for the big man Hammed. He would have to give Hammed an urgent letter, which she wrote quickly. The boy was instructed not to give the letter to anyone but Hammed. Margaret took her warm cape from the chair and hanging it over her shoulders, she pulled the hood over her head. It was getting cold outside and she slowly walked down the tiny street to her old rooms. She opened the door to the bigger room and wrinkled her nose in disgust. The room was as she had left it so many months ago. Tired and in pain, she took off the cape and folding it carefully, she stuck it under the foot end of the big mattress. The jewels and some money were still sewn and secure in the hem of the cape. She would need it later. She opened the chest and placed the little bundle in it. A stronger pain went through her and she crawled into the big bed. She would rest a while until Misses Tippins came back. Margaret fell into a light sleep. It seemed only moments later and Misses Tippins came quietly into the room. Margaret opened her eyes and asked with fear in her voice,

"You had children, Misses Tippins, are those pains normal?"

"Yes, Margaret, they are quite normal. Your inside is squeezing together, so the child will be pushed out. That is where the pains are from. Do not be afraid. You are healthy and strong. Everything will be well. You have slept for a few hours and Patrick returned a few moments ago. He told me, that the innkeeper is keeping you door locked and he gave Hammed my letter. The poor man got very pale as he read it. He went to fetch Misses Bowman the midwife. She will be here shortly. Hammed should be here any moment now," Misses Tippins said and handed Margaret a small glass with some milk she had poured from a little pitcher. She had brought the warm milk along, for she knew that Margaret had nothing to eat and nothing to drink in her tiny rooms. The door opened without a knock and Hammed stood frozen on the spot. He could not believe his eyes. In this filth was his little Miss Margaret about to bear his master's child. His mind had been working feverishly all the way from the mansion to the midwife and to this place. How was it possible that Margaret was carrying master Jack's child. The dates checked out. He had seen the bloody stains on her undergarments himself. Suddenly it dawned on him. Alfred had mentioned, that he had seen Miss Margaret pay the butcher a visit. He had assumed that Margaret was merely paying him a visit since she knew a few people in this neighborhood. Now he found the explanation to the empty pigs bladder, which was found a few months back on the balcony under Margaret's window. He chuckled to himself, as he walked up the stairs to Margaret's old room. She had been very clever indeed and must have been scared to death all by herself all those months. Little did he know, that Gretchen was with her for a big part of this time. He rushed to her bed and knelt next to it.

"Miss Margaret, will you ever forgive me. I had no idea that you were in fact still carrying Master Jack's child. Your little deception worked well. I believed you at your aunt's house until today." He kissed her hand gently.

"Oh, Hammed, I was so frightened. I could not let you or Jack kill my child. You must forgive me. I had nowhere else to go and I told no one but Gretchen the whole story. She was with me at my aunt's house and upon our hasty return to Manchester stayed with me at the little inn on the road to Oldham. The visit to my aunt's house was a disaster. The house was filthy and she is a stingy greedy old woman who would have taken all my money if I had stayed longer." Margaret flinched as a strong pain went through her.

The door opened again and Misses Bowman arrived. Seeing the surroundings, she was not pleased. Misses Tippins and Hammed greeted the midwife and promised to come back later. Both knew, that Margaret was in good and capable hands. Misses Bowman examined Margaret and taking her knitting, she sat on one of the little wobbly chairs. It was hours later and Margaret was screaming. She was screaming at the top of her lungs…

CHAPTER 14

A Child Is Born

Hammed had arrived back at the mansion. Jack sat in the dining hall. He held a glass with brandy in his hand. He jumped up as Hammed entered.

"Tell me it is a jest, Hammed. Tell me that there is no child. Alfred found out from his sister's husband the tavern keeper. He in turn had visited his brother the innkeeper on the road to Oldham. He recognized Margaret being great with child. Did you not follow my orders and give her your special pills. News like this travels fast. Why is she still enceinte Hammed, answer me," he thundered.

"First of all, Jack, Miss Margaret is not enceinte any longer. She bore a healthy son early this morning," Hammed thundered back at him. It was very seldom that Hammed raised his voice. It had never happened that he did not address Jack with 'Master'. He had dared. The look that Jack gave him was disbelief. Hammed was not finished. He had just begun.

"How dare you call yourself a man? A healthy wonderful child as such is a blessing bestowed on a parent by Allah. You call him God. Miss Margaret was alone all these months scared to death that we would still try to kill her unborn child. She hid under unspeakable conditions. She endured hardships that you spoiled brat could not even fathom. I grew up under similar conditions and know what it feels like.

I have not forgotten how your saintly father, Allah bless his soul forever, gave me a place to live and enough food and education that children in my country only dream off. With your request to have your own flesh and blood terminated, you violated the trust and legacy this wonderful kind man left behind. This angel child is now one of the less fortunate that your father always helped. If he knew, he would rise from the grave and box your ears. You have turned into a stupid drunkard who cannot see the forest for the trees. I have been patient with you and overlooked your increasing short temper tantrums. I have been patient with your increasing forgetfulness because you fell fully clothed into your bed drunk as a sailor on shore leave. I will not be patient with you any longer. I will not lie for you any longer. I will not clean up your vomit. If I see you take another drink, I will do what your father cannot do any more. I will beat you senseless. Let me add one more thing. No one in this household will come to your aid. As a matter of fact, no one in this city will lift a finger to help you. I however will help Miss Margaret in any way I can. Do not concern yourself; I will not take a farthing from your account. I have saved enough to money of my own," Hammed hollered that the walls shook.

Frightened the servants had listened at the door. What would the master's answer be? Would he dismiss Hammed? Would he dismiss all of them? All of them held their breath. They all knew, that Jack was not drunk just yet. He had only seconds before Hammed, entered the dining hall. Hammed stood with his arms crossed in front of his chest and sent Jack a dark look. Carefully and slowly, Jack placed the glass on the little table. He began to laugh. He had never seen his faithful Hammed like this. He did believe him however to beat him senseless. Hammed stood a few inches taller and was very muscular.

"So you would actually lay a hand on me. Did you forget that you are my servant?" Jack asked, still laughing.

"I do not see any humor in this situation. Furthermore, I have always been and will always be your friend first and foremost. A friend who cares about his friends self destructive ways. I will not stand by any longer and watch you destroy yourself and other lives around you. You are way on your way of doing exactly that. The spirit drink has turned

179

your liver to poison and your mind into a demon. When you are drunk, you turn into this evil being that I do not even recognize. You must stop this insanity and take care of your responsibility. Which is your child and it's mother. Miss Sibylla is dead and will not come back. Life does go on. I will not let you make any excuses any longer. Hiding your grief and heartache in the bottle will make your problems only worse. How long has it been, since you were able to perform in the bedchamber? I can tell you. It has been nine months. Before that you had problems and you have not been near a Lady after Miss Margaret. You know why? Because I gave you a potion as well that night. It does not only give you the impression that you are dreaming. It also helps to perform in the bedchamber. Ask your big friend, Thomas Crandall. He will tell you. He is as concerned as I am. He noticed every day that you drank very much and asked me often to do something. I hesitated and the result was that the problem got worse. I will not be quiet any longer. Choose life and friends and love or be a lonely alcohol bloated doddering fool in a few years time in an empty mansion that no one will dare get near too. Believe me my friend, I will not be around any longer to see it," Hammed finished nodding his head.

"After all these years you would leave me? I cannot believe my ears Hammed." Jack sat stunned. He thought for a few long minutes before he spoke again. He hated to admit it, Hammed was correct.

"Very well, perhaps you are right. I will not make any promises. I admit, I do enjoy the drink. Like you said, it is not worth loosing all I have worked for all these years. What Margaret and the child concerns, I leave it up to you. However, you must understand that I do not love her. I never will. She is sweet and the mother of my child. I did not wish for it. I was tricked into it, remember? So do not preach responsibility to me as to the child's welfare. I will give you money to get her a small place of her own. I will make sure that she has food and clothes for herself and the child. Nevertheless, I will not have anything to do with her. I will not welcome her back into my house. That is my final word on it. She should have known, that I was not having any other interest in her person as to business. She was to become one of my 'ladies'. I invested plenty of money in her. This sort of disobedience is the reward for my kindness, Hammed."

"I admit, that much of the blame lies on my shoulders, Jack. Miss Margaret is a proud little creature. She was hurt and angry. You were the one to order the child killed in her womb, if indeed there was one. No matter how old or young a female is. The mother instinct will protect any life growing within her. I should have known this. Which brings me to the next subject. Miss Margaret is at her old little apartment in the poorest section of town. I will go and rent her a nice little cottage outside of town. The child will have plenty of fresh air and space. With your permission, I will take her things from her room and bring them to her. The bed she is laying in as we speak is dreadful as is her entire surrounding. The poor little child could get sick in this drafty room." Hammed wrinkled his brow concerned.

"Go then and take what you see fit. I have decided to sell this mansion anyway. That is what I wanted to speak to you about last night as you suddenly had urgent business. My friend Thomas sent word, that there is a potential buyer and I will move back to Spain," Jack said quietly. He seemed suddenly sad. Hammed noticed an asked,

"I have the feeling that something else is amiss besides the insane notion to sell this place. What is it?"

"You remember, that Thomas received a letter from his wife many months ago. He was to return to America at once. The letter he received did not specify the emergency. I found out this morning in the letter he wrote me. His daughter got killed in a riding accident. My poor friend is beside himself with grief. His wife is losing her wits. She is acting strange and needs constant care. He has not been at sea for months now," Jack worried.

"Oh, I am so terribly sorry to hear that. Captain Crandall is such caring man. To have to go through something so sad is heart wrenching indeed. I hope he will be at sea again soon. It will help him take his mind off this tragedy. No parent should have to bury their own child," Hammed said sadly and shook his head in disbelieve. A look on the little clock on the mantle let the big man realize how late it was getting. There were so many things to do. Renting the little cottage. Taking

Margaret and the child there after the furniture had been taken to her new home. Making sure that there was enough firewood to stay warm in the coming months. Convincing Jack to let Elizabeth stay with Margaret and the child. At least for a few months until she had regained her strength. At this moment, Hammed was glad his Master had not dismissed him and the whole staff. He would not push his luck any further this day. He would approach the subject tomorrow. He excused himself and hurried out the door, where he almost ran over the eves dropping servants. Elizabeth cried as she saw Hammed coming out the dining hall. She was certain to loose her position. She had heard every word and felt sick to her stomach. Poor Miss Margaret had been all alone and with child. She would go and visit her as soon as she would find the time.

Hammed wiped Elizabeth's tears away with his dumb and whispered,

"I shall talk to Master Jack in the morning. I will try and convince him to let you stay with Miss Margaret. You will still be paid the same wages as in this house. So dry your tears and smile. Everything will work out." Before the stunned little maid could answer, Hammed had quickly walked outside, where the carriage was waiting. He signaled Alfred to go. It would be dark in a few hours and he had to take care of many things.

Jack was left alone with his thoughts in the dining hall. Without thinking, he reached for the glass of brandy. Realizing what he was holding in his hand however, he suddenly smashed the glass onto the wall by the fireplace. The sound from the braking glass alarmed Elizabeth, who was about to go up to her little room. She turned on her heel and ran back to the dining hall.

"Master Jack, I heard glass break. Are you hurt? Is everything all right?" she asked fearful as she saw the broken glass pieces and the stain on the wall. She started to pick up the pieces with shaking hands and placed them into her apron, which she had ruffed with her left to carry the broken glass. Jack watched the little maid and said nothing. He had seen how fearful the girl was. Hammed had been right all along. Things would have to change. He felt suddenly like an old man. Here he was, wealthy beyond believe. Not a worry in the world, so it seemed. Yet there was this nagging emptiness inside him that he could not explain. He had tried to fill this void with the bottle and almost lost his dearest friend. His servants were frightened of him.

"Elizabeth, please send Mister Potter to me with some tea. I shall be in the library," Jack ordered the maid with a soft voice.

Elizabeth almost dropped the glass again from her apron. Quickly she curtsied and smiled,

"Yes Master Jack, at once." She hurried from the room to find Mister Potter. She found the old servant in the kitchen polishing the silver spoons.

"Mister Potter, the Master wishes some tea. He is waiting in the library," the maid spoke, while she shook the glass from her apron into a small barrel with trash and ashes from the fireplace.

"I cannot believe my ears. Elizabeth, are you certain this is what the Master ordered?" the old man asked grinning.

"I am certain as my mother has gray hair on her head," Elizabeth answered.

Mister Potter took the tray with the dainty cup and a porcelain kettle filled with aromatic hot tea, which his wife handed him and took it to his master.

Meanwhile Hammed was on his way to see the owner of the little cottage. He had done business with him before. He had sold him a shipment of special wood. The man builds instruments and was reasonably wealthy. He found the man and haggled over the price of the rent. After a little while they agreed on a price and Hammed rented the cottage for two years. The cottage had four lovely rooms each with a small fireplace and one big kitchen with a big fireplace for cooking. Behind the house were a little garden with herbs and some vegetables and several fruit trees. The previous inhabitants must have taken great care. The house and the roof were in good repair. Hammed was satisfied. Miss Margaret and the child would live in comfort and warmth. He would have the furniture brought the next day. Miss Margaret would have to stay for one more night in this dreadful room above the laundry kitchen. Tomorrow everything would change for the better. Hammed ordered Alfred to take him to the young mother and child. He had taken a few pieces of wood from the mansion and wanted to make sure, that the little room was at least warm. It was almost dark as he arrived at the little street where Margaret was resting in her room. Quickly he grabbed the wood and climbed up the stairs to the room. He knocked softly and to his surprise, Misses Tippins opened the door. The table had been cleaned and scrubbed. The small fireplace crackled merrily. The old musty pile of clothes behind the trunk was gone and the floor had been swept clean. Margaret and the child were in the big bed sleeping.

"Misses Tippins, this mattress must be still moist from last night. How can she sleep in this?" Hammed asked concerned.

"Not to worry, my fine fellow. We dried it all up with hot stones and then I turned the mattress. We took Margaret to the other bed across the hall for a little while. Young Patrick helped me clean up this place. It will have to do for a while." The older woman let out a sigh and sat on one of the little stools.

"I have some wonderful news for Miss Margaret. She is going to move from this place. My master allowed me to rent a little cottage just outside of town and not far from here. The rooms are lovely and there is a big kitchen and a small garden behind the house. I will have her furniture from the mansion moved to her new home by the morrow. I am certain she will love her new home. And the child will be playing soon in the little garden eating from its fruit trees. I believe there are apples and pears and plums as well as cherries. I noticed carrots and cabbage and other vegetables growing. Among the weeds I saw a few herbs. So you see, Misses Tippins, Miss Margaret has a wonderful little home of her own." Hammed smiled and put a piece of wood into the fireplace.

"I cannot believe it, Hammed. Is your master not curious about his son? He is moving the girl as far away from him as possible and is not even trying to visit her and his child. I mean, it is good that she will have a warm comfortable place to live. However, the child needs a father. I am only glad that poor Margaret can count on you as a true friend. Please watch out for her and the little boy. I must go and give my husband his supper. I shall be back in the morning." Misses Tippins had risen from the little stool and put a hand on Hammed's arm.

"Thank you for all you have done for her. May God bless you."

"I believe I did it also for my own self, Misses Tippins. I was the one who plotted to bring my master and Miss Margaret happiness. A wise man said to me to be on guard, it might bite me in the ass," Hammed chuckled. "I see now that this man was correct. I have to make amends. I have to correct the damage that I created. Miss Margaret was correct to protect her child."

"What is done is done, Hammed. Perhaps some day it all will work out," Misses Tippins said, padding Hammed's arm and left the room.

The tiny baby was stirring. Hammed got up from the little stool and took the small bundle carefully from the bed beside Margaret's arm. Gently he caressed the little cheek with his finger. The little boy turned his head and sought the finger with his tiny mouth. Hammed smiled. The child was obviously hungry. Hammed could not help himself and a tear ran down his dark cheek. Such beautiful child should make any father proud. Why was Jack so stubborn? If only the old man Enrico was still alive. He would be so proud to call this little perfect child his grandson. There must be a way to bring father and son together. 'May Allah show me the way' Hammed thought as he softly rocked the baby in his big arms.

The door opened quietly and the young boy Patrick tiptoed into the room. He saw the big man holding the baby and smiling whispered:

"Misses Tippins told me to stay the night here. I am Patrick. I must care for the fire. I will bring the other small mattress and lay right here on the floor. Misses Tippins will pull my ears, if I let the fire burn out," the boy said and left the room to come back moments later with the small mattress. He placed it on the floor in front of the small fireplace and sat on the mattress.

"Are you the baby's Dah then, Mister?" Patrick asked curiously. Hammed shook his head and grinned ruefully at Patrick;

"No, son, I am not the child's father. My master is the father of this beautiful boy." Patrick did not understand.

"Where is he then? Why is he not with his child and his wife? Why is he sending his servant? Is he ill?" Patrick questioned innocently.

"It is a long and complicated story, Patrick. Miss Margaret and my master are not married. I think you are correct, my master is ill. He will get better soon and then he will see his son." Hammed spoke almost to himself.

"Patrick, when Miss Margaret wakes up, tell her that I will be back in the morning with some good news. I must return to my master, he needs me," Hammed said into the quiet. Patrick was lying on the mattress playing with some wood chips. He looked up and grinned,

"I will tell her, Mister. Not to worry, I will be here until Misses Tippins brings food for Margaret." He put another small log on the fire and lies back down on the mattress. Hammed knew that Margaret would be watched over for the night. He carefully placed the baby next to the sleeping girl and quietly left the room. The carriage stood in front of the shoemakers shop. He walked briskly up the narrow street and entered the shop. Alfred sat with Mister and Misses Tippins by the kitchen table drinking hot tea.

"Let us go back to the mansion, Alfred. We still have many things to do," Hammed said to the coachman. He planned to pack Margaret's furniture on one of the big wagons, which were used to transport wares like fabrics and wood from the ships to the warehouses and later to the many shops in the city. The stable boys would earn some extra coins this evening. Hammed was well pleased. It had been a long day and he was tired.

The furniture was loaded on the wagon and would be taken to the little cottage in the morning. Hammed sat in the big kitchen and drank his tea. He had found out from Mister Potter, that Jack had ordered tea and then went to bed early after finishing entries in the books. Hammed slowly rose from the chair and grinning he sought his own bed. He had requested from Mister Potter to wake him up at dawn.

A soft rapping on his door woke Hammed up. Quickly he took his bath and cleansed his teeth. Smiling he remembered the first bath he had in his life. He could still see Leila standing with the big spoon over him all dripping wet. In his mind he could still hear Jack's laughter. Where had all those carefree days gone? Now they were both grown men and so many things had happened. Hammed wondered, what Allah had in store next. He certainly had a great sense of humor about it. A new life had been created and would not be stopped from coming into this world. It was the great creators way to show his all powerful might. Hammed laughed to himself. He had seen the extend of Allah's humor just last night. As the furniture were moved from Margaret's room, one of the stable boys found twelve little green pills under the cushions of the big couch. Puzzled he had handed Hammed his find. Hammed placed the pills in a little box and vowed to save this little box as a reminder, that the creator of life is not to be interfered with his plans. Life was a wonderful mysterious voyage in which all creation travels and partakes.

Hammed dressed and went to Jack's rooms. He shook the sleeping man gently on his shoulder and said quietly:

"Master Jack, it is time to rise. Morning has broken and we have work to do." Jack opened his eyes and stretched. He felt wonderful. His head was not aching and he remembered everything that went on the night before. He flung the cover aside and jumped out of the big bed. While Hammed helped Jack to slip into his robe, he said:

"I believe I spoke harsh words yesterday. I must beg your pardon. After seeing your beautiful son and Miss Margaret, I was extremely angry."

"Hammed, I forgive you. What I am having a hard time forgiving is myself my friend. How could I have been so blind? I only saw yesterday how frightened my servants had become. The little maid Elizabeth had the look of a haunted deer in her eyes," Jack said, walking with Hammed to the baths. He let Hammed take his robe and climbed into the big tub.

"Speaking of Elizabeth, Master Jack, I believe it would be best to have the maid take care of Miss Margaret and your son for a while. Miss Margaret is still weak from giving birth and will need some care. Permit me to take the maid to the cottage where I will take Miss Margaret later this day. The furniture are all packed and will be moved this morning to her new little home," Hammed spoke, while he had lathered and washed Jack's hair. Slyly he added, "the child resembles you very much indeed. He has dark hair and his eyes are big and shaped like yours."

"Who is helping the laundress, if I let Elizabeth take care of Margaret. I will get cold suppers if Misses Potter is doing more chores in this

187

house." Jack pretended to whine and ignored Hammed's last sentence. The answer was forthcoming in form of a bucket of cool water, which Hammed poured over his Master's head in one swooping motion. Jack shook himself startled and send Hammed a dark look.

"I did not realize the water had cooled down that much." Hammed smiled sweetly and handed Jack a towel. Hammed turned and reached for Jack's robe on the marble bench.

"Before you kill me with your kindness, Hammed, I will give you permission to take Elizabeth to live in Margaret's house. You will have to hire a new girl then. Answer me one question, Hammed. Who is running this household?"

"You are running this household, Master Jack. I am merely your humble servant and most loyal friend." Hammed helped Jack into the robe.

Both men were sitting in the dining hall eating their morning meal. Hammed took a bite from his bread.

"So, you think he resembles me?" Jack asked into the quiet. Hammed almost choked on his bread. Cleverly, hard pressed to hide his mirth he answered with a serious face matter of fact:

"He will be a handsome man some day." Nothing else was said. Hammed hoped, that Jack had taken the bait. He knew, that his part was done. It was up to Jack to do the rest. Hammed would not volunteer any more information. Slowly he sipped his coffee and watched Jack from beneath his eyelashes. Hammed placed the empty cup on the table and looked at the little clock on the mantle. He jumped up from the chair:

"I shall take care of the furniture yet. I will also find a girl this morning to take Elizabeth's position. Will I find you in the library when I return?"

"I will write some letters and then I must go to the warehouses. Some new fabrics will be delivered today. I must be there. I should be back here later this afternoon, Hammed," Jack said, wiping his lips with the napkin. He took his cup and drank his coffee. Hammed bowed and hurried out the door.

Chapter 15

Burning Bridges

Fourteen months had passed and it was the Christmas month. Margaret had been moved from the tiny rooms above the laundry kitchen into the spacious cottage just outside of town. Once again life seemed to change for the worse. Elizabeth had agreed to marry Hammed. Their relationship had indeed developed into a romance since Hammed visited the cottage often. The young couple expected their first child by the end of April. Elizabeth was five months pregnant and it became more difficult to serve Margaret with each passing day. Hammed took Elizabeth back to the mansion and had hired Elizabeth's younger sister Laura to help Margaret around the house and with the child. Laura was a fresh-faced girl of fifteen with ash blond hair and green eyes. She moved into the room at the cottage that was once occupied by her older sister Elizabeth. Margaret had learned to do many things for herself. She knew how to make sweet scented soap. She could cook any dish that Misses Potter had cooked at the mansion. She could sew and mend her own gowns. She could knit and crochet. She made her own perfume and had succeeded in creating a delicious smelling fragrance to be sold to wealthy ladies in and around Manchester. Each shipment that came from the orient, brought oils and essences to Jack's big warehouses. Hammed sold some of the oils and essences with Jack's permission to Margaret which she used in her perfumes and soaps. Many times Hammed came with big baskets full of fruits and vegetables for Margaret and her son.

Justus had learned to walk and was speaking a few words already.

Many times Margaret had received letters from her aunt Delia. In every letter aunt Delia complained about not having enough money to repair the house and the barn. With each letter she received, Margaret became increasingly more irritated with the old woman who seemed to think that Margaret owed her something. A few days before Christmas Margaret sent her aunt a letter, explaining that she had born a child and her husband had died. She was in need of money herself and could not spare anything. Margaret never received another begging letter from her aunt.

Hammed and Elizabeth visited Margaret and Justus for the celebration of the Christ child's birth. It was a wonderful day for Margaret and little Justus. Hammed had succeeded in asking his Master for money to purchase

some gifts for Jack's little son Justus. Jack had given Hammed a large amount of money. It was far more than Hammed could have ever expected. He purchased wool and fabrics, dishes and a new bigger bed for little Justus.

Heavy laden with gifts, Hammed and Elizabeth arrived at the little cottage. He handed Margaret a pouch with the rest of the money that Jack had given him. It would take care of her and little Justus for many months to come.

What Margaret could not understand was Jack's refusal to visit and see his own son. The fact that Jack knew about his son and still did nothing but send money and gifts with Hammed, made Margaret angry and bitter. She vowed, that some day Jack would beg her to be a part of her and Justus's life. Hammed promised to help in any way he could.

Fate would have it, that Jack had different ideas. Thomas Crandall would be arriving in the spring to bring the family with him, which wanted to buy the mansion. Jack had immediately made travel arrangements to go to Spain and buy a big house near Madrid. Hammed had no choice as to travel with his master. Since Elizabeth was in a delicate condition, she was left behind at the mansion. Hammed promised to be back for the birth of their first child. Elizabeth visited Margaret and told her the news. Margaret was shocked. She could not understand, that Jack would move so far away from his son without having seen him once. Now that Elizabeth was to be a mother herself, she could understand Margaret's feelings of anger and frustration. She agreed to Margaret's suggestion to stay for a few months with her and her younger sister at the cottage. If the child decided to arrive early, Margaret and Laura would be there to help. Hammed and Jack returned from Spain on the first day of April and Elizabeth moved once again into the mansion. It was April the eighth, as Elizabeth went into labor. She gave birth to a healthy little girl in the early morning hours of Saturday April the ninth, which she named Mabel. Hammed sent a message to Margaret, that his wife and daughter Mabel were both healthy and happy. He was ecstatic and proud. What made him sad was the fact that Margaret and Justus would have to be left behind as soon as Elizabeth would be strong enough to travel. Only a few days later on Tuesday April the twelfth, Thomas Crandall arrived at the mansion with the new owners Ira and Ruth Goldberg. The price for the mansion was agreed upon and Jack started sending his personal possessions and some of the furniture ahead to his new house in Spain. Everything was on its way and Elizabeth insisted that she was well enough to travel by the end of the month. After a tearful farewell with Margaret and Laura, Hammed and Elizabeth departed on April the twenty fifth with Jack for their new home in Spain.

Mister and Misses Potter would stay at the mansion and would continue to serve the new owners Ira and Ruth Goldberg. It was merely two days later, as disaster struck. Margaret woke up to the sound of Justus's crying. By some misfortunate coincidence a log had rolled out of the fireplace in the huge kitchen and the whole house filled quickly with smoke. Margaret screamed for Laura to wake up and handed her the crying child. Laura grabbed a blanket from the bed and wrapped Justus in it, while she ran with the child in her arm out of the house. Margaret ran back to her room an began to throw her clothes, shoes and personal things as well as her two empty trunks out of the window in the back of the house. The smoke was getting thicker and her eyes burned. She could not stay in the room any longer and flames and thick smoke blocked the way through the kitchen. She had no choice as to climb out of the window herself. Quickly she gathered all the things she had thrown out and carried them away from the burning house.

She stuffed the belongings she had saved into the empty trunks, as some of the neighbors came running with buckets and filling them at the well tried to extinguish the fire. It was no use. Besides the stone walls there was nothing left but ashes. Once again, Margaret was left without a home. She had saved however the pouch with the money and sent for a carriage. One of her neighbors had been kind enough to let her, Laura and Justus stay the night at their home. She thanked the people and had her trunks loaded onto the carriage. She had to find a way to earn money again. All her oils and essences had perished in the fire. Hammed who always sold her these things at a low price, was on his way to Spain. There was no one left to help her. She had to rely on herself. She ordered the coachman to take her to the mansion. Perhaps the new owners would know exactly, where she could find Jack. All she knew was, that he had moved to a big house near Madrid. He had to help her and his son. Mister Potter answered the door at the mansion and pleasantly surprised he greeted Margaret Laura and little Justus.

"Miss Margaret, what a wonderful surprise. My wife is in the kitchen and is baking some honey cakes. Go and have a nice visit with her. I must go to town and order some more food. The new people will give a ball in a few days time."

"Mister Potter, would it be possible to talk to the new owners. I must find Jack. My house burned down last night and I have no place to go with my son. Oh pardon me, this is Laura and she will need a new position also. I am not able to pay her wages any longer," Margaret said sadly while pointing at Laura. She held Justus by his little hand.

"I am sure we can find something for your friend, Miss Margaret. We will talk more when I come back. I must be on my way now. There are so many things still to do. Oh, I almost forgot. Captain Crandall is still here. He will love to see you again, Miss Margaret," the older man said and while he took his cape from his arm and flung it around his shoulders.

"Very well then, Mister Potter, I shall wait in the kitchen and have a visit with Misses Potter. Come, Laura, this way." Margaret pointed into the direction of the door to the big kitchen. Laura followed Margaret with Justus on her hand into the kitchen. Misses Potter turned at the sound of the door opening and said joyful:

"Oh, Miss Margaret, how nice to see you again. I was wondering how you were and your little son." She wiped her hands on her big apron and took both of Margaret's hands in her own.

"Let me look at you. You have changed, child. Motherhood becomes you. Ah, is this the little man?" She looked around Margaret and noticed the tiny boy hiding behind Laura's big skirt.

"Yes, Misses Potter, this is my son Justus. He will be two years old this October. Oh, it is so wonderful to see you again. The lessons you gave me were indeed helpful. I can cook on my own and I was able to teach Laura a few of your recipes. Tell me, Misses Potter, are the new owners kind people?" Margaret asked. Misses Potter had reached into a bowl and held a freshly baked honey cake. She bent down and tried to coax little Justus from behind Laura's skirt. The child saw the delicious treat and quickly reached for it. Misses Potter smiled and ruffled his little head lovingly.

"The new people are indeed kind and generous, Miss Margaret. In a few days time we will have a great ball here at the mansion. I asked the new Misses for some more help in the kitchen. There is much work to be done. She told me, that she would trust me and my husband to hire some more help. She is a lovely lady."

"Oh, Misses Potter, this is wonderful. Laura here is currently without a position. I have some sad news. My wonderful little house burned to the ground last night and Laura will not be staying with me any longer. I have to go to Spain and find Jack. He must take responsibility for his son. I saved some money and a few of my things last night. However, it is not enough to pay for Laura traveling with me. Please Misses Potter, Laura is a hard worker and will be a great help to you. You do not have to look any further."

"I am so deeply sorry to hear about your misfortune, Miss Margaret. Of course I will take Laura into my kitchen. It is only odd, that sometimes some others bad luck is a blessing in disguise after all. I am sure that the new Misses will let you stay in one of the rooms on the second floor until you can make your travel arrangements. Her daughter will be arriving here in a few months. She is expecting her first child any day now and will be moving in with her husband and the new baby as soon as she can travel. I shall speak to Misses Goldberg as soon as she comes back. She is in town to have her gown fitted for the ball," Misses Potter said while she had made some tea and was pouring the aromatic liquid into three cups. Margaret, Laura and Misses Potter drank their tea, while sitting around the big kitchen table. They chatted for a while, until Mister Potter came back from town.

Not long there after, the wife of the new owner of the mansion returned also. Misses Potter started cooking and Laura was helping her. Upon hearing the big front door, the older woman quickly dried her hands and left the kitchen to talk to her new Mistress. It did not take long and Misses Potter returned to the kitchen with a big smile.

"Miss Margaret, Misses Goldberg wishes to see you in the dining hall. I believe she can help you. Leave the child here, Laura can watch him. I can do the rest of the cooking myself," the older woman suggested.

"Wonderful, Misses Potter. Thank you for helping me. Is Mister Crandall with her?" Margaret asked while she quickly smoothened her skirt and checked her hair for loose strands.

"Mister Crandall is resting in the guest room. He will be down for the midday meal in a little while," Misses Potter answered.

Margaret walked through the big entrance hall and knocked on the door to the dining hall. A female voice came from within:

"Come in please." Margaret entered the dining hall and saw a lovely woman sit in one of the big chairs by the fireplace. Her hair was jet black and pulled back to the nape of her neck into a thick braid. Warm dark brown eyes looked at Margaret motherly and somewhat curious. The woman remained seated as Margaret walked closer and curtsied:

"It is a pleasure meeting you, Misses Goldberg. My name is Margaret Ziegler. I thank you for seeing me," Margaret said softly.

"Please, Miss Margaret, won't you sit down. The pleasure is all mine." The woman pointed at the other chair with an elegant gesture. Margaret sat shyly at the other chair and waited respectfully for the Lady to open the conversation. Misses Goldberg smiled and said,

"I hear from Misses Potter, that you suffered a great misfortune. I am sorry that this happened to you, especially since you have a little child. I am going to be a grandmother any day now and I can't wait until my daughter gets here with the baby. We do have enough room and you may stay here with your son until you can make your travel arrangements." Misses Goldberg smiled friendly. She poured Margaret a brown liquid into a cup and handed it to her.

"Would you like some chocolate, Miss Margaret?" Margaret took the little cup and sniffed the thick dark drink. It smelled wonderfully delicious. She took a tiny sip and said smiling:

"Thank you, Misses Goldberg, I never tasted anything as delicious. How is it made?"

"It is made from the fruits of the cacao tree which are ground into a fine powder. I am surprised that you never heard of it. It was introduced into Europe by the Spaniards who learned its use from the Aztecs at the time of the invasion by the Spanish adventurer Hernan Cortes in 1519. England knows its use for over one hundred years already. The place where I come from manufactured chocolate only a few years ago in Massachusetts in 1765. It can also be made into various kinds of confectionery. I love the taste of it." Ruth Goldberg twinkled at Margaret like a conspirator.

"I must seem ignorant indeed, Misses Goldberg. I also never heard of a place you call Massachusetts or the Aztecs. I merely know, that the world is a big round place and there are many lands I would like to visit. Unfortunately I do not have the financial means to travel far. I must use my meager savings to go to Spain and find the father of my son. Since the fire destroyed almost everything I had, I need his help desperately." Margaret spoke quietly while fussing with her skirt.

"Misses Potter told me that you are a hard worker. From what I understand, you were able to support yourself and your son ever since his birth. If it is not too personal of a question, how did you do it?" Ruth asked.

"I used to make perfume and soaps and sold my products to wealthy women. All my oils and essences were destroyed last night. Hammed used to sell me these items at a low price. Now that he is gone, I cannot afford to buy them from another merchant. They all would charge me much more and I would not be able to make a small profit," Margaret answered truthfully.

"Ah I see, so you would beg the father of your son for help? What if he will not help you? Then you would be stuck in a strange land with your son and could not even understand the language, child. I believe you could find a better way. Think on it, a woman is not helpless and you have proven that. Why would you want to be dependent on a man once more? In my homeland many women work to support them self. You can do the same. All you need is a little help. Like I said before, you may stay here in my house and think about it some more. We will find a solution," Ruth said resolutely.

"I thank you again for your kindness, Misses Goldberg. Perhaps you are correct. I worked before and I can do it again. I am also afraid you might be right about the father of my son. He never visited once and merely sent his servant Hammed with gifts and money to my house. I still cannot understand how a father can deny his own flesh and blood. When my son gets older, I have to tell him that his father did not want him. Justus is his only child and should be his heir some day." Margaret sounded bitter. She sipped her chocolate with her eyes lowered. She did not want the kind woman to see her tears of anger and frustration welling up in her eyes.

"The trunks in the hall are yours I gather? I will have them taken up to your room. Let us have some lunch first. It is always better to think on a full stomach." Ruth changed the subject quickly. She had noticed the tears. She rang the little bell on the small table next to her chair and bade Mister Potter to have the meal served.

Moments later, the door opened again and Thomas Crandall entered the dining hall. He walked over to Ruth and kissed her hand.

"Hello, Ruth, did you have a successful visit with the seamstress?"

"Ah yes, Thomas, the gown is lovely and will be delivered tomorrow. Meat my guest, Miss Margaret Ziegler," Ruth introduced.

Since Margaret sat with her back toward the door, he had not seen her features at first. He turned to see Ruth's guest. Merely for an instant his heart contracted painfully and he hoped his thoughts would not be reflecting in his features. Politely he greeted Margaret,

"Miss Margaret, what a pleasant surprise. I did not expect to see you here. Do you know my friends the Goldberg's then?" Kissing her small hand, he kept her hand in his big warm one for a few moments longer than he should have. Softly, Margaret pulled her hand back, blushing.

"Captain, I know Misses Goldberg merely from today. I was visiting Mister and Misses Potter. Misses Goldberg was so kind to receive me today. I suffered a great misfortune and I assumed that either Mister or Misses Potter could tell me exactly, where I could find Jack. Perhaps you do not know this, I bore Jack's son on October the fourteenth in the year of our lord seventeen hundred seventy two., Margaret stated proudly.

"I do not understand, Miss Margaret. How is it that you are still here then and not with the father of your child? Does Jack know that he has a son?" the big captain asked concerned.

"Yes, Captain, he knows and it is a long story." Margaret answered.

"Let me do the mathematics here for a second. Would it have anything to do with the night of your birthday?" Captain Crandall asked.

"You assume correctly, Captain, it was the night of my fifteenth birthday as I was drugged and became enceinte," Margaret answered with a bitter undertone in her voice.

"So, I was right all along. It bit Hammed in the ass," he stated, chuckling softly.

"I beg your pardon, Captain?" Margaret questioned.

"I was witness to this outrage, Miss Margaret. I saw Hammed put something into Jack's drink and questioned his motive for his doings. I had no idea what was going on. Only later in the kitchen did Hammed explain to me, what the purpose of the pill and the drops were, which Hammed had given the both of you. I warned him, that actions like this could backfire. No one likes interference with his or her life. I assume you are angry with my friend Jack. It seems obvious that he does not care about the child. Oh what a rat. I should kick his behind. Does he not know what a blessing a child is?" Captain Crandall thundered.

"Obviously he does not realize anything, Captain. As for the kicking, Hammed did get very angry with Jack the day of my son's birth. He told me himself. Jack does not drink any more spirited beverages." Margaret giggled despite herself.

"Let us have our meal first. Shall we sit by the table?" Ruth interrupted. The door to the library opened and a middle-aged man of medium built with thinning hair and a full beard walked into the dining hall. He walked toward Ruth's chair and kissed her on the forehead:

"Hello my dear, who is our lovely guest?" he asked smiling.

"Ira, my love, this is Miss Margaret Ziegler. She will be our guest for a while. Miss Margaret and her tiny son have no place to go. Her home burned to ashes last night," Ruth explained to her husband.

"Oh, how terrible, of course you may stay in our home as long as you wish, Miss Ziegler. I am Ira Goldberg," he nodded to Margaret who curtsied.

"I am eternally grateful, Sir. My son and I thank you from the bottom of our hearts. You and your lovely wife are kind indeed. May God bless you and your family," Margaret said sincerely.

"Miss Margaret, I had no idea that your home burned down. How did this happen?" the big Captain asked concerned.

"I do not know exactly, Captain. I woke up because my son was crying. The house was full of smoke and we barely escaped with our lives. I was able to save some of my personal possessions however by throwing them out of the window. A nearby neighbor and his wife let us stay the rest of the night and we were able to bathe and dress our self," Margaret explained.

"I wish I could do something to help you and your son, Miss Margaret. This is tragic to say the least," Captain Crandall said sadly. He truly wished he could do something for her. However, she must never know, how he really felt. After all, he had a wife that was his responsibly. Suddenly he dropped his piece of bread that was in his hand.

"I do have a fabulous idea. It may be the solution to your problem,

Miss Margaret as well as mine. In a few days time I will return to America. My wife is in need of constant care. You and your son can come with me and you take care of my wife. I will pay you generous wages and you can stay in the guesthouse as soon as it is refurbished," he said exited.

"I do not know anything about the medical profession, Captain. Is you wife bedridden?" Margaret asked.

"Oh no, it is nothing like that, Miss Margaret. Her mental state is fragile and she needs constant looking after. She tried to commit suicide a few times. I am merely afraid to leave her alone at home while I am at sea."

"Oh I see, so I would not have to administer any medicine?" Margaret asked.

"No you would not have to do anything like that. The doctor will take care of that. He visits my house once a week. All she needs is a companion who will be there at all times. Please, Miss Margaret, say yes. You would help me very much. I do not like strange people in my house. The lady who is with my wife presently is old and somewhat forgetful,." he chuckled.

"It seems like a wonderful idea, Captain. However, I do not have enough money to give you for the fare. I believe it would cost much to travel that far. Furthermore, I have never been near the sea, let alone on a ship, Captain. The thought frightens me to be on a ship for a long time," Margaret admitted. She was not certain about this part of adventure.

"The sea can be indeed a bit stormy this time of year, Miss Margaret. However, I have traveled by sea just about all my life and I am still here. As for the fare, you would not have to pay anything. You would be doing me a great favor by looking after my wife," he pointed out.

"Oh, Miss Margaret, you see, we found a solution. You will be able to make your own money and would not have to beg the reluctant father of your child for anything," Ruth remarked, clapping her hands exited.

"I believe you are correct, Misses Goldberg. Since I do not know for certain that Jack would help me, I have to rely on myself. It is settled then. I shall go with my son to America," Margaret agreed, wiping her lips with the spotless white linen napkin.

"Wonderful, Miss Margaret. I could not agree more. You must stand on your own two feet and take care of your son. Speaking of which, I have heard much about your little son, Miss Margaret. Where is he?" the big Captain asked.

"He is with Laura and Misses Potter in the kitchen. I suspect he is stuffing his little mouth with the delicious honey cakes Misses Potter baked earlier," Margaret laughed. Ruth rang the little bell and moments later Mister Potter entered the room.

"You rang, Misses Goldberg?" The older man bowed.

"Please, Mister Potter, would you have Laura bring Miss Margaret's son to us. We are also finished eating. You may clear the table," Ruth said.

"As you wish, Misses Goldberg." Mister Potter bowed again and left the dining hall to fetch Laura and little Justus.

It did not take long and the door opened. Laura entered with the little boy on her hand. Upon seeing his mother, he wiggled free from Laura's hand and ran toward her with tiny still somewhat unsteady steps.

"Mama, mama, kitty." He pointed to the door.

"Ah, I see your son met our cat," Ruth laughed and filled a small glass with warm milk. She handed Margaret the glass. Margaret pulled Justus on her lap and held the glass for the little boy to drink some of the milk.

"What a beautiful child, Miss Margaret." Thomas smiled at the little boy. Justus shyly buried his little face in his mother's chest. Slowly he turned his little head again and looking at the big captain, he smiled back. Captain Crandall took the tiny little hand in his big one.

"Hello, Justus, your mama and you are coming with me on a big ship. Would you like to see the big ship?"

"Sip," Justus peeped at the big man and nodded vehemently, everyone laughed.

"If you will excuse me, I must go back to work in my study. Thomas, would you please come with me, I have a few things to add to the list of merchandise." Ira rose from his chair and walked to the library with

Thomas in his wake. Ira Goldberg was as Jack had been, a merchant. He dealt mainly in rare woods and precious metals.

"Miss Margaret, I have a few things to go over with Misses Potter. She might have mentioned to you, that we are giving a ball in a few days time. So feel free to use any of our carriages if you decide to go to town. Drake is our coachman and will bring your trunks up to your room. Most of the rooms on the second floor are still furnished yet. However, the first door on your left has a big bed and some lovely furniture still in it, from the ladies who occupied this room once. I believe her name was Gretchen and before her it belonged to Miss Fiona. Yes I think these were the names Hammed mentioned," Ruth smiled at Margaret. Margaret curtsied and thanked Ruth:

"Thank you, Misses Goldberg. I believe my son is ready for a nap. I shall take him to my room and rest a while myself. I did not get much sleep last night."

"Good, Miss Margaret, go and sleep a while. I will have Laura wake you for dinner," Ruth answered and left the dining hall.

Margaret took Justus and carried him upstairs to Gretchen's room, which would be her own for the next few days. It seemed strange to her that she was once again back in this great mansion. It seemed only yesterday, that she had lived in the other room at the end of the hallway. She decided to see her old rooms one more time as soon as little Justus was asleep. It did not take long and the little boy's eyes closed. Quietly, Margaret walked the long hallway and opened the door to her old rooms. They were empty save the beautiful carpets. Slowly she walked toward the big window and looked out over the big balcony into the park behind the house. She remembered the long walks she had taken while she still lived here. She felt tired and went back to her sleeping son. She lie down next to Justus and closed her eyes. Her mind began to wander and she tried to picture America. What would this place be like? Would people be dressed the same as here in England? Would everybody speak with such funny accent as Thomas Crandall and the Goldberg's? Margaret smiled and soon was fast asleep as her tiny son was.

Chapter 16

Hidden Jewels

Margaret stretched leisurely on the bed, where her son Justus was still sleeping. Carefully, not to wake the child, she got up from the bed and only now did she notice, that all the furniture were still in the room as Gretchen had left it. Hammed had told her many months ago, that Gretchen had not returned to the mansion. Realizing, that Gretchen had only taken two of her trunks with her as they visited aunt Delia, she opened the door to the closet. Perhaps she could find one or two gowns that would fit her if she took the hem up. Since Margaret was able to save only some of her things, she could certainly use a few more things. To her utter amazement, she found that just about all of Gretchen's things were still there. Quickly she selected five of the prettiest gowns, under garments and slippers and stuffed them into her trunks. If the gowns were still there, perhaps she would find some hairpins and powder in the little vanity, which was similar to the one she had owned. She opened the drawers and with a little cry of delight, Margaret reached for the brushes and little combs she found. Suddenly she stopped. One of the little combs seemed to be stuck in the back of the drawer, which was unusually thick on the bottom. She pulled and gasped. The bottom of the drawer came loose and Margaret stared in shock. Lying in the drawer was a necklace almost identical to the one she owned. Merely the stones were red.

She found rings and bracelets, ear bobs, smaller necklaces and a pouch. Quickly she pulled on the drawstring and poured the contents in her hand. Margaret gasped once more. Among small precious stones she found a small miniature of Fiona. It must be a fortune what she held in her hand. Margaret's heart leapt for joy. She would be able to live on this for a long time to come. She wondered however, why Fiona had not taken her jewels with her. This was mysterious.

Perhaps she had forgotten all about the secret little compartment, as she had to leave the mansion so many months ago. Still, Margaret could not understand, that a Lady would forget her most priced possessions. She had to find out. Without hesitation, Margaret stuffed the stones back into the pouch, grabbed all the jewelry and placed everything on a linen square. She bound the four corners of the square together and hid it under her clothes in one of her trunks. She would never mention this find to anyone. The little miniature of Fiona was stuffed in the pocket of her skirt.

Little Justus woke up and Margaret brushed his thick dark hair after changing his nappies. Satisfied she took her son by his little hand.

"Come my little darling, mama is taking you for a walk in the park. We still have time until dinner," Margaret said smiling. She wandered with her little son to the back of the mansion along the many small paths. Suddenly a tiny rabbit hobbled across the path and startled Margaret. Justus pointed to the animal and peeped,

"Mama, kitty."

"No, Justus, this is not a kitty, this is a rabbit," she explained to her son. He wiggled free from his mother's hand and followed the little animals path. Justus ran as fast as his little legs could pump. The rabbit went out of sight. Margaret had followed her son and took his hand again, as she suddenly saw something in the grass next to a big beautiful old oak tree. She bent down to pick up the object. It was a lady's slipper. It looked strangely familiar to her. However, the weather seemed to have done its dirty deed and the color was not recognizable. It almost looked like one of Fiona's slippers. Margaret shook her head and let the slipper fall back to the ground where she had found it. For some strange reason, a shiver went up and down her spine. The sun began to set and Margaret walked slowly back to the mansion. It must be almost dinnertime and Margaret took Justus to the baths. She washed his little hands. Justus had picked up stones and twigs from the ground and his hands were dirty. She brushed his little blue velvet suit and went back through the big hall to the dining hall. Mister Potter was busy setting the table.

"Oh, Mister Potter, I have some wonderful news. I am going with Captain Crandall to America. His wife needs care and I shall work in Captain Crandall's house. He promised to pay me good wages. Is it not strange, how sometimes things have a way of working out after all," Margaret stated.

"I am happy to hear that, Miss Margaret. My wife will be delighted also. We were worried that you would go to Spain with your little child and have no one to take care of you. Thank the Lord, you and little Justus will be safe," the older man said relieved.

"Mister Potter, I found this in the room I am staying in. Why did Miss Fiona leave this beautiful little miniature here?" Margaret handed Mister Potter the miniature. His face changed suddenly. Sadly he looked at the lovely face on the miniature. Quickly he handed the item back to Margaret and continued setting the table.

"I am not supposed to tell you anything, Miss Margaret. It is a tragic thing that happened to poor Miss Fiona," Mister Potter whispered.

Suddenly Margaret had a sinking feeling in her stomach. However she wanted to know the truth. She had to find out what was going on.

"Who told you not to tell me what, Mister Potter? What happened to Fiona? Please I have to know," she insisted, her voice shaking.

"I had to promise Hammed never to tell you, Miss Margaret. He is gone now and I suppose he is not coming back here. In any case, he must never find out, that I told you what happened the day after your birthday. You do remember, that Master Jack got terribly angry at Hammed and the other ladies. He was especially angry with Miss Fiona. After saying her farewell to you that evening, we all assumed that she had called a public carriage to take her to London, where her father still lives. She had dismissed her little maid and given her a generous amount of money. The next morning I went to Miss Fiona's room to see if the walls and carpets would have to be washed for the new girl that was to be expected in a few weeks. To my surprise I found all of Miss Fiona's trunks and personal things still there. I spoke to Hammed about it at once and he became very concerned. He had Alfred, myself and the stable boys search the ground. Hammed's suspicion was confirmed. One of the boys found Miss Fiona hanging from a tree."

"Oh no, this is terrible. I cannot believe that Fiona would do such thing," Margaret cried, the color draining from her face. She let herself slowly down in one of the chairs by the fireplace. Now she could explain to herself why she had found all of Fiona's jewels. She felt sick. The door opened and Ruth entered the room with Thomas. Both looked at Margaret and Ruth asked concerned,

"Miss Margaret, are you feeling well? You are pale. Perhaps you should lie down. I will have Mister Potter bring you some food up to your room."

"I am sorry, Misses Goldberg, I feel indeed not too well. The excitement from last night has weakened my nerves. I shall follow your advice and rest. A good nights sleep will do me good and I will feel better tomorrow." She got up from the big chair and curtsied to Ruth and Thomas. As she reached for her son's hand, Ruth suggested,

"Please leave the child with us, Miss Margaret. I will have Laura take care of Justus and she will stay with him in the room next to yours. That way you will get your rest and will not be disturbed."

"Once again I thank you for your kindness, Misses Goldberg. I shall leave my son in your and Laura's care," Margaret gladly agreed. Bending down, she gave Justus a kiss on his little forehead and gently pushed him toward Ruth. Misses Goldberg took his little hand and walked with him to the big dining table. Margaret watched as Ruth placed Justus on her lap and fed him a slice of orange. She knew, that her son was in good hands and went slowly to her room. With a heavy sigh Margaret sat on one of the chairs and tears steamed down her face. Poor Fiona must have been heartbroken. It was typical of Hammed not to say anything. He wanted to protect her in his own way. She would not forgive Jack however. He should have been kinder and more understanding. Margaret got angrier at each passing minute. It seemed that this rich brat refused to take any of the responsibility for any of his actions. Some day she would show him. She would hurt him the way he had hurt her and Fiona. As soon as she had enough money, she would find him and make him sorry for what he had done to her and his son. Margaret wiped the tears from her face with an angry gesture. She had to find a way to take her mind of Jack. Looking on the small desk in the corner, Margaret saw paper. She found a quill and a small bottle with ink and wrote a letter to Misses Tippins.

Dearest Misses Tippins.

I am writing you to let you know that my son and I are well and healthy. Jack has moved to his homeland Spain and I am taking my son to America. I have a position offered to me in Captain Crandall's house. His wife needs care. I will be able to save my money which will be generous wages paid by the Captain for looking after his wife. I must tell you that I am somewhat frightened about the long voyage on his big ship. Nevertheless, I cannot pass up a wonderful opportunity as such. Some day I shall be wealthy and come back to visit. Give my best regards and wishes to your dear husband and Patrick. I shall be eternally grateful for all your kindnesses you have done my child and me. I wish you well and good health. You shall always be in my thoughts.

Thankfully yours, Miss Margaret Ziegler.

She dribbled the hot wax on the folded letter and pressed the small seal into the wax. She decided to send the letter in the morning when the new coachman would go to town. She could not bring herself to say farewell to

Mister and Misses Tippins in person. It would break her heart to look into the old woman's kind face, knowing that it might be the last time. She wrote another letter to Gretchen. Hoping that it would find her well and happy. Once again Margaret explained in her second letter, what happened in the past eighteen months and what she was about to undertake. Margaret promised Gretchen, that she would some day visit as soon as she was wealthy in her own right. She also promised to write and stay in contact from the new land she would live in. Satisfied, Margaret signed and sealed the letter and placed it on top of the first. She felt hungry and sat by the little table, where Mister Potter had placed a tray with food earlier. Since Margaret was writing at the time, he did not want to disturb her and quietly had left the room. Somehow he was not certain that he had done the right thing by telling Margaret the truth. He would not mention this to his wife. She would most certainly get angry with him. On more than one occasion she had called him an 'old gossiping fool'. She was not a pretty sight when she got angry and was quick to throw a big spoon after him now and then.

It was a few days later in the first week of May and the carriage was packed and waiting to take Thomas, Margaret and Justus to Liverpool where they would board the Captain's ship. Thankfully and sadly, Margaret said her farewells to the Goldberg family and Mister and Misses Potter.

"We have to be on our way now, Miss Margaret. The tide will not wait for us," Thomas grumbled. He hated tearful farewells and after seeing Misses Potter hugging and kissing the little boy for the ninth time and wiping her tearstained face on her big apron, he had to bring an end to it. Taking Margaret's arm, he helped her into the carriage. Gently he took little Justus from Misses Potter's arm and placed the child next to his mother in the carriage. Justus did not know, what all this weeping was about. He was excited. He would take a ride in the carriage. He was fascinated with the big horses and stood up on the seat. There were so many things to see outside. It did not take long and Justus got tired. Margaret placed her son's head on her lap and soon he was asleep. Slowly the carriage made its way along the roads toward the harbor of Liverpool.

Liverpool was a loud and exciting place. Margaret had not expected anything like this. The noise and the different smells were almost overpowering. Awestruck she climbed out of the carriage with Justus in her arm. She stood for a moment and took a deep breath. Justus wiggled and wanted to get down from his mother's arm. Slowly she let him down to stand on his little feet. Quickly she grabbed his little hand as he started to move. She was frightened and with her other hand she held on to the Captains arm. He padded her hand and said proudly pointing at a huge vassal fastened with thick ropes on the pier:

"There is my ship, Miss Margaret. This is where you will spend the next few weeks on. How do you like it?"

"Oh it is magnificent," Margaret cried. The beautiful three-mast Caravel took her breath away. Thomas picked up little Justus and carried him over the gangplank onto the ship. Margaret had not let go of his arm and followed him with tiny steps along the gangplank. She was frightened to death of falling into the water. She breathed a sigh of relieve as she felt the planks of the big ship under her feet. Thomas was hard pressed not to show his mirth. Carrying Justus still on his arm, he motioned to the door.

"Let me show you to your cabin, Miss Margaret. I will have my cabin boy bring your trunks. Please make certain that Justus is staying with you. A ship is a dangerous place for a little boy," Thomas explained. He had led Margaret along a narrow hall to a door which he opened for her.

"This is your cabin, Miss Margaret. Make yourself at home. If you need anything, my quarters are next to yours. This cabin is spacious and comfortable. Ira and Ruth stayed in this cabin on their way over. Get some rest, I must get back on deck to take care of things there." Thomas placed Justus in Margaret's arm and hurried back on deck.

Margaret stepped into the cabin and looked around. She was surprised how spacious and richly furnished this cabin was. The big bed and all the other furniture were fastened to the floor and walls. Merely the chairs could be moved. The heavy furniture would stay in place even in a storm. She found it all fascinating and slowly put Justus down onto the floor. She hoped that there would be no storm along her voyage. A soft knock on the cabin door startled her out of her thoughts. A young boy about fifteen years of age stood outside in the narrow hallway as she opened the door.

"Hello, Miss, the Captain told me to bring your trunks. I'm Bart. Actually, my real name is Bartholomew, but everyone calls me Bart," he grinned. He pulled one of Margaret's trunks into the cabin and promised to be back shortly with the other one.

"Thank you, Bart, I am Miss Margaret and this is my son Justus." She pointed with a nod toward the little boy. A few minutes later, the boy came back and pulled the second trunk into the cabin. Margaret thanked him with a smile and glad to be alone, she realized that she was tired. She looked toward the bed where her son had climbed on too. Justus had fallen asleep. Smiling she covered him with a small blanket and undressed to lay on the bed herself. Closing her eyes, she could hear the commands shouted up on deck. This exciting day had taken its toll. Soon she was asleep. She was not aware of the ship softly rolling out to the sea.

It was a few hours later, as she woke. She realized that Justus was not next to her in bed. Quickly she sat up and saw her son kneeling in the window seat. Apparently he had climbed onto one of small footstools to reach the window seat. Wide eyed he stared out of the thick glass window.

"Justus, what are you doing?" Margaret asked.

"Bath, bath." He pointed out of the window excited. Margaret walked over to the window to see for herself. Laughing she agreed with her son:

"Yes, Justus, this is a big bath indeed. Come, let us change clothes. Perhaps we are able to go up on deck and see the big sea."

After changing her son's nappies and clothes, Margaret brushed and braided her hair and took one of her warmer gowns from one of her trunks. The air was getting cooler. She was fastening the last of her little buttons as a knock sounded from the door.

"Miss Margaret, are you awake? Cook is about to serve dinner in my cabin. Would you please join me?" Thomas called.

"We shall be with you shortly, Captain. Please be patient but a moment," Margaret called back.

"Very well, I shall await you and your son in my cabin," he said.

Margaret could hear his heavy footsteps receding from the door.

209

"Come, Justus, let me brush your hair. You must be hungry also."
Margaret had brushed her little son's thick dark hair with a few gentle
strokes. She lifted him from the chair and he made back for the window
seat. She grabbed his little arm and scolded,

"No Justus, you may not go back to the seat to look at the water.
Captain Crandall is waiting for us."

He protested loudly.

"No, Justus look water."

Irritated, Margaret gave her son a slight pad on the little bottom.

"You will be a good little boy this instant, Justus. Mama is getting
angry with you." Her voice rose slightly and momentarily Justus
stopped fussing. He was not used to seeing his mama angry all that
often. Margaret checked her appearance once more with a quick glance
in the mirror and walked to the Captains cabin. She knocked and
Captain Crandall bade her to enter. His eyes widened slightly in
appreciation:

"You look beautiful this evening, Miss Margaret. Please have a seat
over here. Justus will sit next to you. I had some pillows brought in, so
the little man can reach the table." Thomas smiled and ruffled the
child's hair.

"Thank you, Captain, it was thoughtful of you," Margaret said,
while seating Justus on the chair with the pillows. Seating herself she
asked, "Captain Crandall, would it be possible for us to go on deck
later? I should like to show my son the big sea. He seems to be quite
taken with this big 'bath' as he calls it," Margaret chuckled.

"Of course you may go on deck. However, please make certain that
Justus does not leave your hand. Hold him tight. Oh, another thing.
Please do not pay any attention to my men. They are rough natured and
cuss sometimes. I would not like for you to be offended," Thomas said
while breaking off a piece of bread from the freshly baked loaf.

"Thank you for the warning, Captain. I do not mind a little rough
jesting. As I was lodging in the little inn on the road to Oldham, I heard
rough talk quite often. Not all that was said was suitable for a lady's
ears. Nevertheless it made me laugh," Margaret spoke and handed
Justus a piece of bread.

210

The captain said nothing. He had heard the whole sad story in detail over the past few days. He could not understand, that his friend would refuse to see his own child. His heart painfully contracted as he watched Margaret spooning some of the delicious soup into her son's little mouth. His daughter would have been about the same age as Margaret. He could still see his daughter in his mind as she rode like the wind on the big black stallion he had given her on her birthday. He had been in England as the terrible accident happened and his head groom had told him later. It had been a beautiful day and she wanted to ride. The groom saddled the horses and went with her through the forest and into the field. Laughing she had given the big black beast the spores and raced away. Not wanting to lose against a girl, he had given his own stallion the spores and raced after her. Just as he was about to catch up, her horse stumbled and Kristin flew over the horse's head. She landed on her head and did not move. With a cry of despair, he brought his own horse to a halt and ran toward the motionless girl on the ground. Gently he cradled her as she opened her eyes and spoke barely audible to his ears:

"Where is Papa, it is getting so dark. I am cold." Her beautiful blue eyes had stared sightless into nothing as her head rolled slowly to the side. He had prayed:

"Oh God please no, she is only fifteen. Please let her live."

God had not heard his groom's prayers.

"Captain, is everything all right?" Margaret asked. She had noticed his far away look and the painful expression on his face.

"I am sorry, Miss Margaret," he snapped out of his thoughts, "it is nothing. I was merely thinking of home," he admitted the half-truth.

"I believe I understand. You have been away for a long time and must be longing to be home again," Margaret assumed.

Finishing her meal and wiping her son's face with the napkin, Margaret stood up and took Justus from his chair:

"If you would excuse us, Captain, we should like to walk on deck for a few minutes and then retire. Again, thank you for your kindness. Good night."

"Good night, Miss Margaret," he said softly, "please remember to keep Justus with you at all times. Lock your door at night so he cannot wander off." The Captain had risen from his chair and opened the door for her.

Margaret slightly lifted the hem of her skirt and with Justus on her other hand in a tight grip, she climbed on deck. They were able to stay merely for a few moments. The breeze from the sea was cold and damp. It was dark and she could hardly see anything. Shivering she pulled Justus back down into the narrow hallway and went back to her cabin. Thinking that she could not afford for her or her son to get sick, she gladly entered her own warm cabin.

Justus climbed back onto the window seat once more and tried to see the water. Disappointed he came back after a few minutes and said,

"Mama, dark there, no water. Justus play."

"Very well, Justus, you may play with your toy. I shall get it for you." His mother opened one of her trunks and pulled out a box. Ruth Goldberg had bought the box with toys from the toy maker in town. In the box was a little stall with several painted horses and sheep carved from wood. Justus loved to play with his new toys and kept him self busy for hours. Margaret walked back to the door and locked it tightly. She went back to her trunks and sifting through her belongings, she found what she was looking for. She pulled out the little bundle with all the jewelry and stones she had taken from Fiona's vanity. Carefully she opened the bundle and inspected the rings, bracelets, necklaces and ear bobs. She had not dared to open the bundle in the mansion. She did not want to have to explain to anyone how she came into her treasures possession. On board this ship however would be enough time to sew all the jewels in the hems of her gowns and capes. She would not take the chance of having it stolen. Her own jewels, which she had received on her birthday and the next day from all the other girls, were still safe and securely sewn into her winter cape, which she had rescued from the fire. Margaret took one of the gowns from her trunk and biting the thread, she opened up a small portion of the hem. Carefully and with tiny stitches, she began to sew every piece of jewelry into her gowns. She kept herself busy with her work for many evenings.

America
1772—1774

CHAPTER 17

The New Country

The rest of the voyage she would stitch her embroidery or play with Justus who had won the hearts of all the men on deck. However, Cook was his favorite. Many times he had given the little boy sweetmeats and slices of orange. It was May the twenty first as Margaret woke up from the shouting on deck. She assumed that something had happened and began to dress quickly. Justus still slept in the big bed. Closing the door quietly behind her, she rushed on deck to see what the shouting was all about. Captain Crandall saw her concerned face and smiled,

"In a few hours we will land in New York harbor, Miss Margaret. We made fantastic time crossing the ocean. Thank God the weather held out except for the little storm we had a few days back," Thomas said happily.

"I must admit, it frightened me a bit and I felt sick to my stomach. Nevertheless, I trusted you and your crew to get us safely through the storm. I remembered you telling me, that you had spent most of your life at sea and as you told me it is merely a small storm we are experiencing, I felt safe. How can we ever thank you," Margaret smiled sincerely.

"You do not have to thank me, Miss Margaret. I am glad you agreed to come with me and take care of my wife. I can be at sea and do not have to worry, that she is left alone with an old woman, who sometimes forgets her own children's names," he laughed, his eyes twinkling merrily.

"I remember a woman like this, Captain. I knew a boy, his name was Patrick. His grandmother could tell stories from far past, but she could not remember what happened a few moments ago. I hope I am not getting to be like that when I am getting older," Margaret said wrinkling her brow.

"No one knows, what the future will hold in store for either one of us. We have to take it day by day. Looking back, I would certainly change a few things myself, if I would have known what would happen," Thomas said with a rueful expression on his face.

"I know just how you feel, Captain," Margaret agreed.

"Look, Miss Margaret, can you see the land over there to the west." He had placed one arm around her shoulder and pointing with his other hand in the distance. "That is where we will land nearby. This is called Gibbet Island. A pirate was hung there in 1765. Before that it was called Oster Island," Thomas explained.

"Is this America then?" Margaret asked.

"You mean that little island? Oh no, Miss Margaret. This is merely a tiny part of it. My country is enormous. It stretches all the way to the west for over three thousand miles, where another ocean begins, which is called the Pacific Ocean. Perhaps some day you will see for your self."

"Perhaps I will, Captain. You must excuse me please, I must see to my son. He was still sleeping when I came on deck. Would it be permissible to bring him up on deck later?" Margaret asked, slipping from his arm.

"Certainly, Miss Margaret. The sea is calm and if he will stay on your lap, you may sit with him over there on the ropes in the front. They will not be used to fasten the ship in the harbor." Thomas pointed with his head toward a big coil of rope.

"Wonderful, Captain, Justus will like that and I am longing to see land and feel it under my feet also," Margaret laughed. She turned and hurried back down to her cabin. Justus was sitting on the floor with the little cabin boy Bart and playing with his toys. He heard his mother enter the cabin ran toward her.

"Mama, Justus hungry."

"Cook sent us our meal I can see. Let us eat then." Margaret had noticed the tray with food on her table and sniffing the aroma from the freshly brewed coffee. She thanked the cabin boy and picked up Justus from the floor. After changing his nappies and clothes, Margaret and Justus ate their morning meal. She could hardly wait to go up on deck again. Quickly she drank the last of her coffee and taking Justus by his hand went up on deck.

Holding her son tight, she sat on the big coil of thick rope and pointed to the closer coming land.

"Look Justus, this is our new home America." Justus stretched his little neck as far as he could and looked fascinated at the water and the land. His mother watched quietly as the big city drew nearer and grew bigger. The weather was beautiful warm and she felt wonderful. It seemed that America had ordered the sunshine for her arrival. She wondered how many people were living in this big city. She did not want to disturb Captain Crandall, for he had taken the wheel and steered the big Caravel himself into the harbor.

Thomas supervised some of the cargo to be unloaded and other items were being brought onto the ship in big crates. Margaret could hardly take her eyes away from all the fascinating sights. Captain Crandall came walking toward her and Justus.

"Miss Margaret, it might take a few hours to load and unload. Perhaps it is best if you and your son go down below. I will have you called as soon as we sail again. You are both not used to the strong sunshine and could burn your face and arms. A sunburn is painful and takes days to heal," he said concerned. He helped Margaret to get up from her seat on the ropes and went back to his crew. Margaret took Justus to the cabin and put him on the bed for a nap. It had taken a few hours to reach the New York harbor and he was tired. It did not take long and he was asleep. Margaret decided to work some more on her embroidery until the Captain would call. Just the other night, the Captain had explained to her that they would merely stop in New York to deliver and take on cargo. After that the caravel would take the south route toward Yorktown by sailing along the coast and with good wind could reach their destination about by nightfall the next day. Margaret made certain, that all her belongings were packed securely. After checking her trunks, she picked up her embroidery once more and waited for the call to be able to go on deck again. It took a few hours and Justus was already awake and sitting by the window seat as the little cabin boy Bart knocked on the door. He told Margaret, that the captain was about to set sail again and she would be welcome to come up on deck with her son if she wished to do so. She took her seat once more on the ropes and stayed there with Justus on her lap until cook had served dinner in the captain's cabin.

It was the next morning, as Margaret woke up to the knocking on her cabin door. Quickly she pulled her light robe over her shoulders and opened the door. In the hallway stood cook personally with a tray in his hand.

"It is the best I could do this fine morning, Miss. The Captain is already on deck and had his breakfast early," he smiled.

"Thank you, cook, oh what is this?" Margaret's eyes had fallen on something long and yellow on the tray.

"It is a fruit called banana. We took a load of this fruit on board last night. You have to peel the yellow skin and eat the flesh on the inside. The little fellow might like this I reckon. Here, let me show you." He had put the tray on the table and took a banana to peel it. He broke of a piece and handed it to Margaret.

"I never tasted anything like it cook. It is delicious." Margaret rolled her eyes and chewed. Justus had woken up also and climbed down from the bed.

Margaret took the rest of the banana from the cook and broke of another small piece to let Justus try it. He seemed to like it as he munched.

"More, mama," he demanded. Smiling, Margaret lifted her son onto the chair and handed him the rest of the fruit.

"Enjoy Miss, I must get back to work." The cook said and left the cabin. Margaret peeled one of the hard-boiled eggs and handed it to

Justus. He ate the egg and tiny bits of ham that Margaret had cut from a slice on his plate.

After he had eaten everything on his plate, he reached for another banana.

"So you are still hungry. Very well then, let me help you peel this fruit." Margaret laughed. While Justus ate his banana, Margaret washed herself and dressed. She washed and changed her son and sat back on the chair to have some more coffee. Justus climbed to the window seat and looked out. After a while he got tired of it and he went back to play with his toys. Margaret had taken up her embroidery again and it was almost noon, as someone knocked on the door. It was the Captain,

"Miss Margaret, I would like to show you something. We are sailing close to the coast and there are a few sights I would point out to you."

"I should like to see that, Captain. My son fell asleep a short while ago and I would not leave him here alone." Margaret worried.

"I shall send the cabin boy Bart down to watch him," Thomas offered.

"Thank you, you are indeed thoughtful. In that case I should like to come with you on deck, Captain." Margaret smiled at Thomas as he gently took her arm.

Up on deck, Thomas told the little cabin boy to watch Miss Margaret's son.

The boy hurried down below. Once again, the sunshine was warm and a slight breeze from the northeast sped the ship along the coast. Thomas pointed to the rear toward land and explained,

"To our right back there is Long Island. If we were to go on shore right here, we would reach Monmouth in the state of New Jersey. On our left down there is the state of Delaware that was established by a Swedish trading company in 1638. We will stay on this course and in a few hours we reach the state of Virginia where we live. Virginia was colonized in 1607 and the first city there was called Jamestown. We shall land in Hampton which was established in 1610 by settlers from Jamestown."

"Was this land always here with empty space before or did other people live here?" Margaret asked.

"Yes, Miss Margaret, this land was always here. Up until a Spanish Noble man sailed of course and discovered this land, there were people here who had lived here before. The Spaniards name was Christopher Columbus. He believed himself in the Indies and therefore called the first people he encountered on this land 'Indians'. He did not have the modern technical instruments as we have today. Although he used a compass, he did not have a sextant which we sailors use today," Thomas said proudly.

"Is this instrument telling you, where to go then?" she asked.

"Not directly, Miss Margaret. A sextant tells me, where I am at when I look at the map. It is an optical instrument to measure angular distance between any two objects. Actually two men invented it not too long ago. One of them was an English mathematician. His name was John Hadley. The other inventor was an American named Thomas Godfrey," he explained.

"I should like to know, what happened to the people who were called Indians. Are they still here in this country?" Margaret asked concerned.

"Yes, they are still in this country. Most of them are living further west. They live in homes made of animal skin and furs. Their costumes might be foreign to us; however, they care for and love their families as well as we do. Merely their skin is slightly darker as our own," Thomas pointed out.

"It is all so fascinating, Captain. I should like to hear more. Perhaps after our meal you could tell me some more. I have the feeling, that my son is going to wake up soon and might be hungry," Margaret worried.

"Let us go and have lunch then, Miss Margaret. I shall await you in my cabin," Thomas agreed and took her arm to lead her to the door.

Justus sat on the floor together with the little cabin boy Bart and played with his toys as Margaret entered the cabin. She thanked Bart and quickly dressed her son. After having their meal at the Captain's cabin, Margaret took her son back up on deck. Even though they were sailing a few miles off the coast, the land seemed within reach.

Margaret could hardly wait until they would anchor at Hampton. It would not take long and she would be able to walk on land once again. Together with Justus on her lap she watched fascinated, as the ship turned slightly to the right and the land came closer. She could see buildings and people. She could see fisher boats and strange looking beings. It did look almost like in Liverpool. People were running and shouting.

Margaret could hardly believe it. She had land under her feet again. Her trunks were safe and securely tied to the open carriage. Justus sat next to her and stared in childish wonderment at the people and landscape. The carriage traveled northwest toward Williamsburg and it would take only a short while, to reach Captain Crandall's home. Thomas sat across from Margaret and Justus. He began to speak.

"Miss Margaret, I must inform you about the reason that my wife is in such condition. About two years ago our daughter died while riding her horse. She was thrown and fell head first to the ground. My wife was beside herself and was never the same since this happened. She was not able to forgive me for giving the horse to my daughter on her birthday. The doctor said, that my wife would not be able to have any more children, which makes the whole situation even worse. That is the reason she tried to take her own life a few times. You see, my daughter was about the same age as you are. I thought it might be good for Cynthia to have you and your son in the house. It might give her a new outlook on life. Can you understand that?" Thomas asked.

"Oh, I am so terribly sorry about your daughter, Captain. I had no idea. Of course I will do my best to be a good friend to your wife. I could not even imagine, what the poor woman must have felt. I am a mother myself and I believe I would go mad if something would happen to my son. Perhaps you are correct and your strategy will work to all our advantage. I know that Justus can charm his way into any body's heart." Margaret smiled and lovingly ruffled her little son's hair.

"I have no doubt about that, Miss Margaret. My whole crew loved the little boy. Especially Bart and Cook." It was dark and Margaret could see some lights from afar.

"I see lights over there, Captain. What is it?" Margaret pointed to the left.

"This is my home, Miss Margaret. We are here," Thomas said.

As he had finished his sentence, the coachman had brought the carriage to a halt; he climbed from his seat and opened a large wooden gate. They must have done this many times, for Thomas climbed into the coachman's seat and lead the horses through the gate to stop once again. The coachman closed the gate behind the carriage and took his seat back on the coachman's seat. Together they drove in front of the huge white house. Thomas jumped down from his seat and helped Margaret out of the carriage. At that moment, the big door in the center of the house opened and a man came running toward the little group with a lantern in his hand. Margaret stopped in her track and stared terrified at the man. His skin was almost black. He flashed a big smile at Thomas with his big snow-white teeth:

"Welcome home, Captain. The Misses is upstairs resting. She ain't feelin' too well."

"Thank you, Joseph, it is good to be home again. Joseph, this is Miss Margaret and her son Justus. She will be staying with us and keep my wife company," Thomas introduced. He turned toward Margaret and saw her terrified expression.

"Oh, poor Miss Margaret, I gather you have never seen a black person before. This is my loyal servant Joseph and he does not bite," he added with a soft chuckle.

"I am sorry Captain, I believe I made a complete fool of myself. Indeed I have never seen a person with such dark skin, except here in this new country. It was quite a frightening sight at the harbor already. Is this man an Indian then as you told me?" she asked somewhat shy.

"No, Miss Margaret, Joseph is from a continent called Africa. Actually, his ancestors were brought to America in 1690. You shall see many people like Joseph on my land. They are my slaves and work for me," he explained.

"Am I to understand that I am a slave? I do not understand the difference, Captain," Margaret wrinkled her forehead.

"No, Miss Margaret, you are not my slave. You shall be paid wages.

A slave works for free housing and food. Do not worry; slavery is quite legal here in my country since 1650. Furthermore, I am a good and kind Master and do not punish any of my slaves without good cause. Let us go inside the house now, I am famished." Thomas said and took her arm. Margaret took her sons hand and the three people walked into the big house, while Joseph and the coachman took care of the luggage.

The hall was well lit with several oil lamps along the walls. A beautiful staircase in the middle of the hall led up to the second floor. Margaret noticed several doors partially hidden by a masterful crafted banister. To her left were big glass doors leading into the dining room and the study. To the right were several big wooden doors leading to the kitchen, baths and the Captains private rooms. At their entrance into the hall, one of the doors on the upper floor opened and a woman came walking down the stairs. She had golden blond hair, which was braided and unusual greenish blue eyes. Her slender nose sat straight over full red lips that reminded Margaret of the shape of a heart. She had heard noises from her window and came to see who her late callers were. Suddenly she lifted the hem of her skirt and ran the rest of the staircase into the Captains waiting arms. She embraced him and kissed Thomas on both cheeks like she would greet a good friend.

"Tom, my dear, I did not expect you back so soon. Oh what a wonderful surprise. Please introduce me to our guest." She had freed herself gently from his embrace and looked softly smiling at Margaret.

"Cynthia, my dear, this is Miss Margaret Ziegler your new companion and her son Justus from England. She will be staying with us. I thought it might be best to dismiss old Adele Kaufman." He winked at his lovely wife.

"How thoughtful of you, Tom, what a wonderful husband I have." Cynthia let her lips curl into a sweet smile and gave her husband another kiss on his cheek. Turning toward Margaret she said,

"Welcome to our house, Miss Margaret. I am Cynthia Crandall as you might have guessed." Just for an instant did her brow furrow as she spied the child. Catching herself, she smiled again, "what a beautiful little child you have," Cynthia said as she bent to greet little Justus who hid behind Margaret's skirt. Margaret curtsied and greeted Cynthia,

"Thank you, Misses Crandall. I am grateful to you and your husband. The Captain was so kind as to offer me a position here in your beautiful home. I hope his decision meets with your approval." Margaret smiled.

"I believe my dear husband has all of our best interest at heart, Miss Margaret. Our dear Adele is old enough to be my grandmother and seems to forget just about everything she did only moments ago. You seem to be in need of employment and my husband thinks, he cannot leave me alone," she said somewhat ruefully, smiling at Thomas.

"Yes, dear, I only have your best interest at heart. It would be nice however to have something to eat. The last meal we had was lunch and I am hungry." He laughed and placed his arm around his wife's waist, giving her a loving squeeze. Once again Cynthia freed herself gently from his arm.

"Oh, of course you all must be hungry, where are my manners. Let me ask Ophelia to cook something for our guests and us. Miss Margaret, I will have Joseph show you to your rooms and bring your luggage up. Please join us for supper in about one hour." Cynthia called for Joseph to take the trunks up to the three adjoining rooms to the left on the second floor.

"Oh pardon me, Captain, it was my understanding that my son and I would stay in the guesthouse. I would not wish to impose any further on your privacy," Margaret worried. She had noticed how Cynthia had pulled away from her Husband and was under the impression that the Lady was merely modest and did not want to show any affection in front of strangers.

"Nonsense, Miss Margaret, I will not hear of it. The rooms upstairs are a lot more comfortable as the little guesthouse. Furthermore it would have to be cleaned and painted after Adele moves out from there. Please stay in the house for a few nights at least. If you still wish to move in the guesthouse after seeing it, we will have it made up for you. Adele is staying there and we will have to give her some time to move her things back to her daughters house on the far Westside of the property," Cynthia suggested.

"Oh, I did not know, Misses Crandall. Of course I shall be happy to stay in your house. Perhaps it would be best for the old Lady to stay where she is. The dear Lady might get confused if she would have to move," Margaret agreed concerned.

"It is settled then, please make yourself at home," Thomas smiled, while his wife nodded and hurried toward the kitchen to find the cook Ophelia.

"Please, Captain, I believe you should dine alone with your wife tonight. I do not feel comfortable being there on your first night at home. Be so kind and have some food brought to my rooms so you can be undisturbed." She had also noticed, that Thomas had looked with a certain longing at his wife. The last thing Margaret wanted to do is be witness to any more tenderness between husband and wife. She felt pain and anger that Jack had not married her and had never looked at her like this. She felt envious.

"Perhaps you are right, Miss Margaret. Thank you for understanding. I will send Joseph to your rooms with your meal as soon as Ophelia is done cooking." Thomas agreed gladly. He was indeed longing to be alone with his wife and thankful, that Margaret had the understanding. He still hoped that Cynthia would be in his arms again. She had refused him ever since their daughter had died. Perhaps tonight after a romantic dinner would be the night. Perhaps tonight he would give her the gift he brought back from the orient. The little box and its content had been in his luggage for many months now. For many months he never had the nerve to give it to her. Oh, perhaps tonight he would…

Still a little wary of the big black man, Margaret followed him with Justus on her hand to the second floor. Joseph took one of the oil lamps from one of the tables in the hall. He walked along the long hallway and climbing yet another staircase at the left end of the building to the third floor, Margaret noticed six doors. Joseph opened the first door on the left for Margaret and let her and Justus pass to enter the room. The room was almost as big as the one she hade lived in at the mansion in England. She liked what she saw. To her left in the corner stood a small square table with four chairs. On the left wall further into the center of the room was a small fireplace. A few inches further yet were a small window and a lovely small desk and a chair beneath the window. Straight away from her were two bigger windows with a little table in between them. To her right on the wall stood a big couch and a low table in front. Two comfortable chairs were placed on the other side of the low table. This was obviously the sitting room. Joseph lit the oil lamps in the room and bowing he left to fetch the luggage. Margaret opened the door next to the couch to her right and found a smaller room with a big bed and a nightstand. The headboard of the bed had been pushed against a wall she was facing. Yet to her left were two identical windows to the ones in the sitting room. So why was this room smaller than the other? Walking around the bed, she found yet another door across the second window. Opening this door, she could see nothing. It was too dark to make out anything. Curious she went back to the sitting room to take one of the lamps. Walking back to the bedroom, she found that the other smaller door led to a closet where her clothes would be stored. Satisfied, Margaret nodded her head and smiled. It was more than she had expected. She would live here and work here and raise her son here.

She heard Joseph coming back with on of her trunks. It was the smallest one and contained her son's clothes and toys.

"Where do you want this, Miss?" Joseph asked wiping the sweat from his forehead.

"Please place my trunk and that of my son, which is this one, in the closet in the bed chamber. I will take care of my things tomorrow," Margaret decided.

"Ah Miss, the little man has his rooms across the hall. Natty will take care of him. The Lady has ordered it to be so," Joseph grinned.

"And who is Natty?" Margaret asked slightly annoyed.

"Natty is my granddaughter Miss. She's seventeen and a good girl. She will watch the little boy like it was her own Miss. Don't you worry none."

Joseph said proudly. Like a conspirator he added,

"Natty can even read and write and she can count too."

As soon as he finished his sentence, a young dark-skinned girl stuck her head around the door and flashed Joseph a big smile.

"Ah, there you are grandfather. I was told to come up here."

Upon seeing Margaret and the little boy, the girl curtsied,

"I'm Natty, Miss, and I was told to watch the little boy. Actually my name is Nathalie. My Grandparents call me Natty." She smiled her broad smile at Margaret. Margaret was still a little hesitant to let this dark girl take care of her son. She did not want to offend the Captain however and said,

"Very well then, Natty. I am Miss Margaret and this is my son Justus. The small trunk contains my son's things. Perhaps you could take his nightshift out and get him ready to retire. It has been a long day and a long voyage indeed. Before he goes to sleep, he will dine with me here." Natty had opened the small trunk and pulled out the little boy's nightshift. Upon closing the trunk, Natty's finger made contact with one of the studs. The stud had a sharp edge to it and cut the girl's finger. Instantly the girl cried out and stuck the injured finger in her mouth to suck the blood away. Fascinated, Margaret had watched as she noticed, that the girl bleed as red as any other normal person. Her mind was made up right then. If the girl bleeds red, then merely the skin is darker. There would be no other difference. Margaret took her cape off and placed it over one of the chairs. Rubbing her hands together, she realized the chill in the room. Even though it was the month of May, there was a slight chill in the air. Turning toward Joseph who moved toward the door to get the rest of her luggage, Margaret asked:

"Joseph, would you be so kind to bring some wood after you brought all our luggage. It is cool in here and I do not want my son to get a chill."

"I'll make you a nice fire, Miss, as soon as I am done with your trunks,"Joseph promised. Bowing once more, he left the room.

Natty had taken Justus by his little hand and he did not mind at all, that the friendly girl was so dark. To him, the last few weeks had been a wonderful adventure with new things and new people to discover. All the people he had met so far were all nice. All the ladies in his mind were as nice as mama. Obediently he let Natty take his hand and followed her to his rooms across the hall. Margaret however wanted to see her son's rooms and followed. Pleasantly surprised, that her son's rooms were as spacious and friendly as her own she noticed two beds, slightly smaller as her own, in the room. There were also a small table and two chairs and a smaller candle stand, however with an oil lamp. Her son would have plenty of room to play. Watching Natty, she saw that the girl had begun to undress Justus and chattering merrily with the little boy about horses and dogs and cats on the property, she pulled the nightshift over his dark head. Margaret was satisfied. Yes, she would like it here. She would live here and save her coins she would earn. Some day, she would have a house of her own. Some day she would take her son and would go back to Europe. Some day she would find Jack. She would have revenge...

CHAPTER 18

Friendly People

Margaret woke with a start. What was that noise? It sounded as if a door had slammed and shook the walls of the house to its foundation. Only a few seconds later another door was slammed. Curious, she swung her legs out of the bed. She slipped into her robe and went into the hallway to see where the rude person was, which woke not only her but also the entire household. She could see no one in the dimly lit hall and ascended down the stairs to the second floor. The picture that greeted her was disturbing and frightening. The big captain stood clasping the banister with his hands until his knuckles turned white and softly cussing said to himself,

"Damn the woman to hell. I can't take this any longer. How long will she punish me? It wasn't my fault. It was an accident. She didn't even open the gift I gave her."

Angry he pushed himself from the banister and stomped down toward his study. Margaret stood for a long while, trying to decide what to do. Obviously there was more to his marriage than the happiness she believed existed. Margaret wanted to find out more. How could she do it without being considered nosey? She had an idea. Quietly she went down to the kitchen and poured a glass of milk. With the glass of milk in her hand she walked to the door to the study. Upon her soft rapping, the captain's voice inside the room bade her to enter.

"Oh, Miss Margaret, it is you. I thought you are asleep." Thomas said somewhat absent-minded.

"I was asleep, Captain, until a few minutes ago. I woke up terribly thirsty and got a glass of milk. I saw light in your study and thought this perhaps a good time to ask you as to my duties as far as the Lady is concerned. I realize it is late, but I should like to be informed. Please Captain it is important to me that I know exactly what is expected of me," Margaret said softly smiling.

"All I expect of you is to keep Cynthia company and be a friend to her. As I told you, she is not to be left alone for any length of time. That is basically what is expected of you. In the future however remember please that we have servants and slaves to fetch food or drink. I do not want you to take a fall and injure yourself in the halls or on the stairs." Thomas still seemed angry. Not wanting to push him any further, Margaret thought better of it and curtsied.

"Of course, Captain. I shall remember the next time. Good night then."

His heart painfully contracted as he saw the hurt in her eyes. He wanted to call out to her. He wanted to reach out and...Oh god, what was he thinking. He could never tell her how he felt. He had a wife and responsibilities.

Quickly turning on her heels, she closed the door to the study quietly behind her and took a deep breath.

Tiptoeing back to her rooms, Margaret sat for a long while in one of the comfortable chairs, slowly sipping her milk. Perhaps Natty could shed some light on the mysterious happenings in this house. Margaret would ask her son's new nurse in the morning. Finishing her milk, Margaret went quietly back to her bed.

The sun had just begun to rise, as Margaret woke up in the morning. She swung her legs out of her bed and walked over to the window. The sight that greeted her was magnificent. Looking down, she could see a beautiful enormous garden with all sorts of flowers already in bloom. Huge trees, which she had never seen before, stood toward the edge of the garden, which was surrounded by a stone wall. A forest seemed to extend beyond the stone wall as far as the eye could see. The small walkways were swept and kept clean from leaves and weeds. To her surprise, Margaret saw a small pond nestled back in the right corner of the garden and totally surrounded by a small fence. The pond and its surrounding walkway could be entered through a gate, which was closed at the moment. To the left behind the big trees and close to the stone wall, Margaret saw a small house. 'This must be the house were the old Lady is living.' Margaret thought. Still, it was bigger than the cottage she had lived at in England. Perhaps she should not have been so hasty and agreed to move here into these rooms. The garden house looked far bigger and more private. For now however she would hold her tongue and not approach the captain. Perhaps in time she could move into the small house without offending the captain or Cynthia. Time would tell. A soft knock startled Margaret out of her thoughts. It was Natty with little Justus on her hand. Upon seeing his mother, the boy ran toward her on his fat little legs and Margaret bending down, scooped her laughing son up into her arms and swung him in the air.

"Good morning, my little love." Margaret greeted him with a loud kiss on his rosy cheek. His little arms went around her neck and hugging his mother tightly, he said:

"Good morning, mama, I like it here. Natty is nice too. She tells me stories."

"I know, my son. I like it here too. Now go with Natty and wash up. Do not forget to cleanse your teeth," Margaret warned.

"Yes, mama," the little boy said. Kissing his cheek once more, Margaret placed her son on the floor were he ran back to his nurse. He stuck his little hand in her big brown hand and together they left the room. A little wave of jealousy went through Margaret as she saw her son place his hand trustingly in the other woman's hand. It was still early in the morning and the house seemed quiet. Margaret decided to sit in her dayroom and write a letter to her friend Gretchen, as she had promised to stay in contact. She would let her friend know that she had arrived safely in America and found the work and her new home much to her liking. The people were pleasant and some of them very dark-skinned indeed. Perhaps some day in the future Gretchen could come and visit here and see for herself. She folded and sealed the letter and placed it on her desk. Perhaps the Captain or the coachman could take the letter to town to be shipped to Europe.

Thinking and considering her wages, plus the jewels in her clothes and the amount she could save, Margaret figured that it would take about five years before she could return to Europe. But return she would. She would be able to purchase a house and furnish it with her savings and still have money to live. However it would take some time. She tried to envision Jack's face when he would see her again. A woman, fairly well situated in her own right and not dependent on his mercy. Her lips curled into a bitter smile. Once again she was startled and snapped out of her daydream by a knock on her door. Upon bidding the caller to enter, Margaret was surprised to see Joseph enter her room with yet another dark-skinned girl.

"Good morning, Misses Margaret. This is another one of my granddaughters, Patty. She will serve you. Natty and Patty are cousins. They are the daughters of my sons Nathaniel and Matthias. Patty here is fifteen and if she ain't behaving' just rap her one behind her ears." He flashed Margaret a big bright smile with his snow-white big teeth.

"Thank you, Joseph," Margaret couldn't help herself but laugh at his funny remark and accent, " I am not in the habit however, to hit and smack people. I am sure Patty will be as good a girl as Natty is." Margaret chuckled. Turning to Patty, she said,

"Good morning, Patty. I am Miss Margaret. You may help me dress after I take my bath. I am certain that breakfast will be served soon. I do not wish to be late." With that, Joseph was dismissed and he bowed and left the room.

Margaret's trunks had not been unpacked yet and pointing at them, Margaret said to Patty:

"My gowns and other personal things are still packed in there. Find me the blue gown with the silver stars. I shall wear it today." Margaret ordered. Patty curtseyed and went to open the trunks to hang the gowns into the big closet.

"Where can I find a tub to take a bath, Patty?" Margaret enquired while Patty shook out the wrinkles from the gown she held in her hands.

"It is straight across the hall from your bedroom, Miss Margaret.

There is a big tub. If you turn the knob on the wall, the water will come out into the tub," Patty finished proudly.

Having seen something similar as Patty described, in Jack's house, Margaret was not surprised at such comfort in the captain's house as well. She remembered that Hammed had told her once, that Jack and Thomas had lived in Istanbul for a while, as they were still boys. Both families seemed to have adapted and taken advantage of this fine invention, which led the water through pipes into a room. Margaret had still no idea how this wonder of modern technology worked. She only knew it worked and she would be able to take her baths as she had been used too in Jack's house. Not moving however, Margaret stood and watched Patty bustling back and fro to hang and fold her belongings. Realizing that her Mistress was waiting, Patty asked:

"Is there something else I can help you with, Miss Margaret?" The girl had assumed that Margaret was perfectly capable to handle something as simple as taking a bath by herself.

"I was accustomed to having being washed by my servant in Europe. Are the servants here in this country different, Patty?" Margaret asked somewhat astonished as she noticed the nonplussed look on Patty's face, almost bordering on revolted.

"Good Lord, Miss Margaret!" Patty exclaimed, "I would not be allowed to touch another grown person on his or her naked skin. My pa would tan my hide somthin' fierce until I'm black and blue."

"Oh, I had no idea that costumes in this country somewhat differ from where I come from. Very well then, Patty. I promise not to tell anyone. I do however need some help with my hair. Will you help me to wash my hair?" Margaret asked smiling. Deep down she was glad that she did not have to be touched and parade as God had fashioned her in front of another person.

"That I can do, Miss Margaret. Just knock on the wall when you are ready to have your hair washed. I'll be there in a flash." Patty was relieved. She had feared that her new mistress would insist on being washed. The girl had never heard of such nonsense as washing another grown person. Shaking her head and continuing folding and hanging Margaret's clothes, the girl giggled as Margaret had left the room and pulled the door shut behind her. It must be a very strange country where Miss Margaret had lived before. Margaret opened the door to the bathing room and gasped surprised.

Though a bit smaller, the room was almost identical to the one in Jack's mansion. Merely the big massage tables were missing. Taking some of the small jars and vials from the shelves, she sniffed at every one and inhaling the sweet fragrances of soaps and bath oils she noticed each jar was labeled. There were fragrances of rose, freesia, sandalwood, gardenia, lilac and some she had never heard of. After smelling the jars with the strange names hyacinth and jasmine, she decided on using the new exotic fragrance, jasmine. Margaret poured some of the oil in her bath water. Climbing into the big oak tub with the steaming water, Margaret washed her own body with the sweet smelling soft soap. After rinsing and sitting down on the seat in the tub, she took the big wooden spoon, which was used to stir the bath oil into the water and knocked on the wall. Only moments later Patty entered the room and began to wash Margaret's hair. After rinsing several times with the water from the wooden buckets next to the big tub, Patty took one of the huge towels from the shelve and discretely turning her head and lowering her eyes, she held out the towel so Margaret could climb out of the tub and wrap herself in the towel. Clad thusly, Margaret sat on one of the little wooden stools and taking a smaller towel, Patty began rubbing and drying the mass of glorious hair until it was merely damp. Taking Margaret's robe from the other chair, Patty held it open for her Mistress. Dropping the towel where she stood, Margaret quickly slipped into her robe and bound the sash. She was pleased with her servant's modesty and tact. She began to like this new country and its costumes better as each minute passed. Not waiting for the girl, who kept busy with cleaning away the towels and the big tub, Margaret went back to her own rooms to quickly change from her robe into her under things. Just as she tied the drawstring on her underskirt, Patty came back into the room. The blue gown had been carefully placed on the already made bed. Merrily chattering about her family and the new baby her mother would have in a few days' time, the girl helped Margaret into her gown. Margaret noticed that the girl had a keen sense of observation and might also know what was going on in this house. She decided she must win Patty's total confidence and trust if she wanted to find out anything about the captain and his wife. It would take some time and Margaret, despite her youth, had learned to be patient. She knew that everything would come and be revealed in its own good time. At this very moment it was time to go downstairs. Her stomach rumbled as to verify her thoughts of breakfast. Patty had brushed out Margaret's hair and free from tangles parted it in the middle and braided it into a single braid. Winding the long braid around her hand, the girl fastened it with a few hairpins artfully at the nape of Margaret's neck. Looking very mature and elegant and quite the young lady, Margaret checked her appearance once more in the mirror. Satisfied she smiled at Patty and said,

"Will you tell Natty to bring my son to me. I should like to have my morning meal with him."

"Oh, the young master had his meal some time ago while you were bathing. He was very hungry and Natty took him downstairs to the kitchen. I saw them walking down as you knocked on the wall," Patty answered.

For a brief moment Margaret's brow wrinkled. She was used to taking care of her son and to give him his meals ever since he was born. Not pleased by this she lifted the hem of her gown and without answering the girl rushed out the door. She would have to talk to the captain about this. To have a servant was one thing. However, nobody would take the time away from her, which she spends with her son at the table to eat. She would see to it that this was not to be repeated. The door to the dining hall was wide open and Margaret saw the captain sitting by the long table having a slice of freshly baked bread, which he buttered and added a few slices of thinly sliced ham. He was about to take a bite, as Margaret entered the room. She noticed Cynthia's absence.

"Good morning, Captain. Will your wife join us for our meal?" she asked.

"My wife is not feeling well this morning. She suffers from a headache. She will keep to her bed today. Cecilia, the cook's daughter will stay with her. You will have the whole day for yourself," he answered and bit in his bread. Chewing and wiping his lips with the spotless white napkin he washed the bread down with several sips of hot aromatic coffee.

"I trust you slept well." Thomas quickly changed the subject, forestalling any more questions concerning his wife. Margaret instinctively knew that the subject of Cynthia was closed upon hearing his almost gruff answer. Seating herself, Margaret poured some coffee in her dainty cup and took a sip. She reached for the basket with the bread and spreading some butter and honey on it, began to eat.

"Thank you, yes, I slept very well indeed," she answered in between bites. Nothing else was said. To approach him with the little matter of her son, Margaret would wait until he had finished his meal. She remembered Hammed's words. Not much if anything at all was accomplished on an empty growling stomach. Sated and satisfied, people were more apt to listen and give an inch than being distracted by delicious smelling food. This was the way Jack and Hammed had conducted every business transaction. At first there would be a generous meal and then merchants would be willing to lower their prices to both parties satisfaction.

So, Margaret waited until Thomas sat back in his chair and delicately belching behind his elegant hand, signaled that he was done with his breakfast. However, pouring himself another cup of coffee, he reached into his pocket and drew out a strange looking object. Margaret had never seen anything like it. Fascinated she watched as he reached into his pocked once more and held a little round box in his hand. He opened the box and reaching in with three fingers took some of its content, which looked to Margaret like dirt, to stuff it into the funny looking object. To her horror he reached for a candle on the table and held the flame directly on the wide opening of the object where he had stuffed the dirt. The other smaller end of the object was between his lips. Wide-eyed and horrified that the Captain would blow the whole state of Virginia to kingdom come, she shrieked and motioned to flee. She thought it was this certain powder that Hammed had spoken of once. 'Oh God have mercy, he is gone mad and is going to kill himself and me too.' She thought. It was then that Thomas looked at Margaret and noticed her apparent terror. Not able to help himself, the Captain began to laugh that his sides ached. Realizing that Margaret had never been present when he smoked his pipe on the ship, he blew out the smoke and laughed until tears were running into his beard. Hardly able to draw a breath between laughter, he put a reassuring hand on Margaret's arm and wiping the tears away with the back of his other hand where he still held his pipe, he wheezed,

"Miss Margaret, I don't know what you were thinking just yet. The look on you face suggests something horrifying indeed. What I am doing is merely smoking my pipe."

"Forgive me that I am not able to share your humor, Captain," Margaret said somewhat aggrieved, "I thought you wanted to kill yourself and the whole household. Hammed told me once about a powder which explodes with a great horrible noise and could break stonewalls as well as people into many pieces. That is what I thought it was," she finished red-faced.

"No, Miss Margaret, what I stuffed into my pipe is called tobacco. Once it is lit, it merely smolders and to some men it is a relaxing pastime. I am one of the few who enjoys smoking a pipe after a meal," Thomas explained. Why would she think that he wanted to kill himself?

Sniffing, Margaret realized, that the blue smoke had an aromatic fragrance to it and not too unpleasant. She wondered, if it tasted as strange as it smelled.

She vowed never to find this out. Her mind went back to the important issue, her son. Before he found an answer to his question however, Margaret spoke after wiping her lips with the napkin.

"Captain, I wish to talk to you about a small matter. As you know, I have raised my son up until now on my own and would be grateful if he is to take his meals with me, his mother. While I was bathing, my son had his meal with Natty in the kitchen. As well meaning, as Natty was this morning to feed Justus, I insist that this is not going to happen again. My son is very precious to me and the times we spend together as well." Margaret had spoken in a soft but firm voice; her face had a strangely mature look to it.

'Ah, the little mother hen is showing her claws' Thomas thought. This would prove to be a problem. Before he had the fight with Cynthia, she had mentioned a few plans she had as to the child's welfare and education was concerned. Cynthia loved children. She had taken an instant liking to this beautiful child at first sight. As he realized only now, Margaret had not been mentioned at all in Cynthia's plans. Perhaps he did not have to worry about Cynthia's plans after all. After the terrible fight last night, he was not certain. It was Cynthia's idea, to appoint Natty to be the child's nurse. He knew that Natty was only loyal to his wife. Natty and his late daughter grew up together and had been more like sisters. He remembered one day as Natty and his daughter were playing by the little pond. Cynthia had been sitting on a chair reading, as Natty fell into the pond and almost drowned. At his daughter's terrified scream Cynthia dropped her book and jumped into the pond in her gown to pull out the child. Even though, the pond was merely three feet deep, Natty had not been able to find the ground with her feet and had been helplessly splashing and bobbing in the water. Natty and her whole family were eternally grateful to the lady of the house. There would be almost nothing they would not do for her.

"I shall talk to my wife about it as soon as she feels better," the Captain promised.

"I do not understand, Captain. I was under the impression that you ordered and appointed servant's duties. That is why I came to you with my request to have my son with me at mealtime," Margaret said somewhat disturbed. It was unheard of in Jack's house that a woman would presume the appointing of duties as far as servants were concerned. There it was the Master or the Stewart who ordered things done. Perhaps this was another one of the strange and new costumes she would have to get used too.

"All the servant's and slaves in this house answer to my wife and to me. Since I am gone many months out of the year, it has become a habit more then a costume, Miss Margaret, that my wife is in charge. Since this is more a female issue I assumed it would be better to have my wife talk to Natty. Natty loves my wife very much and coming from me, well, it would perhaps sound more like an order then a request. Please understand, Miss Margaret, I am still the master in this house. However, there are certain things a woman is capable of doing more softly and delicately than a man." Thomas drank the last of his coffee and rose from his chair. For him the matter was taken care of and closed. He had business to attend in town and did not want to be late. Nodding his head slightly he suggested,

"Please feel free to explore the grounds. The day is promising to be sunny and warm. Do not wander too far into the woods behind the garden. The woods are tricky and you could get lost. I have business in town and must be on my way. I shall see you tonight here for supper."

"Captain, before I forget; I should like to have this letter sent to my friend Gretchen in Europe. Please be so kind and take it to town with you."

Margaret handed him the letter she had placed in the folds of her skirt earlier, while Patty had brushed her hair.

"Certainly, Miss Margaret. I shall see to it that your letter gets shipped. Another small matter, since we are living together under one roof, please call me by my given name, which you know is Thomas. May I call you Margaret?" She nodded her consent.

"Do not fret about your son's welfare. He is in good hands."

With that he took the letter from her hand and turned to hurry out the door before Margaret could say another word.

'We shall see about that,' Margaret thought. 'If he is not talking to his wife this very moment, then I certainly will do so. It would not be considered impolite to pay her a visit and enquire about her headache. There is nothing wrong or suspicious about being courteous and perchance bring up the little matter with my son.' Finishing her meal, Margaret watched for a moment yet another servant coming through the door and clearing the table. The woman was just as dark-skinned as all the other servants Margaret had met so far. However she seemed older and great with child. Margaret remembered Patty telling her, that her mother would be having another child in a few days' time. 'This must be Patty's mother then,' she thought and felt sympathetic toward the woman. In between doing her work, she kept rubbing her back. Margaret remembered her own confinement as she was carrying Justus. Many times her back had ached as if it would break. It was almost impossible to get comfortable in the last few weeks of her pregnancy.

She knew that she would not want to go through this again any time soon. If Jack would have married her, then it might be another matter. However, he did not marry her and was living somewhere near Madrid in the lap of luxury and without care. Anger seemed to sweep through Margaret's whole being like a burning wildfire. She had not been aware, that she was clutching her napkin in her hand until her knuckles turned white. Here she was all alone with her little sweet son among strangers in a strange house in a strange country with strange costumes. Then some little chit comes and does not ask her permission to feed her son. She would not have any of it. She looked into the woman's face and saw little beats of sweat running down her forehead. It was strange for the room was pleasantly cool. Suddenly the woman seemed to breathe a heavy sigh. It was then that Margaret saw a puddle building beneath the woman's feet. Horrified, Margaret gasped and her hand went over her open mouth. Margaret realized in an instant, that the woman's water just had broken. She was about to give birth to her baby. The woman smiled and said:

"Don't worry, Miss, it's not my first one. I got nine others. This will be number ten and hopefully a boy this time." Calmly she carried the cups and plates on the tray out to the kitchen. Only a few seconds later another young girl about twelve or thirteen years old came running into the dining room with a bucket and a big rag. She began to mop up the little puddle from the wooden floor. Stunned and unable to move, Margaret sat on her chair. How this woman could be so calm and still work, while she was about to give birth to a child, was a mystery to Margaret. The young girl had finished mopping the floor and smiled at the fine Lady sitting by the table.

"Ma said it would still take some time before the little one is born. We all hope it's a boy this time. We ain't nothing' but girls with Patty being the oldest," the girl chattered while wringing out the rag.

"How can your mother still work like this girl?" Margaret asked.

"She's used to havin' kids, Miss. She always says that being with child ain't a sickness. So she's always gettin' mad when we do things for her and she hollers at us to stop fussin'." The girl giggled. Shaking her head, Margaret rose from her chair and asked,

"What is your name?"

"I'm Tammy, Miss. It's short for Tamara. I'm the second oldest. Then there is Sammy, that's short for Samantha. Then there is Tulip. Her real name is Dahlia. But we think she ain't that pretty. So we call her Tulip. Then there are the twins Rose and Mary. Pa is teasing Ma about them two. He says she's been too close to the kitchen garden for too long. Then there is Caroline, Charlotte and the little one is Cindy. Ma named her after the Captain's wife because she wants to honor the Lady. So she said. I think Ma ran out of girls names," the girl answered with a sweet curtsy and giggled again.

In spite of herself, Margaret had to smile. This was a strange country indeed. However the people were open and friendly. Perhaps she was a bit hasty and should think on the matter with her son some more. After all, no harm had been done and her child was safe and protected. As it seemed by a girl who was part of a large family and knew how to handle and raise children. Furthermore, her days would be filled with keeping the Lady of the house company. Margaret decided that it was not so bad to have someone else look after her child. She would speak to the girl on her own and merely suggest that her son should have mealtimes with his mother. She would figure out a way and the appropriate words to approach the girl later. Catching herself in her thoughts, Margaret said to the girl more in statement than in question,

"You are all living here on this property, yes. I have not seen any servants' quarters. Where is your house?"

"We live by the stables, Miss. It's the building out the door and to the right. If you walk along the walkway, you'll pass the old well and by the big tree you would turn left. Its faster to run over the lawn." Tammy giggled again.

"You mean to tell me that you live with the horses?" Margaret was incredulous.

"No, Miss, we live in the rooms above the stables," Tammy laughed.

"Ah now I see," Margaret said relieved and had to laugh also. She could not imagine anyone living together with animals. Horses were beautiful animals but the stables at Jacks house always had a certain odor to it. She was sure that the horses in this country smelled not any different. How could one live so close to them? Curious Margaret asked Tammy,

"Does the bad smell from the stables not offend you and your family?"

"What smell are you talking about, Miss? There ain't any bad smell that I know of. My cousins would get a good one with the belt if the stables would smell bad. My cousins Nathan and Luke have to clean there every day. The fresh hay smells nice and we like it there," the girl said proudly.

"Perhaps later I shall take a stroll to see the horses and meet your cousins, Tammy. Would you go now and see how your poor mother is doing. She might need help," Margaret suggested, afraid that the girl would find another subject to chatter about. She wanted to explore the grounds and see the little garden house close up. Bobbing another curtsey, Tammy took the bucket and hurried back to the kitchen. It seemed to Margaret, that this whole family was working and serving here in this estate. They all seemed to be happy to be here and serve the Captain and his wife. Perhaps it was a good thing that she had come here. Anger could wait, curiosity took the upper hand and Margaret decided to take her walk in the huge gardens. For the moment, Margaret's soul found peace. No revenge, for the moment…

CHAPTER 19

The Visit

Breathing deeply, Margaret wandered through the huge garden toward the little guesthouse. The house seemed to be in good repair from the outside. Curious as to what the inside of the house looked like, Margaret softly knocked on the door. It seemed that there was no answer. Just as Margaret turned to leave, the door slowly opened and an old woman stuck her head out. She wore a robe over her nightshift. Her face was wrinkled and her thinning hair was as white as the snow. Squinting, her dark lively eyes seemed to wander from Margaret's face over her entire form and back to the face again.

"Who are you?" The old woman had a surprisingly strong voice and with a strange accent that seemed somewhat familiar.

"Pardon the intrusion, I am Miss Margaret Ziegler. I am a guest of Captain and Misses Crandall. I was wandering in the garden and saw this charming little house. I hoped to greet the owner and have a nice chat." Margaret answered in half-truth. She did not know if the old woman was aware that Margaret was to take her position as Cynthia's companion.

"Well then, come in and sit. The coffee is almost done. Would you like a cup?" Without waiting for Margaret's answer, the old woman opened the door wide and went back into the house. Lifting the hem of her skirt, Margaret climbed up the two small steps to enter the house.

The inside of the room was dark since the heavy curtains on the windows were drawn and it took a few moments for Margaret's eyes to adjust to the darkness. Surprised, Margaret looked around to find the old woman. She was not in this room and it was then that Margaret saw another door. 'Perhaps the old woman is in the room behind that door. She was still in her nightshift as she opened the door. Ah, she is getting dressed. This must be her bed chamber then.' Margaret thought. However, the old woman was still in her nightshift and robe as she entered the spacious sitting room. She carried a tray with two cups a small pitcher with milk a pot of steaming coffee and a small dish with sugar cookies. Placing the tray on a small square table and filling the two cups with coffee, she pointed at one of the chairs by the table while she sat on the other chair:

"Sit, child, and have some coffee. I take mine with milk. Would you like some milk in your coffee?" Again without waiting for Margaret's answer she added a small amount of milk to the coffee in Margaret's cup. Hiding a smile, Margaret sat and took a sip from her coffee. She had to admit, that the dark liquid somehow had a lovelier and sweeter taste to it as plain black coffee. Somehow the old woman with the sharp eyes reminded Margaret of the old shoemaker's wife Misses Tippins. Although, the woman sitting by the table was somewhat slimmer and taller than Misses Tippins.

"I think I forgot to introduce myself. I am Frau Adele Kaufmann. What was your name again child?" the old woman fell into Margaret's thoughts.

"My name is Margaret. I am pleased to meat you Frau Kaufmann," Margaret responded.

"Frau is German for Misses. You may call me Adele." The old woman explained. "Many years ago we lived in Germany. My husband Alwin died a few years back. He was a good man, my Alwin." Adele said.

"Oh, I am very sorry to hear that. I know how devastating it is to lose someone dear. My mother passed away when I was nearly fifteen years of age. I have lived in England since birth. However, I do have a good friend, Gretchen. She also lives in Germany. That's why your accent sounded so familiar to me," Margaret said exited, "the city she lives in is called Dresden. I also know a little German."

"How odd, we also lived in Dresden for a while," Adele mused. Merely for an instant, her forehead seemed to wrinkle even more if such thing was possible.

"Oh please tell me something about this city Dresden and its people and your life over there, Adele. Gretchen mentioned something about great buildings there and a big river near the house she grew up in." Margaret clapped her hands like an exited child.

"I hope you have some time little, Margaret, for the story I am about to tell you is a long one. It is the story about my life in Dresden." The old woman crackled softly.

"Please tell me, Adele. I do enjoy learning and hearing stories of other countries and people." Margaret smiled.

"Very well then, sit back and listen." Adele took another sip from her coffee and began to speak,

"When I was a young girl, I was a maid at a very wealthy lady's castle near the Elbe River. She was old and enjoyed her garden, especially in the summertime, where she used to sit every afternoon to have her coffee. Many times several of her lady friends sat with her to enjoy and admire the abundance of flowers and shady trees in this beautiful garden. The old countess was generous and loving to all. She knew that her gardener Alwin and I were in love and planned to get married. Since we married in the beginning of summer, she gave us permission to have our wedding in her private little chapel and the wedding feast was going to be held in her garden. Some of the old lady's friends were invited to join us in the celebration. As we were making rather merry with dancing, eating and drinking, a little servant boy came running across the lawn and handed the countess a note. Upon reading the note, her eyes got wide and she clapped her hands to silence the musicians. Standing up, she announced, that the King Friedrich August was hunting nearby and was about to pay her castle a visit. We all got very exited and took it as a good omen that the king was coming for a visit on our wedding day. Not long thereafter the king arrived. With him were several people from court and a beautiful lady.

My countess greeted the king and she explained to him and the lady, that we were celebrating our wedding. The king smiled at the lady and she blushed. One of my friends stood behind me and whispered to my husband and me, that this was the king's mistress Anna von Cosel. He had just recently gifted the lady with a beautiful castle nearby. The name of the palace was Schloss Pillnitz. My heart was in my throat as the king and his lady walked toward us and congratulated us on our marriage. It was then, that the lady noticed the wreath of flowers on my head. She said that she had never seen beautiful red flowers like this before and asked me, where I found them. My husband explained to her and the king that these flowers had come from a small bush in the old countess' garden. He had planted the bush himself and took care of it. However, he had no idea where the countess bought the bush. The old countess had listened and told the king, that a friend had given her this plant a few years back. This friend was an old sea captain and brought this plant for her from one of his trips to the Orient. Since she was a collector of rare and exotic plants, she had asked the old captain to bring her some plants from far away places. The bush with the red flowers was called Camellia. The king's mistress interrupted and said that she did not care where this plant came from as long as she would have it in her own garden. The king smiled and asked my old countess if he could have the plant for his lady. The countess had no choice as to curtsey and to say, yes. After all, the king was asking her and no one would dare to say no to the king. The king told my husband to bring the little bush to Schloss Pillnitz the next day. I was sad for my countess. I could see that it hurt her to have the gift from her dear friend taken away at a spoiled woman's whim. My husband squeezed my hand and whispered that he would take care of it.

I had no idea, what he was talking about. The king and his people remained for a few hours and nothing more was said about the plant. As I was sitting by the table, I could feel the young lady's eyes on me and my beautiful wreath. I felt like slapping the smug smile from her powdered face. My dear old countess was heartbroken and retired early as soon as the king and his entourage had left. Early the next morning my husband was ordered by the countess to dig up the plant and bring it to the king's mistress. My husband told the countess, that there was no need to dig up the plant in her garden. As he was given the plant several years back, he had cut off a small sprout from it and had planted the sprout in his mother's tiny garden. His mother had been at the French court and had enjoyed the gardens there also. To please his French mother, he had gifted her with the little sprout, which was by now almost as big as the original plant had been. Furthermore, if the bigger plant had died, there was still hope that the slightly smaller one would thrive. He was also the only one to know, how to take care of this plant, for it was very sensitive to the cold and would die if not treated properly. He had learned his craft from his father, who had been a skilled gardener at the Castle of Brissac in the Loire Valley for a while, where he had met Louise, my husbands mother.

My husband had covered the bush every fall with hay and built a small glass house around it to give the plant light and protect it from ice and wind. He doubted that the gardener in the young lady's service would know this. The plant he would take to her palace would in all likelihood die in the next winter. So it was agreed, that my husband took the plant from his mother's little garden and brought it to the king's mistress. My old countess was happy that she could keep her bush and a pact was made, not to tell anyone about this. Time went by and fall came, followed by a harsh winter. In the next spring I found myself with child. I had told the old countess, that my child would be no problem, since my husband's mother would take care of it and I could stay in my lady's service. It was a wonderful time and we were very happy. Fate would have it, that the king's mistress invited my countess one day.

As the guests took a walk after their meal in the park at the palace, my countess was curious about the plant my husband had brought to the palace.

As Alwin had predicted, the Camellia had indeed, died. My countess pondered for a while if she should tell the young lady about the other plant. Honest and generous as the old lady was, she offered to have my husband take another sprout from the plant in her own garden. To the young lady's question how such thing was possible, since she considered herself the only one having to have had such plant, the old lady told her the whole story and what my husband had done. The young lady got furious and told the king about my husband's little deception. The king ordered my husband's arrest. Distraught and sad the old countess rushed home and told us that the king's men would take my husband to the dungeon. We were both frightened and afraid that our child would never know his or her father. We decided to flee. The countess gave us a generous amount of coins and her own carriage, which would take us to a little inn outside of the city. From there we would take the public carriages, making our way toward the sea. Gathering a few of our meager belongings we rushed to the waiting carriage, which the countess had ordered to wait outside. The horses and carriage would be back in time before the king's men would arrive. My countess would not be accused of having aided our flight. She could say in truth that she did not know where we went. Whipping the horses was something, Karl the coachman did seldom. The night of our flight Karl's whip smacked countless times on the poor animals back, driving them onward. He was ordered to be back before dawn. At such speed, we reached the little inn shortly after midnight. The next public carriage would go early in the morning. Afraid that the king's men would find us, we decided to walk to the next town. We could not wait for the carriage. With our bundles on our back we wandered all night and the next morning. As soon as we saw horsemen on the road, we hid behind trees and bushes during the day. It was far less dangerous to walk at night. So we rested during the day in the forests and fields and walked only at night. We bought our food at the little markets in the small villages, avoiding the inns. We realized, that we could save our money for inns and carriages and slept for a few hours during the day in old barns and abandoned huts. We took baths and washed our clothes in rivers and ponds. After weeks of wandering, we realized the landscape had changed ever so slightly. We saw vineyards and the people spoke a different language. My husband got very exited, for he knew this language. His mother had thought him enough to converse passably in French. We found our way to the road, which led to Calais. From there we would, with luck and the money we had saved, be able to board a ship to England. We were exhausted and happy to reach our destination soon. It had become difficult for me to walk many hours at once and we needed to rest more frequently. The child in my belly had grown and had started to kick softly at first. With each passing week my belly got bigger and the kicks stronger. To avoid any further mishaps, we made up this story to tell people why we were on the road to Calais. We would say that my husband's sister had recently moved to England and needed his help repairing her house. Also that we intended to purchase a small cottage near the sisters house. Finally we reached Calais. However, finding a ship to take us was an entirely different matter. We realized that we did not have enough money for the voyage. Living on the road for months and buying food and drink to survive, had depleted our purse quite heavily. We rented a small room in one of the little inns near the harbor and my husband worked for a few weeks at the harbor, unloading and loading cargo from the ships. It was the end of August, that Captain Crandall's grandfather Max Crandall met my husband. Alwin had carried a bulk of wool and slipped as he lugged it onto the ship. The old Captain Crandall grabbed Alwin's arm and prevented him from falling into the water. Thankful my husband told the Captain, that I, his wife would have been left destitute if he had fallen and in all likelihood being crushed between the big ship and the pier. He told Captain Crandall, that I was about to have a child in two months time. The Captain told my husband, that his wife was also with child and it would be another five months or so, before his wife would give birth. However, his child would need a wet nurse and if I was healthy and strong, I could take this position. Delighted, the Captain found out from my husband, that he was in truth a fine gardener. Alwin came home very exited and told me to pack our belongings, which was not much. Together we hurried back to the pier where the Captain waited on his ship. We were given a small cabin and began our long voyage to America. Only a few days after our arrival here on November the first in the year of our Lord seventeen hundred and thirteen, I gave birth to my oldest daughter, Sonja. She is living a few miles up the road behind the forest. Sonja grew up here in this house and got married a few months before the current Captain's father Paul. Master Paul's wife and Sonja were with child at nearly the same time. Unfortunately, the master's wife died in childbirth and my Sonja was the young Captain's wet nurse. Captain Thomas was born on the fourteenth day of October in the year of our Lord seventeen hundred and thirty five."

"Oh, how wonderful, my son was born on the same day nearly two years past," Margaret interrupted the old woman.

"You have children?" the old woman asked. This little girl was no more than a child herself. How could she have a child already?

"Did your husband come with you?"

"No, my husband passed away," Margaret lied. Quickly to avoid any further questions on the subject and remembering her mother's demise, she added, "he died of inflamed lungs this past January. The doctor was not able to save him."

"Ahww, what a tragedy. The poor man did not see his child grow up. Just like the Captain's poor mother," old Adele crooned sympathetically.

It was odd, that the young woman was not wearing black. Did she not still mourn her husband? The older woman could not help it but ask,

"Did you love your husband?"

Margaret's sharp eyes had not missed the look from the old woman at her dress. Her mind responded as quickly as before,

"Yes, I did love my husband, Adele. However, the black dresses I wore in England were left there by mistake. A servant had forgotten to load one of my trunks onto the ship," Margaret lied once again.

"Oh, this is terrible. I hope nothing important or valuable was left there."

"Not to worry, dear Adele. It was merely a small trunk with a few gowns. Whatever is of value is safely with me." Lying became easier as each minute passed. Margaret had finished her coffee and her eyes had well adjusted to the semi-darkness in the room. Getting up, the old woman cleared the table and carried the tray back to the other room. Looking around, Margaret was surprised to see a shelf with many books. Getting up, she walked over to the bookshelf and found volumes on gardening, cooking and a number of other subjects. A few books with symbols and curious drawings and numbers captured her interest. Margaret took one of the books and thumbing through it she saw circles divided into twelve parts. Next to each of the circles was a name, a birth date and some strange words, such as Margaret had never heard. Shaking her head, she placed the book back on its place. On the lowest shelf near the floor, partially hidden behind some handwritten scripts stood a round ball made of glass. Curious, Margaret picked the glass ball up and found that it was very heavy. She could not explain the use of this ball and finding nothing inside the glass while looking through it, she placed it back on its little stand of cast iron. She would have to ask the old woman, how this strange ball was used. Next to the little stand with the ball were a folded piece of silky clothes with some foreign looking symbols stitched on it. She had never seen anything like it. Way in the corner of the shelf was a small box. As Margaret reached for the box, Adele came back to the room.

"I see you found my cards," the old woman chuckled.

"Oh, I was looking at you books and saw this strange ball sitting here. How does one use it?" Margaret asked.

"If you promise not to tell anyone, especially not the Captain or his wife, I will tell you. The Misses would tell Ophelia, the cook, and she would put a voodoo spell on me," Adele said fearful.

"I promise not to tell a soul, Adele. What is so dangerous and mysterious about a simple glass ball and cards?" Margaret wondered, hiding a smile.

"Ah, this is not just an ordinary ball child. It's a ball made of crystal. I bought from a Gypsy queen many years back. The old queen taught me how to use it. She also gave me this deck of tarot cards. I use both items to tell the future," Adele spoke in a hushed voice.

Stunned, Margaret stood for a moment in silence. She had heard of fortunetellers before but never had she encountered one in person. It was getting more interesting by the minute. Curious and inquisitive by nature, Margaret silently thanked her lucky stars for this piece of good luck. She would find out, if she would be with Jack in the future. Hopefully, God would not mind. After all, knowledge of what is to come is not cheating fate. It was merely preparing for it before disaster could strike one unaware and change destiny for the worse.

"Oh, please, Adele you must tell me my fortune. I should like to know what the future holds for me," Margaret almost begged.

"Very well then, child, in order to do it correctly, I must know the year and the day of your birth. It will be helpful if you also know the exact time and place when and where you were born. From this information, I will draw a chart, which is called a horoscope."

'Ah, these must be the strange drawings with numbers and circles I saw earlier in her books,' Margaret thought.

"Can you give me the information I need?" Adele's voice was pulling Margaret out of her thoughts.

"I do have my birth papers in my rooms. The information you need is all written down there. I know my day of birth and also the place. I never saw a necessity to memorize the time of my birth," Margaret giggled.

"Bring it to me later this afternoon. I must warn you, it may not be all pleasant what I find in the charts. It will take a few days until I am done. Do you still want to know everything?"

"I want to know if I am going to stay here in this country for long or if I am going back to Europe one day to find the f…" Margaret almost said 'the father of my son'. She caught herself in time and said, "to find the family I believe still exists somewhere in Spain."

Adele knew, that the young girl had wanted to say something else and was hiding something. In time she would find out what it was. It was a good thing that she pretended to go senile. People were more apt to talk freely in her presents. She had time to listen when people thought she would not understand anymore. Many times she made people believe, that she had forgotten things that were said. Adele was eighty years old and wished to sit in her little house to draw her charts and maps. It was so much more interesting than sitting with Cynthia and her young friends, drinking tea and chattering mindlessly about others. Although she felt genuinely sorry for the young woman loosing her child, she wished to God, that Cynthia would stop blaming her husband for the girl's death. Adele knew that Cynthia had not shared her bed with the Captain since their daughter, Kristin, had died.

It had been only last night, as she had, unintentionally, become a witness to the horrendous fight between husband and wife. After their supper, Cynthia and Thomas had entered the bedroom and the door to Cynthia's day room stood slightly ajar, where Adele had been with Cynthia until the Captain's arrival. Adele had fallen asleep on the chair and was roused by voices from the next room. Since Adele was not aware, that the Captain had returned, she got curious as to whom the man's voice belonged to. Quietly she moved toward the door and saw the Captain with his arms around Cynthia's waist. The little wooden box, which he had given to her, was in her hand. As he bends to kiss her lips, Cynthia turned her head and his lips merely made contact with her cheek.

"Cynthia, please, it has been many months since I held you in my arms. Can you not understand that I am a man? I long to be with you again." He nuzzled into her hair, his breath ragged.

"I am sorry, Thomas, I do not desire to be in your arms. I cannot forget. Kristin was my only child and you know well, that the doctor said I couldn't have any more children. I feel like my own soul left with her and my body is just an empty shell. I don't know if I will ever feel anything again." She flung the wooden box on the bed and had placed her slender hands on his chest, pushing him away.

"Damn it, woman, Kristin was my daughter too. It hurts me just as much as you. However, we are still among the living. I wish I could change things but I can't bring her back. She id dead, we are not." His eyes were dark with anger and penned up frustration. Her hand lashed out and made contact with his cheek.

"Bastard," she hissed, "she would be still alive if you would not have given her this great black beast of a stallion. You knew she was used to riding on her gentle little mare. How could you think that she could handle a wild animal as *Thunder* ?"

"Because she had ridden him before, without any problems," he hollered back.

"Do I have to remind you that she had ridden him before under mine and the groom's supervision in the corral. That was the only time she had been on *Thunder* before you allowed the groom took take her in the fields behind the forest," Cynthia screamed back.

Rubbing his burning cheek, he realized that it made no sense to talk to Cynthia any further at the moment. Turning, he stomped out the room and slammed the door behind him that the entire house shook. Merely a second later, the door opened again and Cynthia hissed,

"Get a mistress if you are hot to bed someone, or give me my divorce. It will never be me again in your bed."

With that she slammed her door just as loud and furious as he had done.

Margaret still waited for an answer from Adele. Seeing the girl looking questioningly at her, Adele snapped out of her own thoughts and asked,

"Do you have any idea, if your distant relative is male or female?"

"I believe it is a man," Margaret answered a bit too quickly. Adele hid a smile. She had heard all she needed to know. The girl was obviously in love with a man other than her late husband. The charts would tell Adele more. She could hardly wait. Respectfully, Margaret curtseyed,

"I shall see you later this afternoon then, Adele. Thank you for the coffee and the story."

"Perhaps when I am done with your chart, you will tell me about your country and the people there," Adele said slyly. Nodding, Margaret turned and left the little house. Shaking her head and remembering the content of the little box, which Thomas handed his wife before they fought, Adele felt a twitch of guilt that she had opened it. It had been a magnificent necklace of rubies and sapphires. It must be worth a king's ransom.

CHAPTER 20

Love and Nature

Margaret was jubilant. Her mother had seen a fortuneteller once and everything the old crone had said, had come true, according to her mother. Margaret would know in a few days, if she would be with Jack. Enjoying the warmth of the sun, after she had been sitting for hours in Adele's house, and it was still early in the afternoon, Margaret decided to walk into the forest. She opened the small gate in the stone wall and wandering along the path for a while, she saw a clearing to her left. Making her way slightly downhill toward the clearing, she found a little lake and a breathtaking view of the forest surrounding the lake and a small waterfall in the distance to her right. The water was crystal clear and Margaret could see some big fish swimming leisurely near the shore by the reeds. Drinking in the beautiful view and the stillness around her, which was only interrupted by a few birds singing, she sat in the lush thick grass near the shore. Lifting the hem of her skirt and tucking it into her waistband, she took her shoes and stockings off and stuck her toes carefully into the water. Margaret winced, for the water was as cold as ice. Glad, that apparently nobody was near; she playfully splashed the water with her feet. Suddenly something seemed to have dropped out of the sky into the water and making a splashing sound. Little ripples where waving across the water in a circular pattern toward her feet. The little object seemed to swim very still out into the lake. Suddenly the little object went under water, to appear just about as quickly as it had disappeared. A fish had bitten into something attached to the little swimming object and it was now that Margaret saw a thin line from the object toward the shore on the other side of the reeds. Margaret could not say, if she was more distressed about having to share her beautiful peace with someone or the fact that the poor fish struggled and wiggled on the other end of the line, trying to free himself. Margaret had never seen someone fishing and it was a spectacle for her to watch the fish being drawn nearer and nearer toward the shore. Slowly, not leaving the fish out of her sight, Margaret got up and taking her stockings and shoes, she crept silently toward the other side of the reeds, where the fisherman was obviously sitting. Her hair got tangled on a low branch and pulled out the pins, which held her braids at the nape of her neck.

The man was bare-chested sitting on a blanket and wore a big straw hat, which hid his features. His back was turned toward Margaret. He did not see her. He was busy, taking the big fish from the hook and winding another big worm onto the hook, he cast his fishing rod out again. Margaret noticed, that some blue smoke escaped from under the big straw hat and the smell seemed familiar. At that moment, she stepped onto a small twig and at the cracking sound, the man spun around to see who dared to invade his leisure. Margaret stared into the Captain's face.

For a long moment he stared back at her. His heart began to beat faster and he chided himself a fool. Her skirt was still tucked into her waistband and her shapely bare legs were visible up to above her knees. He caught his breath, for the girl standing before him, was a lovely sight. Her long thick hair had come undone and was hanging down to her waist, fetchingly catching the golden sunlight. The slight soft breeze blowing an unruly strand of her hair into her face. In her blue dress with the little silver stars and with bare feet and her hair waving in the wind she looked like a little enchantress of the forest.

"Margaret, I had not seen you. You startled me." He smiled, got up from the blanket and was walking a few steps toward her. Somehow he seemed happy to see her. To her great astonishment he added softly, "I have been thinking about you just now." Margaret's heart skipped a beat as she noticed the look in his eyes and the softness of his voice.

"Oh, Thomas, I am sorry. I did not mean to startle you. I believed myself alone here by this beautiful lake. I took your advice and took a walk on the grounds to discover this wonderful place. I had no idea, that you are back from town," Margaret said blushing. She had noticed his glance at her bare legs and her hands went to her waist to pull the hem of her dress down to cover her legs again. Perhaps she had misunderstood the soft smile and the huskiness of his voice.

"No, don't," he said quickly, and placed his big warm hand over her small one, "do you have any idea, how beautiful you look at this moment, Margaret?"

She could not believe her ears. Hardly breathing, she looked up into his face. His hand had remained at her waist and slowly he was pulling her toward him. Her heart pounding, she was unable to move. Her body was pressed against his lean hard one. Since Margaret had no memory of the one night Jack had taken her, she was innocent and naïve as to what really went on between lovers. Not even in her wildest dreams would she have thought about another man but Jack touching her and making love to her and yet, somehow his touch seemed to turn her whole inside and her belly began to flutter strangely. To stunned to move, Thomas was offered no resistance as his lips came down on her soft mouth. An unfamiliar tingling sensation went through Margaret's whole body, as she felt his velvety tongue entering between her lips, caressing and seeking her sweet little tongue. She had never been kissed like this and she had to admit that it was wonderful. Her mind was numb and her young healthy body began to ache for something. She had no idea, what it was. Still kissing her, his hand went from her tiny waist to her bodice. Expertly, though with shaking fingers, he undid some of the lace, slipping his hand into her bodice and softly caressed her full firm breasts. The sensation as his thumb teased her nipple, was devastatingly delicious and her knees almost buckled. The secret place of her womanhood began to throb and ache, like something belonged there to soothe the unbearable longing away. Instinctively, Margaret pressed herself against his body, straining for something

257

unknown. Her arms went around his neck. She was kissing him back. Her little tongue darting and fencing with his. Without a word, he gently pushed Margaret down onto the soft blanket. Pulling the open dress from her shoulders, he exposed her lovely full breasts. His mouth closed over her nipple and his tongue flicked softly over the hardened little nub, driving her young body frantic with longing. He worshiped her generous breasts thusly for a long while. Slowly, not to frighten her, his hand went down to her thigh, softly caressing the silky white flesh. Her eyes were closed and she gasped as his hand went further up her thigh to the throbbing place.

"It's alright, Margaret, I will not hurt you. Let me love you a little." He whispered huskily, his breath quickening. She had never dared to hope, that this big handsome man would take any interest in her as a woman. Obviously, she had not seen the forest for the trees.

"Oh, Thomas, I never..."

"Hush, I know. You were never touched by another man as Jack," he breathed into her mouth.

His finger had found her and gently rubbing her stiffening little angry nub of womanhood, she felt a wonderful sensation building in her lower belly. Whimpering her hips were moving and seeking more from his insistent hand. Her hands tangled his dark hair as his mouth once more played havoc with her sensitive nipples. Her whole body seemed like liquid fire, her nether lips moist and opening. He knew she was almost ready to receive him. He opened the rest of the laces on her dress and with one swift motion he pulled her up to completely undress her. Quickly he slipped out of his pants and Margaret stood for a moment, staring at him. She had never seen a man nude before, except the drawings in her studies of the human anatomy at Jack's house. Though twenty-three years her senior, he was magnificent. His broad chest furred with a mat of dark hair. His arms and legs strong and well muscled. Somewhat fearful, Margaret gasped as she lowered her glance. His rampant manhood big and engorged, ready for combat. Seating himself down on the blanket again, he gently took her hand pulling her next to him to tenderly push her back onto the blanket. Seeing the fear in her face, asked softly,

"Margaret, do you remember anything at all of the night your son was conceived?" His hand was on her fluttering belly as if to quiet the tense uproar within.

"No, I do not remember much. I felt feelings that I never felt before. That much I know. Hammed had given me a powerful potion, which left me even to the next day like in a dream, which turned out to be a nightmare. I felt sore," she answered softly, relaxing under his gentle touch and soft voice.

Gazing into her beautiful eyes, his lips found her mouth once more and the hand on her belly moved lower to tease and find her aroused core. Playfully he flicked his tongue over the tip of her tongue. The sensation left her breathless for a moment. Trailing a chain of tiny kisses down from her soft throat to the onset of her firm and aching breasts, he nuzzled in between the valley of those orbs; to move his head lower to her belly. Margaret, thrashing her head back and forth and her hands clutching the soft blanket, felt him parting her nether lips with his fingers and his mouth gently closing over her angry little knob of womanhood. His flicking tongue intensifying the delicious tingling sensations in her lower region, until she felt her whole body becoming liquid and she cried out. Her hands had moved to his head and grasping his dark hair, instinctively arched her back to keep his feasting mouth and tongue continuing this wonderful torture. She did not want him to stop. Still the sensation was building and building until she felt her inside explode into convulsions of unspeakable pleasure. Tasting the salty sweet tribute of his ministrations on his tongue, Thomas swiftly moved between her soft thighs and entered her moist soft warmth with his big throbbing maleness. Upon feeling his organ within her, Margaret thought she would be torn asunder. As he began to move, the feelings of pleasure came back and as if her hips had a life of their own, she began to meat him stroke for stroke. Faster and harder he pumped into her exited flesh. She wanted more.

Her legs wrapped around him, driving him deeper yet. Each wave of pleasure washing over and through her whole body was more intense than the one before until she felt herself tense and a feeling went through her, like she had never experienced before. She heard the unearthly sound she made and at the same time she heard him cry out his pleasure. It was the last sound she heard before fainting in his arms.

Gently Thomas kissed her pale face and pulled her close to him. Holding her in his arms, he whispered,

"Oh, my little love, you don't know how long I waited. Now I can give Cynthia what she has been asking me for. She can have her divorce and you are going to be mine. You will give me the heir I need."

Margaret stirred in his arm and opening her eyes, she saw in his face what she had feared. A man had fallen in love with her. The man she had thought and considered above approach. The man was married to another woman. This man was holding her in his arms and had given her pleasure beyond belief. A pleasure she never knew existed. Merely thinking of it sent a thrill of sexual excitement through her lower body. She knew at that moment, that she wanted more of these delicious feelings. His arms were still tightly around her and her hand went to his now flaccid manhood.

Catching her hand with his, he chuckled and said:

"No, my Maggie, I need a little rest. I am not eighteen any more."

"But I thought we could do this again. It feels wonderful. I loved the feelings, when you loved me with your tongue and your man root. I never felt anything like this before. Please Thomas, I want more of you inside me again."

"I will be rested in a little while, Maggie," he reassured her, "meanwhile we can have some wine and cheese. It's in the little basket behind the bucket with the fish. Would you like to pour us some wine?"

"Yes, Thomas, I should like that. I am merely fearful of someone coming by and seeing us here," she said.

"Not to worry. It is my land. Strangers will not come through here and all my slaves are busy working. None of them are having any business here. They know, that I would punish them if they are lazy and sit by the lake. So you see, you have nothing to fear." Thomas lit his pipe.

"What if your wife would walk by and saw us?"

"My wife would in all likelihood be glad that I am not bothering her with bed sport. She has denied me for a long time and repeatedly asked me for a divorce. So put your mind at ease. She will not bother us. Furthermore, she is in her bed nursing a headache, as I told you this morning."

"I am so sorry to hear this, Thomas. I knew something was amiss as I saw you last night standing in the hall. I woke up from a loud noise. So I walked down to see who had made such noise. I saw you standing by the banister and cussing. I knew something was wrong. I did not have the courage to ask any questions in your study," Margaret confessed.

"Yes, Maggie, we fought again last night. She herself suggested that I get myself a mistress. She wants to be left alone." Thomas blew out the blue smoke.

"I do not know if I like the idea of being a mistress to anyone, Thomas. I intend to go back to Europe some day," Margaret said somewhat aggrieved.

"To find what, Maggie? A man who does not even care if you and your son are dead or alive," Thomas said angrily.

"He must acknowledge his son as his heir, Thomas. Justus is his firstborn son and no matter how many children he has after that, MY son is his first."

"You were never married to him, Margaret. You were supposed to be one of his escords. Have you forgotten that?" he said patiently.

"What has marriage to do with my child? Explain that to me."

"In any country it is only the children of a married couple who will inherit their wealth and estates. So it is by law. No court in this or any other country would help you to claim anything for your illegitimate son. It is a sad but unshakable fact, Maggie. However, if you would marry me, your son would be entitled to a part of my estate and fortune if I legally adopt him. Do not count on Jack. He does not love you, Maggie. I do..." he had said it.

He had said, what he had felt for a long time. He had fallen in love with the girl the first time he laid eyes on her.

Trying to be a good husband and the knowledge that she was to be one of Jack's escords, he had never had the courage to even admit it to himself. Now he knew, that no other man than Jack had touched her and he was not ashamed any longer. He had for a long while considered himself a romantic fool and much too old for her. For the past few months, the little voice inside had insistently told him, that she had a son by a man, who was merely three years younger than he was. She would learn to love him and forget Jack. Never did he betray his feelings with so much as a gesture or a word. He had hoped, that Cynthia would get over Kristin's death and forget about divorce. He had wanted to be a faithful husband and stand by his wife. Cynthia had not forgotten. After the night before, he had decided to grand her the divorce. However, he had not dared to hope for Margaret ever being in his arms so soon. She had been in his arms merely minutes ago. With any luck and on God's good grace, he would have his heir in a year's time. He repeated his words,

"Marry me, Margaret, and give me a son."

Not believing her own ears, Margaret asked,

"You love me, Thomas? You want to marry me?"

"For a long time, Maggie. At first I did not even want to admit it to myself. I feared being to old for you. Yes, I want to marry you as soon as I get divorced from Cynthia."

"Oh, Thomas, I never would have thought that a man could actually fall in love with me. After Jack rejected my son and me, I thought I was not good enough to be loved. I merely saw you as a good and kind friend. Just now in your arms I felt for the first time in my live, that I was desired. My mother was the only person to tell me, that she loved me," Margaret said sadly with tears welling up in her beautiful eyes. Quickly he reached out and pulled her into his arms where she snuggled close to his chest.

Kissing the top of her head, he pulled her closer and his hand went to her wonderful breasts once more. Looking up, she willingly accepted his mouth coming down on her quivering lips, while he whispered into her mouth:

"Hush, my love, I am here with you. I will never let anything or anyone hurt you again. Oh, my Maggie, I do love you so very much." There was an almost painful expression on his face, as he spoke those tender words. The age-old dance of adoration had begun anew, as he caressed and kissed her. As he gently entered her tight warmth, he wondered and hoped, that she would love him with a fraction of feelings that he had for her. He would be a happy man indeed. He would talk to his lawyer tomorrow and with any luck, he would be divorced soon. He was a patient man. Time would tell…

CHAPTER 21

Meeting the King

Meanwhile, Jack had settled on the outskirts of Madrid in Spain. The local nobility had welcomed him with open arms, for he was obviously a wealthy and honorable merchant. Several of his neighbors, wealthy, but not of nobel birth, had daughters of marriageable age and high hopes that Jack would choose a wife soon from among their girls. To his faithful servant and friend's joy, he had not touched any spirit drinks since they had left England. At balls and festivities where Jack would be invited, he drank juices and coffee. Nobody would question his choice of beverage, since he had told his new friends and neighbors that he was raised in Istanbul and his faith being Muslim, forbade consuming spirited beverages. Hammed had seen to his master getting regular exercise every morning. Swimming in his pool and briskly walking through the huge park-like garden at his new home contributed therefore to Jack's body being lean and well muscled. The little pouch, which his once flat abdomen had developed in England, disappeared and his soft and flabby arms and legs became rock-hard and strong. The high wall surrounding his entire estate guaranteed total privacy and he swam in the nude and walked through his park merely in his trousers, leaving his upper body exposed to the sunshine. The result was a wonderful even and golden-brown healthy tan, which let his white teeth appear whiter yet as soon as his handsome face turned into a smile. Hammed was happy and proud of his master. Befitting his station as chief steward, Hammed and his wife Elizabeth had moved from their temporary lodging within Jack's mansion into the newly build smaller house, which had been set back in the huge park a few hundred feet from the mansion. Hammed had hired an army of staff to clean and cook, to keep the grounds and pool as well as stables spotless. A nurse was hired to take care of his infant and his wife Elizabeth was put in charge of kitchen and laundry staff. Hammed had carefully selected servants with the best reputations to do their services thoroughly and with great efficiency. The whole household and their lives seemed to run quietly and serenely. Until one day all this would change somewhat.

Hammed came running through the great hall and looking for his master, he hurried to the study. Jack sat by his desk and made entries into his record books. Exited and without knocking, Hammed entered.

"Master Jack, I beg your pardon for disturbing you. A page just delivered this invitation to a great ball at the Conte's house. Your presence is requested and all the nobility from the city will be there. The page said that he had heard a rumor, that the king might be there as well, Oh, Master, it is so exiting. If the rumor has any truth to it, you shall meat the king. Imagine, Charles the III. He greatly favors commerce and trade Master. Perhaps it is Allah's face shining upon you with favor, that you shall meet the king and offer your services as a merchant of the finest wares. Oh, I can hardly contain myself." Hammed handed the letter of invitation to Jack. With a chuckle he opened the envelope and reading the card, let out a whistle.

"It seems, the rumor has merit. King Charles will be at the ball. Perhaps you are right, my faithful Hammed, and I can present myself to his majesty. I would be foolish to miss such great opportunity. The ball is in two weeks. Go and bring the seamstress and the cobbler to me. I must have new clothes and new boots also. There is not much time, hurry."

"Yes, Master, at once." Hammed bowed shortly and hurried out the door.

Jack leaned back in his chair and thought that this might be his chance to a great fortune and a well-respected name in the future.

Two weeks later, Jack stood in front of the mirror and he nodded satisfied. He wore a pair of black velvet trousers with thin silver threads and a burgundy jacket made from the finest brocade with heavy silver and gold embroidery. His white shirt from silk had fashionable ruffles on the wrists and front. His boots were flat and made from the softest leather coming up to his knees. He was dressed elegant and richly. His dark beard around his chin and his thin mustache above his lips were cropped short. Helping his master to hang the black velvet cape around his shoulders, he handed Jack his soft kid gloves. Not to outshine his master, the otherwise colorful dresser Hammed had toned down to simple white and silver pantaloons made from silk and a peacock blue velvet cape over a snow-white shirt. His white and silver turban was from the same material as his pantaloons. Looking at his master, Hammed flashed a big smile, showing his white teeth and said:

"I wonder how many hearts are you going to break this night, Master Jack. I should not be surprised if the some ladies should offer their daughters in marriage to you again." Laughing, Jack responded,

"You know, what I think about marriage, my dear Hammed. I like my freedom and the fact that I do not have to answer to a woman about my whereabouts."

"Yes, Master, I know it too well. However, you are not getting any younger and you need children. Who will inherit all of your wealth if you do not marry?"

"I do not need children to leave all I have to a person I love, Hammed. Should something happen to me, you are my choice. I know my father would approve." Jack had become serious.

"I could never accept such generosity, my Master. I was born to serve you. This was Allah's will. However, there is, as you know a child from your seed. If you do not marry and sire more children, then he should be your rightful heir. It was not the poor child's fault to be born out of wed luck. To this day and my everlasting shame, I deeply regret what I have done," Hammed said sadly.

"Do not fret, my faithful Hammed, as you said, if it is God's will or

Allah's as you call the everlasting creator, we will find him and his mother."

"Master, no one knows, where Miss Margaret went and the world is a big place indeed. All your letters have been returned unopened. It is as if the earth had swallowed her and your son. We can only hope that Elizabeth's younger sister Laura is still with her and will let us know what happened and why she is not responding."

"Yes, Hammed, I think we will have to wait until Elizabeth hears from Laura. This is indeed our only hope. However, we cannot let the king wait. It would make a terrible impression and he might get angry with me. Come, the carriage is waiting." Both men hurried to the waiting carriage.

Slowly, the carriage made its way toward the Conte's villa. Both men were sitting in silence, hanging on their own thoughts. Each in his own way. Hammed was the first to speak,

"Master Jack, it just occurred to me. Perhaps we should send a letter to the new owners of your old mansion in England. They might know, if Miss Margaret and your son have moved from the little cottage."

"Oh, Hammed, I can't write to these people. I do not even know them well enough. What should they think about me, if I am not even know the whereabouts of my child and its mother," Jack worried.

"You are not in England any longer and should not worry what people think about you. Furthermore, we could write them, that we have not heard anything from your son. Tell them, that the letters and money you send for your son came back and you are worried. This is in fact the truth now. Is it not?" Hammed probed.

"Hammed, sometimes you are just like an old meddling woman. Of course I am worried. I am not as cold and heartless as I seemed to be not to many months ago. I have done a lot of thinking and I wish to God, I could change a few things." Jack took a heavy sigh.

"Does that mean you wish your child by your side, Master?"

"It means I want to know where they are, so my son gets enough to eat and a roof over his head. It does not mean anything else you old schemer,"

Jack laughed. He knew, where this conversation was leading, if he let Hammed have his way. He could not blame his faithful friend and servant. He wanted his Master happy.

"Ah, I can see the lights shining from the villa, Master. We are almost there. Oh, look all the carriages," Hammed cried excitedly. Bending forward to see out the window, Jack whistled softly through his teeth.

"The nobility from all of Spain must be here tonight. I have a funny feeling, Hammed. Perhaps it would have been better to respectfully decline the invitation."

"Oh, Master, are you mad? I have a feeling it will be an important night for you. Since when are you shy of people? You are about to meet the king. The KING Master," Hammed almost shouted.

"Calm yourself, Hammed. People can hear you. We must make a graceful and dignified entrance. You are starting to sound like your sweet little wife," Jack chuckled.

"Forgive me, Master, I am exited. In all the years in England, hardly anyone of the nobles so much as acknowledged or invited you, save for a few small parties. Here you are respected and welcomed," Hammed pouted.

"You forget, my good Hammed, that the enterprise I had undertaken, was somewhat of a daring and let us say, delicate nature and most definitely not to the fine lady's taste. Many of them were mad at me. After meeting my girls, a few of the husbands went home and told their powdered and perfumed wives to take a bath," Jack laughed merrily. Hammed had to laugh also that his sides ached.

The carriage had made its way to the big entrance door and serious with great ceremony, Hammed bowing low, helped his master out. From under his dark lashes he noticed several ladies casting Jack longing glances. He was hard pressed not to show his mirth. Walking closely behind Jack up the wide stairs to the villa entrance he also noticed some dark looks toward his master from some of the ladies husband's. Entering the great hall, the major-domo ceremoniously announced Jack, after Jack had whispered something in his ear.

"Don Giaccomo Emanuel Viego and his friend Hammed ben Hassan."

Several elegantly dressed people were standing in little groups conversing. At Jack's and Hammed's entrance they grew silent. A short heavyset man with eyes as black as coal and dark beard came toward Jack, both of his pudgy jeweled hands outstretched.

"Don Viego, how wonderful that you could join us this evening," The fat little man smiled, shaking Jack's hand.

"I am honored by your invitation, Conte de Mondego. Thank you for including me in your festivities," Jack bowed.

"Come Don Viego, let me introduce you to some of my friends. A few of them are anxious to meet you. I had told them about the fine quality of your wares. I am the envy of many, who saw the jewels I purchased from you and gifted my daughter with on her birthday," the Conte chattered. He had taken Jacks arm and led him toward the back of the hall, where a group of gentlemen stood and laughed about a ribald jest one of them had just told.

Conte de Mondego introduced Jack to several of the older gentlemen and as if he had always been in their midst, Jack found himself laughing and conversing with ease and great charm. Suddenly there was a murmur going through the hall and a shout from the door rang through the hall.

"The king is arriving." A few moments later the monarch came walking through the wide opened double door, followed by his entourage. After being greeted with great ceremony by Conte de Mondego, he was led through the hall up to a small dais, where he seated himself on a small throne, which had been especially brought into the great hall for this special occasion. The present ladies and gentlemen had curtseyed and bowed deep before their ruler. At a wave of his hand, the musicians started playing and the people went slowly back to conversations and refreshments. Jack watched from some distance, while still standing among the group of several gentlemen, that the king seemed to watch a few of his subjects at first, before he told his own servants to have them brought before him and have them introduced to him.

Conte de Mondego stood next to the king and seemed to introduce some of his close friends to the monarch. Both men were looking in the direction where Jack and the other gentlemen stood. The Conte smiled and said something to the king. A servant came walking toward Jack's group and bowing before him, he told Jack to follow him. The king wishes to see him. Jack's heart leaped to his throat. With his faithful Hammed in his wake, Jack followed the servant toward the king's throne. Bowing deeply, Jack said, "Your highness wishes to see me."

Coming to his side, the Conte said,

"May I present Don Giaccomo Viego, your majesty."

"Conte de Mondego tells me you are a merchant from England. Are you English by birth?" the king asked suspiciously. Perhaps this young fop had changed his name to a more Spanish sounding version. All of Spain knew, how Charles felt about the English.

"Oh no, your gracious majesty, I was born here in Spain and raised in Istanbul. After my parents and brothers perished in the great earthquake while on a business venture in Lisbon, I moved to my uncle's house in Manchester. Since he did not have any other family, I became his heir," Jack explained, his knees slightly shaking.

"Ah I see, tell us, Don Viego, for we are curious. What brought you back to Spain?"

"The climate brought me back to my homeland your majesty. England is cold and foggy. I merely remained there until my uncles estate was settled after he had passed away," Jack lied smoothly. Hammed held his breath.

"I am glad to hear that you have decided to come back, Don Viego. Welcome back to Spain," the king said somewhat relieved.

"Thank you, your majesty," Jack bowed again. It seemed he was dismissed. Jack was about to turn, as the King spoke again:

"Wait, Don Viego, we have not given you permission to leave."

"I humbly beg your pardon, gracious majesty. I was under the impression of being dismissed." Jack quickly bowed again.

"I have one more question Don Viego. Are you married?"

"No, your majesty, I am not married." Jack answered with a sinking feeling in his stomach.

"Is there a reason for a young healthy fellow as you seem to be, not to be married to a fine young lady?" the stern voice of the monarch queried.

"No reason in particular, your majesty. I am a merchant and many times I travel for several months out of the year. I simply did not have the time to choose a bride," Jack answered in half-truth. Hammed shifted nervously from one foot to the other.

"Very well then, my young friend, we wish you to consider that our beloved Spain needs fine sons and daughters. You may go." The king had said it with a smile. However, it seemed to Jack, that the king had given him somehow an ultimatum. Bowing once more, Jack turned and made his way to the farthest corner to calm his breathing. This was really all he needed. This pompous ass of a king telling him to sire sons for his damn navy and daughters to breed more sons for the same purpose. This was not boding well. Hammed had followed Jack to the little alcove and saw the dark look on Jack's face.

"Master, be careful, the king is still watching," he cautioned in a low voice.

"I don't care if God is watching me at this moment, Hammed. You heard what he said," Jack whispered. Pretending to casually talk to his servant he smiled as Hammed handed him a glass of water from a nearby little table.

"I believe it would be best to make up an excuse to go home, Hammed. I do not wish to remain here any longer," Jack suggested.

"We cannot leave and offend the king, my Master. It would be a terrible rudeness and you might find yourself out of favor with the friendly little Conte de Mondego as well."

Jack knew that also and they decided to remain the entire evening, staying out of the king's sight as best as they could. Perhaps the monarch would forget and not even give the simple merchant another thought. It was not to be so.

The king was wary of the English. This young man had obviously lived in England for some time. Where would his loyalty lie? The king was not a man to leave anything to chance. If Don Viego would be bound by marriage to a young Spanish woman, he was less likely to be troublesome in the future. Waving Conte de Mondego closer, the king whispered something in his ear. Blanching, the Conte bowed and seemed distressed. Jack and Hammed had watched the little scene with great interest. What could the king have said to the poor Conte, that the fat little man had turned several shades of gray? They were about to find out the next day.

Jack had arisen early to enjoy his swim and walk in his park together with Hammed. Both men walked at a quick pace toward the house, as Elizabeth came running down the steps.

"Master Jack, there is a man here to see you. He said it is of great importance. He is waiting for you in the hall." The young woman pointed with her hand to the inside of the house.

"Does this man have a name, Elizabeth?" Jack asked somewhat annoyed that the early visitor had interrupted his daily routine.

"He said his name is Conte Pedro Alfonso Mondego," Elizabeth said quickly. She had sensed Jack's mood and was not about to anger him any further. Both men looked at each other in surprise. What would bring the Conte out at this early hour? Jack wrinkled his brow.

"Tell Conte de Mondego, I should join him presently. Hammed, my robe." Hammed had grabbed the silk robe from the garden chair and helped his Master to slip it on. Tying the sash while hurrying to his hall, Jack saw the little fat man pacing and wiping his sweaty hands on his trousers. Hammed had followed Jack and sent his master a meaningful look. Both men knew that Conte de Mondego was a man with the patience of a Saint. Something awful must have happened to agitate him thusly. At the sight of Jack and Hammed, the little man fumbled nervously with his pocket from his jacket, withdrawing a little cloth and wiping his forehead.

"Conte de Mondego, you honor my house," Jack said in greeting.

"Ah, Don Viego, the honor is all mine. Please may we talk in private?" The Conte eyed Hammed suspiciously. Elizabeth still stood at the entrance to the kitchen and sent her Husband Hammed a curious glance.

"My dear Conte, Hammed is my most trusted friend and servant. He is privy to all my affairs. Please feel free to talk in his presence. Let us go to my study. If you would follow me please." Jack motioned elegantly to the door to his study. He let the Conte enter and calling through the hall to Elizabeth, who had opened the door to the kitchen:

"Elizabeth, bring refreshments to my study."

"At once, Master," Elizabeth complied.

The Conte stood in the study and was kneading the little cloth in his hands.

"Please, Conte de Mondego let us sit and talk." Jack invited the Conte to a group of comfortable big chairs standing around a small table, which was made from the finest mahogany wood and its legs were beautifully carved and covered with gold leaves, giving the impression of climbing vines. The top of the little table was covered with a heavy sheet of glass, where Elizabeth placed a tray with freshly squeezed orange juice and some heavy gold painted glasses. Patiently waiting for the maid to fill the glasses and finally closing the heavy carved door behind her, the Conte took sip from his glass. He sighed a deep breath and began to speak.

"Don Viego, let me tender my apologies for disturbing you at this early hour. However, the reason I am here is not voluntary. I am here at the king's request." He wiped his forehead again and Jack held his breath. Hammed standing next to the Conte's chair and out of his line of sight lifted and wrinkled his brow meaningful and shrugged his shoulder. The glass in the Conte's hand shook ever so slightly.

"The king's request?" Jack was incredulous. He had yet to hear what the true reason for the little man's visit was.

"Let me come to the point, Don Viego. I am here to offer you my daughter's hand in marriage." Jack almost dropped his glass. Recovering from his shock, Jack placed the glass on the table with a thud and jumped up from his chair.

"Surely you must be jesting, Conte de Mondego. How can I marry you daughter? I am not nobility. I am a simple merchant. Furthermore I have no intention of getting married at this point. As much as I am honored by your offer, I respectfully decline," he almost shouted.

"My dear Don Viego, I had told you that the king requested it. The whole idea is not of my making," admonished the Conte.

"Oh, now I see,." Jack slapped his hand on his forehead, "it was what the King told you last night. Is it not? Why? Why would he let you sacrifice your noble daughter?" Jack grumbled low.

"I do not question his majesty's reasons, Don Viego. I am his most humble and faithful servant and loyal to the crown of Spain," the Conte said proudly.

"I cannot make any sense of it, Conte de Mondego. Have I done something to offend his majesty? Why would he force me into marriage with your daughter?" Jack shook his head in disbelieve.

"Perhaps this will explain more."

The Conte handed Jack a sealed letter, which he pulled out of his pocket. Snatching the letter from the Conte's hand, Jack noticed the seal of the crown. With shaking hands, he broke the seal and began to read. Slowly he sank back onto the chair and his eyes stared disbelieving at Hammed. Wordlessly he handed the letter to Hammed and the big dark man read aloud,

Don Viego

We are pleased to welcome you back to Spain. It has come to our attention that your merchandise is of the finest quality. Therefore we shall order a number of items, which are listed below. We also wish to honor a fine and honest merchant as you undoubtedly are, by offering you the hand of Contessa Sofia Anna Isabella de Mondego, daughter to my dear friend and loyal subject Conte Pedro Alfonso de Mendego. At the advice of our royal council however, that a nobel lady could hardly enter into marriage with an untitled Gentleman, we deemed it appropriate to grand you the title Baron.

Henceforth you shall be known as and addressed with
Baron Giaccomo Emanuel de Viego.

We wish you happiness and a long prosperous life, Baron de Viego.

Signed King Charles III

A long list of items was added to the letter. Hammed's eyes flew over the requested merchandise and he sharply whistled through his teeth. Jack's coffers would increase tremendously at the sale of all sorts of fabrics, jewelry and various other items such as wood and furniture, oil and lamps.

At hearing the content of the letter, the Conte seemed less agitated. He had feared to give his beautiful daughter to a mere merchant and the other nobility would laugh at his expense. At this turn of events, his sweet Sofia would be a Baroness. It was not all that bad after all. The Conte liked Jack and he knew the young man was very wealthy and his daughter would lack for nothing.

"May I be the first to offer my congratulations on your new title Baron de Viego. I am happy for you," the Conte broke the silence.

"Thank you, Conte de Mondego, it seems I woke up this morning to be granted a title a wife and a great amount of gold. But at what price?" Jack said bitter. "It also seems, that I have not much of a choice."

"Do not be angry, my dear Baron de Viego. My daughter is beautiful and gentle. I know you have not seen her. She is presently visiting in the country with her aunt. That is the reason I did not have the pleasure to introduce her to you last night. Here, see for yourself." The Conte handed Jack a tiny miniature from his waistcoat pocket. Almost reluctantly, the young newly titled Baron de Viego grabbed the miniature and his eyes beheld the most beautiful young woman he had ever seen. Her wavy waist-long hair was raven blue-black and shone like polished ebony. Her large eyes of an unusual violet bluish color looked intelligent and at the same time sparkled mischievously at the beholder. The sparkle was aided by a mysterious little smile, which her full rosebud lips had curled into. Her nose was slim and straight. She had the look of a devilish charming little angel. Jack could not help himself as smile back at the little picture. The Conte as well as Hammed had noticed. Hammed had moved to behind his master's chair and took a look at the miniature in Jack's hand.

"You are correct, my dear Conte, you daughter is breathtakingly beautiful," Jack admitted, "how old is she?," he asked.

"Sofia celebrated her twenty first birthday on the second day of this April past," Conte Mondego answered.

"Is it not unusual that a girl of her age is not married?" Jack asked.

"She was betrothed when she was sixteen. The man she was to wed, died suddenly two weeks before the wedding. They knew each other from childhood and Sofia was heartbroken for a long time. Understand please, that Sofia is my only child. I did not have the heart to force her into another relationship. When my wife died several days after Sofia's birth of a high fever, I promised on her deathbed that Sofia would marry only if she would love the man. My wife and I had not seen each other before the wedding day and she had been very frightened. In time she learned to love me. Nevertheless, she did not want our precious daughter to have to go through the same experience. For the past six years I have indulged Sofia and I fear I spoiled her terribly. However she is a good chatelaine and knows all housewifely arts and duties. As gentle as she is at other times, she can be headstrong at times and has a temper. But she has not fallen in love since poor Leandro died."

"Now you want to force her into marriage with me on the king's orders?" Jack asked. He somehow felt sorry for the poor girl, who obviously had no idea of her intended fate.

"That is why I must ask you to court my daughter, Baron de Viego. I do not wish this any more than you do. However, the king has been known to deal harshly with his disobedient subjects. Properties have been confiscated and many have been impoverished. I do not have any desire to be one of them. If you agree to marry my daughter however, I will personally inform his majesty, that there will be a wedding in the future. That should placate the king for a time and you will have some time to get to know my daughter and vice versa. I shall pray that she is going to love you. My dear Baron, I do have no quarrel with you and I like you. From what I can see, my daughter would live in comfort and in elegant surroundings. Please think on it. To refuse the king would mean you have to flee this country. I would be at his majesty's mercy and my daughter as well. There is no other way."

The little Conte sat back in his chair and took a sip from his cool sweet orange juice. Jack thought for a moment. The crown of England had dealt with disloyal people as harshly as the king of Spain. There was not much difference in that respect. He did not want to leave Spain again. The Conte was correct. There was no other way. Unless…

"Very well my dear, Conte de Mondego, I agree to your terms. However, if your daughter should not learn to love me and should in fact dislike me within the next six months, we will have to find a different way out of this ridiculous situation," Jack said to Hammed's amazement. He knew instantly, that Jack had another plan, which he did not share with the Conte. The little man smiled broadly and relieved he stood up and stretched his hand out to shake Jack's.

"You will not regret your decision, my dear young friend. Please be gentle with my daughter. She is all I have." Jack had risen from his chair and shaking the Conte's hand, he asked,

"When is your daughter expected back from her visit with her aunt? I should like to call on you as soon as she is back in town."

"I expect her back by the end of this week. I shall send a messenger to you, to let you know. I will introduce you as the son of a dear old friend of mine. The rest I shall leave up to you Baron de Viego," the Conte smiled.

Jack could not help it; 'Baron de Viego' had a nice ring to it. He smiled back.

Hammed on the other hand had yet to find out, what Jack's plan was. He didn't buy it for a minute, that his dear master Jack was suddenly so agreeable to matrimony. He couldn't wait for the Conte to get into his carriage and drive away. Jack stood by the entrance door and turning he gave Hammed a boyish grin. 'Allah have mercy' Hammed thought.

CHAPTER 22

Seeing the Future

Margaret sat in her room on the big couch. She had tried to read. The book however was lying in her lap and her eyes stared dreamily into the distance. She had walked the distance from the lake to the house, after bringing some semblance of order back to her dress. After being in Thomas' arms for hours, the air had gone chilly. The sun had hidden behind some clouds and it had threatened to rain. If the weather would hold however, Thomas had promised her to meet her by the small hunting lodge on the other side of the lake. He explained to her, that she would have to follow the little path around the lake to a group of huge pine trees next to the waterfall. The little path would swing up to the right and after passing an old mill; she would see the lodge at the distance. Both agreed, that Cynthia was not to be made aware of their affair for the time being. In the presents of his wife and servants she would have to pretend to be merely his friend and companion to Cynthia. As soon as his divorce would be granted, Margaret would become his wife. Thinking about his kisses, Margaret felt a thrill of pleasure through her body. She wished, he would be divorced soon. It seemed that her life had taken a turn for the better. She was not certain, if she would love Thomas as much as she had loved Jack. She was certain however; that the big captain would make her happy and her son would be safe and his heir some day. After all, he was much older and would not live forever. Her revenge would have to wait a little while longer. In fact, time was on her side and while safe and secure, she could strike when Jack would expect it least. Many years from now. She would be a wealthy woman.

Margaret looked toward the window and heavy rain was pouring down. It was getting dark and she lost hope to be in Thomas' arms tonight. With a heavy sigh she placed the book on the little table and leaning her forehead against the window, she remembered her promise to Adele. Quickly she rummaged through her little desk and finding the papers she had been looking for, Margaret grabbed her cape. She flung the cape over her shoulders and hurried down to the back entrance of the house. She pulled the hood from the cape over her head and ran along the path toward Adele's little house. Margaret knocked on the door and moments later Adele opened.

"Ah there you are, child. I thought you had forgotten to bring me your information. Come, sit, but take that wet cape off first. Pull the chair to the fireplace and hang the cape over it so it may dry."

After hanging her cape on the chair, Margaret sat down on the chair by the table. She handed Adele her papers and the old woman took paper and quill to copy the information she needed. The Paper from the church, which had recorded Margaret's birth, was laying on the table and the old woman scribbled intensely. Dipping the quill into the little inkpot, she somehow misjudged her aim and the inkpot tipped over, spilling black ink partially over Margaret's birth records. Adele cried out:

"Oh no, this is terrible. Half of your name is blocked out by the black ink." Quickly she dabbed the ink from the paper with a large piece of linen, which she seemed to have magically pulled from her pocket.

"Oh, do not fret, Adele. I did not need these papers in all my life except for now. My name is something I remember well," Margaret laughed. Soon, she hoped, her name would be different anyway. She would be Misses Crandall. She had to find out, if it would take long until her wedding day. If the old woman could see things from the future, perhaps she would see how long she would have to wait. It was worth a try.

"Can you not tell me anything from my future with this crystal ball or perhaps with your magical cards, Adele? Will I ever get married…again?" she quickly added. Adele finished her notes and said,

"I could try it. Let us see, if my crystal ball will reveal something." Adele went to fetch the crystal ball from its shelve and placed it on the table. She took three candles and placed then strategically around the Crystal ball and dimmed the lights on the oil lamps in the room. She lit the candles and sat back on her chair. Folding her hands, she mumbled a prayer and placing her hands on both sides of the crystal ball, gazed for a few minutes. Margaret watched the old woman in fascination. She hardly dared to breathe. Then suddenly the crystal ball seemed to get foggy. However, Margaret could not see anything specific. Adele's eyes were narrowing and she began to speak,

"The spirits show me a ship and you and a male child are traveling on it to a distant land. I see you wearing a beautiful dark gown. The child is about four years of age. The ship is hiding in the fog. It has vanished from my sight. Ah, wait, I see you standing on a cliff by the ocean. The child is holding your hand. The child is speaking to you. You look sad. I see a man in the distance. He is watching you and the child. The man is on a horse. He is holding a little girl on his lap. The girl is perhaps one year old. The man is riding off. The vision is gone."

Adele leaned back in her chair. She seemed exhausted and closed her eyes for a few moments. Margaret could not make any sense of it. Her mind was working feverish. That the child on her hand had been her son was clear. Justus would be four years old in two years and five months. Suddenly it dawned on Margaret. Thomas would take her and Justus on his ship to accompany him on his voyage. That must be the reason; Adele had seen her on a ship. Of course, it must be Thomas' ship. The man on the horse is Thomas with their daughter in his arms. Adele had said, that the little girl would be about one year old. It would mean that she would bear Thomas a daughter in about one year's time. Oh, he would be so happy. It was wonderful to know, what the future would be. Margaret smiled and decided to keep this to herself for the time being.

"Well, child, was this vision helpful to you?" Adele's voice fell into her thoughts. Margaret shook her head,

"Not very much, Adele. However, I do plan to travel back to Europe some day. Perhaps your vision confirmed my plans. For the man on the horse…I can only guess that it was a stranger with his child. He might have been taking a leisurely ride with his daughter and saw me by accident."

"Yes, perhaps it is so. Oh listen, I believe the rain has stopped."

Adele got up from her chair and parting the heavy curtains on the window, she nodded. She was glad for it. The rain was good for the flowers, but not for her old bones. The moisture made her knees and hands ache. Margaret had moved behind Adele and saw the moon rising from behind the mountain in the distance. Taking her cape from the chair by the fireplace, she swung it over her shoulders and facing Adele, she yawned delicately.

"It is getting late, Adele. I best go to my rooms. Thank you for your time. I wish you a good night." She grabbed her papers from the table and made for the door.

"Good night, child. Come back in a few days. Your horoscope should be finished by then," Adele called after her.

Margaret stood for a moment outside Adele's door and tried to decide, what she should do. Should she walk to the little hunting lodge? If Thomas were not there, she would make the walk for naught. She turned and saw, that the light in Thomas' study had saved her a long moonlight walk through the woods. Sidestepping little puddles, she hurried back to the big house. Quickly she ran up to her rooms and taking off her cape, she flung it on the chair. Patty entered from the bedchamber with a pile of clothes in her arms. Slightly startled, she looked at Margaret:

"Miss Margaret, I didn't hear you come in. I was about to take your clothes to the laundry. The captain has been asking for you. He said you should have dinner with him. The Misses is still in her rooms and he doesn't want to eat alone. Dinner should be ready in a few minutes. Do you need anything?"

"No, Patty, I can manage on my own. Go take care of the laundry. I will be down in a few moments. Tell the captain, that I am back from my visit with Misses Kaufmann and will join him for dinner," Margaret ordered.

"Yes, Miss."

Patty bobbed a quick curtsy and flew out the door with the laundry under her arm. Quickly, Margaret reached for her brush and began to untangle her windblown hair with it. Not bothering with braiding it, she simply bound it with a small ribbon at the nape of her neck. Checking her appearance once more in the mirror, she dabbed her lovely smelling perfume behind her ears and in between the valley of her breasts. It was her favorite fragrance, which she had made up while she still lived in England. She had called it 'Midnight starburst'. Since she detested the heavy musky scents of some perfumes, she had experimented with a different mixture of oils and dried flowers and seeds. The result had been a deliciously fresh fragrance, which smelled like a garden of spring flowers after a night of gentle rain.

Satisfied sniffing, she wrinkled her little nose appreciatively with a smile and left the room to go downstairs.

Ophelia was setting the table in the dining room and the captain stood by the little table near the wall to pour himself a glass of wine. Margaret watched his movements for a few moments and a thrill of excitement went through her, as she saw his elegant strong hands. These hands had caressed and loved her body tenderly and inflamed her passion only a few hours ago. She felt her knees tremble at the memory of it and the secret place between her thighs throbbed longingly. As if he had sensed her presence, Thomas turned and gave her a warning look. Ophelia was still in the room and bustled with the dishes. Aloud he greeted her:

"Ah, Margaret, I am glad you could join me for dinner. My wife is unfortunately unable to join us. Please, sit down. Would you like a glass of wine?"

She felt a little stab of jealousy as he mentioned his wife. She knew however, that it was said for Ophelia's benefit and smiling she answered,

"Yes, please, Thomas, I should like that. I hoped I am not late for dinner. I did have a nice visit with Misses Kaufmann this afternoon and time passed quickly." She took the glass from his hand and slightly brushed his finger as she looked into his eyes.

"I trust you had an enjoyable afternoon then?" He smiled meaningful.

"Oh, indeed, my afternoon was lovely and I hope to have many such pleasant afternoons in the future," she said blushingly. Ophelia finished setting the table and taking her big empty tray, she hurried back to the kitchen, closing the door behind her. For a moment, Thomas looked at Margaret and suddenly placed his glass back onto the little table, he pulled her close and his lips came crushing down on her sweet mouth. Fearing that Ophelia would return at any second, he released her just as suddenly and motioned with his head to the big table to sit down. Margaret, with trembling knees and pounding heart, took her place at the table and the door opened again. Ophelia rolled a serving cart into the room and placed the delicious smelling food on the table. Suspiciously Margaret ogled a large tray with a fish laying on it. Thomas had followed Margaret's glance with his eyes and said smiling mischievously:

"I went fishing today and got myself a fine catch as you can see. This is a large mouth bass, Margaret. Before I went fishing, I shot two rabbits and this is a delicious rabbit stew as only our dear Ophelia can make it. Am I right, Ophelia?"

He reached over the table and padded Ophelia's hand. Ophelia smiled proudly and answered,

"And I ain't tellin' anybody my secrets. There ain't a better cook around for miles. So you better start eatin' before it gets cold."

Ophelia bobbed a short curtsy and left the dining room. Margaret had not eaten anything since morning and she was ravenous. Piling her plate high with mashed potatoes and rabbit stew, she added little carrots glazed with honey and little green peas seasoned with tarragon and melted butter. Thomas had been correct. It was delicious. Ophelia was an excellent cook. Margaret had eaten with gusto and amused, Thomas watched her as she mopped her little mouth with the fine linen napkin. Seeing his look, Margaret blushed and quickly grabbed her glass with wine.

"I like a woman who can enjoy her food. Women picking around on their plate go on my nerves," Thomas chuckled. Margaret kept sipping her wine smiling at him suddenly shy of him and said nothing.

"Ah, before I forget, Margaret, I will be in town for a few days to take care of some business. I also want to talk to my lawyer to start the divorce. I should be back by the end of next week." Thomas lit his pipe.

"Oh, I will not be able to see you until next week?" Margaret asked pouting.

"Yes, Margaret. The reason I will stay near the town is a few friends, which I expect back from the Orient any day. We agreed to meet at the little inn just outside of the town on the road to Washington. This is a long way and I do not want to make this trip every day until my friends arrive. If I go later, I might miss them if they have arrived already," he explained.

"Oh, please, Thomas take me with you," Margaret said quickly. At his surprised expression she explained,

"I too have some business to take care off. Jack gifted me with a few jewelry items, which I may not need any time soon. I wish to place them in the vault of the bank. I do not want to loose them. They are worth a lot of money. I also want to go and sell some of it and deposit the money for saving. Perhaps you could help me with that. You see, I am terribly ignorant when it comes to such dealings. However, I do know from Hammed, that money is best saved in a bank, for it draws interest, as he called it." she smiled winningly. Thoughtfully he scratched his chin for a moment and said,

"Very well then. I will help you. Since there is not much suspicious about you opening a bank account, you may come along. Perhaps you could have some new gowns made as well. This would be a good excuse for you to stay in town. I know the owner of the little shop, which sells the most wonderful fabrics. I know it, because I supply him with these fabrics," he chuckled.

"Oh, how wonderful," Margaret clapped her hands excitedly, "I will tell Patty to pack my small trunk. But, Thomas, who will watch your wife. She will ask, why I am not with her in the next few days. Then there is my son. He will be terrified if I am gone."

"From what I understand, the little man is keeping himself busy, chasing the ducks, playing with the kittens and puppies and will have no time to miss you for a few days," Thomas laughed, "as for Cynthia, I will tell Joseph, that Patty is to keep an eye on her. That way, she will not insist to come with you."

It had not even occurred to Margaret, that she had not seen her son the whole day. Suddenly she felt a pang of guilt. She would bring him something lovely from her trip to town. She realized, that it had some good sides to have a nurse watch her son. She decided to concentrate on her relationship with Thomas for now and leave her little son in the trusted care of Natty. She would make it all up to Justus, as soon as she was safely married and they were a normal family. Thomas seemed to sniff something and asked,

"Margaret, I love the fragrance of your perfume. Did you buy this in England?"

"No, Thomas, I did not buy my perfume. It is my own creation. I used to make and sell perfumes and soaps in England to support myself. The fire had destroyed all my essences and oils. I was merely able to save my little book with the recipes and the small bottle of my own perfume. I wish, I could make more of it. However, I would need the oils and essences to do so. There are certain dried flowers also, which I used. I saw some of them in the garden. Perhaps I am able to purchase some oils and essences in town."

Margaret shrugged her shoulders.

"There will be no need to buy anything, Margaret. Have you forgotten, that I am a sea captain trading in just such tings? My warehouse is full of those things and is at your disposal. Take whatever you need and make your perfumes and soaps. I can see the light in your eyes shining when you speak of your products. You must be very good at it, from what I can smell."

Thomas smiled and sniffed again appreciatively.

"Oh, Thomas, that is wonderful. I will need a room where I have water and a small stove to cook my soaps however. I do not think that

Ophelia would be to pleased if her food started smelling like wildflowers. She may not want to share her kitchen with me and my pots," she said twinkling.

"There is a little shed next to the stables. I will have it cleaned for you and you will have your little stove there also. As for the water, the old well is next to it. We don't use it, having running water from the pipes. It will serve your purpose though. If you need water, have the stable boys bring you a few buckets. That should solve this little problem," he suggested.

"Thank you, Thomas, I shall make a list of what I need tonight. I will need some pots and a few other things, which we might be able to get from the copper smith in town."

Dreamily she turned the stem of the glass in her hand with her fingers. Margaret could hardly believe her good fortune. Indeed, she had completely forgotten, that it had been Thomas, supplying Jack's warehouses. Now it would be even better for the simple fact that she did not have to pay for the otherwise expensive oils and essences. Though she had been able to buy them from Hammed at a great discount, she was jubilant. She would now get it for free and could make her wonderful perfumes and soaps. She had already taken a fancy to some of the exotic smelling fragrances in the bath chamber. She would make better ones yet.

Drinking the last of her wine, Margaret stood up,

"I will instruct Patty, what to pack, Thomas. At what time are we departing?"

"I will ride on horseback very early, Margaret. I will instruct Joseph to have the carriage waiting for you, as soon as you are ready. You may take your time. Meet me at the 'Longneck Swan'. I should be there after I talk to my lawyer by the noon hour."

As much as he had doubted the idea of taking Margaret was a good one, he suddenly looked forward to it. They would be alone for a few days, away from the prying eyes of his servants and Cynthia.

Not feeling any remorse, he grabbed her hand and placed a burning kiss on her palm. Margaret's heart skipped a beat and her face got flushed with the heat from her quickening pulse. Reluctantly she withdrew her hand from his soft lips and fled the room. She heard his soft chuckle behind her. Taking two steps at the time, Margaret ran up to her room and called for Patty. The girl was obviously not back from the laundry room yet and Margaret sat on the chair to catch her breath. She would be in his arms for the next few days.

'Oh, my dear Lord, I think I am falling in love. I can hardly wait to feel his hands and mouth on me again. I never thought that lovemaking could be this wonderful. I believe we will be very happy together,' Margaret thought. The door opened and Patty returned. The girl told Margaret, that her grandfather had ordered her to keep an eye on the Misses. Miss Margaret had business in town for a few days to have some gowns made. Since there would be several fittings, it was best to stay near the seamstress. Margaret confirmed Patty's information and asked the girl to tell Misses Kaufmann, that she would be back soon. She would talk to Misses Kaufmann as soon as she got back from town. Patty promised to give the old woman the message and started packing Margaret's small trunk. She could not figure out, how her mistress would manage without her. However it was not her business and only shaking her head, she kept her mouth shut and folded several dresses into the trunk. Her work done, she bid Margaret a good night and sought her own bed. Margaret was too exited to sleep and taking her book, she read for several hours. Finally shortly after midnight, she felt her eyes getting heavy and she closed her book. She cleansed her teeth and quickly washed her face and neck using the little china bowl in her bedchamber, she slipped into her night trail and went to bed. She would have to tell her son in the morning, that mama would be gone for a few days and would bring a new toy for him.

She hoped that Justus would not fuss and cry when she left. The promise of a new toy should placate the child and Margaret could concentrate on her business and Thomas. It had not only been a ruse to per sway Thomas to take her along, as she told him she wanted to open up a bank account. She fully intended to use her lessons from Hammed to her advantage. He had said that one little beetle made a tiny speck of dung. However a thousand little beetles made a big pile of dung. She had laughed at his comparison, but she had understood quickly what it

287

meant. One coin in the bank would give a hardly noticeable percentage of interest. Many coins would draw interest on the interest. She had her mind made up to become wealthy and independent. Her goal had not changed in light of her relationship with Thomas. She would never be dependant on a man alone. Even if she would stay for many more years in this country as she had planned, she would keep adding to her account whatever she could. She knew from an early start, that life can be fickle and fate can deal hard blows. If she had enough money, she would be able to deal with life's rough turns in a better way. Her perfumes would help her account to grow at a fast rate. She knew that it would take only a very little time until the local wealthy ladies would know her products. Yes, she would be a wealthy woman in her own right and through her own business. She would also be a respected wife and mother to Justus and the children she would bear Thomas. Oh, life was wonderful and as Hammed had said many times, Allah's face was shining with great favor upon her humble self. Hugging her arms around her, Margaret turned on her side and snuggling deep into her soft bed, she closed her eyes and with a smile on her lips she fell asleep.

CHAPTER 23

Love at First Sight

"Master, what is on your mind? I have seen this certain look before and as far as I remember, it meant trouble for someone other than you," the big servant asked suspiciously, following Jack back to his study.

"If the king thinks, he can lure me into a marriage with a damn title and a generous order, which I neither want nor need at this point, he is sadly mistaken. I felt pretty good about myself without being called 'Baron'," Jack growled.

"What do you intend to do then?" Hammed asked, "as our dear Conte de Mondego pointed out, you have not much of a choice. I cannot see a reason for the King's strange request however. Why would he give you a title and an order of merchandise as big as this one?" Hammed waved the paper in front of Jack.

"Because he is trapping flies with honey instead of vinegar, my dear Hammed. I suppose the king is well informed about my wealth and adding two and two, he assumes that in order to amass such riches, one must be very industrious indeed. Fact is, that I am richer than some of the nobility here in this country and he knows that also. Now think, Hammed, I have lived in England for a long time. The king does not like the English. He is making certain that I will not be disloyal to the crown of Spain, should any trouble arise. Furthermore, he is just starting to strengthen his navy and needs money. Where better to borrow money, then from his loyal subjects. I have never gotten involved with the court of England for just this very reason. Here I am, back in my homeland and the first thing I am getting is a title and a wife to assure my loyalty. It is clear, what the king is trying to do. If I have children by a Spanish wife, I am not much of a thread to the crown." Jack finished and poured another glass of orange juice, which he emptied in a few big gulps.

"Perhaps it is not all that bad, Master. If you don't like your wife, then we will go on many long business trips and she can stay home," Hammed grinned, "from what I could see on the little miniature however, she is indeed outrageously beautiful. Her creamy white skin must feel…"

"Enough, Hammed," Jack roared, "I will make her hate me and the king can go to hell. If we both do not like each other, the Conte will find a way to safe his precious daughter from an unhappy marriage. You have heard what he said. He is the king's friend. Damn, there must be a way out of this ridiculous situation." Jack pushed an errant strand of hair from his forehead with an impatient gesture.

"There is another way, Master, but I don't think you will like it. We could move back to England. Another option would be Istanbul, which you loved," Hammed suggested.

"I do not want to move again, Hammed," Jack whined, "this would be indeed the last resort if we don't have any other options left. We still have a few days to decide, since the little Countess is expected back next week. Now let me see the order from the king. I merely read the letter before and I am curious, how much we would profit from the sale." Jack reached for the paper with the order written on it. "Heavens, what does the king want with all of this material? This is a very strange order, Hammed. Besides oil and lamps, he wants some jewelry, wood, perfumes and spices. There are just a very few small amounts of silks and laces ordered. The rest is all wool, and tons of it. The fabrics he ordered could clothe an army." Suddenly he clapped his hand against his forehead as he saw Hammed nodding and smiling brightly.

"Precisely, Master, have you not told me a few moments ago, that the king of Spain is strengthening his navy? There you have it. The cloth is for his soldiers." Quickly Jack estimated in his head, how much profit he would make and looked astonished at Hammed.

"Dear sinners and saints, I would be richer yet by about a tenth of my entire fortune. What am I to do, Hammed?"

"Fill the order and wait, Master. A decision made in haste, never brings any good. In any case, Countess de Mondego might be a charming young lady and make you a good wife after all. If she is not, have your banker transfer all your money to Istanbul, where you still have your open account and sell this house here in secret. No one would be the wiser and you would be much wealthier than before," Hammed advised.

"Ah, my dear faithful Hammed, what would I do without you. Very well, I shall wait and see. Now go and tell that charming wife of yours, that I am famished. It is time for our morning meal."

He padded with his hand on Hammed's shoulder in a friendly gesture and turning he walked into the hall toward the dining room.

It took a few days for the king's order to be filled and delivered. To his surprise, the king's treasurer paid Jack in full. Not taking any chances however, Jack had his banker transfer this large sum to his bank in Istanbul. Depending on the further developments by the end of the week, he intended to sell the house as Hammed had suggested. He hoped to God, the Countess would not like him. He did not want to get married.

It was the last Saturday in June on the twenty fifth day in the year of our Lord seventeen hundred and seventy four as Conte de Mondego's little messenger arrived. The boy had ridden the distance from the Conte's house to Jack's at breakneck speed and breathlessly, he handed Hammed the letter he carried. Hammed told the boy, that his horse needed rest and would be cared for by the master's groom. Elizabeth took the boy in the kitchen to rest and gave him food and drink. Jack's life would never be the same. The messenger boy had brought an invitation to a small intimate party at the Conte's house. Not to be obvious and letting his daughter know about the king's order, the party was covered under the guise of a friendly card game, which the Conte did enjoy so much. There would be two other gentlemen present together with their wife's. Senior de Domingo and Conte de Alvarez. Jack had met both gentlemen at the night of the fateful party as he was introduced to the king.

Coincidently, Senior de Domingo was the owner of a large fleet of merchant ships and lived near Barcelona. He had visited his old childhood friend Conte de Mondego for a few weeks and would return home soon. Jack had wanted to talk with him about business, as the king called him. Unfortunately, after the talk with the king, Jack's mind had not been with business any longer. Perhaps another opportunity would present itself tonight, to talk to Senior de Domingo. He had spoken to Hammed about it and the big loyal servant could not have been happier. Thanks to Allah, his master's mind was foremost on being a merchant. In time, he hoped, Jack would accept his fate and marries the Countess as ordered by the king. After all, what great harm could it do, since they would be traveling several months out of the year. With any luck, Jack would be able to make an arrangement with Senior de Domingo and the business would flourish like never before. Hammed had prayed for Allah's guidance and he felt at peace with the situation, though Jack still seemed to struggle against the creators will. Carefully choosing his clothing, Jack made certain he was dressed elegantly and taking great pains with his personal appearance, he had Hammed barber his beard and mustache, which was cropped short and merely surrounded his chin and lips. Flashing his servant a smile, showing his brilliantly white teeth contrasting his bronzed skin, he asked,

"How do I look, Hammed?"

"Ah, Master Jack, the little Countess will fall in love with you at first sight," Hammed teased. Jack gave him a sour look.

"Traitor, I should have known you would be like that," Jack grumbled.

Hammed could not help it and chuckled. Jack had decided to cover the relatively short distance to the Conte's house, which was about two miles on horseback and mounting their horses, Hammed blew his wife Elizabeth a kiss as she stood by the steps and waved to him. They rode in silence for a while at a leisurely pace, enjoying the sunny day and the slight breeze coming from the east. Glancing in the direction from where the wind was blowing, Hammed broke the silence and asked:

"To the east is Barcelona. Is this not where Senior de Domingo has his home?"

"Yes, Hammed, I believe so. Speaking of Senior de Domingo…Do you think it a good idea to approach him tonight about a business venture? Though my dear friend Thomas Crandall is still contracted to bring me the merchandises from several countries, I would not mind expanding the trading business and add furs and other various items to my list." Glad to hear his master responding exactly as Hammed had wanted him to, he hid a smile,

"Yes, Master Jack, I believe it would be a wonderful idea. Come to think of it, I believe it quite convenient how everything is working out. If you marry the Countess…" Jack raised his hand and waved his finger back and forth.

"This is not what I wanted to hear at this moment, Hammed."

"Please, Master, hear me out. Assume you could talk Senior de Domingo into renting you cargo space on his ships and bringing you additional wares to sell…Conte de Mondego and Senior de Domingo are old friends, more like brothers I would say. You are to marry Conte de Mondego's daughter. I do not believe that Senior de Domingo would say no to a merging business with his best friend's daughter's husband. Now think further, if you are married to the Countess, we would have a perfect excuse and could move to Barcelona to be a little farther away from the king's reach. Out of sight out of mind as your father, Allah bless his kind soul, always said. We would hardly have to fear any other involvement with the crown. There are too many wonderful opportunities to pass up, Master. If I were you, I would marry the Countess if she would be as ugly as my late father's old donkey. But she is not ugly. She is beautiful and if my instincts are correct about her from the picture, she is charming and intelligent. Many men in the past and present have been and are still to this day forced into marriage with a woman, to amass more riches and power. A marriage of convenience but not of love. Pah, how obscene to think of it, to sire children on a less than pretty woman with a mind of a beetle. Consider yourself fortunate, Master, that Countess de Mondego seems to be neither. Give her and yourself a chance to get to know each other. You heard what Conte de Mondego said as he paid you this fateful visit. He will personally inform the king of the upcoming marriage, but not when. It will give you and the Countess plenty of time to learn about each other. Would you not agree?" Jack had listened to Hammed's speech silently and indeed it gave him pause for thought.

"In all my life I have been a free man to do as he pleases, my dear Hammed. Never was I forced to do anything against my own will. But I see the wisdom of your words. Very well then you old schemer, I shall give the Countess a chance," Jack grinned.

Hammed sent a silent prayer of thanks to the great all-knowing creator. He knew that Jack was a proud man and the King had injured his pride as the ruler took away his choice. But even the king was a person who obeyed Allah's will, whether he knew it or not. The big man was breathing a sigh of relieve. Now perhaps Jack would concentrate on courting the Countess and stop struggling against his fate. It would all work out to everybody's satisfaction. Jack would get a beautiful wife and hopefully many sons and daughters in the future. They would move to Barcelona and make a greater fortune yet with the help of Senior de Domingo. The Conte would be happy and content, knowing that his daughter was in a loving relationship and happily married raising her children and the king would leave them alone.

Hammed considered his plan for the future foolproof and pointing into the distance, he happily announced,

"Look, Master, we are almost there. I can see the Conte's house." Kicking their horses slightly, both men quickened the animals' pace and a few minutes later they dismounted the horses in front of the big staircase at the Conte's mansion. The horses were taken away to be cared for by the grooms and Jack, followed by Hammed, walked up the stairs. A servant opened the big entrance door and bade them to follow him to the elegantly furnished parlor. Upon their entrance, Conte de Mondego jumped from his huge comfortable chair and his hands outstretched he greeted Jack,

"Ah, my dear Baron de Viego, I am honored by your visit. I am happy you accepted my invitation." Both men shook hands and Jack answered,

"As always, the honor is mine." Jack bowed. Besides the three men there was no one else in the room and Jack said apologetically,

"I hope we are not too early, Conte de Mondego. I thought your friend Senior de Domingo would be playing with us tonight. Did he change his mind?" The Conte shook his head and said,

"Alfredo and his wife are resting upstairs in their rooms. They should be joining us within the hour. We planned to play cards tonight. I hope a friendly gamble is not offensive to you Baron," the Conte smiled.

"Not at all, Conte, I am looking forward to this evening." Many nights, Jack and Hammed had played cards and Jack had found he liked the game and was actually becoming very good at it. He had learned quickly to memorize discarded cards and therefore won frequently. It should prove to be an interesting evening after all. At that moment, the door opened and Hammed held his breath. Jack stood with his back toward the door and had not seen the person walking into the room. Looking around Jack's shoulder, the Conte said cheerfully,

"My dear child, come and meet Baron de Viego. He is the son of an old friend I told you about," the Conte said twinkling meaningful.

"Baron de Viego, meet my daughter Sofia," he proudly announced. It was then, that Jack turned and his heart seemed to stop for a moment. His eyes beheld the most exquisite creature he had ever seen. The painter of the miniature must have been blind. He had done the girl's real beauty no justice. Finally, Jack found his composure and bending, he placed a gallant kiss on the outstretched hand of the sweetly smiling Countess.

"Baron de Viego, it is my pleasure to meet you. My father told me only recently of his friendship with your late father. I was very sad to hear that you had lost your entire family." Jack was still holding Sofia's hand in his and seemed to be somewhat aggrieved as she gently withdrew it from his.

Hammed had watched the little scene with great interest and was hard pressed not to show the smirk that seemed to develop on his lips.

He was ready to eat his turban, if Jack was not already falling in love with Sofia.

Wisely however, he kept his composure and stood straight his arms crossed behind his back and with a serious face next to his master.

Sofia glanced at Hammed and at her silent question in her face, Jack said,

"This is my faithful friend and servant, Hammed."

Jack knew that the big man's face was a bit to stern and he reached for his arm to draw him closer to greet the Countess. While he was drawing him near, he quickly pinched the arm and said smiling sweetly,

"Hammed's advice is invaluable to me, even though sometimes he seems to know more than mortal men do, or I personally care to know."

Hammed folded his arms in front of his chest and greeted the young Countess eastern fashion with a respectful bow.

"I am pleased to welcome you to our home, Hammed."

The Countess had folded her arms in the same way as Hammed had done and bowed her head slightly. Twinkling mischievously she continued, "We all should follow intuition more often, as your friend here obviously does. But where are my manners, please do sit down and be comfortable. I must go to the kitchen to see if cook is following my instructions. We shall dine in an hour."

With that she swept her father a quick sweet curtsy and hurried from the room. Jack peeped at Hammed from below his dark thick lashes. Since the Conte had walked back to the group of chairs and a big couch, his back was for a few moments turned toward Jack and Hammed. Merely for an instant, the big servant cracked a smile. As soon as the Conte turned and still standing waved Jack and Hammed with an elegant gesture to sit, Hammed's face was as stern and serious as it had been before.

Hammed seldom sat when his master went to parties or had guests on his own. This time he made an exception, since Jack had given him a hardly noticeable signal with his eyes. It would have been impolite for Hammed to stand. Jack had introduced his servant also as his trusted friend. Therefore he was allowed to sit in his master's presence at the

Conte's friendly invitation. As the three men talked for a while about trivial things, the door opened and Senior Alfredo de Domingo and his wife Viola joint the party. Politely, Jack and Hammed rose and greeted the gentleman and his tiny wife. Not long thereafter, Conte de Alvarez and his charming wife arrived.

Conte de Mondego had strategically placed Jack next to his daughter Sofia, at the dinner table as a servant announced that dinner was served. To Jack's amazement, the Countess proved to be not only a charming hostess but also seemed to be highly intelligent and deeply interested in his business. He found himself talking about business with her as he would with Hammed. As the servants were ordered to clear the table, Conte de Mondego suggested to have the after-dinner-drink back in the parlor and to start their card game. Knowing already, that Jack and Hammed did not consume any alcoholic beverages, Conte de Mondego ordered fruit juices and coffee for his other two guests. Hammed poured him self a glass of mango juice and Jack preferred his favorite orange juice. Handing Jack his drink, Hammed stood discretely by the table and waited until all the men had taken their seats. On Jack's signal, he sat on one of the empty chairs. At previous parties, the other nobles had questioned Jack's servant being treated as their equal and was allowed to sit on the same table. Jack had admonished them politely, that Hammed was not merely his servant, but also his most trusted friend and advisor with a brilliant mind.

The nobles had accepted his eccentricity indulgingly since it was rumored that Jack had lived in Istanbul for a while and it was said, costumes in the east were different from their own. The Ladies had made themselves comfortable in the cozy corner with the huge chairs and small side tables. Anticipating, that the women would sit there, Jack had taken his seat at the small end of the card table after Conte de Mondego had chosen the chair facing the door. He was able to watch Sofia sitting on the couch and the two other ladies in the big chairs. Hammed had taken the chair next to Jack and he could see both, his master as well as Sofia. The men played for a few hours and Jack played terribly. His mind and his eyes wandered to the corner, where Sofia was sitting and her tinkling laughter could be heard quite often. More then once she had glanced at Jack and caught his eyes looking at her. She blushed most becomingly. Besides Hammed, Conte de Mondego had also noticed that Jack's face seemed to soften as he looked in direction couch. Conte de Mondego could not be happier. Jack had missed the understanding and indulging look between his loyal Hammed and the Conte. The other gentlemen were deeply involved in the game and had noticed nothing.

'Thank God or Allah or whoever is in charge up there, I listened to Hammed. He was correct; the Countess is very charming and smart. Not to mention her beauty. Only an angel could look like that,' Jack thought and found he was suddenly not so much opposed to married life any longer. Still he would take his time. The men around the table had talked about politics and seemed to be quiet for a moment, as Hammed slyly steered the direction of the conversation to business.

"Master Jack, did you not tell me to remind you, that you wanted to thank Conte de Mondego for the king's grand order of fabrics. The warehouses are nearly empty since we made the delivery."

"Ah thank you, my dear Hammed, you are correct. I nearly forgot." Jack caught on to Hammed's little hint.

"The order from the king you brought by my house not too long ago was indeed grand. How can I ever thank you, Conte de Mondego. I found myself wealthier as I could have ever hoped for from merely one order. And all for the reason that you are his majesty's friend. Thank you, Conte, from the bottom of my heart," Jack smiled and his eyes twinkled merrily. That his talk had a double meaning was only clear to Hammed and the Conte. The older man smiled back just as merrily and answered,

"You are indeed very welcome, my young friend. I shall inform his majesty, that his order is greatly appreciated by the young merchant in question." Hammed almost choked on his juice, trying to hide his mirth.

Turning to his friend Senior Alfredo de Domingo, Conte de Mondego explained,

"My young friend here is a fine merchant as you are, my dear

Alfredo. As I understand he was titled Baron de Viego by his majesty for the prompt delivery and excellent quality of his wares."

"A title for merchandise?" Alfredo was incredulous.

"You know, how eccentric his majesty can be at times. One never knows what our beloved king will do next." Pedro de Mondego chuckled. "We are not to judge his majesty's reasoning and should rejoice in my young friends good fortune."

"Well then, I drink to your good fortune, Baron de Viego," Alfredo lifted his glass to drink a toast:

"Here is to the king, may he live forever."

Politely, Jack and the other men lifted their glasses and echoed, "Hear, hear."

Placing his glass back on the table, Alfredo asked,

"If I may ask Baron de Viego, how large was the king's order?"

After Jack sent Hammed a warning look, he named the figure of the merchandises and it was Conte de Alvarez' turn to almost choke on his wine.

"Dear heavens, what is the king doing with all that fabric?" the man asked.

"I can only assume that the king is clothing his navy. But like our dear Conte de Mondego said, we are not privy to his majesty's mind. I got my payment in full from the king's treasurer and I did not ask any questions."

The evening had proven to be enjoyable for Jack after all and Conte Pedro de Mondego was not surprised as Jack asked him, while saying his farewells if he may have permission to call on his daughter. The permission was given and Jack courted Sofia for three months. Both young people had indeed fallen deeply in love and to Pedro's great joy, the wedding was celebrated on November the first in the year of our lord seventeen hundred and seventy four. On August the twenty sixth in the year of our Lord seventeen hundred and seventy five, the young Baroness was safely delivered of a healthy and beautiful daughter. Jack was ecstatic as was Hammed and Pedro. To honor the memory of Sofia's dear mother as well as his own, Jack decided that the child was to be named after both grandmothers. Proudly he announced his newborn daughters name to Pedro. Baroness Loenora Lucrezia de Viego. The old Conte wept with joy.

As Hammed had predicted, they all moved from Madrid to Barcelona. A short time later, Pedro's friend Alfredo agreed to combine their merchant trading business and seeing that Jack was indeed everything Pedro had promised, and more, he gave Jack the option to buy several ships from his fleet. Alfredo's son Vincento de Domingo protested loudly. Alfredo was not to be moved in his decision. Vincento had become every father's nightmare. He was lazy and several angry fathers of ruined girls had threatened with violence. His indeed generous allowance was spend in taverns and heavy gambling debts amassed, which Alfredo in turn had to cover. Alfredo began to see in Jack the son he always had envisioned. A family man with pride, honor and a good sense for business. Jack, Sofia and their little daughter were the picture perfect ideal of Alfredo's sense for a happy family. He even accepted Hammed, his wife Elizabeth and their child as friends of the family. Elizabeth had finally succeeded and after writing many letters to England, she had found her little sister Laura. She had to laugh at the discovery that Laura was serving in the old mansion. To Hammed's great consternation, Laura had answered, that Miss Margaret had moved and she was no longer in her service. Unfortunately, she had no knowledge of her former Mistress' whereabouts. Margaret had forbidden the girl to give anyone any information as to where she went. She had told the girl before her departure, that she would get in contact in her own good time and when she deemed it right. So Laura had no choice as to deny any knowledge of Margaret's new location.

It was not her business, what the wealthy people did and she kept quiet.

CHAPTER 24

The Horoscope

Margaret remembered those many months back, as morning had broken and after taking her usual bath, Margaret dressed in her soft green velvet gown. Quickly she ate her breakfast, which she ordered Patty to bring to her room. Joseph carried the little trunk down to the hall and called for the carriage to be brought around. Before Patty came to her rooms, Margaret opened all the seams of her gowns, where she had hidden her jewels and stuffing them safely in a pouch, she hid the pouch under her gowns in the little trunk. Margaret took her book along and reading; she sat in the carriage, which took her to the little inn. As she hoped, Justus had not even fussed as she bade him 'good bye' and he ran off, Natty hard on his heels, to play with the kittens in the stable.

Patty told Margaret, that the Captain informed Misses Crandall of Miss Margaret's temporary absence. Poor Miss Margaret had lost much of her gowns in the terrible fire and needed some new ones made. 'How clever of Thomas' Margaret thought and a little feline smile stole itself around her lips at the memory of it. He made certain, that no one had any inappropriate suspicions at the moment. Including and foremost his wife was not to suspect their affair. If she could accuse him of any infidelity during their divorce proceedings, she could make his life a lot more complicated. Thomas spoke about this to Margaret as they made love by the lake. Margaret agreed, that, since Thomas' character was above reproach, his good name as well as her own reputation as a virtuous widow should not suffer through vicious gossip. Whatever was said after the divorce could not harm either one of them. He then would be free to take another wife and no one would be the wiser, if it turned out to be Miss Margaret. Passing the time, by reading her book and alternatively thinking, Margaret reached the inn and waited in her room for Thomas. It was as he had promised, shortly after noon the hour and he told her, that the lawyer had started the divorce. He had set up another meeting in a few days with Cynthia's lawyer and so far everything seemed to go well. His friends, which he expected had not arrived yet and they took advantage of the early afternoon, to open up Margaret's bank account, after she sold the jewels at a generous price to a local jeweler.

They had taken separate rooms at the inn and Thomas promised her to visit her room later that night. Since Thomas paid for both rooms, he introduced Margaret as the widow of his friend to the curious innkeeper.

He knew the man well and told Margaret, that he was an incurable gossip. He must not suspect anything. After an incredible night of passion, Thomas took Margaret to the little shop to select some fabrics for her new gowns. A visit to the seamstress followed and back at the inn, Thomas finally received a message that his friends had arrived in town. They were waiting for him at the saloon and Thomas went to see them. He told Margaret to wait for him at the inn, he would return later that night. Thomas met his friends every afternoon and returned to the inn to have late dinners with Margaret.

Time passed quickly and Margaret felt like she was in a dream. Her days were filled with reading, embroidery and the fittings for her gowns. She befriended the innkeeper's daughter and walked in her company to the seamstress' little shop. She had been able to purchase pots and pans from the copper smith and also a few wooden spoons for her soap making. True to his promise, Thomas let her select all the oils and essences from his warehouse, which she needed for her perfumes. The warehouse was located a half hours ride by carriage on the road to Washington and was surrounded by a high fence. Well guarded by several huge dogs and a young man and his son stepped out of the little house, which stood a few steps away from the warehouse. Upon seeing Thomas, his face lit up and he greeted him with a big smile. He called his son to greet Thomas and sent him to help Margaret. Both men talked outside, while Margaret made her selections in the big warehouse, after the young boy had shown her the section where she would find all she needed. The fragrance of this section of the warehouse was almost overpowering. Lugging the boxes outside, the boy packed them safely onto a wagon, which would be sent to the Estate. As soon as Margaret arrived home, she would be able to produce her soaps and perfumes. She already told the seamstress and her helpers about her products as the ladies sniffed appreciatively. Smartly, she wore her own fragrance and telling the girls at the shop, that there are other fragrances available and now she had several orders to fill. As much as she enjoyed being with Thomas, especially when he held her in his arms, Margaret could hardly wait to get home and start making her products. Quickly she learned how to be a shrewd little businesswoman and promised the seamstress and her helpers a large discount on soaps and perfumes, if her dresses would be ready by the end of the week. The twelve girls must have been working around the clock and as promised, Margaret owned four new gowns as she went back home. She had not forgotten to purchase a few toys for her son and he squealed his delight as his mother handed him little cats and dogs carved from wood. He also was the proud little owner of a wooden horse, where he could sit on. The wooden horse was fastened to two long pieces of wood, which were bent and the horse would swing like a rocking chair. Justus insisted on feeding his horse and Natty took him laughing to the stables to get a hand full of hay.

Patty returned into her little Miss's service and Cynthia decided to move back to her parents. She left a message for Thomas, that she would get in contact with him through her lawyer. Since Thomas had obviously started the divorce proceedings, she saw no need to remain in his house any longer. The servants and slaves would stay in this house. She would not need them. Cynthia took all her belongings and her rooms glared empty at the surprised Thomas. 'It is just as well' he thought and Margaret could not help but being gleeful at this turn of events. Remembering her promise to Adele, Margaret went to the little garden house the next afternoon. Adele had finished Margaret's horoscope and was excitedly waiting for Margaret's visit.

"I am glad you returned safely, child. Did you have a pleasant trip?"

"Yes, Adele, I had a very successful trip. I own four new gowns and I am also able to make my perfumes and soaps again as I used to do in England,"

Margaret answered proudly.

"Come, let us sit by the table, I will get the coffee," Adele said and hurried to the little kitchen to come back with her tray. Filling the cups, she went to the bookshelf to fetch the finished horoscopes. Seating herself, she took a sip from her coffee and started interpreting Margaret's charts,

"You were born under the sign of the waterman Neptune. This sign is called Aquarius. There are some powerful aspects in you chart. You see here, the moon was in the hour of your birth in your second house. That means you have a restless soul and will do much traveling. Travel will mean separations, which the sun opposing Uranus confirms. Jupiter trine Uranus means you will travel to exotic lands, which seem strange to you. You will have to be careful not to be too overoptimistic as Jupiter suggests with its square to Neptune. Saturn in your second house tells me, that financial and material security is very important to you. There is something going on here in your first house, which I am not quite clear about. It could mean some major trouble in your thirties however. I had done some charts before with similar dark spots. All those people went through some rough times as soon as the were thirty years and older. The moon is also showing me a certain spot, which suggests that you are a spiritual person and might even be very interested to investigate the unknown forces. Jupiter in Scorpio tells me that you have the power to make miracles happen my child. The Moon trines Mercury and I wouldn't be surprised if you could charm the scales of a fish. You are persuasive and you know what you want, which is property. You want to be your own Mistress. Venus is sitting in Capricorn and that tells me you have a sharp sense for business. You are thrifty and you have good common sense. Don't ever loose it," Adele said and took another sip.

Margaret sat still for a moment and could not believe that the old woman knew so much about her. It was true that she was thrifty and wanted her own business. Since she had traveled to this country and everything seemed strange to her at first, the stars had told Adele about that also. But Margaret wanted to know more. She wanted to know about the future, which she intended to spend with Thomas. Taking a sip from her coffee, she leaned back and spoke a bit irritated,

"Thank you, Adele, that was very revealing indeed. However, do the stars say something about my future? It seems to me, that all the stars have told you is the events that already have happened and traits that are my current characteristics. I should like to know, if there is a man in my life once more and if I will have any more children."

'So that is the direction the wind was blowing from' Adele thought, 'if you only knew, that I know more then what you want me too'.

"I anticipated as much, child, and I have drawn a chart for the future. Here it is. The planets from your native chart and the planets in the chart of the future combined are telling me some strange things. You will not be living here for long and you will indeed go across the ocean to a different land. I had drawn this for the next forty years to make certain that I don't miss an event, which would have lead to another one earlier and vice versa. Beware my child; it is in your nature to be vengeful. If you let your feelings overrule your heart and mind, you will do great evil with it. I always see two roads in every interpretation. God has given you the choice to take either one. I see you surrounded by wealth and a dark man. There are children here. One is undoubtedly your own son. The other child has a female vibration in your chart. It could very well be the future wife of you son, for she is not as strong here as a natural child would be. With the female presence in your chart comes a haunting past and great tragedy in the future."

It was then, that Adele's eyes got wide for merely an instant. How could she have missed that? She had looked at the charts before Margaret's visit. Margaret stared at the paper and did not notice. Adele stopped speaking and Margaret looked up to see Adele's lips tightly pressed together. She would not tell the girl, what she had seen. It was impossible. Adele was shocked, but did not betray her emotions she felt, with any gesture or a look.

"Is that all you see, Adele?" Margaret asked a little concerned now.

"Yes, my dear girl, that is all I ever needed to see. Just remember, that God is watching you and has given you a choice to be either good or evil. I am a little tired now and I wish to rest a bit. Reading charts is always draining my strength so much," Adele excused her self. Taking the hint, Margaret drained her cup and got up from her chair.

"I am a little tired myself, Adele. The past week in town was tiresome indeed. All the fittings and shopping has worn me out. I might come by another time so we can chat."

"That might not be possible, child," Adele said quickly, "I am going to stay with my daughter. Since the Misses is gone, I am not needed here any longer and I can be with my daughter. She always wanted me to come and live with her. Up until now, I rejected the idea. Now there is nothing holding me back and I will enjoy the time I have left with my family."

"Then I wish you well and many happy years with your family, Adele. I am going to miss the pleasant times we could have had. But I am also happy for you. I can understand your daughter that she wants her mother by her side. I wish that my mother would still be alive to help me. Many times I would have needed her advice," Margaret said sadly with a heavy sigh.

"Farewell, Adele, I shall write to you," Margaret promised and took a few coins from her little pouch to place them on the table in front of Adele.

"May I take my horoscopes with me, Adele?"

"Oh, child, this is too much money for the horoscopes," Adele counted the coins, "yes of course you may take the papers with you."

"Nonsense, Adele, you have worked very hard on all this." Margaret turned and was heading for the door.

"God keep you safe, child, farewell," Adele said as Margaret closed the door behind her. It had been a strange interpretation. Margaret went to her rooms and placing the papers in front of her on the table, she stared at it for a long time. She learned from early on to memorize details and words, which others would miss. Therefore she remembered every word that Adele had said. Not to confuse things in the future, Margaret took a sheet of paper and quill to write it all down word for word. She had to find out, what Adele had meant with the dark man. Who was the girl in her chart? Patty came to the room and told Margaret, that the Captain wishes to see her. He would be waiting for her in his study. Checking her appearance in the mirror, she took the brush and handing it to Patty, she sat on the little chair. Patty brushed Margaret's hair and parting it in the middle, twisted the mass of auburn hair into a soft knot to fasten it with hairpins at the nape of Margaret's neck. As always, Margaret dabbed some of her favorite fragrance on her wrist, behind her ears and in between the valley of her breasts. She told Patty, she could have the rest of the evening off. She would manage without her and her silky skirts hissing, she swooped out the door to go downstairs. Politely she knocked on the big door to Thomas' study and was bidden to enter from Thomas' voice within. Joseph was with him and Margaret stood in the doorway.

"Thank you, Joseph, that is all. See that my orders are obeyed. See that Miss Margaret and I are not disturbed." She heard Thomas say as he saw her entering the room. " Yes, Captain," Joseph bowed and turned to leave.

"Ah, Margaret, I have something important to talk to you about," he said.

He waited until Joseph had closed the door behind him and his eyes started to twinkle. Opening his arms wide he laughed:

"Come here to me, my little witch. You have enchanted me and I can hardly wait to see you. Where were you all afternoon?" Margaret snuggled into his embrace and somehow she felt safe. Only the tone in his voice irritated her a little. They were not married yet and she was free to do as she pleases. Avoiding his question purposely, she purred,

"I was longing to see you too. It feels so good to be safe in your arms, Thomas."

Thomas however was not fooled. He knew that Margaret avoided his question intentionally. He also realized, that at his question, her eyebrow had raised for merely an instant. Nevertheless, he had seen it and he asked again in a different tone of voice while kissing the top of her head,

"Where were you all afternoon, my sweet Maggie? I wanted to talk to you and I could not find you." Margaret heard the longing and concern in his voice and softening she answered,

"I was with Misses Kaufmann this afternoon. She is moving back to her daughter and I was saying my farewells."

"What?" Thomas looked at her in total surprise, "I was not informed of her intentions to move. Why is she leaving us now?"

"She said that she wants to be with her family. I can hardly blame her. She is alone in this little house and your wife is gone. She feels that she is not needed here any longer. The woman is over eighty years old, Thomas, and she needs to be needed," Margaret said wisely.

"Very well then, I will arrange for her things to be moved to her daughters house. Oh, I almost forgot, I still owe her last month's wages. Could you do me the favor and bring it to her before she leaves?" Margaret nodded in agreement. He opened his desk and pushing a little hidden button, he pulled out a big pouch with money from the secret compartment that had popped open. He counted some money onto the desk.

"I will leave this here for you, so you can give the money to Misses Kaufmann tomorrow morning."

"Why can't you give Misses Kaufmann the money yourself, Thomas?"

"That is what I wanted to talk to you about, Margaret. I must leave very early tomorrow morning. I received a message this afternoon that my ship is ready to go to sea. The minor repairs are done and I have some big loads waiting for me in India and Batavia."

"Oh, you leaving me so soon?" she pouted.

"I must, Margaret. If I do not go, somebody else will take my cargo and sell it to the merchants. I would miss out on a great sum of money my dear."

"I understand that, Thomas. However, I thought we would have some more time together," she wheedled.

"We have the rest of our lives, my little love. I am a sea captain and this is my business. I will be gone only for a few months," he crooned softly as he pulled her back into his embrace, nuzzling her soft neck. Margaret's hands went to his chest and softly pushing him so she could see into his face, she asked,

"But Thomas, what about your divorce? I thought you would have to sign papers for it?"

"I took care of that this afternoon, Margaret. I gave my lawyer full power of attorney to sign any documents in my stead. With any luck, my divorce is already granted when I return."

"Besides making my perfumes and soaps, what am I to do in all this long time?"

"I hoped you would be the lady of the house in my absence. I had just spoken to Joseph about it and told him, that you would supervise the running of my estate," he said matter-of-factly.

"Dear heavens Thomas, I do not know anything about running an estate as big as this. What if I do something wrong?" she exclaimed.

"Don't worry, my little love, Joseph is capable and will take care of most things around here. You would merely take charge of the kitchen and laundry business. There are quite a few people here and they all have to be well fed and clothed. That will be your responsibility. You will have to give Joseph the money for the food and repairs he is in charge off. It will not be difficult and you will have the perfect opportunity to learn. I know you can do it and will make me proud." He caressed her soft cheek with his finger.

"I know I can do it, Thomas. Thank you for trusting me. But it does not change the fact that I am a little scared." Margaret took a deep breath.

"Thank you, my sweet little future wife. I knew I could count on you. Now let us have dinner, I am hungry. But I'm not only hungry for food. Come to my rooms after dinner. We will have to be careful. Make sure no one is going to see you. You will have to find a way to dismiss Patty early."

"I already told Patty to take the rest of the night off. She went home to her family." Margaret smiled mischievously and pressed her body against his suggestively. Moaning, he gripped her upper arms and pushed the giggling young woman away to hold her at arms length.

"Dinner first, Madame," he laughed softly, "little witch," he mumbled.

After another incredible night of love making, Thomas kissed the sleeping Margaret and whispered,

"It is time for me to leave, my love. You must go to your rooms now, before the servants are up." Reluctantly, Margaret clung to him and did not want him to leave. Lovingly, he kissed her and pushed her gently out the door, saying,

"I will send a messenger, when I return. I shall bring you the material for your wedding gown my love. Now go, I love you, Margaret."

Flinging her arms around his neck, she kissed him one last time and said,

"Come back to me safe, Thomas, I love you too." Rejoicing, his heart had leapt in his chest. It had been the first time she had said these words. She went to her room unseen and slept for a few more hours, since it was still dark as Thomas left. Margaret paid Adele as she had promised and to her surprise, Adele gave her some of her books. If Margaret chooses, she could learn the science of astrology on her own. Adele saw in the charts, that Margaret would be interested and had a sharp intuition. Adele knew everything by heart and did not need the books any longer. She also gifted Margaret with the deck of Taro cards and a thick notebook where she had written the meaning and interpretation of the cards. Margaret thanked Adele and after saying her final farewell, waved after the small carriage, which rumbled slowly along the road through the forest. The carriage was being loaded with a few personal items that Adele possessed and had been waiting for the old woman outside the little gate. The big wagon with all the furniture and other things took a different road around the forest a few hours later.

Margaret kept busy with making her soaps and perfumes and the delicious smelling products quickly became highly sought after. She began to sell to

several different towns and had needed more help. She went to town and talked to the man guarding the warehouse. He agreed to let his son work for Margaret. The thirteen-year-old boy Jimmy was hired to drive the finished products to several stores in town and also adjoining towns. Besides making soaps and perfumes, Margaret learned quickly the running of the estate and was praised highly by Joseph. The Misses had left just about everything to the servants and his capable hands after her daughter's death and he was happy about Margaret's iron little fist with which she ruled. She was careful with spending money unnecessarily and many times small repairs were done using material that was already present at the estate. Thomas had left a large amount of money in the little hidden compartment of his desk and told Margaret, how to work the combination of lever and button to open it. Soon Margaret added another bag of money to the already present one in the desk. She traded a small portion of her own products for meat, eggs, vegetables, cheese, fruits and flower with the local farmers. They were happy to have their nagging wives of their back. Even the farmer's wives heard about Miss Margaret's fine soaps and perfumes. The money that Margaret saved by doing so was originally intended to buy food with. Even further she went with saving. If any of the servants needed a new piece of clothing, she had one of the seamstress's girls sew it for a piece of soap. Joseph shook his head in wonderment as she proudly named the figure of their savings in household monies. Yet another third bag had been stored in the desk, which was filled entirely with her own coins. It did not grow much, for she took this money to her banker every week. Under her rule and with Joseph's help, the estate was well run and no one had reason to complain. Ophelia regarded Margaret's advice highly. She too hated waste and many times it happened, that Margaret simply sat in her kitchen for lunch and ate left over soup and meat from the night before with the servants and her son. She still remembered the hard times in England when she went to bed hungry. She had an ally in Ophelia there, who told Margaret about her ancestors and how they were brought starving and naked to this country, to be sold into slavery. The Lord God had been good to her family and brought them to a kind and generous master. Many were not that lucky and suffered terribly at their master's hands. Here, her whole family was safe and lived in a clean home and there was always enough to eat. The Lord be praised for his mercy and kindness.

Margaret agreed. She had to think about her own fate and found that her life was getting better every day. A well-respected man was going to be her husband. He trusted her with his home, which she learned to love and managed it well. Her son was healthy and happy in their new home and seemed to grow stronger and smarter every day. The servants and slaves respected her and her products had earned her a lot of money. Life could not be better. Thomas' lawyer stopped by and he was happy to announce, that the divorce was final. He entrusted Margaret with the papers, sealed in a packet, which she carefully placed in the desk. In the evenings, Margaret studied her books of astrology and was learning quickly about aspects and how to interpret horoscopes. She even tried to draw up a chart for Patty, who giggled and shook her head about the nonsense of having a husband and children. Margaret smiled indulgingly and kept her findings carefully written in her notebook.

After nearly four months, Thomas returned and announced to his astonished but happy servants and slaves, that Miss Margaret was to be their new Mistress. The wedding was celebrated one week before her son's second birthday on Friday October the seventh in the year of our Lord seventeen hundred and seventy four. Thomas became 'Papa' to little Justus and on his birthday, which was also his own, Thomas gifted his little stepson with a pony. His wife ordered a new robe for him by the seamstress and she had personally embroidered and monogrammed it. Thomas promised his new wife, that he would stay home for a few months to be with his family, which he had never done before, while he was married to Cynthia.

They were a happy family and celebrated Christmas surrounded by some friends and neighbors, which Thomas knew for years. Easter was nearing and Thomas finally decided to go to sea again. Margaret knew that this day came and she happily told him her wonderful little secret. He would be happy and hurry home to her. She was carrying his child and it would be born under the sign of the archer by the end of November. She had been correct, Thomas was ecstatic and promised his wife to be back as soon as possible.

The last night before his departure, he made love to her tenderly at first and then suddenly with a passion such she had never known him to possess. Frantically and happily weeping, she clung to him and gave her own passion free reign, desperately trying to ignore the little nagging voice inside her head, which seemed to say that this would be the last time she would hold him in her arms. She had come to the realization, that she loved her husband with all her heart. She was carrying his heir and their life was perfect.

And suddenly her life crumbled around her like a house of cards. A messenger came to her home and brought the news. Thomas' ship had been found drifting without crew near the little island of Belitung, which was located between the Islands Borneo and Sumatra. Enquiries to any survivors at nearby Islands brought nothing. The captain and his crew seemed to be lost at sea and dead. There was talk of a terrible seaquake being responsible for the captain's and his crew's death. The quake produced a tremendous title wave that swept over several ships in the area. Some had been fortunate and survived. The captain seemed to be one of the lesser lucky ones.

Margaret screamed, and screamed, and clutching her abdomen she fainted. When she woke up, the doctor was by her bedside and told her, that she had miscarried the baby, which would have been a little girl. Margaret wept bitterly. She was inconsolable for several weeks. The servants were frightened and Joseph got more concerned every day. The master was dead and Margaret was a woman who would need another man. She could not go on and run the estate all on her own. Since she was the soul heiress to the property and even the abandoned ship, she would either have to sell or marry again. Joseph loved his little mistress dearly and he had an idea. Knocking softly on her door in her new rooms, which she had moved into after the wedding and had been Cynthia's before, he stood by her bedside and said,

"Ma'm, I don't know what to do. The messenger from the former mistress was here again and she demands payment for her support. Should I give her the household money or do you want the lawyer handle the situation?" There was a stir.

"What do you mean, Joseph?" Margaret raised herself from the pillows. "I am not responsible for her welfare. My husband is dead and the spoiled bitch better learn to earn her own money. She will have none of mine." She swung her legs from the bed and paced the room. Joseph hid a smile.

"Then you better talk to the lawyer, so she will leave you in peace."

Margaret had done exactly that and to her relieve she heard after a few weeks of negotiating with Cynthia's lawyer, that Cynthia would bother her no more. She spoke to Joseph several times and came up with a fantastic solution to their problem. The monies for the ships repair were sent to Singapore, with a friend of the late captain, where it was docked. One of Thomas' friends had been introduced to Margaret as Steve Daniels, was an officer on a different ship. Margaret made him an offer to captain her ship and continue the trading business for her. He agreed and was the proud new captain of his late friend's Caravel. Margaret had decided to hire the young man from the warehouse in town to help Joseph steward the house for her, while she would go on a trip. She would go to Europe on her husband's ship with her new captain. She decided it was time to leave for a while, since there was talk of war and revolution. She would not be stuck in the middle of it with her child. Perhaps she would be back soon or in a few years, when the situation was resolved and matters were settled between the politicians. She finally gave in to Patty, who wanted to go with her. Patty was young and didn't have any romantic involvement to keep her in America. She pleaded and reasoned with Margaret. No one could service her mistress as she could and teaching a new girl was frustrating at best. And what would Miss Margaret do in a strange country all by herself with a little child. She didn't even speak the language of this new country. How was she supposed to give orders to have her hair done or which gown to press. Laughing, Margaret told the happy girl that she would stay in her service. Natty however would have to stay at the Estate. While on the trip, Patty would have to watch Justus. To hire someone new, would be costly. A new trustworthy nurse could be hired if Patty was unsuitable, wherever Margaret was going. And she was going to Spain…

Chapter 25

The Voyage and a New Home

It was Monday the twenty fourth day in the month of June in 1776 as Misses Katrina Margaret Crandall left America. It had been a strange coincidence, that the port authorities had written Margaret's papers, noting her first name as her middle name by mistake. Her true Middle name, which was Katarina, was named first with the second 'a' missing entirely.

Instead of Margaret Katarina Crandall, she had become Katrina Margaret. Now she remembered the reason why. Adele had spilled ink over her name and the church authorities were not able to see correctly if name or middle name was written first on her records to copy them wrong also onto her certificate of marriage. The port master had done the same and Margaret had kept her lips tightly closed. She did not want to stay any longer to straighten this little error out. There had been a few shootings before she had left and she was becoming more frightened each day. There was a rumor and she had heard about this man George Washington or whatever his name was. The rumor was about revolution and war. Joseph and his whole family were scared to be left alone on the Estate. Margaret had never liked the idea of slavery and by law, she was now the owner of many slaves. Remembering the blood on Natty's finger, she shuddered. No one should be a slave. If there was a law to promote slavery, then there must be a law, to promote faithful and good slaves to at least the servant status. After speaking with her lawyer, he agreed, that it was perfectly legal to free a slave. So Margaret had her lawyer draw up papers of mannerism and the slaves on her Estate became paid servants. Joseph was legally made her steward and her lawyer would attest to it, should any questions or problems arise. No one had left the Estate and had thanked her, praising her and the Lord Jesus with songs and promises to be faithful and loyal only to her. She had written a short letter to her young German friend Gretchen, that she was returning to Europe and would get in touch as soon as she was safely settled in her new home. She had not heard from her dear friend in all the time she was in America and hoped her latest letter would find her in good health. She intended to settle in Spain for a while and keep on making her fine soaps and perfumes. She wrote that she had made some fine profits from her work and every woman should try it. It would always be good to have an extra income, without having to depend on a man. Then, depending on certain circumstances, she would either stay or move back to England. She signed the letter with her maiden name, thinking that she would have to get into lengthy explanations later on. She had mailed the letter and took the carriage to the small ship that was waiting in the harbor.

Many months ago, captain Steve Daniels and his new officers had gone to Batavia with prove of ownership from Margaret and after the repairs had been done to his satisfaction, he brought the 'Undine' home.

Accompanied by her servant Patty, her son Justus and captain Steve Daniels, she boarded her ship, which she had renamed 'Undine'. Since Margaret was still in mourning, her gown was black velvet with merely a small edging of crème colored lace around her neckline and the short puffy little sleeves. She stood on deck of the ship, one hand holding the railing the other holding her son. Her elegant dark dress billowing in the wind as she watched the land slowly getting smaller. Suddenly an icy shiver went up and down her spine and through her. She remembered Adele's vision. Tears sprang to her eyes as she thought about it. Adele had indeed seen the future.

Her gown was dark and her son was holding her hand. She was on a ship, which was now her own. She had been standing there for a long time and the distant land seemed to be a mere dark line on the horizon. Even though the sun was shining brightly, there was a fresh breeze and Margaret went with her son on her hand to her cabin. It was the same cabin she had inhabited as she came to America. It had been refurbished and newly painted, as was the whole Caravel. Margaret could not believe that she was on her own ship and was wealthy beyond her wildest dreams. She had come to America virtually a pauper. Patty had taken Justus to her own little cabin and Margaret stretched out on her big bed to rest. She missed Thomas terribly and a few tears slid down her soft cheeks. Impatiently she wiped them away with the back of her hand and reached for the cup of iced water flavored with lemon juice and honey. Drinking a few sips, she fell back onto the pillows and lay awake thinking.

The new captain Steve Daniels had suggested to take the Straight of Gibraltar to stop in Morocco and take on cargo. Then they would sail along the Mediterranean Sea along the coast of Algeria to also stop in Algiers, where Thomas had rented a medium sized warehouse in case that he would ever have to leave cargo behind. Steve knew, that there were still wool and oil as well as spices stored. Margaret could easily sell most of the cargo in Barcelona where they would go on land. Margaret agreed, since it would have been a waste of cargo space to sail on a nearly empty ship. The ships hull held provisions and several big crates of Margaret's perfumes and soaps. Wisely she had emptied the section with essences and oils of her own warehouse and had ordered them to be loaded onto the ship. She would be able to make her products for a long time to come, without having to buy anything. Though she was wealthy, it never hurt to have more. She was determined to sell her wares to the Spanish nobles as she had sold them in America.

As if Neptune would favor her voyage, the ocean remained calm and they reached Morocco without incident. They loaded barley, dates, tangerines, carpets and leather into the cargo space, after Margaret had haggled the sellers of their wares down to a price, which brought them near to tears and claimed to be impoverished. At first they were insulted to have to deal with a mere woman. However, they were amazed and in awe to hear from Steve, that Margaret was the owner of the ship. Steve Daniels had served as an interpreter and was near tears also, laughing. On they went to Algiers and emptied out the warehouse there. As Steve had told Margaret, there were several bulks of wool, and crates with oil and spices. To her great joy, Margaret found a few small crates. Opening one of them, she saw it was filled with exotic essences she could use to make her soaps. The crates all appeared to be the same and were painted with the same markings. She did not open all of them and assuming, that all the other smaller crates were filled with the same merchandise, she had them loaded onto the ship. Again she was back on board the 'Undine' and soon she would land in Barcelona, Spain. Little Justus had been extremely well behaved during the whole trip and was adored by the young captain Daniels and crew alike. Laughing at first about his many questions, captain Daniels quickly realized, that the boy had a sharp mind and remembered everything he was thought. His little mind seemed like a sponge and absorbed even the difficult to understand nautical phrases and the difference between longitude and latitude. He learned how to read a map and the compass. Margaret was in her cabin with her embroidery, as the little cabin boy knocked on her door and told her that they would be landing in Spain soon. Margaret jumped up from her seat and ran up on deck. In the distance she could see the harbor of Barcelona.

After several hours, they had finally landed in the bustling noisy harbor and Margaret had not left captain Daniels' side until all the cargo that had not been sold off right away, was safely stored in one of the warehouses she had rented. Paying the harbormaster their fee, she jumped with her son and Patty into a carriage, which Steve Daniels had hailed and was on her way to a comfortable little inn, which the harbormaster had recommended. Besides embroidering, Margaret had used the time on her ship to learn some of the Spanish language so she would be able to make herself understood. Her command of the language was passable and she was able to convey to the innkeeper, that she was in search for a house, which she could either rent or buy. She preferred to rent however, since it was not certain, that she would stay indefinitely. The innkeeper sent his little son to fetch the steward of a wealthy banker in town. The banker owned several houses in and around Barcelona and might be able to help her. She had arrived at the inn around noontime and resting together with her son on the big bed in her room, she was awakened by a knock. The little boy had returned and brought instead the steward, the banker Don Dorango in person with him. Don Dorango was waiting downstairs. Quickly Margaret instructed the dozing Patty, that she would return soon. She was to watch Justus. Margaret found Don Dorango to be a pleasant middle aged man with thinning hair and elegant manners. Gallantly, he bent over her outstretched hand and kissed it,

"Madam, it is my pleasure. I am Don Dorango and I understand you are looking for a house to rent. I might be able to help you." Margaret smiled and something suddenly warned her inside, not to reveal her name. She knew, that Jack was here in Spain and did not want him to know, that she was near. Since Jack knew her married name, Crandall, also and might suspect something, she introduced herself with her maiden name, which she had changed from Ziegler to Brickmaker. Gretchen had told her a long time ago, that Ziegler is the German version of Brickmaker. Sweetly and accentuating the American accent, Margaret greeted Don Dorango,

"The pleasure is all mine, Don Dorango. I am Donna Katrina Brickmaker. I would need a small villa for an indefinite time and at reasonable price. I prefer the quiet country side and perhaps near the sea. Would you have something like this available?"

He agreed to show Margaret a little secluded villa, which the Banker was willing to rent out a few short miles from here. He assured her, that it was exactly what she was looking for and she would be pleased. Indeed the next day, Margaret caught her breath, as she saw the magnificent little villa just past a little town called Sant Adria. The house was set high on the reddish cliffs and overlooked the Mediterranean Sea. The price was agreed upon and Margaret moved into the little villa, which was partially furnished. There were several unused little rooms on the ground level, which she would use as her workrooms. Industrious and skilled as she was, Margaret quickly became known as Donna Katrina, the widow from America. Donna Katrina made the finest soaps and perfumes in all of Sant Adria. She had hired some more servants from town for the kitchen, laundry and gardens and one girl specifically to help her in her little workshop. Shrewdly she had sent a small bottle and a small piece of her finest products to the innkeeper's wife, thanking them for their invaluable help, not forgetting Don Dorango. Needless to say, that the orders began to increase in numbers. Every evening, when her work was done, she took a walk with Justus on her hand along the cliff side to reach a point stretching out into the sea. There she stood with her son by her side and let the breeze caress her face and play with her hair. Lovingly, she ruffled her son's dark hair and remembered, that he would be four years old in a few weeks. She thought about poor Thomas and her eyes filled with tears. If only her little girl had lived. She would not be standing here by the cliff alone with only her son by her side. Looking up into his mother's face, Justus asked,

"Mama, why are you crying?"

"I am deeply saddened by papa's death my son. I miss him terribly." The air was mild and the evening was warm. Suddenly she felt an ice cold shiver up her spine. Upon realizing, that she was standing by a cliff with her son by her hand and she was sad, she whirled around and saw in the distance a man riding a horse. The man seemed to have something in front of him on his lap. He had been watching her and riding away, his back was turned toward Margaret. It couldn't be...

Adele, oh dear old lady, she had not seen any more in her crystal ball. This much was clear to Margaret. If Adele had seen the future, then there were forces at work, which most people denied and feared. Margaret was not a person to give in to fear. She wanted to know more. Quickly, she pulled her son back to the little villa and rummaged through her old notes. It had been a long time since she had read them last. She studied her notes and charts every night and learning more and more, began to interpret her horoscope. She came to the same conclusions as Adele had told her so long ago. However, as proficient as she had become, she found several aspects, which Adele had not even mentioned. Concentrating on the missing links, Margaret made some astonishing and frightening discoveries. To her, the charts seemed to tell her that her lover and her son were linked somehow. Only the lover was placed in the distant future. What would it mean? Margaret got even more confused, as she found a female presence somehow relating to her lover. It was frustrating and she tried to consult the taro cards. Even they seemed to conspire to confuse her more yet. The cards were suggesting great wealth, separations, travel, intrigues, great evil and even death. There was also a young man and a female to be noticed. She regretted, that she had not bought the crystal ball from Adele. She wanted to learn to use the power of the crystal ball and see for herself, if she could glimpse into the future. She was determined to succeed and after several months of searching, finally had been able to purchase one from a group of gypsies. She set up a small room on the second floor with a small round table, a comfortable chair and a bookshelf for her notes and books. She had selected several of the fine carpets from Morocco for her self and one of them was placed in her private little room. Patty and the other servants were strictly forbidden to enter the room and after her work was done and her walks with her son, she locked herself in the little room every night. She lit the candles and placed them exactly as she had seen Adele do it and placed her hands on both sides of the crystal ball. For months, nothing happened. Then a thought struck her. She remembered Adele saying a prayer before the vision had come to her. Which prayer had the old woman mumbled? This must be the reason that the crystal ball was still silent. She had to find the prayer. How could she find out and how could she ask Adele? 'That's it,' her mind screamed. She must write to the old woman. Margaret waited patiently for an answer.

Then the long awaited day arrived. With him, captain Steve Daniels. The young captain had successfully acted in Margaret's behalf and had bought and sold cargo, which she had instructed to be, besides her usual wares, fur. It brought Margaret great profits. Captain Daniels had made a voyage back to America to find the country in uproar. Since he did not want to involve himself into politics, he had made a quick turn around and nearly missed the messenger, which brought a letter for Miss Margaret to the ship. He handed Margaret a letter, which she snatched from his hand. Margaret recognized the handwriting and impatiently opened the folded and sealed pages. While Steve poured two glasses of iced orange juice, she sank in the chair and read the letter. Suddenly, she laughed and taking absent minded the drink from Steve's hand, she said,

"Dear me, I should have known. It's so simple." He gave her a questioning look and she explained, that she merely wanted to know about the secret to a certain recipe. She did not want to explain anything about her dealings with the unknown. He might think her a witch and that was all she needed. Superstition and ignorance had done many innocent women great harm. Though knowledgeable with herbs for medicinal purposes and other potions, these women were considered witches and the devils disciples by jealous and envious people. Margaret liked the warmth of a good fire. However, being burned alive at the stake was not her idea of comfort. She carefully guarded her secret studies and sessions under the guise to work on recipes for her new and wonderful smelling products. Since all the servants knew, which great success Donna Katrina had with her products, no one dared to disobey and enter her special room. Folding the letter, Margaret stuck it in the pocket of her skirts and smiled at Steve,

"You will stay for a while of course." It was a statement and not a question.

"I seem to have not much of a choice. If it is not too much to ask, may I take advantage of you hospitality for a few weeks? Let us see then, if things in America have settled. I am frightened for my parents though. They live near New York on a farm and my brothers are there to help. But I wish I could be there to see what is really going on. Yet I do not wish to be in the middle of a war," he sighed heavily.

"You do not have to ask. Of course you may stay as long as you wish. In time we will know more. Meanwhile we could use my ship to trade between Spain and Algeria. The carpets and the leather from Morocco also seemed to find great popularity. If I remember correctly, an old acquaintance had great success with dealings in Lisbon. It is not far to sail around southern Spain and go up along the coast to reach Lisbon that way. Then there is another city, which would interest me. I would buy some wares from Istanbul. I have heard many fantastic stories about the city and some day I might even venture there to see for myself. Perhaps we can combine business with pleasure and I shall go with you, if we receive a trading permit from the ruler there. Wouldn't you agree, that trading with Istanbul would be a very profitable enterprise?"

"I wouldn't be opposed to it," he grinned boyishly. It had never occurred to her, that Steve Daniels was a handsome young man. She knew very little about him except him having been good friends with her late husband. From below her lashes she watched him as he poured himself another glass of refreshing orange juice. He was standing as tall as Thomas had been. He was slim and had long legs where Margaret could see muscular thighs and well formed calves rippling under the tight black pants.

His dark blond hair wavy hair was shoulder long and bound with a small ribbon at the nape of his neck. He sported an elegantly short cropped blond mustache and beard around his full sensual lips. His nose was straight and slim in between his gray-green eyes, which twinkled merrily when he laughed. He turned toward her and quickly she lowered her glance to see the wedding band on her finger. Thomas was dead and would never return. She was young and healthy. Getting up from the chair, she excused herself,

"I must see to your rooms and our dinner. Make yourself at home. I will be back shortly."

"Thank you. I appreciate your kindness. The evening is beautiful and there is hardly a breeze. Would you mind if I sit out on the veranda?" Steve asked as she opened the door.

"Of course not. There are some pillows in the chest by the wall. Please get one for me also. I will join you in a few minutes," she called back over her shoulder. She called one of the servants and ordered the rooms next to her own for Captain Daniels to be made up. The girl curtseyed,

"Si, la Donna Katrina."

Margaret smiled as she remembered how her new chosen name had sounded from the girl's lips. It had sounded something like

'Brickmocker'. She had given up trying to teach the girl and the others and told her servants to address her by her first name, which was according to her papers now legally, Katrina. Quickly she ran up to her little private room and placed Adele's letter on the bookshelf. She would get to try her visions later. It would not be this evening or the next or the next.

Margaret and Steve sat in the big chairs on the Veranda and enjoying the mild evening. Sipping their cool orange juices, they talked about the success of the new merchandise she had added to her trading business. Furs seemed to be in great demand and as she had seen on her first try, brought indeed high profits. Steve placed his glass on a little table between the chairs,

"The man I sold the merchandise to, was very exited about it. He wants more from us. I heard he owns a great merchant fleet together with his partner. He also started to trade in furs and was very disappointed about the low quality. He told me, that there were trap markings all over the furs and he stopped buying. He wanted to know, where I found such fine quality and naturally, I did not tell him. I promised him however, that I would speak to the owner of the business and would get back to him. If the owner agreed, I would tell him where to find the high quality furs."

"Naturally I will keep our source of merchandise to myself," Margaret laughed.

"Ah, wait, there is more. Up until this point, I had not told the man, who the owner of my ship and the business is. He was surprised to hear that a woman would be so bold to own and run a merchant trading enterprise. He asked me the name of the ship and I had told him it is the 'Undine'. He shook his head and said that he had never heard the name," he chuckled.

"Of course he would not know. You know that I renamed my ship. I felt after my husband's death, that I should make a complete new start on my own, including a new name for the ship. Since the clerk in America, writing my certificate of marriage already exchanged my first and middle names, I thought it might be a good idea," Margaret giggled.

"Oh, Misses Crandall, that is terrible," he wrinkled his forehead.

"Not at all, my dear Captain," Margaret smiled charmingly, "I have a suggestion to make and a request. Since we are business partners, hopefully for many profitable years to come, I think it would be appropriate that we call each other by our first names. Only remember, that here in Spain I am called Katrina. Please don't confuse my poor servants with calling me Margaret. Furthermore, I changed my last name back to my maiden name. I do not want any of my late husband's acquaintances throughout Spain and the rest of the world nagging me with painful questions about his death," she said ruefully.

"I couldn't agree more, Katrina. I also hope to be sailing in your service for a long time. The percentage you are paying me from the sales is very generous and more than any other merchant would give me and I love the ship. I am very proud to be your captain," he smiled.

"Well now that is settled and I am happy that you are my captain. I never can thank you enough for bringing the 'Undine' back from Batavia. What would I have done without you, Steve."

"You don't have to thank me, Katrina. Thomas was my friend and I loved him like one of my big brothers," he said seriously, "furthermore I like helping a damsel in distress." He grinned rakishly.

"I can see that you have been Thomas' friend, his charm has rubbed off on you," she laughed softly.

"Dinner is served, la Donna Katrina," the little maid said as she entered the veranda.

"And about time it is, I am famished. Come, Steve, let us go to the dining salon."

Gallantly he took her hand to help her up from the chair and placing her hand on his arm, he led her to the table. His grip had been gentle yet firm and she could feel his muscles through his thin silky shirt. She could feel his body heat through the shirt and quickly she sat on the chair, which he had held for her. Her face was flushed and he noticed.

"Please, bring us some cold juice, it is terribly warm in here," he ordered the little maid. The girl curtseyed and hurried of to fetch the juice. Thankful that Steve had accredited her red face to the heat, she said,

"Tomorrow night I shall have dinner served out on the veranda. It is much more pleasant out there."

She was fanning her face with the napkin.

They ate in silence and decided to return to their chairs out on the veranda.

Steve had taken his boots off and stretched his legs to touch the cool tiled floor with his hot feet. They could see the sea and the moonlight was reflecting in the water, painting a long streak of silver onto the dark waves. The dark shadowy outline of a ship passing slowly through the far end of the silver streak on the horizon. Patty came with Justus on her hand out to the veranda to bid his mother a good night. He had not been aware of Steve's return and his eyes lit up as he noticed the captain sitting in the chair:

"Uncle Steve," he threw his arms around the captains neck, " I missed you. Did you bring me my compass?" Steve pulled Justus on his lap.

"Yes I brought you your compass, Justus, as I had promised you." Steve laughed, "Patty, in my trunk is a small blue piece of cloth. Please bring me what is wrapped in it," he ordered the girl, who quickly brought the requested item from Steve's trunk. Steve handed Justus the small compass and the child ran exited to his mother.

"Look, mama, I have my very own compass. Now I can become a sea captain like papa and uncle Steve," he said proudly. Margaret laughed and paddled his bottom lovingly.

"If you do not sleep enough, you shall remain tiny and will not be able to see the big waves coming toward your ship. So your compass would do you not much good. You will need strong arms to steer your ship, my son. Now off to bed with you." She kissed her son's forehead and he bowed before Steve, clutching his precious gift to his little chest:

"Thank you, uncle Steve, and good night." He was ushered from the veranda by Patty:

"Come, little Jessy, I'll read you a nice story like Natty used to do."

"We can't forget my prayers first, Patty. Natty said it is very important," the boy remarked seriously.

"Since when did Justus become Jessy, Katrina? Does he not mind his changed name?" Steve laughed.

"Oh no, he likes to be called Jessy. Thomas used to call him thusly and now everybody else does, including myself," she answered.

"What a delight he has become, Katrina. He has a very sharp mind. You must be so proud as his father would be, were he still alive."

Many months back, Margaret or now, called Katrina, had been introduced to Steve and another friend by Thomas as a widow. Up until now, she had not thought about it and somehow, she felt that she owed Steve the truth.

"He still is alive, Steve." She said low. He looked at her as if she had gone mad.

"Katrina, I believe there is an afterlife, but people who have died, don't come back," he said ruefully.

"No, Steve, you don't understand. My son's real father is still alive and well. Thomas and I agreed to tell everyone that I was widowed to save Jessy from the stigma of being born a bastard child. He was born out of wedlock and I did not want to give anyone lengthy explanations."

"My god, Katrina, does this man know that he has a son?" he asked concerned.

"Yes, Steve, he is aware of the fact." Katrina said bitterly and sighed.

"Let me guess, he was married and you were his mistress. The bastard took advantage of you and left you to fend for yourself," he said scathingly.

"No, Steve, he was not married and he did not wanted to get married to me either. He felt that I wanted to trap him into marriage by presenting him with a child. He refused to even see his son. Were it not for the kindness of his steward Hammed, I should have been left destitute. Hammed convinced his master, to send me money so I could feed and clothe my son. He even bought a small cottage for us in Manchester and we lived there until a fire destroyed it. Meanwhile, Jack had moved away and I was helpless. I went to his old mansion and wanted to find out, where he had moved. I found Thomas instead and he took us to America. Thomas and Jack had been friends since childhood and I had met Thomas in Jacks house. Upon his return to America, Cynthia asked Thomas for a divorce. We fell in love and you know the rest."

"Did you ever find out, where this Jack went?" Steve asked.

"No, not yet," Katrina answered in half-truth. She believed it would be best if Steve did not know, that Jack had moved to Spain. She had to find out first, if he was here in this country or perhaps had moved away again. He must not be warned or suspect, that she was near. She still had her heart and mind set on revenge. How she would go about it, she did not know yet. That was something she would have to plan carefully. In time she had hoped, he would get married to another woman. Her original plan was to destroy his happiness and marriage with presenting his wife with her husband's son. Then she thought about it some more and feared that the lady would perhaps be forgiving and stay with Jack. All her efforts would be in vain. No, she would have to find something, which would hurt him as deeply as he had hurt her. She would think on it some more.

"It is a strange coincidence, that the name you have mentioned as Jack's steward is the same as the man I dealt with. His name was also Hammed.

Ali and Hammed seem to be the only male names in the Orient," Steve said jokingly.

"And what did you say, his master's name was?" Katrina asked chuckling.

"I didn't say. The Hammed's master, which I dealt with, is a very wealthy Baron. He lives right here in Barcelona with his wife and little daughter. His name is Baron Giaccomo de Viego." Katrina turned white and the glass in her hand dropped to the tiled floor, smashing into a thousand little pieces.

Quickly she recovered from her shock and mumbled an apology,

"How clumsy of me. Please be careful and watch your feet." She called for the girl to sweep up the broken glass.

"Katrina, is something amiss? You are as white as a sheet and looked like you have seen a ghost," he said concerned.

"It must be the heat. I should have known better as to wear this heavy velvet gown. If you will excuse me, I should like to lie down in my rooms.

I will see you in the morning."

Carefully she lifted the hem of her skirt and stepped over the remaining broken glass, which the little maid swept up.

"Yes of course, Katrina. I hope you feel better tomorrow. I'll see you for breakfast. If you don't mind, I am not tired yet and would like to sit here for a while."

"Not it all, Steve, please stay here as long as you wish. Good night." She hurried to her rooms and sat in a big comfortable chair. Her mind reeled.

CHAPTER 26

Dangerous Paths

Hammed was excitedly running into Jack's study. Without knocking, he entered and rubbed his hands joyfully,

"Master Jack, I have just come from a meeting with the American captain, I told you about. His name is Steve Daniels. He agreed to talk to the owner of the *Undine,* which is the name of the ship that has brought these fine quality furs. Perhaps the merchant is going to share the information where these fine furs can be bought. Now here is the surprise. The owner of the ship and merchant is a woman from America. She is, according to captain Daniels, the widow of a wealthy merchant and they had a little son. I did not want to be impolite and ask too many questions at a first meeting. Next time I see him I will ask the woman's name." Jack placed the quill he had held in his hand, back into the little inkpot and leaned back in his chair, to muster Hammed with an amused smile.

"Wonderful, Hammed, if we can find the source for those fine furs, we could send all our ships to buy them. Oh, what a tremendous profit we could make." Jack was jubilant.

"We just have to be careful not to make the lady merchant suspicious. She might want a share of the profits, if she is going to share her source," Hammed cautioned.

"I would not mind giving her a small percentage, Hammed. From what I heard from you, she is a widow and is raising her child alone and might need all the help she can get," Jack admonished softly.

'This is not how you thought several years back, when your own son was born and Miss Margaret was alone to fend for herself and the child', Hammed thought, but kept it to himself. Since Hammed didn't answer and looked indeed crestfallen, Jack padded his shoulder and suggested,

"Perhaps we can find out, where this merchant lady lives and invite her to our next ball. If she is beautiful and intelligent, she might soon find a new suitor from among our single friends, especially Vincento," he chuckled.

"Ah, marriage becomes you, Master Jack. I can see that you want everybody as happy as you are. Allah be praised for you finding your wonderful wife and having your sweet little Nora."

"Yes, Hammed, I am happy for the first time in my life and I feel I don't deserve either one of them. Neither my beautiful wife nor my darling little Leonora. She is growing every day and her grandfather spoils her too much. Just yesterday he brought a new doll for her again, which would make that number twenty in her collection. I wonder, what he will bring her on her second birthday next week," Jack laughed.

"Speaking of Nora's birthday, Master Jack; The invitations have all been sent out. Since you suggested to invite some friends, do you think it a good idea, to perhaps invite the lady merchant? Her son might enjoy playing with the other children from your friends."

"I think this is a little too early yet, Hammed, Speak to this captain Daniels at first and find out a little more about her and the boy. I do not want any hard to control children around Leonora. She is spoiled enough as it is," he finished with a rueful sigh.

"Very well, Master Jack, it should not be easy however. captain Daniels is very young and protective of his female Master. From what I understood, the child is little yet and she lives out in Sant Adria by the red cliffs."

"I rode out there the other day, Hammed, as my wife insisted to visit her father's dear friend Senior Alfredo de Domingo and I saw a lady

331

with a small child standing by the cliff. Perhaps this was the lady from America. I know the house you speak of. It once belonged to my wife's father until he sold it to Don Dorango, our banker. Don Dorango is renting out several of his houses. Perhaps we can find out a little more about the lady, if I speak to Don Dorango. Go and fetch Sergio, I will send him with a message to Don Dorango."

"At once, Master Jack." Hammed bowed slightly and hurried out the door.

The messenger returned and told Jack, that Don Dorango would be able to come by the house later in the afternoon. Jack waited patiently while playing with his little daughter in the pool. Little Nora liked the water and splashed happily, in her father's arms, while Sofia sat watching them in a big lawn chair. Hammed's own little daughter, Mabel sat next to Sofia on the lawn and played with one of Nora's many dolls. Mabel promised to be a beautiful woman some day. Her rich creamy skin was somewhat darker and her hair was raven black, which shimmered bluish in the light. Her large eyes were a stunning sky blue and almost piercingly looked into the world. She had celebrated her third birthday on April the ninth and had not understood, as papa told her, that mama would soon have a little brother or sister for her to play with. She was happy to play with Nora's dolls. Indeed, Elizabeth would be giving birth to her second child any day now and Hammed was ecstatic. Elizabeth had begged Hammed, to let her sister Laura come to Spain and Hammed finally had agreed, after speaking with Jack. So, Laura would be arriving soon and Elizabeth was happy to have a small part of her family with her and some help with her children.

It was late in the afternoon as Don Dorango arrived at the mansion. Jack bade him to follow him into his study. After offering refreshments, the men sat in comfortable chairs and Jack looked at his visitor.

"The reason I asked you here, Don Dorango, is of a delicate nature. Let me start at the beginning. A few days ago, Hammed was able to purchase some very fine furs from a merchant ship, which belongs to a merchant from Sant Adria. The captain of the merchant ship spoke to Hammed and promised, to disclose the source of the high quality furs to us, after he had spoken with the merchant. You can imagine my surprise, that the merchant turned out to be a woman. She seems to have moved here not too long ago and from what I understand, she is a widow with a small child. By any chance, Don Dorango, do you know of the woman I speak of?"

"Indeed I do know the lady in question, Baron de Viego. She rented the little villa by the red cliffs from me," Don Dorango answered.

"Did she tell you her name?" Jack asked.

"Yes, Baron de Viego, she did. I could hardly rent out one of my finer houses, without knowing the name of my tenants," Don Dorango answered and asked slightly concerned in return, "why do you want any information on this woman Baron?"

"It is very simple, Don Dorango. My dear Hammed suggested to invite the lady and her child for my daughter's second birthday party. Since I don't want any troublesome incidents, I wish to know a little about the lady and her child. Please, Don Dorango, can you tell me some more?" Jack insisted.

"All I know is, that the lady is a young widow and her name is Donna Katrina Brickmaker. She came here from America after her husband's death and took over his merchant business. She seems a very charming and beautiful young lady of quality and the little boy is a very smart little fellow of about four or five years of age. She is very industrious and besides running her late husband's business, she makes the most wonderfully fragrant soaps and perfumes. She sent me some of her products after I rented the house to her. That in itself speaks of a lady of good breeding, Baron. As I showed her the house, the child was with her and she called him Jessy, I believe. Does that help you in any way, my dear Baron?"

Don Dorango did not like to disclose his costumers private affairs. However, Baron de Viego was one of his best costumers together with Senior Alfredo de Domingo. He could not afford to lose either one of them to another bank. Furthermore, he was able to purchase some items from Jack's warehouse at a great discount. He did not see any harm in telling Jack all he knew about Donna Brickmaker. It seemed he was merely concerned about his precious little daughter's welfare.

"How young do you estimate Donna Brickmaker to be?"

"Oh, Baron de Viego, I am terrible at guessing a lady's age. I would say she is no more than her early twenties."

"Thank you, Don Dorango, yes it was indeed helpful what you have told me. You see, some of my friends here have children about Jessy's age and it would be lovely for the little boy to make some new friends here. I know the villa out by the red cliffs is somewhat isolated and he may not have great opportunities to find playmates," Jack said sweetly.

"Of course, Baron de Viego. I am certain that Donna Brickmaker will appreciate your kindness and concern toward her son. If that is all, I must be getting back to my business," Don Dorango said and rose. Jack escorted the banker to the door and bid him a good day.

"Hammed, to me," Jack shouted, after he had closed the door behind his visitor.

"Here I am, Master Jack." Hammed stuck his head out the secret door to a small room, which was cleverly hidden in the study behind a bookcase. Jack kept his wife's jewels and precious metals there. He chuckled softly as he thought about how Don Dorango's face would light up, if he knew the treasure that was hidden there. However, Jack had no intension to store his wife's jewels and his gold and silver at the bank. Banks might get robbed or worse, the king could freeze assets at any time, if he had need of raising funds for his purposes.

"Well, my dear Hammed, you have heard what Don Dorango said. Donna Brickmaker is very young yet and according to our dear banker beautiful," he laughed. Both men knew, that the banker's wife was less than handsome and he considered his wife to be beautiful.

"Do you really want to invite Donna Brickmaker to your daughter's birthday party, Master Jack?" Hammed asked still a little concerned.

"Of course I will, Hammed. I wish to speak to her myself about the source of the fine furs. Perhaps she will tell me," Jack mused.

"Shall I send Sergio, Master Jack?"

"Yes, Hammed, send Sergio to me. I am going to write the invitation myself this time."

"What if Donna Brickmaker declines?"

"Think, Hammed, she is, according to Don Dorango, a good

mother. She will grasp the opportunity to have her son find some friends here in this country. I will add a few well-meaning words to the invitation as to her son's happiness. Furthermore, if she is a strong and beautiful woman, our dear Vincento might take a liking to her. I invite him as well. Perhaps we can do Alfredo a favor and his son might straighten out his life, if he falls in love with a woman." Jack smiled smugly.

"Oh, Master Jack. I remember your dear friend Thomas saying once to me that meddling could bite someone in the ass, if you pardon me," he cautioned.

"Nonsense, Hammed, I don't think it is the same. Vincento is a very handsome man. He just needs the right woman to keep him in line. If he would not be so lazy and gamble, he would be a fine catch indeed."

"Allah forbid, Master, if the poor woman would fall in love with Vincento, he might gamble her fortune away. Could you sleep with that on your conscience?"

"From what I understand, Hammed, the woman has been able to amass a great deal of money. She is not just giving it to any man," Jack pouted.

"You have no idea, what a woman in love will do for a man, Master Jack. I strongly advice against the idea to bring the two together. Your wife would have your ears for breakfast if she knew, what you plan to do. Furthermore, we know merely her name and her approximate age. She could be a devil in disguise and just be friendly in public." Hammed looked concerned.

"Don't you dare tell my wife on me, Hammed. Sofia is a gentle soul and I love her very much. She might even start to nurture a friendship with this merchant woman. Can't you see how this could benefit the business? Furthermore, I do not want my wife to be concerned about anything but my dear little Nora and me. So, go and fetch Sergio for me in a little while. I will write the invitations first," Jack ordered.

"Yes, Master Jack, as you wish," Hammed said with a heavy sigh. He couldn't help the uneasy feeling, which seemed to creep into his inside. Perhaps he would be able to warn the poor woman about Vincento's drinking and gambling, without his master's knowledge.

Sometimes he felt like boxing Jack's ears. In many ways, he was still selfish and did not think of the consequences. Though he stopped drinking, he still behaved egocentrically at times. Hammed was not fooled for a minute, that Jack did not needed to do Alfredo a favor. He wanted Vincento out of his own hair. The young man had a habit of dropping by the house quite frequently to borrow money, when his father had refused him. Gentle and kind as Sofia is, she was not able to say no to the handsome and charming devil. Here was the whole reason for Jack's trying to interfere. Hammed went to the kitchen and looked for his wife. Elizabeth sat by the table and was drinking a glass of milk. Seeing the dark look on her husband's face, she knew that something was wrong.

"Hammed, my love, you look as if you could rival the storm clouds in England. What is it?" Hammed sat next to his wife and placing his hand lovingly on her big protruding stomach, heaved a sigh.

"I really don't know what to do, Betty, my Love. Jack is about to do something foolish and it might even be cruel. I don't want the parties involved hurt. I also don't want Jack angry at me for warning the persons in this scheme of his. Give me some advice my dear."

"My poor dear," Elizabeth crooned softly, "go and pray to Allah for advice. Any advice I could give you, is coming from a mere woman with a soul and feelings. If someone is about to get hurt, I would tell you in an instant to stop it at any cost. Let your own mind be your guide and ask the creator. Set your mind at rest my dear. Allah knows that you are trying to prevent something terrible. He will not judge you and will bestow his favor upon you for obeying his laws."

"Thank you, my sweet Love, I knew I could count on you. Ah, what would I do without you," He gently kissed his wife's hand and asked, "do you feel like taking a walk with me through the gardens later this evening?"

"I should like this very much, my dear husband," Elizabeth smiled at him with a mischievous smile. Though she was not able to couple with him at regular fashion, his mouth and hands could move a Saint to sin. They would go to their little place with the very soft grass in the far corner of the Estate. It was well hidden behind thick bushes and trees.

Both believed, that in this spot, their second child was conceived and it was now considered to be a very special little place, where they had made love many times.

"I shall see you later then. I must go and fetch Sergio for Jack." Hammed kissed his wife's cheek and hurried to do his master's bidding.

Jack sat in his study and was trying to think of the right words to write to Donna Brickmaker. He must not make her suspicious, that he had made inquiries about her. Dipping the quill into the inkpot, he wrote,

Honored Donna Brickmaker

It has come to my attention that you have newly arrived in our country. By mere coincidence did I find out from our banker Don Dorango, that you have a small child. My daughter's second birthday party is to celebrated next week on August the 26th. Some of my friends have small children also and I believe, your child might enjoy meeting some new playmates. Please honor my house with your presence and join our small festivities.

Baron Giaccomo de Viego

Satisfied, Jack sat back in his chair and his eyes flew over the invitation once more. Her folded and sealed the paper and wrote a second invitation to his dear friend's son Vincento de Domingo, that he was invited to celebrate Leonora's second birthday party. He was sealing this letter, as Sergio entered the study and bowing asked,

"Baron de Viego, Hammed said to report here. I am to deliver some messages again?"

"Yes, Sergio, take this blue letter to Vincento de Domingo and the white letter to Sant Adria. Out by the red cliffs is a single villa. A lady lives there by the name of Donna Brickmaker. Give this letter to her and wait for the reply. Take *Candra* to ride out there. She is one of my fastest horsesl" he ordered.

"Yes, Baron, I shall be back in a few hours," Sergio grinned and bowed again. He loved the big horse *Candra* and was happy to ride her. There was not one day, that he did not sneak into the stables and fed *Candra* some apples or carrots. Quickly, Sergio ran to the stables and had one of the grooms saddle his favorite horse on the Baron's orders. The groom looked disbelieving at him and chuckled,

"What kind of message is this, that the Baron would let you ride *Candra*?"

"I have no idea, I can't read a sealed letter, you dolt. Now hurry, the Baron is waiting for an answer from a lady out by the red cliffs in San Adria," Sergio said with great importance.

"Ah, a lady it is, huh?" the groom sneered while placing the heavy saddle onto the horses back.

"It's none of my affair or yours, what the Baron does," Sergio grumbled.

"Well then, off you go and be careful. The road out by the cliffs is very dangerous in the dark. So you best hurry and bring *Candra* back in one piece," the groom said and gave the horse a loving smack on its backside.

Sergio was a fine horseman and had been around horses all his young live. His father was a groom at Alfredo de Domingo's Estate and young Sergio had been able to ride the horses to exercise them every day. He rode like the wind and reached the de Domingo house in less than an hour. It would take him another two hours or so to reach the villa by the red cliffs. With any luck, it would still be daylight when he entered the road up there. Unless he would take the shortcut. Sergio had taken this narrow and steep path many times and knew his way to the villa well. Before Senior de Domingo had sold it to Don Dorango, he had delivered many messages to the former tenant of the little villa. Gently padding *Candra's* neck, Sergio smiled,

"You don't have to run like the devil, *Candra*, we will take the little path to the villa. It will save us over half an hour."

Sergio arrived at the foot of the red cliffs and carefully led the horse up the narrow path, instead of going around the long winding road, which would lead through San Adria and then slightly up the hill toward the red cliff villa. He had been correct and it was still daylight, as he arrived at the end of the little path and the villa came into his view. Dismounting *Candra*, he delivered the white letter to one of the servant girls, saying,

"I have an urgent message for Donna Brickmaker and I am to wait for the reply."

"Please come to the kitchen and take some refreshments. I will give the letter to Donna Katrina at once," the girl said and led Sergio to the kitchen.

She poured him a glass of orange juice and handed it to him,

"Donna Katrina is still in her workroom making soap. Wait here, I shall be back soon."

Sergio sat and sipped the delicious cool juice and waited patiently. The sun was beginning to set and it was getting dark outside. The girl returned and told Sergio, that Donna Katrina would write a reply as soon as she was finished in her workroom. A small boy entered the kitchen and asked the girl for some milk. Turning, he saw Sergio and curiously asked,

"Good evening, who are you?"

"Good evening, I am Sergio and I am a messenger. What is your name?"

"I am Jessy, mama calls me that, because papa liked to call me Jessy also," the child said with a small grin.

"Well met, Jessy. Say, do you like horses?"

"I used to have my own pony in America. Mama promised me to get one for me on my birthday. I am going to be five years old," Jessy said with great importance.

"When is your birthday Jessy?" Sergio smiled. He liked the bright little boy and gave a friendly little wink to the girl, peeling oranges. The girl blushed and lowered her glance.

"My birthday is in October on the 14th day. Are you going to bring me a gift, Sergio?"

"Perhaps I will," Sergio said and asked, "what is it you want most Jessy?"

"A new papa, Sergio. My papa died at sea. He was a great captain and the ship belongs to mama now."

"Ah, there you are, Jessy, come and wash up, dinner will be served soon." Patty had entered the kitchen and took Jessy's hand.

"Remember my birthday, Sergio," Jessy called back as Patty led him from the kitchen.

"Do not worry, I will not forget, Jessy," Sergio called after the boy and laughed. He remembered his youngest brother who was six years old and was a little scamp just like Jessy. Sergio with seventeen was the oldest of six children and he liked to be around children. Life was so simple around the little people. It only got complicated around the older people.

Finally the door opened and the dark skinned girl handed him a letter.

"Here is Donna Brickmaker's answer. Take this to Baron de Viego."

Sergio quickly grabbed the letter and giving the saucy little kitchen maid another wink, under which she blushed again, he hurried back to his horse. He pondered to take the road down this time. The night was dark and he had only the moon to light his way. However, it was getting late and he wanted to get the message back to the Baron as soon as possible. Furthermore, there might be an extra coin in it for him. Sergio took the little path.

"Damn that boy, Hammed. It is passed midnight. Where in Allah's name is Sergio?" Jack thundered.

"I wish I knew, Master Jack. Perhaps Donna Brickmaker decided to let Sergio stay the night. The road can be treacherous at night," Hammed tried to calm his master.

"Sergio knows better. I told him to wait for the reply and it was urgent," Jack snapped.

"Nevertheless, perhaps Donna Brickmaker has more sense than you and will not let the boy ride down the road at night. Especially with a fine horse as *Candra,*" Hammed snapped back.

Jack gave him a dark look and grumbled,

"Sergio is a fine horseman and knows the road up to the villa. He also loves *Candra*."

"Precisely, Master Jack. Sergio would not endanger *Candra* and take the risk of her injuring herself on the rocks. Be patient until morning. If he is not back by then, we will send some men to search for him," Hammed spoke with more calm than he actually felt. He had an uneasy feeling in his stomach. Perhaps it was nothing or perhaps it had been Elizabeth, telling him of a slight backache earlier. Both men went to their own quarters to sleep.

It was around three in the morning, as a frantic knocking woke Jack.

"Master Jack, Master Jack, the groom just came to me and told me that *Candra* is back at the stables. *Candra's* left front leg had a big scratch and blood on it. Oh, Master, I am sick at heart. We must go and search for Sergio. He might be lying out there on the road injured and helpless." Hammed was wringing his hands in dismay.

"Call the men together, Hammed. We will go at once." Jack rubbed the sleep from his eyes. Quickly he dressed and within half an hour, five of his men were mounted and ready to go. Jack told one of his men to ride to Senior de Domingo and find out if Sergio had been there. He would meet him at the foot of the road to the villa. The men rode in silence and daybreak was near, as they reached the road. His other man was waiting for him, with six of Alfredo's men already. One of Alfredo's men spoke,

"Pardon me, Baron, I know the area well and so does Sergio. He might have been taken the little path up over there." He pointed to a hardly noticeable path, which would lead up to the end of the road, emerging near the villa. Hammed turned ashen.

"Allah have mercy," he mumbled.

"Very well the, you take your men and take the path up, my men and I will take the road. We will meat on the top of the hill," Jack ordered.

Jack, Hammed and the other four men rode slowly up the long road and looked carefully on both sides of the road for any sign of Sergio. A man came riding after the group at high speed and Hammed saw him waiving frantically and shouting something. The group waited and as the man came near, Hammed recognized him as one of Alfredo's men. Short of breath, the man panted,

"Baron, we found Sergio. His horse had stumbled and he hid his head. He is bleeding and his arm hurts also. He is alive. Come quickly." He turned to race back down the road with six other men in his wake. They reached Sergio and the other men merely a few minutes later and Jack jumping from his horse, knelt by Sergio.

"If you were not injured already, I should beat you senseless for taking the path at night. You could have fallen down the cliff side and be killed you little idiot. What would I have told your father then."

"I am sorry, Baron de Viego. *Candra* got spooked by a night bird. She lost her footing and stumbling threw me. I was caught of guard and I reached for the reign as she ran. But my arm hurt and she got away. How did you find me?"

"You have to thank *Candra* for that, my boy. She made it home and the groom got alarmed as you were not with her." Jack softened as he saw tears developing in the boy's eyes.

"Oh, dear *Candra*, she will get all the carrots she can eat," Sergio sniffed.

His head ached terribly and he had a nasty gash, which was still bleeding a bit. He was happy to be alive however. As the men placed him on one of the horses, he winced. His arm was broken and he saw, the limb had swollen to almost twice its normal size. Hammed took his turban and without a word, wrapped the boy's broken arm tightly. At home the doctor would take care of the rest.

"Oh, by the way," Sergio reached into his shirt with his healthy arm and withdrew a letter, "here is Donna Brickmaker's answer." He held the letter out to Jack. Jack took the letter and while the group slowly rode, he read. His features turned into a smile.

CHAPTER 27

Merciful Blindness

Katrina was beside herself with feelings of hatred, anger and envy. Over and over she read the invitation, which Jack had sent her. He had a daughter and a wife and she had been left to raise her son alone. If not for the sweet kindness of strangers and her beloved Thomas, she would have been destitute perhaps for the rest of her life. Her mind was made up. She would hurt this man in the worst way possible. However, she must find out about his habits and where she could wreck his life to bring him to his knees. What better way, as to accept his invitation and present his wife with a son he had. His wife would leave him with his daughter. Katrina thought for a while and wrote,

Honored Baron de Viego

I wish to thank you for your gracious invitation. Your concern for my son's welfare is touching and I appreciate your kind thoughts. I accept your invitation. I am deeply grateful for including my son and myself to the festivities of your daughter's second birthday.

Katrina M. Brickmaker

Katrina sealed the letter and called for Patty to give her answer to the messenger. She would have to find a way to talk to Steve. She did not want him to talk to anyone about her and give her secret away before she could strike. Steve however, must never know, that Baron de Viego is in fact her son's father. Patty returned with little Jessy on her hand to kiss his mother good night. She pulled her son on her lap and looked into his face. It was disconcerting, how much he resembled his father. Confused and with mixed feelings, she kissed his cheek and wished him a good night. To Patty's great astonishment, she quickly placed the child back on its feet and turned abruptly, so the girl would not see the tears well up in her eyes. Pretending to write in her inventory books, she bent over her little desk and Patty, shaking her head, took her little charge's hand to take him to bed. Jessy had noticed patty's puzzlement and finishing his prayers, he said quietly,

"I think mama is still sad about papa dying Patty. Do you think that papa can see me from heaven?"

"Oh yes, little Jessy, papa can see you. Papa is with God and baby Jesus and he is an angel now, so he can watch over you." Patty gently placed her hand on Jessy's hair and stroked the child's forehead with her thumb. In a soft voice, she began to tell him a story about princes and princesses and soon his eyes closed.

Katrina however was unable to sleep. She had looked for Steve and had found that he had sought his bed. Not wanting to disturb him, she went to her little workroom and sat on the little wooden stool. Whenever she was excited or sad, she had found that work would take her mind of her troubles. Looking for one of her essences to make her perfume, she noticed the vial was near empty. She remembered the crates she had found in the warehouse in Algiers. She went to the little storeroom and finding the iron to pry one of the crates open, she pulled back the lid. Strangely, there were several oddly shaped objects wrapped in pieces of clothes. She took one of the objects and felt it was heavy. Slowly she began to unwrap it and gasped in horror. In her hand was a gun. Quickly she dropped it and began to unwrap the other pieces of clothes. She found boxes with black powder and ammunition as well as more guns. She could not make any sense of it.

"Dear God, what did Thomas want to do with all these guns?" she asked out loud. He could build a small army with all this. Suddenly, a thought struck her and she remembered that there was unrest and talk of revolution in America, before she had left this country. Could her dear gentle Thomas have been involved in all this? Opening the other crates, she found two more with guns and accessories. The remaining twelve crates contained her essences and oils. Carefully, she wrapped the weapons and boxes of powder and ammunition back into the clothes and closing the lids, she placed some empty crates on top, which she filled with essences and oils. No one must ever know, that she had found the weapons. Taking some of her essences and oils, she carefully locked the door to the little storeroom and placed the key in her skirt pocket. She would have to make certain, that her workroom was always fully supplied with her ingredients and necessary items, which she needed to make her products. She could not allow the girl, which helped her during the day, to fetch them for her any longer. Taking a big bottle of pure alcohol, she poured some of it in a small earthenware bowl. Setting the bowl aside, she filled an identical bowl with water to bring it to a boil. She looked for certain flower pedals and found the jar was empty. Annoyed, she went back to the storeroom and brought the needed flower pedals back, which were in a linen bag. She filled the jar with the pedals and taking some, she crumbled them into one of the earthenware bowls. She had not noticed the small crack in the bowl. Placing the bowl over a small metal dish with burning oil, she stood patiently to wait for the pedals to cook. Coming closer, she tried to smell the fragrance of the vapors coming from the bowl. Suddenly, there was a flash and a loud crash.

She screamed as she was thrown against the wall behind her. Her eyes burned terribly and her face hurt. Feeling her face, she found, that it was wet. She tried to open her eyes to look at her hand. She could see nothing. In a flash, she remembered what happened. She had mistaken the bowl of water, with the bowl with alcohol. She had to get help, for she could hear the fire crackling. If it would reach the other bottles with alcohol and vials with oil, the villa would explode. Crawling along the wall, she found the doorknob and opening the door, she screamed again. She could hear rushing footsteps and the voices of her servants. She heard Steve's voice roar,

"Damn it, don't just stand there, go fetch the doctor." Suddenly she felt herself swept up into strong arms and carried up the stairs. She could hear water splashing and knew, that the fire was being extinguished. Moaning, she held onto the neck of the person carrying her. She knew it was a strong man and she heard him panting as he rushed her to the sitting room couch, where he gently placed her down. She heard his voice and recognized Steve.

"My God Katrina, what happened?"

"I was making perfume and mistakenly placed the bowl with the alcohol on the fire instead of the water. My face hurts terribly and I cannot open my eyes. The burning is horrific, Steve. I am not able to see. My god, Steve, I am blind," Katrina whimpered softly and very frightened.

"I have sent for the doctor, Katrina. He should be here soon. Hold still, I am going to pour water over your eyes to wash them out." She felt the water pouring over her eyes, which he had opened with his fingers as gently as he could. She felt the water running over her face and it stung her. She winced again.

"What happened to my face, Steve?" she asked in a shaking voice. The pain of her stinging eyes was incredible and she felt herself getting faint. She heard Steve's voice from far away before she fell into darkness,

"You have a nasty gash on your cheek. The doctor will have to sew it."

She had no idea, how long she had been unconscious and when she came too and feeling with her hands around her, she felt her own bed. Gingerly she felt her face with her hands and discovered her eyes and face were covered with bandages wrapped around her head.

"You must lie still, Katrina, here, drink this," Steve's voice could be heard and she felt something being held against her lips, "it will help you sleep and lessen the pain. The doctor gave it to me before he left. He said to be sure you drink it all." Obediently, Katrina drank the liquid down and flinched at the bitter taste of it.

Falling back into her pillows, she remembered, why she had been in her workroom in the first place. She had been unable to sleep, since she had read Jack's invitation and had thought of her revenge. 'Oh dear, the invitation…I am unable to go. I am blind and disfigured for the rest of my life. It is all his fault. Dear God, I never hated anybody as much as I hate Jack. Damn him to hell, he will pay some day.' Mercifully, the drug worked fast and she fell into a healing sleep. Steve sat by her bedside dozing, as she spoke after many hours,

"Steve, please tender my apologies to Baron de Viego for me. I believe I am unable to attend his daughter's birthday celebration," she said ruefully.

She felt hot and her whole body was bathed in sweat.

"You are running a fever, Katrina," Steve felt her forehead, "what is this about a birthday celebration?"

"I received an invitation from the Baron. I answered that I would be joining the festivities," Katrina said low and quietly.

"Don't worry, I will send a messenger to the Baron. The doctor should be here again later this evening. He will change your bandages and give you something for the fever. Just lie still and save your strength," Steve crooned softly, taking her hot hands in his big cool ones.

"Where is Jessy?" Katrina asked fearful.

"He has been told, that mama has taken ill with a stomach ache and must stay in bed for a while. I did not let him see you like this. I anticipated your fear of him seeing you with your face all wrapped up," Steve calmed her.

"Thank you, Steve," she squeezed his hand, "that was very thoughtful of you. May I please have something to drink? I am terribly thirsty." He responded by holding a glass of cool orange juice to her lips. Greedily she drank in big gulps and fell back into her pillows, exhausted. She felt herself getting drowsy again and her mind wandered to her childhood. She saw her mother baking bread and Misses Tippins cooking in her kitchen. Little images of a happy time, long past, were brought to her mind by the high fever and soon she was asleep once more.

Steve was getting worried. The doctor had told him, that the injuries to her eyes were indeed severe. He had removed several tiny splinters from the exploded earthenware bowl out of her eyes. It was highly unlikely, that Katrina would regain her full eyesight, if any at all. After stitching her cheek, he also assessed the wound on her lovely face, which of course would leave a scar and fading in time, might be hardly noticeable. Steve, knowing her whole story, felt sorry for the young woman he had grown very fond of. Pondering, how miserable and unfair life could be sometimes, he thought about his own fate. He was exiled by his own choice from his country and did not know, if his family were still alive and well. It was so unfair, that Thomas had to die before he was able to bring the weapons to America. Then again, where had Thomas hidden them? He had promised to bring the load back from his last trip, which had lead him to the islands of Sumatra and Borneo. Suspecting, that the weapons might be hidden in the warehouse Thomas shared with a friend from England, he had eagerly accepted Katrina's proposal to have the *Undine* repaired and bring her home. He had found nothing. Ah, he remembered Thomas telling him, that this certain friend had also moved to Spain. Unfortunately, he had never mentioned his name. Perhaps Katrina would be able to help him, as soon as she was feeling better. He had to be careful however, for Katrina had no knowledge of her late husband's activities in politics and Steve had no intention of telling her about it. The big captain had supported the appointed commander of the newly created continental army, George Washington. Thomas had spoken highly of this big man. Washington had liked to ride horses and was a fine surveyor. Thomas had met him at Culpepper County, where Washington was an adjutant since 1753. Unfortunately, he had to resign his commission in 1754 and offered his services to volunteer as aide-de-camp to the British general Edward Braddock. Braddock was mortally wounded in an ambush by French forces and Indians and Washington barely escaped with his life. While war had been declared between the French and Britain, Washington had managed to keep the Virginia frontier relatively safe. This had gained the big colonel Washington the admiration of many, including Thomas. Now, the weapons, which

Thomas had promised, could not be found and Steve hoped, that his country was able to free itself from the intruders without them.

Katrina moaned and seemed very hot.

"Thomas, oh, Thomas."

She threw her blankets off in her restless sleep and Steve's eyes got a glimpse of her shapely soft legs. Her nightgown had slipped and exposed her thighs. Trying to calm the restless woman, he placed his hand once more on her hot one. Feverish and delirious, she grabbed his hand and said,

"Oh, my dear Love, I need you so much. Thomas, touch me like the first time we made love by the lake." Slowly, she pushed the resisting hand down her belly to her secret woman's place. Steve did not know, what to do and sat stunned for a moment. Katrina whole body felt hot and he was unable to ignore the moist softness between her thighs. Though it did not seem right to him, his own body responded with a certain stirring in his loins. Slowly and gently, he began to caress her moist pink flesh with his fingers. Katrina seemed to relax under his touch and he could see her face turn into a smile under the bandages. Blissfully she met his touch and her breathing became quicker.

"Thomas, love me with your mouth. I love when you play with your tongue. Oh, my darling, I need you so." She panted and opened her legs wide. Steve knew that none of the servants would enter this room without knocking and he bent his head. He tasted her salty sweetness on his tongue and quickly flicked it insistently over her stiff little jewel of ecstasy. Inserting his finger gently and imitating the act of loving, Katrina arched her back to meet his touch. She cried out her pleasure and instantly relaxed as his brought her to an shuddering climax. She seemed peaceful and Steve pulled the blanket gently over her hips to cover her nudity. He could still taste her pungent fragrance on his lips and he ached. Quickly, he got up and called for one of the servant girls to watch Katrina for a little while. Merely a few minutes later, he had climbed down a small path by the cliffs and taking his trousers and shirt off, he dove into the cool sea. His mind still brought the writhing woman in front of his eyes and he knew, that he did desire her. He must have her and make her happy. This time, she had thought in her feverish mind, that it was Thomas. The next time, she would know, it would be him. He would have to be patient. Her fragile mind was still mourning for her husband and it would take time to heal her spirit. Steve had nowhere to go. The country he loved was in uproar and there was no other lady waiting for him anywhere in the world. He had to accept that, perhaps, his fate would lie with Katrina. Life never brought any certainties or guaranties. He had seen, how quick and unmerciful death could strike at any given moment. It was just too precious to waste, with wishing for something better, when a good thing was right in front of ones nose. Yes, he would stay here in Spain and try to make Katrina happy. In time, she would learn to love him. Slowly, he swam back to shore and pulling his trousers back on, he grabbed his shirt and walked back to the house. He went to his rooms to change his clothes and back to Katrina's bedchamber, where the doctor had just arrived. In a hushed voice he spoke to Steve,

"I just changed her bandages again, Captain. She seems more relaxed and it feels like the fever went down the slightest bit." Reaching into his bag, he handed Steve two little bottles. "Here is some more medication. The one with the blue label will help her sleep and lessen the pain. Give her a small spoon of this only when she needs it. The green label is medication to fight the infection. She should have this three times a day and once at night. Make certain that she takes it. Call me at any time, if there is any change for the worse."

"Thank you, doctor. I will make sure that she takes all of her medication. Hopefully she will get better soon. She had worse already," Steve whispered with an rueful smile. Somewhat fearful he looked at the doctor: "If she would get worse, could she die?"

"I doubt she will die from her injuries, Captain. However, if the fever is rising too high, her brain would start to boil and that could indeed kill her. She needs plenty of fluids and has to be kept cool. To aid the medication for the fever, wrap some compresses around her calves and wrists. Take two parts cool water and one part vinegar in a container and moisten some clothes with the solution. That is all we can do for her at this point."

"I shall personally see to it, doctor. Thank you again." Steve shook the doctors hand and led him to the door. He called for one of the servant girls and ordered to bring a bucket with cold water and some vinegar and towels.

Furthermore he told the girl to bring a big pitcher of lemon flavored water.

Steve sat by Katrina's bedside the whole night, changing her compresses and dribbling the medication to fight the fever between her lips. In the morning, with the help of the little servant girl Anna, he changed her sheets and nightgown after Anna had bathed Katrina's body gently with some cool scented water.

Sitting back in the chair, he told Anna to bring him some breakfast. The girl hurried to the kitchen and came back with a tray of food for the captain. He ate with gusto and sated, he leaned back into the chair to close his eyes. Anna removed the tray and tiptoed quietly from the room. How long Steve had dozed, he was not sure. He woke from the sound of Katrina's voice,

"Steve, are you here?"

"Yes, Katrina, I am here. What can I do for you?" he snapped out of his light slumber and took her hand quickly in his.

"I believe I am better, Steve. I don't feel so hot any longer. Please tell Anna to bring me something to eat. I am famished." Giving her hand a little squeeze, he happily complied. Her hand felt cool in his and he heaved a sigh of relieve.

"I am happy that you are better, Katrina. From what I can see, the wound on your cheek has also stopped bleeding. The bandages are clean. But let me get you something to eat first."

He called Anna and smiling happily the girl flew to the kitchen to bring Donna Katrina a tray with soft boiled eggs, the yolk still running, as Katrina preferred, a thin slice of ham, a small crock with sweet butter, a few slices of raisin bread, a small dish with strawberry jam and a steaming pot of strong coffee with milk. While Steve buttered the bread for her, She sipped some of the coffee and ate her eggs. Slicing the bread for her into tiny little squares, he fed it to her with tiny bits of ham, which he had cut. Chewing was still very painful and after she had braved three slices of bread with ham and little dollops of jam, she leaned back in her pillows.

"Thank you, Steve. That was so very sweet of you. I feel much better now."

"I am glad to be able to help you, Katrina," Steve stated simply. He had poured himself a cup of coffee and sipping purposely noisily the hot aromatic liquid, he saw Katrina relax. She had to know and be certain, that he was near and would take care of her. To take her mind of her injuries, he began to talk about the trading business.

"Katrina, I have made a decision. We should concentrate on trading more spices and fur for a while. Pepper is as you know in high demand and is bringing great profits. Here is my proposal for the future, Katrina. We need another two ships. Hear me out," he said quickly as she had raised herself from the pillows and wanted to say something. "India is our main source for pepper. In order to reach India, we have to go all the way around Africa and sail up the Indian Ocean to reach Bombay. With three ships, we could make ten times as much as we have been able to make now. Ship one would go back and forth between Bombay and Suez, where the cargo would be transported to Alexandria to the warehouse, which Thomas rented and is still available for us to hold our cargo until I arrive with the *Undine*, to bring it through the Mediterranean Sea here to Barcelona. While ship one is busy filling our warehouse, ship three can sail up to Greenland, to get our fine quality furs. As I had spoken to this Hammed, he told me that Baron de Viego has a whole fleet doing about the same as I intend to do. Merely, he gets his furs from a different source and I am not going to reveal about the trappers in Greenland unless you want me too."

"Oh no," she interrupted quickly, "he is not going to find out anything. I have been thinking about this for a while Steve. It came to my attention, that this Baron de Viego made inquiries about me. Please don't ever tell him or this Hammed anything about me or Thomas. Since he is a merchant also, he might have known my husband and would figure out, where we get the furs from," Katrina lied convincingly with logic.

"Of course I would never tell anything about you or our sources, Katrina. Now tell me, what do you think about my idea of buying two more ships. I know this shipyard owner in Norway and he would sell us two of his ships at a very low price," he pushed.

"How low?" She pondered the possibilities and found Steve's proposal made a lot of sense. Steve named a figure and she caught her breath.

"You are correct, Steve, it would be very profitable if we could save all this time to go around Africa. Furthermore, you would be home here more often. Until things are settling in America, you might want to consider this your home for the time being." She sought his hand with hers stretching her arm out and he took it in his. Placing a gentle kiss on the back of her hand, he smiled.

"Thank you, Katrina. I intended to stay and have to ask you another question. How many warehouses did Thomas have all together?"

"As far as I know, there is the one big warehouse in Virginia. Then one in Algiers and besides this one here in Barcelona, I believe he spoke of another in Istanbul. Why do you ask?" she asked with a strange quiver in her voice. Of course, that's it, he had forgotten Istanbul. Trying to make his voice sound more nonchalantly than he felt, he answered,

"I was wondering, if we could perhaps store some of the furs in Lisbon, if there would have been a warehouse there. Ship number three would not have to make the trip all around Spain and could drop the cargo of much sooner, for me to pick it up."

It sounded logical and Katrina had not noticed any change in his voice, nor was she able to see his exited look. Damn, he had to go to Istanbul. He had to find out, if the weapons were still there. It would be what Thomas wanted, if he were alive. But how could he leave her behind. She needed him. He had a wonderful idea. He would tell her that he would go to Norway at once to purchase the two additional ships. There would be nothing suspicious about his leaving. Since the trip to Istanbul and Norway would take a few months anyway, he would tell her, that he was forced to spend the winter in Norway due to weather conditions. Nevertheless, he would stay in Spain until he was certain that Katrina was well enough and out of danger. It would still take a few more weeks. The doctor had agreed, that there was no danger any longer. The wound had healed nicely and to his immense joy, Katrina had regained some small sense of her vision. She was able to make out shadows and could even distinguish bright colors. He had given her a solution, with witch she would have to wash her eyes daily and keep them covered. Steve knew, that Katrina was in good hands as he left for Istanbul. Anna had promised him to not leave her side until he returned. As Steve took his leave of little Jessy, the boy asked,

"Uncle Steve, will you bring me something from Norway?"

"Of course I will bring you something. What would you like to have Jessy?" he laughed.

"I would like a puppy. We had big dogs in America and I miss Hercules. He was my favorite," Jessy said with shining eyes.

"Well then, I shall bring you a fine dog from Norway Jessy. Do you promise to take good care of him?"

"Oh yes, I will take very good care of the puppy. I promise," he wiggled excitedly. He liked his uncle Steve. He was almost as nice as papa had been.

"Uncle Steve," he lowered his glace bashfully, "could you be my new papa, when you come back?" Steve was caught unawares and almost choked on the apple he was eating.

"Ah, Jessy, I believe we have to talk about this some more when I get back. But I will tell you a secret and you must promise me, not to tell anyone about this."

"I promise, uncle Steve, what is the secret?" Jessy whispered wide eyed.

"I like your mama very much and perhaps some day I will ask your mother to marry me. Then I will be your new papa," Steve whispered back smiling. Clapping his hands excitedly, Jessy cried,

"Oh how wonderful, I am going to have a puppy and a papa." Laughing, Steve placed his finger over his lips, to remind the boy of his promise. He answered giggling with the same gesture. In his rooms, Steve wrote a long letter, which he gave to Patty with special instructions. So, Steve set out on his long voyage to Istanbul. He would have to find a way to get the weapons, if there were any, to America. Katrina had given him power of attorney to transfer the funds he needed to Norway and he left with the promise to be back as soon as possible.

Chapter 28

Strong Ties

It was the same time, as Katrina lay in her bed, as Jack had received the message from Steve.

"Oh no, this is terrible," Sofia cried and tears stung her eyes, "the poor woman must be so terrified to lose her eye sight. I wish to God we could do something for her," she wiped her eyes with her fine linen handkerchief, " I cannot imagine not to be able to see my sweet child's face any longer. Oh please, my darling husband, can we not send for doctor De Walt in England."

"Oh, Sofia, I don't know if that would be such good idea. What if the woman refuses to see my former doctor? Let me make some discreet inquiries about her exact injuries first. Then we shall see," Jack tried to calm his sweet wife.

"I was so looking forward to meet the lady. Now this terrible thing happened to her," Sofia sniffed, looking at the short letter of explanation from captain Steve Daniels as to what happened and why Donna Brickmaker would be unable to attend the birthday festivities.

"I know, my Love. Would it please you, if we would invite the child to our daughter's birthday?" He held her close and softly kissed her forehead.

"Oh, Jack, yes it would please me very much. Thank you, oh thank you, my darling." Her eyes shone with joy and love for her handsome husband. She flung her arms around his neck and covered his cheek with many little kisses. Laughing, he sought her lips and she melted into his arms. A knock on the door brought the couple back to reality. It was Hammed, sticking his head through the door and he beamed a radiant smile.

"The doctor is with Elizabeth and it should be a few more hours before we have our child. Everything is going well."

"How wonderful, Hammed. We are happy for both of you." Sofia smiled and gave her husband a sweet look. He had the good grace to blush. Sofia had told him her wonderful little secret just this morning. She expected their second child some time next February. She knew somehow, that it would be a son this time and Jack, upon hearing the news, swung her jubilant around the room. They had decided to wait, telling Hammed about this wonderful news, until Elizabeth had her child delivered safely. On August the 21st in the year 1777 shortly before midnight, Elizabeth gave birth to a healthy boy, which Hammed named Benjamin. Benjamin ben Hassan was a big boy and it had taken Elizabeth many hours of pushing, grunting and sweating to bring forth the child. Radiantly, she beamed at her husband as he gingerly drew near her bedside. Lifting the swaddled infant, she handed Benjamin to his proud and amazed father. The child seemed to look straight at Hammed with intelligent eyes and his little hand grabbed firmly at his father's thumb. Kissing his new son's little hand, he handed him back to Elizabeth and sat beside her on the bed.

"Thank you, my love, for our fine son." There were tears of joy in his eyes, as he gently took her hand in his and pressed it against his cheek. He had never known such happiness as in the few years, in which he was married to this wonderful little woman. Exhausted, Elizabeth closed her eyes and caressed Hammed's cheek. A noise from the door startled the couple from their tender moment and Hammed quickly wiped his eyes. It was the Master's wife Sofia, with a goblet in her hand.

"Elizabeth gave me a fine son, Baroness. I am a fortunate man," he said proudly, getting up from his seat on the bed.

"Jack will be so happy to hear it, my dear Hammed. May I be the first to congratulate you both." Sofia smiled and handed Elizabeth the drink with herbs, beaten egg and red wine, which would help her sleep and regain her strength.

Happily she smiled and drank the strengthening potion. Sofia quietly left the happy couple and pulled the door softly shut behind her.

"Elizabeth and Hammed are the proud parents of a son, Jack." Sofia told her husband as she entered the study without knocking, which she seldom did. Sofia knew, when Jack was in the study, that he did not wanted to be disturbed. Waiving politeness aside in sight of the happy news she had to bring, Sofia saw her husband spin around. She could have sworn, that he had been walking toward the bookshelf at her entrance and he had stopped in his track. She had no idea about the secret little room behind the special bookshelf and Jack wanted to keep it this way. If Sofia knew, she might be tempted to give in to Vincento's begging. He could not allow it, especially since Alfredo de Domingo had spoken to him just the other day, that his son Vincento should not be indulged. Alfredo received a visit from the banker Don Dorango and found out that Vincento forged his father's signature to withdraw a large amount of money. Fortunately, the banker had been on the alert and alarmed by the sum, he had told Vincento, that the bank does not carry such large amount of money. He would have to sent for it to Madrid, which would take a few days. Disappointed, Vincento had left the bank in a fury and had gotten drunk. Upon finding out about his own son's intended deception, Alfredo cut Vincento's allowance entirely and told him to try work for a change.

If he would not be willing to do that, he would have to look for a different place to live. Grudgingly and with no place to go, Vincento had started to oversee deliveries to the warehouses by the docks.

"How very fortunate for both of them, Sofia," Jack said quickly with a sweet smile. He was hard pressed to hide his irritation at Sofia's entrance.

Seeing her puzzled look, he walked to the bookshelf and pretended to search for a certain book. Grabbing one, he said,

"Ah, here it is." More puzzled, Sofia laughed and asked,

"Since when do you read poetry my dear husband?" Frantically, his mind worked to find an answer:

"I wish to look for a poem, which I may present to my daughter on her birthday." He was grasping at straws. Sofia laughed even more.

"I am sure she will listen intently, when you start to recite it, Jack."

Sheepishly he mumbled back, "It is never too early for the finer things in life. Now may I please have some time to find the fitting poem for our daughter," he said with mock anger.

"Very well then, Jack, I will not disturb you any longer. It is late and I shall retire. Good night, my husband."

"Good night, my love, and pleasant dreams." Jack thumbed through the book in his hand, pretending to read a few words here and there. Shaking her head and chuckling softly, Sofia left the study and went up to her rooms.

Quickly, Jack placed the book back onto the shelf and locked the door to the study. Though Hammed knew of the secret room, he did not want his wife or any other servant to surprise him. Opening the secret door, he went to his desk in the study and pulled out a small box. He wanted to present Sofia with a magnificent necklace of sapphires and diamonds on Leonora's second birthday. The surprise would have been spoiled, if she would have caught him with the box in his hand. He chuckled amused as he thought about his wife's eyes. She would love her present. He left the secret room after placing the box with the necklace on one of the shelves and closed the bookshelf door safely. Pulling the hidden little lever, which swung the bookshelf shut, he placed the special book with a small indentation snug to the side of the wood to hide the lever and button. Satisfied, he eyed the bookshelf once more to find nothing out of place and went to his rooms.

To Elizabeth's great joy, her sister Laura arrived from England a few days later and Hammed was glad that his wife would have some help with the children. The next day would be Leonora's birthday and many things would still have to be done. As Hammed entered the study in the afternoon, he saw Jack sitting by the desk with a letter in his hand. Looking up, the

disappointment was clearly visible on his face.

"I trust, the letter you are reading bears bad tidings?" Hammed asked.

"Sofia will be saddened by this news. I had written an invitation for Donna Brickmaker's son to attend the party tomorrow. He was to be accompanied by captain Daniels. Here, read and see for yourself, Hammed." He handed his big friend the letter. Hammed read.

Honored Baron de Viego

As I mentioned in my first message, Donna Brickmaker is very ill do to her unfortunate accident, which left her blind. Furthermore, she sustained a serious injury to her face, which had to be stitched and brought about a high fever, from which she is only now slightly recovering. I took it upon myself to nurse Donna Brickmaker back to health, which makes it impossible to leave her bedside. Therefore, I deeply regret, I am unable to escort her son to attend your daughter's birthday festivities. Nevertheless, I thank you from the bottom of my heart for your kind invitation. We wish your daughter a joyous day and many happy returns in good health and prosperity.

Signed Captain Steve C. Daniels

A little smile formed around Hammed's lips, as he placed the letter on Jack's desk.

"What are you grinning about, Hammed? I don't see any humor in this," Jack snapped.

"It seems to me, that captain Daniels is very fond of Donna Brickmaker. *He* is nursing her?" He let the rest of his thoughts hang in the air. If the young captain loved Donna Brickmaker, then Jack's scheme may not work. Allah be praised for his wisdom. Hammed's prayers seemed to be answered in a most satisfying way. Unfortunately, the woman had to get hurt by all this and Hammed felt a twitch of guilt. He would have to pray some more for the woman's speedy recovery. Perhaps there is still a chance of her regaining her eye sight. Hammed decided to find the doctor, which had been called to tend to Donna Brickmaker's injuries. He must find out, if there was still hope. Somehow, Hammed blamed himself for the accident. However, for now, the young lady would be safe from Vincento after all.

"Nonsense, Hammed, captain Daniels might be nursing her, but I don't see anything strange in it. I place a wager on it, he is hoping for her quick recovery, so he may be going out to sea again. I remember Thomas being this way. His sea legs were always itching," he chuckled, "by the way, I have not heard from my friend in a very long time. I hoped to talk to him about the source of the furs, if we are unable to find out from Donna Brickmaker or her captain. From what we have heard so far about his country, there is great trouble and I hope Thomas and his wife are safe. The poor fellow has been through so much with losing his daughter," Jack said compassionately. Now that he was a father, he could understand his friend's pain. He believed, he would go insane, if something would happen to his sweet little Leonora. The thought made him shudder and his mind went to Donna Brickmaker's son. Sofia's remark came back to him and he felt genuinely sorry for the poor woman, who might never be able to see her child grow. As if Hammed could read his thoughts, he suggested,

"If I may be so bold, Master Jack, you have bought little gifts for all the other children attending the party tomorrow. Do you think it would be a terrible intrusion, if we send the small gift you had selected for her child to Donna Brickmaker's villa? It might cheer her and make the child happy. I would personally see to it, that it gets delivered. That way, I could perhaps find out, if she knows your friend captain Crandall. After all, she is from America and so is he. Usually, merchants know about each other and are fiercely competitive not to step on each other's toes by buying and selling the same wares. Another thought struck me, what if Donna Brickmaker indeed knew captain Crandall and he told her, where to find these fine furs. You know, he is always a gentleman, where ladies are concerned. From what I understand, she owns merely one ship and he might have given her aid in her enterprise after her husband died," he finished.

"Why, Hammed, you might be right," Jack mused, "softhearted as

Thomas is, he may indeed have tried to help Donna Brickmaker, if he knew her. I have in mind to write a letter to America. I will find out, why Thomas did not send word in, what is it now, over two years?"

"Yes, Master Jack, it has been that long," Hammed agreed, "may I have permission to bring the gift for the little boy to Donna Brickmaker's home?"

"Yes, of course you may have my permission. You will go the day after tomorrow and find out, if she or captain Daniels know Thomas. Perhaps we can find out, why we have not heard from him in such a long time. To be frank, I was thinking about Thomas often and I am worried. It is unlike him not to send any messages at all." Jack shook his head concerned.

"I wish I knew, what is keeping the captain, Master Jack. Hopefully by the day after tomorrow, we know more," Hammed smiled encouragingly. He bowed shortly and left his master to his thoughts. Hurrying to the kitchen, he spoke to the cooks about the menu for the celebrations and taking care of all the many little details, including musicians, drinks, the tables and chairs, which would have to be set up on the lawn, to even a small brick outside necessary that had been built just for the occasion. Everything had to be in perfect order. It was close to midnight, as Hammed was finally able to seek his own bed, after going to his wife's room to kiss her and the children in the nursery. Another bed had been placed in the nursery for Laura and she was sleeping soundly with the door to Elizabeth's room slightly ajar. Mabel slept with her thumb in her mouth, her black hair contrasting the snow white pillow. Proudly, Hammed looked at his sleeping son Benjamin. As he gently touched his cheek, the infant moved his little mouth like he was suckling. The big man chuckled softly and kissed the little forehead. Quietly, he tiptoed from the room and sighing contently, said his prayers and snuggled into his pillows. Life was wonderful. He had a beautiful loving wife and two healthy children. What more could a man want. Hammed closed his eyes and slept.

A frantic knocking on his door woke him from a deep slumber. It was still dark outside and grumbling he was Jumping from his bed, to open the door merely a crack. Peeking around the door, he blinked sleepily. It was Laura and she looked frightened:

"Hammed, Elizabeth is not feeling well. Her breast hurts and is very swollen and red. My sister feels hot to the touch. Come quickly," she urged.

"I shall be with you in a moment, Laura, let me fetch my robe," Hammed said wide awake now. Quickly he flung his robe over his shoulders and while running to his wife's room, he pulled it on and tied the sash. His wife was lying in her bed and said,

"Oh, Hammed my dear, Laura is such a fuss pot. It is nothing serious. My breasts are a little sore from nursing and the room is hot," she tried to console her concerned husband, who had taken her hot hand in his.

"No, my dear wife, you are running a fever. Do not lie to me. It may not be serious, but I will send for the doctor anyway. Just lie still and drink some cool juice," he turned and spoke to Laura, "go to the kitchen and bring your sister some orange juice. I shall go to the stables and ride to fetch the doctor myself." Kissing Elizabeth's hot forehead, he flew back to his room to dress. A little while later, he was on the horse to the doctor's house.

The doctor promised to be there shortly and Hammed rode back to be with his wife. Patiently, Hammed waited for the doctor's arrival, sitting on his wife's bed and holding her hot hands, feeding her orange juice. Finally the doctor came through the door and examined Elizabeth. He took Hammed outside and spoke,

"Your wife is suffering from an inflammation of the breasts. It is called Mastitis. Some nursing mothers are known to develop this disease."

"What can be done to cure this doctor?" Hammed asked frightful.

"Alternate warm and cold compresses on your wife's breasts. The cold will ease the pain and the warmth will increase the circulation and promote the milk to flow. Some milk ducts are in all likelihood clogged and your wife should nurse frequently to get the milk flowing. I would also suggest for your wife to sit in a warm tub and gently massage the inflamed areas so the hardened milk will start flowing once more. She will need plenty of rest and lots of fluids. Please make certain, that she is not getting exited in the next few weeks. Anxiety also stops the milk flow and could worsen her condition, which at this point is not very serious." Hammed shook the doctor's hand gratefully and said relieved,

"Thank you, doctor. I shall see that my wife gets everything you ordered."

"If there is any change, please do not hesitate to call me," the doctor smiled reassuringly and took the small bag of coins, which Hammed handed him for his services. Instructing Laura, he ordered a tub to be set up in Elizabeth's room and gently placed his wife into the warm water. He told her, what the doctor had instructed him to do and giggling she said with a mischievous smile,

"Would you do me the honor of massaging my breasts, my dear husband. I find your gentle touch soothing."

"Oh no, my dear, I will most certainly do no such thing," he protested laughing, feeling a tug of desire through his loins. Playfully, she started massaging her breasts and he gave her a sour look.

"First, I am awakened by your sister, frightening me half to death and now you make me ache. For shame, madam," he chuckled and quickly turned to pour her a glass of juice. Obediently, she drank as he handed her the glass and blew him a kiss with her lips. Calling for Laura to help her sister to dry herself, he left the room with a happy grin. Going back to his room, he took his prayer rug and bending three times toward the east, he said a prayer of thanks to the great creator. It was getting light outside and he would have to attend Jack soon. Today would be the great day of the long awaited birthday celebration and many things must be done. Quickly, Hammed hurried from his little house to the main mansion.

Indeed, the festivities had been a great success and it was the next day, as Hammed slowly rode up to the villa by the red cliffs. Sofia had personally packed a small basket with sweets and fruits for the child and his mother. The gift from Jack, Hammed carried in his pocket. Though reluctantly, he left his wife in the trusted care of her sister Laura for a few hours. He was glad, that she was free from fever and her breasts did not ache as much. She nursed the child every two hours and it seemed to help, draining her milk. With much giggling and good humor from Elizabeth, Hammed had changed the cold compresses several times. What a wonderful brave little woman his wife was. He shuddered to think that he might have lost her. There would be no more children for her at any time soon. Hammed knew how to make certain of it. The doctor in England had given him the formula for a potion, which he gave to Jack's ladies to prevent conception. He would have to give it to his wife every day mixed in a glass with juice. One scare was quite enough for him.

Riding up the road toward the villa, he noticed a small boy in the garden. He was playing with a dark skinned girl, throwing a small bag filled with sand back and forth. Hammed smiled at the idyllic scene. The boy seemed tall and strong for his age as Hammed remembered Don Dorango saying, that Donna Brickmaker's son was about four years of age as he had arrived. That would make him five years old now. Coming nearer, he tried to make out the child's features, but he was still too far away. As he entered the drive in front of the villa, a servant rushed toward him to take care of his horse. The servant looked at him in wonderment as he mustered shyly his outlandish garb. Taking the basket from the saddle horn, he strode toward the big entrance door, which opened almost momentarily at his knocking. A servant girl eyed him suspiciously and assuming that Hammed was delivering something in his basket, she bade him to follow her into the kitchen.

"Next time you must take the servant entrance," she said, as she was about to turn to go back to the kitchen.

Forestalling her, Hammed smiled ruefully,

"I am not here to make a delivery, girl, I have come to pay a visit to Donna Brickmaker. Go tell her that Hammed ben Hassan, stewart at the house of Baron Giaccomo de Viego, is here to see her and wishes to bring a gift for her son." He was slightly insulted at the girl's assumption, that he might be a mere delivery boy. Blushing, the girl scampered away to fetch the captain. He would know what to do. A few moments later, captain Steve Daniels came down the stairs and extending his hand, he greeted Hammed with a courteous handshake.

"Hammed ben Hassan, how wonderful to see you. May I ask to what has given us the honor of your visit?" Hammed liked Steve and came right to the reason of his visit.

"I was asked by my master and his wife to bring some small gifts for the boy and his mother, since he was unable to attend our celebration yesterday, Captain. The Baron and his wife wish Donna Brickmaker a speedy recovery and hope to bring some cheer to the child." He handed Steve the basket and pulled a square packet out from under his shirt.

"How very sweet of the Baron and his wife to think of the child and poor Donna Katrina. I am certain he will enjoy, whatever is wrapped in here." Steve smiled and weighing the packet in his hand.

"Oh, but please, Hammed ben Hassan would you come in to the study and have some refreshments." He placed the packet on top of the basket and with his free hand, waved elegantly toward the door to the study. He called for one of the servant girls and ordered some coffee and juice to be brought to the study. Blushing again, the girl nodded at the captain, to sent Hammed a fearful look and the door to the kitchen slammed shut. Chuckling softly, Hammed followed Steve and both men sat in the comfortable chairs by the fireplace. The girl entered the room with her tray and Steve told her to fetch Jessy. Almost running from the room, she went to do Steve's bidding.

"Would you like some coffee or perhaps some cool juice?" Steve asked Hammed, as he was pouring a cup of coffee for himself.

"I prefer coffee, thank you," Hammed answered and took the filled cup from Steve's hands.

"May I ask, how Donna Brickmaker is doing? Have you spoken to the doctor?" Hammed asked politely.

"Katrina is doing much better than last week. Her fever was indeed very high and I feared the worst. The doctor assured me just yesterday, that she is out of danger," Steve answered truthfully.

"I can understand your fear my young friend. Last week my wife gave birth to our second child, our first son and had developed a fever. Believe me, I was frantic with fear myself," Hammed shuddered delicately.

"Oh, my congratulations on the birth of your son," Steve smiled.

"Thank you, I am a very fortunate man," Hammed beamed proudly.

"Please, call me Steve, and may I call you Hammed? We Americans are not as formal as Europeans with all their titles," Steve stated with a grin.

"Of course you may, Steve. Just between us; I never liked all these titles myself. I prefer honesty and chivalry, which cannot be bought with money or a title," Hammed said matter-of-factly.

"My sentiment exactly," Steve agreed, "tell me Hammed, I am curious. You are wearing a turban and I was wondering, if you were born in turkey or India. The reason I ask is, in a few weeks I will sail to Istanbul and you might be familiar with the city by chance."

"No, Steve, I was not born in Istanbul. However, you are correct in your assumption about me being Turkish. I was born not far from Istanbul in the city of Bursa, which is south east of Istanbul and about one hundred miles to travel by land. It is quicker to sail over the Sea of Marmara. You may not know this, but the Baron and I lived for a while in Istanbul until his parents and brothers got killed in Lisbon by the big earthquake. Then we moved to England for a few years until my master decided to return to the land of his birth," Hammed explained, sipping his coffee.

"Oh, how awful to lose the whole family," Steve said compassionately, "I can imagine how he must have felt. Since all the trouble began in my own homeland, I have not heard a word from my family in over a year and I am worried sick."

"Some of my master's ships are sailing to America in a few months time. We are trading in New York and might be able to learn some more details about the situation. Perhaps I can bring you some good news upon their return," Hammed promised.

"Oh how odd, my family lives near New York," Steve exclaimed.

"Indeed, that is a strange coincidence, Steve. Now *I* am curious, did Donna Brickmaker also live in New York then?" Before Steve could answer, the door flew open and little Jessy came dashing through the room with his arms wide open to hug his uncle Steve.

"Uncle Steve, Patty said I near wore her out. I can throw very far and

Patty had to run to catch my toy," he laughed proudly. Lovingly, Steve ruffled Jessy's hair and laughed,

"Your manners, my strong young man. We have a visitor." Turning the boy by his shoulders, so he may greet Hammed, he glanced at the big man.

Hammed sat stiff as a board in his chair and the coffee from his cup dribbled onto the tile floor.

"Hammed, what is it? Are you ill?" Steve asked puzzled.

"I am as well as I can be under the circumstances, that I just saw my master exactly as he looked, when he was a child. I met him when he was about ten or eleven years old and this child here is almost his spitting image." Hammed had recovered from his shock. Steve could only shake his head in wonderment. Stretching his big hand toward the child, Hammed said,

"Hello, Jessy, my name is Hammed and I brought you some gifts from my master." Politely bowing, Jessy's eyes got wide at the mention of gifts and he looked around:

"Gifts, for me? Where are they?"

"Right here you little scamp." Steve held the basket out, which he had grabbed from next to his seat. Politeness forgotten, Jessy fell over the basket and ripped the packet open, which he had taken from the basket at first.

"Oh, it is a book with many pictures in it uncle Steve. Look, here is a dog and a cat and…"

"I can see that, Jessy. There is also some writing under these pictures. So you must learn to read quickly to understand the words," Steve chuckled, turning to Hammed with a wink. Jessy looked at Steve wide eyed and grimaced slyly,

"I can't read this, but Patty might. I don't have to learn yet."

Facing Hammed, he smiled impishly: "Thank you for the book. Could you read it to me?"

Hammed laughed and answered, "You are welcome and no, I will not read it to you. You must learn for yourself, my child. Perhaps your mother will let you visit my master's house and then I will teach you to

read. We could also swim in the pool. Tell me, Jessy, can you swim?"
Hammed looked at Steve, who eyed him surprised.

The boy shook his head in the negative as Steve asked,

"Do you think, the Baron would mind if Jessy would visit you some time?"

"Not at all, Steve. My master and his wife love children and would welcome Jessy to visit."

"Let me speak to Katrina and I will send a message to you," Steve assured Hammed, who had risen from his seat to signal the end of his visit.

Once more, Hammed looked at the boy intensely and escorted to the door by Steve, left the villa to ride the long way back to his master's house. In his surprise about the child's appearance, he had completely forgotten to ask if Steve Daniels knew Thomas Crandall. He couldn't shake the feeling, that he had seen this child before.

CHAPTER 29

Deceptions and a Big Stranger

Before Steve left for Istanbul, he had written a letter to Katrina, which he handed to Patty with the instruction to read the letter to her as soon as he was gone. He never had found the opportunity or the right moment to approach Katrina with Hammed's suggestion. However, he was a man of his word and he wrote in the letter of Hammed's visit, which he had kept from her purposely. He did not wanted to burden her until she had recovered and was strong enough to make the decision about letting Jessy visit the Baron's house. Hammed had sent a message, saying that the Baron and his wife would indeed welcome Jessy in his house and were looking forward to meeting the child in person. Upon hearing Patty reading the letter to her, Katrina was hard pressed not to shriek for joy. It was going to be better than she could have ever planned. Though she cursed the fact that her face was scarred, it presented the perfect excuse to wear a veil in public. Neither Jack nor Hammed or even Elizabeth would recognize her, should she be seen by either one of them.

Several weeks passed and her eyesight had almost turned back to normal. Merely small writing as well as her embroidering seemed to get blurry in front of her eyes. She remembered old master Tippins' spectacles and had some made to fit her needs. It was a few days before Jessy's birthday as she started to set her plans into action. Gleefully she went to her desk and began to write a message.

Honored Baron and Baroness de Viego

Several weeks ago, Captain Daniels received a visit from your Stewart, Hammed ben Hassan. Unfortunately, I was still bedridden and was not aware of his call. Captain Daniels told me of your kindness and the gifts you sent to my son. I wish to thank you for it. Although my eyesight has improved to the doctor's great satisfaction, the scar on my face remains, which forces me to wear a veil in public. Since my son's fifth birthday is to be celebrated shortly, on October 14th I am unable to invite guests to my own home, due to my condition. If your offer is still in force, to let my son visit your house, may I impose one your kindness and let Jessy spend this special day with you and your family? It would mean so much to my son, to see Hammed ben Hassan again and he wishes to thank you in person for his book.

Donna Katrina Brickmaker

It was two days later, as the messenger arrived from Baron de Viego. Katrina eagerly snatched the sealed letter from Anna's hand, impatiently waited until the girl had closed the door behind her and breaking the seal, she read.

Dearest Donna Brickmaker

I wish to express our happiness upon hearing that your eyesight is improving. My wife and I agree that it would be our pleasure to have your son celebrate his birthday at our home. We are planning a small firework at night, as we did with our own daughter. Since it would be too late for the child to be sent home and with your permission, we wish to keep him over night. Our Stewart will personally see to his safe

370

return to your home the next day. He has told us that he met your son on his visit and what a bright child it is. We are looking forward to his visit.

Baron and Baroness de Viego

Katrina almost shouted for joy. Of course there would be many more such visits of Jessy to Jack's home. Jubilant, she told her son and Patty, that he would spend his birthday with the man and his wife, which had sent him the book. Hammed would be there also. Little Jessy was getting exited upon hearing about the fireworks. He had never seen anything like it and listened wide eyed as his mother told him, that there would be wonderful colored lights in the sky.

It was mid morning on October the 14th, as the carriage arrived to take Jessy and Patty to the Baron's home. The Baron and his wife greeted him affectionately and he received the greatest present a child could wish for. Baron Jack as he was allowed to call him, gifted him with his own pony, which would of course have to stay in the stables. However, since he would be allowed to visit any time, he would be able to ride his pony on his visits. Jack wanted to make certain, that the child's visitation would be a frequent occurrence in the future. He had taken an instant liking to the bright little boy, which had for some strange reason taken an almost brotherly interest in his little daughter Leonora. Protective and gentle, he played with the tiny girl and hardly left her out of his sight. Amazed and with indulging smiles, Jack and Sofia watched the children play on the lawn. Leonora seemed to make an extra effort to run and followed Jessy, pumping her little legs, wherever he went.

Hammed had his own thoughts about it however. Yet, he could not make any sense of it. Why in Allah's name was the child, who looked so much like Jack in his childhood, even born on the same day as Jack's own son? Was it coincidence? Of course there were millions of people in this big world and thousands of them were born on October 14th. Perhaps it was Allah's will to bring this child into Jack's life for some strange reason. Who knew, what Allah was thinking? He would nevertheless make it a point to speak with Donna Brickmaker the next day as he took Jessy back to the little villa. Hammed was instructed by Jack, to ask Katrina about allowing Jessy frequent visits, for his daughter had been inconsolable about his departure in the morning. Perhaps it was permissible to have him spend a few weeks at the mansion. It would help her, to regain her strength, without having to worry about the child and it would help his wife, who had seemed to be unable to calm her own daughter as Jessy left for home.

As the carriage drew near the little villa, Katrina stood by the window and peeking from behind the heavy drapes, she saw Hammed walking with Jessy on his hand toward the entrance. Quickly, she placed the veil over her head and dimmed the lights in the room. Her heart began to beat frantically. She hoped that he would not recognize her. She had practiced her American accent and as Hammed was announced to see her, she had him come to the dim study. Bowing before her courteously, Hammed tried to get his eyes used to the dark room. Freeing himself from Hammed's hand, Jessy ran toward his mother and hugging her as she bent to greet him, he piped,

"Mama, I had the most splendid time at the Baron's house. I do have a pony now. I like little Leonora. She is my favorite. Is the scratch on your face still hurting?" He wanted to lift the veil, but Katrina caught his hand and said quickly,

"No, Jessy it's not hurting," she answered, lowering her voice purposely, "who's our visitor?" Turning, she faced with her back toward the draped window, so the light, which seemed to seep through, was shadowing her veil.

"Hammed ben Hassan at your service, madam." Hammed bowed shortly once more. There was no recognition. Her deception seemed to work. With Jessy being led from the room by Patty, Katrina pretended to think about Jack's offer and then agreed to let Jessy go back with Hammed. 'How very thoughtful of the Baron and his wife, to be so kind and think about her health and her son's welfare. Of course she was unable to say no to such generosity. Furthermore, it would make sweet little Leonora happy.' Katrina thought bitterly. It was agreed upon, that

Katrina would be invited to celebrate Christmas at the Baron's mansion, to be with her son. Heavily veiled, Katrina spend two days at the mansion and excused herself on the third day that she wanted to be at home, saying that she expected a message from Captain Daniels any day now and she did not want to miss it. Enviously, she had watched Jack's wife as she seemed to bloom under his loving glances and tender little touches and obviously was expecting another child. Elizabeth's sister, Laura was going on her nerves with her constant questions about America and how long she had been living there and if Jessy had been born there. Naturally, she had lied to all of the girl's questions, but she could not allow herself to get trapped in the web of her own lies. So, Katrina was sitting at home, still making her soaps and perfumes and waiting for Steve Daniels to return from Norway with the two new ships, as he had promised.

Steve returned in the spring of 1778 as he had assumed he would and brought the two new ships, including captains and crew, he had hired. He was surprised at the new developments and a little disappointed, that he would have to wait to give Jessy his present, which was a beautiful male Norwegian elkhound pup, who was nine months old by now. Steve had chosen the dog for its unusual intelligence, friendliness and loyalty. He would be a fine protective friend to Jessy. Katrina sent a message to the mansion, telling her son, that uncle Steve had returned with a present.

Jessy returned home for a few days and refused to go back to the big mansion without his new dog. Sofia insisted and Jack had no choice as to let Jessy bring his dog, which turned out to be a blessing. One day in early summer, Sofia sat by the pool nursing her four-month-old son and for an instant the playing children and the dog were hidden from her view by a big bush. She heard a splash and another and placing her baby on the lawn, she ran toward the pool. Her little daughter Leonora had fallen into the pool and the second splash had come from the dog, which had jumped into the water after her. Holding on to the dog's thick fur, little Leonora was safely paddled back to the side of the pool, where Jessy pulled her out, just as Jack and Hammed came running. They had watched the entire scene from the window of the study and horrified, almost running each other over in the doorway, while trying to get to the pool area had dropped the papers of inventory. The dog, which was named Hercules, like his dog in America, and Jessy, received praises upon praises for saving little Leonora's life. Thankful, Jack hired tutors to educate Jessy in reading and writing at first. What seemed most astonishing was Jessy, loving poetry, and he began making up his own little poems. To Jack's great amusement, the little rhymes seemed to be an adoration of his sweet little daughter. One of them read,

Leonora, Hercules and I, your friends we are
We watch over you and will never be far.

Sofia chuckled and remarked, that he had now found a child in Jessy that was actually interested in the fine arts. Jack however, took Jessy's interest serious and encouraged him greatly to learn.

Katrina knew, that her son was safe and decided to sail with Steve on the *Undine* to the Orient and to America, which would take them many months. Steve had finally received word that his family was safe and the area, which they had moved too in the countryside of Pennsylvania, was relatively trouble free. Katrina also wanted to pay a visit to her house in Virginia and sell it, since it was not a great source of income. She knew, that she would stay permanently in Europe. A Stewart was hired to take care of the little villa and Steve had been able to purchase a fourth ship, which would sail the Mediterranean Sea, while the *Undine* would take Katrina and him to their destinations.

She had taken notice, that Steve seemed to look at her in a different way than before and his smiles were more loving. Very attentive, he never missed the opportunity, to gently brush her hand or arms as he helped her to sit by the table or handing her a drink. She was still a very young woman and her body began to react to his touches and glances. She chided herself a fool, for Steve was a handsome young man. He could have any woman, who was not scarred like she was. To her, the scar was a terrible disfigurement, which he in turn hardly noticed any longer. In fact, her wound had healed nicely and thanks to the doctor's surgery skill, the scar was no more than a thin line, of about four centimeters in length and slightly darker pink as her own skin, under her cheekbone.

The occasion arose one day, as Katrina climbed down the steep narrow steps to her cabin on the ship and stumbled. Since she had no recognition to fear from neither crew nor Steve, she was without her veil. He had been climbing down the steps before her and standing at the foot of the stairs, caught her in his arms, as she was about to fall. Her body was forcefully pressed against his and her face with no more than two inches from his as she had thrown her arms around his neck with an instinct reaction. Their eyes met and for a long moment, he held her close. Slowly at first he lowered his head and then his mouth came crushing down on her lips. She offered no resistance to his probing tongue as his kiss deepened.

She was a widow for a long time and longed for a man's touch. Her body reacted with a tug of desire racing through her and her hands tangled in his hair. Without a word, he swooped her up in his arms and carried her to her cabin, where he placed her gently on the big bed. Kissing her again and again, his hands went to her bodies to undo the laces of her gown. Murmuring softly, she reveled in the delicious tingling feeling as his hands cupped her exposed breasts and his thumb gently rubbed over her hardening nipples. His mouth covered her face with tiny kisses to trail down her soft neck and capturing a nipple between his lips, he flicked his tongue quickly back and forth. Katrina gasped as his hand went to her soft thigh and gently stroked up to her secret place. He found her and his finger rubbed softly in little circular motions over the little digit of ecstasy. His gentle efforts were rewarded as her body tensed and panting, she shuddered her first release.

Quickly he jumped from the bed and undressed to stand naked before her. She gasped as she saw his big engorged manhood.

Thomas had been big enough for her, but Steve was far larger and thicker. As if he could read her thoughts, he smiled rakishly. Pulling her of the bed, he helped her out of her clothes and marveled at the perfection of her nude body. Encircling her with his strong arms, he threw her hard against his lean body, his member rampantly pressing against her thigh. He kissed her again and her hand went gingerly at first around his waist to his buttocks, caressing and softly kneading the firm round cheeks. Her hot little hands sent stabs of desire through him and he lifted her back onto the bed, never releasing her lips from his. Moving himself on top of her, he entered the moist warmth of her gently at first. He began to move and her breath quickened at the delicious sensations. Faster and faster he pumped until she cried her release, which tightened her vaginal muscles around him, contracting fiercely. The feel of it and her writhing body made him spill his seed. Barely conscious, Katrina was in his arms with her eyes closed. Covering her face with gentle little kisses, his lips went to the faint scar. Her eyes shot open and she looked surprised into his face, whispering,

"How can you desire to be with me, Steve? I am ugly now and scarred for life." Her eyes filled with tears.

"Hush, little Kat, don't be silly. You are beautiful and I love you for what and who you are. Not for a tiny little scar that is hardly noticeable any longer," he admonished her softly, placing a little kiss on the tip of her nose.

"You love me?" She was incredulous.

"Yes, my little Kat, I am in love with you for a long time. I just didn't have the courage to let you know my feelings for you. I was not sure, if you would have any feelings for me in return. I am nothing more than the mere captain of one of your ships and I feared you might have rejected my suit," he admitted honestly.

"Oh Steve, I am not sure, if I love you. I am very fond of you. Please give me some time." She smiled and gently caressed his cheek with her finger.

"If that is all you are asking of me, I can wait, Kat. I have plenty of time and I am sure you will learn to love me." He smiled back and quickly caught her finger with his lips to gently nip with his teeth and then kiss it.

"Villain." She tugged his hair and pulled him closer to kiss him. A stab of desire ran through him, as her little tongue flicked over his lips and he felt himself getting hard again still within her softness. They made love again and again as the ship gently rocked and sailed through the Indian Ocean, entering the Arabian Sea toward Bombay, which would be their first stop.

Steve had been in the city before and wanted to show Katrina some of the sights. The *Undine* docked in the low-lying Bombay harbor, a broad, sheltered bay located between the city and the mainland. On Elephants they rode to the ancient temples near Elephanta Island and went from there to the Kanheri Caves on Salsette Island, where Steve showed Katrina the carvings. stemming from the 2nd to 9th centuries. Steve explained to her, that the area had once belonged to the Portuguese, who acquired this portion of land in 1534. The Portuguese had named the harbor *Bom Bahia*, which means *beautiful bay,* from which the name of the city derived. The site was ceded to the English in 1661 and in 1668 it was leased to the British East India Corporation. Fascinated by the sights and the people, Katrina was reminded of home by the men wearing turbans. She wondered, what Jessy was doing.

Merely for an instant, her face crumbled and tears stung her eyes. Sitting in her howdah, she quickly blinked the moisture away and concentrated once more on the sights and Steve. Satisfied she nodded, for she knew, that her son was surrounded by people who adored him.

Further they sailed from Bombay south into the Indian Ocean again and took the route east toward Sumatra into the Strait of Malacca, to stop in the city of Batavia. Entering the port of Tanjung Priok, the *Undine* took on fresh provisions and Steve took Katrina to see the city. He explained, that in 1610 the Dutch East India Corporation established a trading post in Yakatra, and eight years later in 1618 they had built a fort nearby. A year later they seized control of Yakatra and renamed it Batavia. The town became company headquarters and, subsequently, capital of the Netherlands Indies. Batavia had been devastated by a massive earthquake in 1699 and many of the old temples were destroyed. After seeing all the sights, they decided to rest for a few days and lodged in one of the finer inns in the city. Their passion had not abated and Katrina's cries of passion were noticed one early morning by a big man walking by their room. Smiling to himself, the man kept walking and went downstairs to chat with the innkeeper. Seating himself in a secluded and dark corner, the man had his breakfast and said chuckling to the innkeeper, who served him a huge meal,

"The couple in room three might want a big breakfast. I could hear them working up an appetite as I walked by earlier. Save some food for them my good man."

"Ah, the couple in room three, yes, they seem very much in love. They can hardly keep their hands to themselves," the innkeeper laughed. The big man was about to finish his meal, as Katrina and Steve entered the dining room. Sitting with his back toward the door, he heard the innkeeper say,

"Good morning, my Lady, good morning, Captain. Your meal will be there momentarily." Since it was not unusual for a captain to be in the inn by the port, the big man kept eating and drinking his coffee. The innkeeper came to his secluded table and cleared the empty dishes away, as he whispered to the big man with a sly grin,

"Over there is the couple from room three." Turning slightly and curious, the big man saw the couple gazing lovingly at each other and he almost dropped his cup. In a tight voice, he whispered to the innkeeper,

"What are their names?"

The innkeeper looked surprised at the big man, who had grabbed his arm in a tight grip and said,

"He is an American captain and she is Spanish I believe. I heard him calling her Katrina." The big man let go of the innkeepers arm, who rubbed it and shook his head in puzzlement.

"Why do you want to know about this captain? Do you know these people?"

"Katrina, you said? Are you sure?" the big captain asked again. The innkeeper nodded.

"Perhaps I was mistaken," The big captain said low and turning his face, he sipped his coffee. The innkeeper took the empty dishes form the big Captains table and hurried back to the kitchen. The couple had not noticed anything unusual, while the innkeeper had cleared the other table in the dark corner. They did not see the man's face turn once more to look at them. He was almost certain, that he was looking at Steve

Daniels, who had grown a splendid beard. But who was this woman Katrina? She wore spectacles and a veil, almost covering her face. Her lips however reminded him of Margaret. His wife. Thomas had to find out if this man really was Steve Daniels, what he was doing here in Batavia. His heart contracted painfully, as he saw the woman tenderly caressing the man's arm and he remembered back those many months.

A seaquake had brought on a big wave and he was thrown from his ship together with several men of his crew. As the rest of the remaining men on his ship tried to help them, a second wave washed them into the boiling sea as well. Hanging on to a small empty wooden crate, he was driven further and further away from his men, bobbing in the water and trying frantically to swim toward him and any other man, clinging to pieces of floating material. He could still hear there desperate screams in his mind. Drifting in the water for many hours, he felt himself getting weaker and weaker. His chest and his leg hurt terribly. By some miracle, a piece of rope was still laying inside the crate and he tightened it around the crate. He managed to pull his belt off and bound his upper arm to the robe on the crate so his upper body would be prevented from submerging in the water. How many more hours he had been drifting unconscious, he could not remember.

He came to as he heard voices and found himself lying on deck of a small fishing boat. The men asked his name and where he had come from. He could not recall his own name. The fisher men took him on land and left him in the care of their wives. The women took turns nursing the big stranger and attended tenderly to his broken leg and several broken ribs. It had taken many months that he suffered from fitful dreams and flashes of a life he did not remember any longer. Only recently after nearly two years had he regained his full memory and was longing to go home to his wife and child, which he believed he had in the meantime. He was told, that his ship had been found and had been pulled to Batavia were it was, repaired, taken back to America. Keeping his gold wedding band, he had sold his other rings and his pocket watch, which he had bought in England from the Clockmakers Corporation in London and had been his great pride. He decided, that he could buy a new watch, but he must get home to his wife and child.

With the money in his pocket, he would buy passage to America on one of the trading vessels. With any luck, he would run into an American captain, which he knew due to his own seafaring and trading enterprise.

He waited in his dark corner, until the couple left and went quickly up the street to sell his wedding band. He decided to make some inquiries and they usually cost money. He regretted that he had not approached the couple as he saw them in the morning. As he came back to the inn later, they had already left. What he found out, in a few weeks time, greatly disturbed him and he couldn't wait to get home to America. He was sorry that he had not spoken with the man that looked so much like Steve, while he had a chance. They had already left for China and from there would be on their way to America. He must make certain, that he would be there before them. It was not as easy as he had hoped. Thomas had to wait full two weeks until he finally found an American captain, who was willing to take him home. The ship, which took him to America, would drop him off in Panama and from there he would have to find his own way. As he heard Thomas' story, he took pity on him and told him, that he would not charge anything. He would need his money to find his way to Virginia. Thomas made his way by land to the other side of Panama and luckily found a ship, which took him to Havana in Cuba. From there he boarded another small ship, which sailed up to New York, graciously dropping him of in Virginia. He took a mail coach and finally reached his home. As he walked up the stairs to the entrance, Joseph answered the door and almost fainted. He found, that all his slaves had been freed and his wife had taken his ship to Spain. He also found out with great sadness, that upon hearing of his death, Margaret had miscarried the baby. What on earth was she doing in Spain and why was this woman Katrina looking so much like her, with a man that looked like Steve? Margaret would have a lot of explaining to do. He did not wanted to wait for the couples arrival in America. He would go to Spain and find Margaret, his Margaret, his wife.

CHAPTER 30

The Lost Son

Thomas had taken the time, to make some more inquiries about Margaret. He found out, that she had cleaned out his warehouses in America as well as in Algiers of essences and oils, she needed to make her soaps and perfumes. His heart almost stopped as he thought about her, finding the weapons he had hidden. What would she think and what would she do with them. He must make certain, that these weapons got into the right hands. It was in the spring of 1779, as Thomas left for Spain to find Margaret. What he didn't know, was that Jack had become Baron de Viego and was no longer Don Viego. He had hoped to find his long-time friend and business partner. Perhaps, Margaret had gone to him in hopes he might acknowledge his own son. His efforts fruitless, he went to England in the fall of the same year, hoping that someone might know where to find his wife. He remembered Laura had been her maid for a while and he made his way to the old mansion, where the Goldberg's now resided. Unfortunately, Laura was not there any longer. Ruth Goldberg told Thomas, that Laura had moved to Spain to be with her sister Elizabeth. Ruth was unable to tell him the exact location and disappointed, Thomas went back to America. If anyone could shed some light on this mystery, it would be Steve Daniels. Thomas wanted to find him and decided to search for Steve's family. Again he would be bitterly disappointed. Steve's family had moved and no one knew, where too. Finally he resigned from his long search and got back home to Virginia in the fall of 1790, where he officially filed for a divorce from Margaret, due to her absence and his inability to locate her whereabouts. Grudgingly he had to admit, that his wife was lost to him and the divorce was granted in her absence in the spring of 1791.

Meanwhile, Steve and Katrina had some adventure of their own. After they had left Batavia, the *Undine* was heavily damaged in a storm while sailing up toward Hong Kong in the South China Sea. Almost all sails had been ripped to shreds by the sudden storm and the rudder had sustained some damage also. Drifting without maneuverability for four days, the ship was finally spotted by another merchant ship from Manila in the Philippines, where the Undine was towed into the deep sheltered harbor for repair. The experience had frightened Katrina to hysterics and she refused to go back onto the ship again to sail to China. She sent a message to her son in Spain, that they were stranded in Manila for an indefinite time. Steve saw no other choice as to leave her behind. He saw no reason to go to China at this time and sailed for America instead. Katrina rented a small house near the city and patiently waited for Steve's return. She had some of her funds transferred from Spain to a bank in Manila and lived there until the spring in 1779.

Steve returned from America and was happy, that he had finally been able to find his family. Unfortunately, his mother was ill and his brother's had joined the army. He had promised his mother to be back with Katrina. Katrina still refused to set foot on a ship and angry, he had drugged her to take her to his homeland. Going back and forth between fits of hysterics and her own anger as she discovered that she was on the ship, Katrina locked herself into her cabin. A small storm frightened her into a faint and Steve had to break the door open. Upon regaining consciousness, she refused to eat and Steve had an idea. He stuffed a small pipe with some leaves and not inhaling the smoke himself, he began to blow the smoke in her direction. It had the effect he had hoped for. She began to relax and almost euphorically giggled, laughed and began to eat again. He told her that this plant had been around for many centuries already and was a common folk medicine in Asia and China. It is harvested from the Indian hemp plant Cannabis sativa and smoked or eaten for its hallucinogenic and pleasure-giving effects. Indeed, Katrina liked the feeling and began to take small puffs of this pipe on a regular basis during their voyage, which continued without further incidents until they reached America in the fall of 1779. Steve and Katrina took care of the ailing old woman until she died in the summer of 1780. Finally in the spring of 1781, Katrina agreed to go back to Spain under the condition that she would have a large supply of the Cannabis sativa plant to keep away her fears. Steve had talked her out of going to Virginia, for there was still some unrest further south. It would also make no difference, if she sold the Estate or not. She was wealthy and did not need the money desperately. He had received word from Spain, that everything was running smoothly in their absence and her bank account had grown very satisfactory from the remaining three ships, trading and selling.

They arrived back in Barcelona in the late summer of 1781 and Katrina saw her son for the first time in almost four years. She almost didn't recognize him. He was almost nine years old and had grown tremendously. His features had become more refined and his manners were those of a young Nobleman. Courteously, he listened to his mother's adventures and he seemed to be anxious to go back to the family, whom he had learned to love and loved him in return. Katrina had no choice as to let him go back to the Baron's home. Somehow, her son had become a stranger to her and she decided to let him live permanently with Jack and his family. She would bite her time to strike, when the time was right. Up until now, her real identity had obviously not been discovered and for the time being she wanted to lay low. Steve was sailing the Mediterranean Sea again and had asked Katrina to marry him, which she refused. Though she loved him, she did not wanted to share her wealth with any man and for him to control it. They remained lovers and good friends as well as business partners. Twice a year, Katrina would be invited to spend time with her son on his birthday and Christmas. The years went by and before Katrina knew it, her son turned 18. It was to be a big birthday celebration and Steve was unable to accompany Katrina to the festivities. He was on the ship, sailing toward Alexandria.

It was obvious, that Jack and Sofia loved Jessy like their own son Leonardo. Katrina felt like an intruder at the party, until she saw Jessy tenderly kissing Leonora's hand and glanced adoringly into her face. Sick with jealousy and raging, she hid the feelings behind her veil. Leonora was a stunning beauty and at fifteen, her body had developed into a woman's. It was also obvious to Katrina, that Jessy loved Leonora, which was unbeknownst to him, his half sister. Quickly, she excused herself and trying to collect her thoughts, went to the study to sit in one of the big chairs. The drapes were closed and the room was in semi darkness. She heard a noise from the bookshelf and jumped from her seat, to hide behind the heavy drapes.

She saw Hammed coming from the secret room with a small package in his hand. Hammed had been instructed to fetch Jessy's birthday present, which was a gold pocket watch that he had hidden in the secret room. Fascinated, Katrina watched Hammed handling the mechanic of lever and button and hardly dared to breathe. She had to find out, what was in this room. As Hammed closed the door behind him, she jumped from her seat and worked the mechanic as she had seen him do it. Surprised she gasped, as she found necklaces, bracelets, rings and earbobs, worth a fortune. Quickly, she left the little room and closing the bookshelf door securely, and carefully making certain that nobody saw her leaving the study, she went back to the party in the great hall.

Since it was agreed upon, that some guest would stay the night, including Katrina, she had brought a tiny trunk with change of clothes. Katrina waited patiently for everyone to be asleep in their own rooms and crept downstairs to the study with a big empty bag. She stuffed the bag full of the jewelry and back in her room, emptied it out into her trunk. She made two trips to the secret room and satisfied, that not even a ring was left behind, she went to her room to rest until the early morning hours. Quickly, she wrote a note to her son, that she had decided to leave for home, since she expected Steve. She had one of the servants take her small trunk to the carriage and hurried home. No one would suspect her of the theft, for no one had seen her watching Hammed as he came from the secret room. Only the people who knew the mechanic and the rooms existence, were suspect to begin with. She could not believe her luck. Fate hade made a decision for her and aided her revenge. Not thinking, that her plans would destroy her own son's life, she kept quiet and sat like a poisonous spider in its web, waiting for its prey.

As she had suspected, Jessy had asked Jack for Leonora's hand in marriage and Jack had happily given his consent. He had raised the boy since he was five years old and had molded and shaped him into the fine young man that he had become. Leonora's happiness was paramount to Jack and he knew, that she loved Jessy. The wedding was to be celebrated after Leonora's 16th birthday. Tragically, Jessy's dog died and both young people decided to postpone the wedding for a few months. Jessy's pain at the loss of his steady and loyal companion was intense as was Leonora's. The dog Hercules had been with them for many years of their happy childhood. But even in death, he should save the young people one last time from unimaginable tragedy. By mere coincidence, Thomas Crandall had sailed with his new ship to Barcelona. Sitting in a little tavern near the harbor and waiting for his cargo to be delivered, he saw a man on the next table, drinking heavily. He heard the man slurring his words to the tavern keeper,

"So much for family and friends. The fine Baron Jack de Viego didn't invite me to Jessy's and Leonora's wedding." He hiccupped and drank straight from the bottle, finishing the rest of the wine in it. Annoyed the tavern keeper answered,

"Go home, Vincento, you have had enough and I'm sick of your whining." Not believing his ears, Thomas got up from his seat and sat down by Vincento's table. Waving to the tavern keeper, he ordered,

"Bring us another bottle of wine my good man. I'll take care of this man. First I have to talk with him." Gratefully, Vincento took the offered glass and drank greedily.

"And whom do I have to thank for the wine if I may ask?"

"I am Captain Thomas Crandall from America. Say on, my friend, you mentioned a Jack de Viego and a Jessy. Tell me more about your troubles and this family. I'm willing to listen and make it worth your while." Placing a bag of coins on the table, Thomas poured it out and Vincento's eyes popped out as he saw the gold. Reaching for it, he nodded.

"All this trouble started many years back." Pouring another glass for himself, he emptied it and leaned back in his chair.

Glary-eyed and slurring in his speech, Vincento told Thomas everything he knew. From Jack getting a title from the king to marrying Sofia, having a daughter Leonora and a son Leonardo. Jack, merging his merchant trading business with his father Alfredo de Domingo and disinheriting him. Then this American chit, Donna Brickmaker, who had a terrible accident years back, by which her face got terribly disfigured, so she had to wear a veil and Jack taking Jessy in to raise the brat like he was his own son. Now Thomas knew, why he never had been able to find Jack. His company name had changed, as he merged with Alfredo. He had looked for him in Madrid and no one had known of him there. Thomas felt bile in his throat and could hardly believe, what he heard. If he would get his hands on Margaret, he would strangle the bitch. She had hidden her face behind a veil, not to be recognized by neither Jack nor Hammed. He had indeed looked at Margaret; The woman with the veil as he saw her and Steve in Batavia. And suddenly, it dawned on Thomas. Margaret's middle name had to their amusement changed on the marriage certificate to the place, where the first name should have been written. His German was good enough to realize, that she had changed her maiden name Ziegler simply into the English version Brickmaker. He knew, that she had been consumed with hatred for Jack and sometimes mentioned, that she would get back at him some day. Dear God, the woman was insane. She would sacrifice her own son's happiness for her revenge. He hoped, he would not be too late to stop the wedding. Thomas had not said a word and looked like a thundercloud. Getting up from his chair, he pulled the dozing drunkard from his chair and supported him by pulling his arm around his neck:

"Come, Vincento, it is getting dark, lets get you home. I have to pay a visit to Jack de Viego and tomorrow I will see this Donna Brickmaker."

Being very fond of Donna Katrina however, since she supplied his wife with the fine soaps and perfumes at a low price, the tavern keeper had listened in on the conversation and sent his son to the little villa. He was to warn her, that a big angry sea captain by the name of Thomas Crandall was looking for her and would pay her a visit the next day, after going to Baron Viego's house. Katrina could not believe, that Thomas had been alive all along and almost fainted at the news. She realized, that her plans were foiled and that Thomas would expose her. Either Jack or even Thomas might kill her, if they found her. In a mad rush, she had Anna pack her clothes and saying to her servants, that she would have to go to Alexandria to be with Steve who had been injured, she left in her carriage for the harbor. Arriving in the early morning hours, as it was still dark, she knew that her fourth ship was docked there. The older captain was surprised to see her and not suspecting anything to be wrong, as she told him she had to visit a sick friend, followed her orders and took her to Marseilles in France, where she traveled from there over land toward Germany. She hoped, she would find Gretchen.

Meanwhile, pandemonium had broken out at the mansion of Baron de Viego. At first, Jack was annoyed, that he would have to receive a visitor at this hour, as one of his servants knocked on the door to his study.

"Baron, there is a man here to see you and he says it is urgent."

"Who is this man? Does he have a name?" Jack asked and looking at Hammed ruefully. They were playing a game of chess and he was about to win.

"He says his name is Captain Thomas Crandall," the servant announced, and was almost run over by his master, who had dropped his pawn and raced by him into the hall. Jack took one look at his friend and noticed that the captains hair had turned gray. Otherwise his features, safe a few wrinkles were still that of his dear old friend.

"My God, Thomas, I have been longing to see you. Where have you been all those years?" he cried, embracing Thomas in a bear hug and tears of joy stung his eyes. Hammed had followed Jack into the hall and he noticed the captain's face. Though smiling and hugging Jack, he seemed worried and sad. Freeing himself gently from his friends embrace, Thomas held Jack at arms length and placing a heavy hand on Jack's shoulder he sighted,

"We have to talk Jack. I hope I am not too late. Where is Jessy?"

"He should be home soon. My daughter Leonora and Jessy went to a concert. How do you know of Jessy?" Jack asked concerned as he looked at his friend and took his arm to lead him toward the study, where the captain was greeted at the door by Hammed with a deep bow and a smile.

"Welcome Captain Crandall, I am happy to see you again. I shall see to the refreshments." And he hurried to the kitchen to order juice and coffee.

Jack and Thomas had seated themselves in the big chairs and just as Hammed came back to the study, the big captain began to speak,

"Listen well, my friend, for the tale I am about to tell you, will make you angry and very sad." Hammed couldn't help the knot in his stomach getting bigger and pouring the coffee, which the servant had brought to the room, he handed one cup to the captain and one to Jack.

"Tell me, Thomas, the suspense is making me ill." Jack sipped his coffee and looked at the captain in great anticipation. Thomas placed his cup back on the table and leaning back, he began to speak,

"It began many years ago, as you had moved to Spain. I had brought the Goldberg's from America and as you know, these were the people, which bought your old mansion in England. I was their guest and as I came downstairs one day, I found Margaret sitting in the dining hall with Ruth. I was very surprised to see her and found out, that her little house, which Hammed had rented for her and her child, burned to the ground." Hammed gasped and looked wide eyed at Jack, who's brow had furrowed concerned,

"Laura never told us of a fire. She merely mentioned, that Margaret had moved away and she had no idea, where too. But…"

Raising his hand to forestall the question, Thomas quickly continued,

"Both mother and child got out of the house safely and spent the night at a neighbors house. With no place to go, Margaret took her son and Laura and went to the mansion, in order to find out the exact location of your new residence here in Spain. The Goldberg's and I talked her out of following you to Spain and then the thought struck me. Cynthia was still suffering greatly from her depression over our daughter's death and needed a constant companion. I offered Margaret to take her to America, to look after my wife, while I was at sea. As I arrived home with Margaret and her son, my wife asked me for a divorce. Soon thereafter, Margaret and I fell in love and I married her." Another audible gasp from both men. And then Jack grinned:

"Ah and now you are married to Margaret and you want to adopt my son. Am I correct?"

"No, Jack, I cannot adopt your son. Margaret is not with me any longer. I had to go on a voyage shortly after we got married and Margaret found herself pregnant with my child. I was happy about it and promised her, to be back soon. My ship was near Sumatra, as a terrible seaquake hit and a big wave swept me and my crew overboard. I managed to cling to a floating crate and after many hours of drifting in the sea, I was rescued by a fishing boat. The men took me home to their wives, who nursed me back to health. However, I could not recall anything from my life or the accident. It took two years for me to remember and I was anxious to go home to my wife and child, which should be over one year old by now. By sheer coincidence, I had spent a few nights in a little inn near the harbor in Batavia to catch a ship that would be willing to take me back to America. I saw a couple sitting a few tables away as I had breakfast and my heart almost stopped. The man, I knew. He was formally an officer at another ship and had become a captain. The woman however, was the spitting image of my wife Margaret, safe a scar on her face and some dark spectacles she wore. Not certain however, I kept sitting quietly and waited for the couple to leave, so I could go and make some inquiries. I found out, that the woman was living here in Spain and her name was Katrina. The captains name is Steve Daniels as I knew from before."

Surprised, Jack's eyes widened, for he knew Donna Katrina and captain Steve Daniels. Hammed turned ashen. It was just too much for him to bear. Instantly, he had realized, what the captain would have to tell his poor master. Surprised, Jack looked at Thomas and then noticed the big tears, running down Hammed's face. With shaking hands and knees, he poured himself a glass of juice as great sobs escaped his chest. Crushed, Hammed sank in one of the big chairs and Jack looked questioningly from Thomas to Hammed, back and forth. Very concerned, Jack put his hand on Hammed's and asked,

"What is it my old friend? Calm yourself, the captain is alive and well."

"It is not the captain, my Master, it is you I am concerned about and poor Jessy," he sobbed, and turning his tearstained face toward Thomas he said almost inaudible, "please tell my dear master the rest Captain. Oh, Allah, I cannot bear the pain." His shoulders shook uncontrollably as he cried like a child. More puzzled than before, Jack asked Thomas with a sinking feeling,

"We know both, Donna Katrina and captain Steve Daniels, but what in God's name does that all have to do with me and Jessy?" He still was not able to figure out, what Hammed already knew. Before Thomas could answer, the door to the study flew open and Jessy stood in the door, staring at Thomas.

"Papa?" he asked incredulous and took a few steps toward Thomas. Jack jumped up from his seat and was near hysterics,

"Jessy is *your* son Thomas?"

"No, Jack, he is *your* son," Thomas said low. Hammed sobbed loudly. He saw his masters face turn white. He saw Jessy's confused look.

"How can this be?" Jack whispered. The young man in front of him was Jessy Brickmaker. But he also knew, that his friend would never lie to him. Then how did Donna Katrina Brickmaker end up with Margaret's child? He could still not make any sense of it.

"Jessy, what is your mother's name?" Jack demanded. Confused, Jessy answered,

"Katrina Brickmaker, why?"

"Jack, Brickmaker is the English version of Ziegler. Margaret's middle name is Katarina, which was mistakenly written as her first name on our marriage certificate. She changed it all to Katrina Brickmaker. Donna Katrina is Margaret Ziegler and Jessy is Justus, your son." Thomas thundered. An unearthly scream came from the door and a young woman stood white-faced and swaying. With two big steps, Justus was by her side and caught her as she collapsed.

"Oh, dear God, Leonora, she heard everything," Jack whispered and was near fainting himself and sank heavily back into the chair. Immediately, Thomas had assessed the situation and helped Justus to place the unconscious young woman on the couch. Jack was unable to move. His mind reeled and he began to place the pieces of the puzzle together. This snake of a woman had known all along, that Leonora and Jessy, no Justus, were brother and sister. Without saying a word, she would have permitted her own son to marry his sister and commit incest. The immensity of her evil in her lust for revenge began to sink into his brain and he shuddered with great force. Dear God, if the dear dog Hercules would not have died, they would be married by now and Leonora might have been pregnant with her own brother's child. It became clear to Jack that this would have been her plan, to destroy him. Looking toward the couch, he saw Justus tenderly hold Leonora's cold little hand and big tears were silently running down his son's face. He had come to love Justus very much and now he found out, he was in fact his son.

"My son," Jack whispered to himself unbelieving. He had known this dear boy, since he was five years old and suddenly, his heart contracted painfully in his chest. Slowly, Jack got up from his chair and placing a gentle hand on his son's shoulder he turned the young man to face him. His eyes were filled with tears of joy and sadness at the same time and unable to speak, he pulled the crying young man to his chest.

"Father, forgive me, I had no idea," Justus sobbed in his arm. He loved Leonora with all his young heart and now he found out, that she was his sister.

"My son, oh my son," Jack hugged Justus tight, "I know you were an innocent in all this. I must ask your forgiveness. Had I acknowledged you as you were born, your mother would have not been driven this far."

Justus still could not believe, what had happened and gently freeing himself from his father's embrace, asked fearful,

"What will you do?"

"I will kill the bitch personally for this," Thomas fell into the silence with a booming voice.

"Please, don't do this, she is my mother," Justus whispered under tears as great big sobs escaped his chest.

"We cannot let her crime go unpunished, my son. You almost married your own sister because of her hatred toward me," Jack admonished gently.

"I know," Justus said and sank into the chair, crushed. He did not know, what to feel at the moment. His young heart was broken into a million pieces, for the woman he loved, was his own sister. The man, he had considered his late papa in his mind, was a stranger and the man he had learned to love and always looked up too and was supposed to be his father-in-law in a few short weeks, turned out to be his real father. He did not know, if he should laugh or cry at the whole situation. Stunned, he sat in silence and the tears were still running down his young handsome face. His heart had decided on crying, for the pain in his soul was too great. He knew, that he would have to confront his mother.

The next day, Thomas returned from the little villa and told them, that she had fled. The servants had told him, that she had gone after Steve Daniels to Alexandria. Thomas did not believe it. Somehow she must have been warned, for little Anna had told the big captain, that Donna Katrina had taken all of her clothes and personal belongings, which had seemed very strange to the girl. Giving the girl a bag with coins, he had looked around in the house to see for himself. To his amazement and great joy, he had found the crates with the weapons in the little storeroom, who's door he had to break open, since it was locked. He told the frightened girl, that Donna Katrina would not be back and the crates belonged to him.

He had ridden to his ship and sent a few of his men to the villa, to pick up his precious cargo. He had no idea, if it would still be of any help, but it would never hurt to try. They searched for many weeks and had found out from the old captain, that his mistress had sailed to France. From there, Margaret's trail went cold. Justus was heartbroken and could not stand to be around Leonora any longer. Confused in his feelings for her, he left his father's house with a great settlement and moved away to the little villa. Painful as it was for him, he finally decided after three years to redecorate the little room she had locked. As he emptied out her desk, he found a letter from a certain friend, his mother had spoken of at times and was very fond of. She had told him, that this friend had helped her greatly, as she was pregnant and would never forget her kindness. This friends name was Gretchen and she lived in Germany.

Then it suddenly dawned on him. What if his mother had gone to Germany to her friend? He had to find out. Ruefully smiling, he remembered Captain Thomas three years back, as he had come back from Marseilles and was very disappointed. They had found out, that all of Margaret's funds had been transferred to a bank there. Cunningly, she had hired an attorney in France to sell her ships in secret to an English merchant. With no ships to her name and no business to trace her, she had managed to vanish. As they had celebrated Thomas' and his own 19th birthday at the mansion, Jack had discovered that his little secret room was cleaned out. Sofia had hardly worn any jewelry, safe for a few festive occasions and it was only then, that the theft had been discovered. For months, they had tried to find the thief, but could come up with nothing. It was Hammed, who remembered later, that as he came from the secret room to fetch his present on his 18th birthday, he had for some strange reason smelled Margaret's perfume in the study. It was decided, that she must have somehow watched him as he closed the bookcase door and had stolen the jewelry during the night. Her departure early in the morning had been somewhat sudden and the servant, who carried her small trunk to the carriage, added to their suspicion, as he confirmed, that the lady's trunk had been indeed very heavy.

Upon Steve Daniels' return from Alexandria, he was told of Margaret's crime and bitterly disappointed, he went back to America with Thomas. He had of course known Margaret's real name and could only shake his head in disbelieve as he heard the whole story from Thomas and Jack. Justus went to the mansion and not giving any reason other than he wanted to travel a bit, took his leave from his father and siblings. Tearfully, his family watched his carriage roll out of the big drive and Justus looked back for one last time. His father was bent over, his shoulders shaking with great sobs. Flanked by Hammed and Sofia, who had her arms around his shoulders, trying to comfort him. It was the last time, Justus saw his father alive. He would never return to Spain.

CHAPTER 31

Evil Incarnate

Stopping sometimes a few weeks, to rest and see the sights, Justus made his way slowly from Spain through France and Switzerland to Germany and arrived there in the summer of 1796. It had taken him many months to travel and he was nearing the city where Gretchen had lived. The city was in the south east of Germany near the tin mountains and was called Chemnitz. Lodging in a little inn at the outskirts of Chemnitz, Justus decided to wait. He went to find a tutor, to teach him the German language at first. It took several months and a hard cold winter went by, until he could converse passably in German and had made some friends, who enjoyed showing him around and taking him to the opera. One of his new friends was a young doctor by the name of Werner Richter. Werner introduced Justus to the nightlife of Chemnitz. Many times, the young men sat in the Ratskeller having some wine and playing cards. Then Justus decided, that the time was right to find Margaret. He had always been careful, not to run into her by accident. He did not want his mother to know, that he was near. She would not have a chance to escape him. He wanted to confront her and tell her, that he hated what she had done to him and his whole family. But she was still his mother and he loved her in spite of everything she had done. He had also realized, that her mind had gotten confused the last few years as she still lived in the little villa in Spain.

He had caught her several times on his visits to the villa with a funny little pipe and she smoked this terrible smelling tobacco, which seemed to relax her however. He had asked Steve about his mother's habit and he had told him about her fears to be on a ship. The drug had a relaxing effect on her mind and she had begun to smoke these leaves more often. The downside of smoking this pipe was, that the mind became befuddled and the thinking process was slowed. Justus blamed his mother's behavior and inability to think not clearly any longer on this drug, she smoked. He would have to find her and stop this insanity.

It was not as easy as he had hoped and wished for. He found out, where Gretchen had lived, before she had married. Luckily, Gretchen's youngest sister still lived there with her old ailing mother, whom she nursed. The old lady's body was grotesquely twisted. Her bones had become deformed and she told Justus, that she was in constant pain now. She wished, death would come soon to get her home to her husband. Justus just stared at her in disbelief, but kept his thoughts to himself. Though he had learned to pray as a child, he doubted a here-after. Where had God been in all this. If there was a God, he must have been on a long vacation. For all Justus could see, there was sadness, misery and poverty. Feeling sorry for the old woman, Justus left a small bag with money with her daughter, to buy some medication. Grateful, the woman, who might have been a few years older than Justus himself, told him, that Margaret indeed had been there and had looked for Gretchen. She told him, that Gretchen's married name was Klein and she was living with her husband and children not too far away in a part of the city, which was called Borna. Thanking the young woman, Justus left and went to his little room at the inn. He wrote a letter to his family in Spain, telling them that he had decided to stay in Germany for a while. What he did not say, was, that his mother was in Germany and that he was looking for her.

Early the next day, he took a public carriage and went in direction Borna.

Wisely, he had bought some flowers and told the woman opening the door, that he had a flower delivery for a Margaret Ziegler. The woman told him, that Margaret had lived there for only a few days upon her arrival from Spain and then had moved into her own little house to another part of the city's outskirts, called Gablenz. He could not miss it, a carpenter's shop was next door on the road to Augustusburg. It was a red little brick house surrounded by a wooden fence. Justus thanked the woman, who, he later found out, was indeed Gretchen Klein.

For days, he watched the house, which Gretchen had described and saw no sign of anyone being there. The older carpenter who had his shop next to the house, had seen the young man lurking around and after a few days he asked Justus,

"Who are you looking for my young man? I have seen you sitting on the steps of the little church over there for days now and staring at the house down the road. Aren't you a little young to be her admirer?" He chuckled good naturedly, pointing with his head toward the little red brick house, several hundred yards away. Justus blushed and smiled boyishly at the older man:

"You know the woman who lives in this house?"

"I don't directly know her. She keeps to herself and I see her sometimes go to the market early in the morning. She is always wearing this big kerchief around her head and pulls it into her face. My wife spoke to her once or twice and she said that the woman has a scar in her face. So, she is shy of people. My wife says, the scar is not even that big. It almost looks like she is trying to hide from something or someone. Always going out very early or when it is dark already," the carpenter chattered.

It was all Justus needed to know. He knew for certain, that Margaret lived in the little house. The day was rainy and chilly, though it was the beginning of June. His heart began to pound as he turned and saw a figure coming out of the house and grabbing a few small logs of firewood, which were neatly stacked next to the door, she went back inside, without looking up. It had been since his 18th birthday that he had not seen her. It was almost seven years later and Justus would celebrate his 25th birthday in four months. Would she recognize him? He knew, that he had matured and having been very slender in his youth, he had filled out nicely. His chest and back had become broader and his arms and legs were muscular and well proportioned. He was sporting a beard around his chin and a mustache, which he kept immaculately cropped. Many times at the opera or at concerts, he had noticed longing glances from the female audience. Werner had teased him about it and offered, to introduce him to some of his female friends, which Justus respectfully and good-natured declined. The young friend had remarked on several occasions,

"Damn, Justus, if I would have your looks, I would have the women eat out of my hand. Don't you like female company?"

"Of course I do, Werner. I just think that I have plenty of time," he had answered and had always managed to quickly change the subject. Justus had never spoken of his past with his friend. He had merely told Werner, that he was born in England, lived in America for a short while and then moved to Spain, where his family still lived. He did not mention, that his mother was living in Germany.

Now he was standing near her house and he was suddenly afraid. He chided himself a childish fool for it. What could be the worst that she might do? She could send him away and refuse to talk to him. The old carpenter looked at him questioningly and had decided, that he somehow liked this young man. There was something fine and noble in this young man's face and also a great sadness. He had noticed the young man's eyes widen for an instant, as the woman stepped out of the house to fetch the firewood. Loving a good gossip, the carpenter spoke,

"Where are my manners? I am Emil Fassbinder. My wife is just making some coffee. Would you like to come in to my workshop and have a cup of coffee with me? Come on, lets get out of the rain." He stretched his hand out to shake the young man's. Justus smiled and taking the carpenter's hand, he shook it and pulling his elegant cape around himself:

"I am Justus Ziegler and yes I should like a cup of coffee." The old man's eyes widened for merely and instant. The woman's name next door was Frau Ziegler. So, he is somehow a long lost nephew or distant relative. Ah, it was really getting interesting now and clapping his big work-worn hardened hand on Justus' shoulder, he said,

"Then lets go inside." Together, both men walked inside the little workshop, which was attached to the house, where Emil opened the door connecting the workshop to the kitchen and called to his wife,

"Alma, bring two cups of coffee out here, I have a guest." Curiously, the old woman stuck her head out the door, to see who this guest was. Justus nodded friendly and smiled.

"Guten Tag."

The old friendly woman greeted him with a nod and a smile, saying,

"Guten Tag, young man. I'll just be a minute. The coffee is almost ready and I baked a cake. Would you like a piece?" Justus always had a little sweet tooth and smiling boyishly he nodded.

"Yes please, if its not too much trouble." Instantly, Alma pulled the door shut and went about her business in the kitchen.

Looking around, Justus noticed Emil's many tools and some finished chairs in the workshop. There were an artfully carved desk and matching cabinet waiting to be delivered to its new proud owners. On the workbench was a half finished little footstool. Admiring the craftsmanship, Justus let his hand glide over the smooth polished surface of the desk:

"This is beautiful work, Herr Fassbinder. My father used to have a desk almost like this one," he had said it with a sad look in his face. Alma stuck her head out the kitchen door again and said,

"I have set the table in the kitchen, Emil. Come in here. You can't let our guest have his coffee and cake standing up. What's the matter with you."

"Well, you have heard my wife, then lets go into the kitchen. Come in, young man. Here, let me get your cape and hang it up to dry in the kitchen." He opened the door to the kitchen wide for Justus to step in and Justus entered, pleasantly surprised, a neatly kept room. There was a cast-iron stove in the corner with a big pot of hot water on top. Several cabinets were standing against the wall, holding dishes and utensils. In the middle of the room stood a square table with an spotless blue and white checkered table cloth on top. The four chairs around the table had solid wooden backs with little hearts carved out of them. On the chair's seats were seat cushions from the same material as the table cloth. The whole kitchen smelled of the freshly baked cake, which stood in the middle of the table. The fine china cups were sitting on little saucers and matching cake plates were next to the cups. Next to the cake was a small pitcher with milk and a small dish with sugar. The whole scene looked inviting and Justus sat on the chair, which Alma had pointed too.

"Just sit right over here my boy. I'll get the knife to cut the cake." she said motherly, walked over to one of the cabinets and pulling out a drawer, she came back to the table with a big knife in her hand. Emil had hung the wet cape on a hook near the stove and took his seat. Seating herself heavily, Alma reached over and pulling the cake toward her, she cut a few slices, to serve one of them to Justus on his cake plate and then herself and her husband. 'So, that is the German tradition', Justus thought. 'coffee and cake in the afternoon. I could get used to that', as he forked a small piece of the cake into his mouth. Rolling his eyes he grinned.

"Hm, this is delicious. What is it called?"

"Eierschecke," Alma replied and sipped on her coffee to wash the cake down. Emil grinned, for he knew, that Alma was the best cook and baker as their six granddaughters would swear too. Alma had kept quiet until now and the suspense was killing her. Her husband was munching on his cake and for some strange reason, he had not asked the young man any questions yet, which was highly unusual. There must be a reason, that he had not bombarded the young man with questions. Emil noticed, that his wife was taking a breath to ask Justus a question and quickly he forestalled her.

"Oh, Alma, I forgot to introduce the young man to you. This is Justus Ziegler." He said meaningful in hopes that his wife would keep her tongue behind her teeth. Too late. Her eyes widened and she gasped,

"Then you are related to Frau Ziegler next door?" Justus almost choked on his cake and he was hard pressed not to laugh. He had realized, what Emil was trying to do and found the situation hilarious. Now his wife had spoiled everything for Emil. Keeping the laughter in his throat however, Justus smiled charmingly and answered nonchalantly,

"She is my mother." The result was Emil choking and spitting his cake clear across the table and Alma dropping her fork to sit openmouthed staring at Justus in disbelief. Regaining her composure, Alma mused,

"She never mentioned a son as I spoke to her. She just said that she was a widow. Are you sure?"

"I'm very sure Frau Fassbinder," Justus had to laugh out loud now. Since he had found his mother, he saw no reason to be careful any longer. She could not escape him.

"Does your mother know, that you are here?" Alma asked again.

"Not yet, and I want to keep it that way. I want to surprise her," he said with a sweet smile, which reminded Emil of a prickly little cactus. Ah, there was more to this story, then what meets the eye. Alma was taking a breath again and Emil wished for his glue to be handy. He had been a soldier in his younger years and knew, that some captives had started talking, when they felt comfortable in their surroundings. One could not just fall with the whole door into the house as the old saying goes. However, the cat was already out of the bag and what harm could Alma do now.

"How long has it been, since you saw her last?" Emil heard his wife ask.

"Seven years," Justus answered and continued, to keep his mother's half-truth intact, for she had considered herself a widow for a long time after Thomas had disappeared, "after my father passed away, I had to stay in Spain to take care of some business. When that was all done, I decided to follow my mother to Germany. I am here in Germany for a while now and I wanted to surprise her with being in command of the language, which she undoubtedly is by now. My birthday is coming up in a few months on October the 14th and I want to wait until then to surprise my mother. So, please don't say anything to her."

"Oh, you can count on us, my boy. We will say nothing, won't we Emil?" She padded her husband's hand and he shook his head. Justus had finished his coffee and cake and looked to check the time on his pocket watch. He had almost forgotten, that he was to meet Werner to go to a concert later that Friday night. After the concert, they would, as always, go to the Ratskeller to play some cards. Thanking the carpenter and his wife for their hospitality, Justus excused himself, saying that he had promised to meet his friend. The old couple told him once again, that they would say nothing and he should promise to come back any time soon. Justus promised and swore he would keep his promise. He would be back after the weekend by Monday afternoon.

Another young man, whom Justus had met a few months back, by the name of Franz Lindner joint the party this evening to listen to the concert, which was a famous piano concerto from the late Wolfgang Amadeus Mozart, who had died just a few years ago on December the 5th 1791. They would also hear a new piece from this young musician Ludwig van Beethoven, who, it was said, was very talented. Upon hearing him once, Mozart had remarked, that this young lad would make the world listen some day. Justus loved music and he was looking forward to an enjoyable evening. They had agreed to meet at the foyer at the concert hall and as Justus arrived, he saw Werner waiting already. Franz had not arrived and Justus was glad, that he was not late, which seemed to annoy Werner. A few minutes passed and a carriage rolled in front of the hall. From the carriage jumped Franz and helped a young woman out. Justus caught his breath. The woman was incredibly lovely. Lifting the hem of her gown, she sidestepped a little puddle and hurried laughing, with Franz on her arm into the concert hall foyer.

"Sorry we are a little late. Anita could not find her little purse, which of course had to match her gown." Franz laughed, which was rewarded with a not too gentle cuff from the lovely woman.

"Oh Justus, I don't believe you have met my sister Anita," he introduced the young woman, "Anita, meet our friend from Spain, Justus." He had pulled the smiling woman closer. Gallantly, Justus kissed her outstretched hand and heard her say after she offered him a courteous curtsey in greeting:

"At long last I get to meet you. Franz told me, that you once lived in America and then in Spain. You must tell me all about it. I adore hearing stories from different countries," she dimpled prettily and stuck her hand through his arm to be led into the concert room.

Helplessly, Justus turned and made a face at Franz, who's mirth was obvious. Franz loved his sister very much and felt sorry for her. She was married to an much older and very wealthy man, who was lying on his deathbed. At first, Anita had refused to go to the concert. Her old husband had insisted, that she should join her brother and go to the concert. It would do her good, since she had been taken care of him for many weeks now and there was nothing she could do to improve his health. His testicles had swollen and the doctor was unable to help him, as a few months later his kidneys stopped functioning. The retained fluid was seeping through his skin on his swollen legs and lower extremities, which slowly pressed into his lungs and heart. Every breath was agony for him and a major effort. He knew, that he had merely days to live now and that his sweet little wife would be unable to go anywhere to observe the mourning year. The marriage was childless, since he had been unable to couple with his wife since their wedding night over one year ago, which had been disastrous. Unable to perform in the marriage bed, he had concerned consulted the physician and found out the terrible news. There was a cancerous growth in his scrotum, which the doctor was unable to remove. It had spread too far already. Devastated, he had told Anita, that he had no more than about a year to live. Dutifully, she had nursed him, taking turns with a hired nurse until this very night.

Franz could see his sister enjoying the beautiful music and she seemed to like Justus. It was a good start and Franz hoped, that Anita and Justus would become friends. After the concert, they all went in Anita's carriage to the Ratskeller to have a few glasses of wine. Time seemed to fly, as they listened to stories, which Justus told them, without giving his secrets away. He told of funny little adventures as he still lived in Spain and on his long travel to Germany. Fascinated, Anita hung on every word and for the first time in a long time she was able to laugh heartily. Her troubles forgotten for the moment, she drank a little too much wine and got tipsy. Charmingly, she giggled as she hiccupped and Justus was unable to take his eyes of her lovely face. Her warm brown eyes reminded him of a gentle little deer and her auburn hair, which she wore in a soft knot at the nape of her neck shone and sparkled fetchingly with little diamond pins behind her little ears. The bodies of her gown was cut low and showed the onset of her firm breasts, which were not big, but not small either.

A young man had risen from the next table and came walking toward Franz.

"Franz, is that really you? My lieber, I haven't seen you in ages," the young man said, stretching his hand toward Franz who seemed to recognize the young man and a big smile broadened his face.

"Gerald, what are doing here in Chemnitz? Come, sit and have some wine with us. You know my sister Anita and my friend Werner. This is Justus Ziegler, a new friend we met several months back," Franz introduced, "Justus, meet an old childhood friend of ours, Gerald Kunz."

Justus rose and shook the young man's hand. The young people sat for a while and chatted until Anita yawned delicately behind her hand. Franz had noticed and had an idea.

"Justus, My sisters house is merely a few steps from your little inn. Would you mind taking her home?"

"Not at all, it will be my pleasure," Justus agreed. He knew, where Franz lived and since his little inn was in the opposite direction as his friend's house, he also realized, that Franz would have to make a long trip if he took his sister home and then would have to go to his own house. There was nothing unreasonable about the request and Justus happily complied. He also saw, that Franz still wanted to talk some more to Gerald and Werner. He helped Anita gallantly into her cape and taking her arm, led her to the waiting carriage. Drowsily, the young woman leaned back into the cushions and Justus sat opposite her.

"I have never been out this long in all my life. What time is it?" she asked sleepily.

"It is two thirty in the morning," Justus answered as he glanced at his pocket watch.

"No wonder I am tired," she remarked dryly.

"I have to admit, I am a little tired myself. I had a wonderful evening and I very much enjoyed your company," Justus smiled.

"I feel the same and I thank you for the wonderful stories. It has been a long time that I laughed so hard," Anita said somewhat ruefully. Quickly, she told Justus in a few sentences, that her dear old husband was dying and she would be a widow soon. She was sad, that he was suffering but also would be glad, when his suffering would come to an end.

"I am very sorry to hear that. Please do not hesitate to call me at any time. Day or night. I should like to help you in any way I can." Justus had taken her hand in his and looked genuinely saddened. The carriage came to a halt in front of Anita's house and Justus helping her out, led her up the few steps to the door.

"Thank you again Justus for a wonderful evening and for your concern," Anita said and he kissed her hand:

"Please promise me to call on me, if you need anything. I am lodging at the little inn just two streets down."

"I promise Justus and I appreciate your offer," she said sweetly and stepped into the house. Luckily, it had stopped to rain and Justus quickly made his way down the street to his little inn. Waking up later than usual, Justus decided to go to a little lake, which was located a few blocks away. He wanted to rest and enjoy the day, by sitting on the bench in the park by the lake and read a book. The weather had turned and the sun was shining. He visited a nearby old monastery and the church next to it. He admired the high gothic lead glass windows, depicting various scenes from the bible. He spent a day in leisure and going back to the little inn, he sat in the tavern's dining room to enjoy his evening meal, which he washed down with a fine glass of German beer. Just as he placed the empty glass on the table and was about to get up from his chair, a young boy came into the tavern. He went to the innkeeper and the older man pointed in Justus' direction. The boy told him, that Anita's husband had passed away in the afternoon. Since she considered Justus a friend, the grieving widow longed to have her friends and family about her. She needed to make arrangements for the funeral and the luncheon afterward. She would appreciate his and her brother's help. Not hesitating for a moment, Justus went with the boy to the house. Franz had already arrived and shook his new friend's hand silently. Anita entered the library garbed in black. Her eyes were swollen from crying. Though she had not loved her husband, she had been very fond of him and had admired his courage and kindness. Justus walked toward her and taking her hand in his, he said quietly,

"I am deeply sorry for your loss. Is there anything I can do for you at this very moment?"

"I really don't know if there is anything to do. When our parents died, my brother and I were still little. I remember, that our distant relative wrote invitations to friends, to attend the funeral and the luncheon after," Anita said tired and shrugged her shoulders.

"Very well, let us start with sending out notice to all the friends you two know," Justus suggested.

"There are not that many from our side. Walther knew a lot of people however. I just don't know all of them," Franz remarked.

"Wait, Walther kept a book in his desk, with all the names and addresses of the people he knew," Anita said quickly. Franz found the book and took an audible breath. The three young people sat up half the night, writing.

Justus woke up with a start. He found himself in a chair, covered with a small blanket at Anita's house. Looking around, he remembered what happened. Her husband had died and they had been sitting up half the night, writing to friends and relatives. Franz was in the other chair, snoring. Pulling the blanket off, Justus looked at his pocket watch and found, it was already getting close to the noon hour. Remembering his promise to the Fassbinders, he got up from his chair and quietly tiptoed to the desk, to write a short note. He would be back later this evening to help with further arrangements. There was plenty of time yet and he walked quickly to his little inn to wash up and change clothes. He arrived at the carpenter's house shortly before three in the afternoon and was greeted friendly and warm by both older people. Alma started making the coffee and Justus could smell, that she had baked yet another cake. While she was busy in the kitchen, Emil finished some work on a chair. Justus watched in fascination, as the old man artfully carved a design into the backrest of the chair.

"Is it difficult to learn this?" Justus asked.

Seeing Justus' interest, the old man handed him a tool similar to the one he was holding and pointed to a small piece of wood.

"Try to imitate, what I am doing. Just don't carve against the grain in the wood. It will splinter. Be gentle. And be careful with your fingers. The tool is sharp," Emil chuckled. So, Justus sat with Emil in the little workshop and carving the design of a flower into the small piece of wood. Inspecting his handy work, Emil nodded satisfied.

"You have an eye for detail, Justus, and the touch of and artist. Say, do you want to learn some more?"

Eagerly, Justus nodded. He found, that he enjoyed creating something with his hands. Besides learning the trading business at his father's house, where he had kept books on the inventory, he had never learned a different trade. It could never hurt to learn something new, as Hammed had always pointed out. Alma called from the kitchen,

"Come on you two, the coffee is ready." Both men went to sit by the table and Alma served a different piece of cake on Justus' plate. Rolling his eyes again, after taking a bite, he hummed his pleasure.

"This is different from the last time. What is this called?"

"Bienenstich, it's made with honey." Alma chewed and sipped her coffee.

Emil sat and finishing his cake, he said, "Justus, if you are serious in learning carpentry and woodwork, I could sure use some help in the workshop. You see, my two daughter's husbands have no interest and frankly ten thumbs, when it comes to wood. Somehow, my daughters have given me six granddaughters and not one boy among them to be taught, what I know. I have seen your work and I am well pleased." Surprised, Justus looked at the old man and asked,

"How much would it cost me to apprentice, Herr Fassbinder?"

"Let me put it this way, Justus. I heard a wise man once say, that knowledge is free, if you bring your own bag to keep it. And stealing with your eyes is not a crime. However, I will sell you some of my tools at a reasonable price. Can you agree to that?"

"Yes, I will pay for the tools," Justus answered, without hesitation. It had occurred to him, that the money, his father had given him upon his departure from Spain would not last forever. He would have to work on something to support himself. Here was the opportunity do learn an honest trade, from this kind old man, who had made him an incredible offer. So it was settled, that Justus would work in the little workshop. He would start the morning after the funeral, which he had told the old couple about.

Justus went back to Anita's house and was an invaluable help for the next few days. The funeral and luncheon over, the four friends sat together at the young woman's house, playing cards and chatting. None of the three young men wanted to leave the young woman alone in the big house. Since Anita was not able to go out for some time, to observe the year of mourning, it was agreed that they would meet in the evening at her house.

The weeks went by and Justus worked at Emil's little shop during the day and spent his evenings together with his three friends. It was Friday on October the 13th, as Emil and Alma Fassbinder surprised Justus with a fine birthday cake and a small present, which was a new tool. Both older people had kept their promise and had said nothing to the woman next door. Now the long awaited day was there and Justus would surprise his mother on the next day, which was his 25th birthday. Taking great care of his appearance, Justus dressed elegantly. Time had done something to his mind and his initial anger at his mother had given way to anticipation. What would she look like now and what would she say? Though he had seen her several times from the little workshop, she had been too far away, to make out her features with this ugly kerchief pulled deeply into her face. He knew, that she lived a lonely and nearly reclusive life. He had never seen anybody near her house, besides the woman he had seen in Borna, whom he suspected was her friend Gretchen and had visited her twice in all this time.

Slowly, he walked toward her door along the little path, which was flanked by some rosebushes and other little plants. To the side of the house was a small herb garden and Justus could see an Apple tree and a tree with plums. Raising his hand, he knocked on the door. For a long while, there was no sound coming from within the house. Then the door opened a small crack and his mother's voice hiding behind the big kerchief barked in German,

"What do you want, I already paid my taxes to the church." Shocked, Justus noticed the strand of gray hair from under the kerchief as her eyes surrounded by a few wrinkles, squinted without any recognition, at him. For a moment, he did not know, what to say. The first thing that came to his mind was in English,

"Hello mother."

Her hand, which had clutched the kerchief to hide her face, fell away and she turned white. Merely for an instant, she looked like she would faint. Then a slow smile crossed over her face and she drawled,

"So, you finally found me after all these years. Did your father send you?" Without waiting for an answer, she went back into the house, leaving the door open for Justus to follow her. He did and was shocked once more. The house was nearly devoid of any furnishings, safe a cast iron stove a small cabinet to hold dishes, a table and two chairs in the kitchen. The living room was furnished with merely a big chair, a small round table next to it and a tiny desk on which the only source of light, an old oil lamp, stood. There were no carpets on the wooden floors, which squeaked under his steps. He wondered, what the upstairs rooms looked like. Justus had followed his mother into the kitchen and sat on one of the chairs.

"What do you intend to do now?" Margaret asked, seating herself on the other chair.

"Don't worry, my father does not know, where you are," he tried to calm her fears. Relieved, she breathed a sigh and stood up. She pulled a small pot from the little cabinet and filling it with water from a bucket in the corner, she placed it onto the stove.

"I was about to make myself a cup of coffee. Would you like some?"

"Yeah, that would be nice. I found, I have gotten used to this German tradition, to have coffee and cake in the afternoon," Justus smiled. Surprised, she spun around and asked,

"How long have you been here in Germany, that you know of this?"

Up until then, Justus had spoken English to his mother. He answered in perfect accent free German,

"Ein ganzes Jahr Mutter." Which means, 'a whole year mother'. She couldn't help it and smiled at him. While the water was starting to

409

boil, she went to her little desk and came back with a pair of spectacles, which she was about to place on her nose.

"So, now I can see, what I am doing. Let me have a look at you, boy." She stood and stared at her son for a long moment. Besides his father, he was the handsomest man she had ever seen. She remembered as she had seen him last when he was eighteen. A tall gangly boy, a little too slim and with some peach fuzz around his lips. That had been seven years ago. And suddenly, she remembered. It was her son's birthday. He was turning twenty five this very day. Feeling a twitch of guilt, she went wordlessly to a room upstairs and returned a few moments later with a small box in her hand. She held out the little box toward her son and said,

"Happy birthday, Justus."

Stunned, Justus slowly took the little box from her hands, mumbling, "Thank you, mother." He opened the little box and found a cravat needle and matching cufflinks, studded with tiny diamonds and emeralds. He didn't know, whether to laugh or to cry. He recognized this jewelry. It had belonged to his father. Now it became indisputably clear to him, that his mother had indeed been the thieve, which had cleaned out the secret little room. What was the use. He decided not to say anything and stuck the little box in the pocket of his elegant cape. His mother was surprised to hear, that he had started working at the carpenter's workshop next door. She offered for him to move into the house and safe therefore the money for the inn. Furthermore, it would be close to work and he could help her around the house and in the garden. Justus gladly agreed. Over time, he managed together with Emil, to make some new furniture for the little house and still visited his three friends often at Anita's house. It seemed to annoy his mother and she asked one day,

"Why do you always go out in the evening? Where are you going all the time? Do you have a lover? Tomorrow is your 26th birthday and I am making your favorite food tonight. You could stay home this once."

"First of all, mother, I am meeting with some friends in my free time. Second, I don't have a lover and even if I had, it would be none of your affair. I'm a grown man. The reason, that I am not getting involved with a woman, should be clear to you. Because of you, I almost married my own sister. And the reason that I don't want to get married is, that I don't want to have to answer to any nagging questions from a woman about my comings and goings," he barked.

"Pah, I have heard that lame excuse before," Margaret spat and turned back to her stove. Somehow, she felt relieved, that he didn't have a lover. Since her son's return, Margaret had taken more care to her appearance. She was a woman of almost forty two years of age and though her hair had turned gray, she was still a handsome woman. Justus placed his hand on his mother's shoulder and felt sorry for his harshness.

"I'm sorry, mother. I don't want to quarrel with you. We have to leave the past behind us."

Whatever came over Margaret at this moment, no one could say. Slowly, she turned to face her son. He looked so much like Jack and she couldn't help herself. She took his face in both of her hands and kissed his mouth. Softly, he hugged her and padded her back, as he became aware, that his mother's body began to press suggestively against his own. Shocked to his innermost core, he pushed her violently from him.

"Are you mad woman?" The look of forbidden desire in his mother's face was his answer. Shamed to death, he ran from the house. He decided to spend the night, drinking himself into a stupor at the Ratskeller.

CHAPTER 32

The Last Straw

"Hey Werner, isn't that the Spaniard over there in the corner?" A young acquaintance of the friends pointed with his glance to the corner of the tavern. Werner spun around on his seat and looked into direction corner. His face turned from the surprised smile, which the name 'Spaniard' had cost, to a worried frown. His friend was sitting glassy-eyed and his shoulder-long hair, which he always wore bound neatly with a black velvet ribbon at the nape of his neck, disheveled hanging into his face, staring at the glass in front of him.

"Dear heavens, something must be wrong. We have missed him for our card game tonight at Anita's house. I have never seen Justus drink more than one or two glasses of wine. So far, I count three empty bottles on his table. Let me see, if I can find out, what is eating him," Werner spoke to his companion. He rose from his seat and the other young man chuckled,

"Looks like female trouble to me, Werner. If I were you, I would stay out of it."

Werner turned and whispered furious, "Justus is a good friend, Johannes, and I will not let him sit there alone to drink himself to death." Johannes rose also and answered, "Have it your way, man, I was about to leave anyway. Well, I'll see you another time then." He turned and left the tavern. Werner walked over to the table and forcing a smile said,

"Hello, Justus, fancy to meet you here. We missed you at the card game tonight. Did you forget?"

Justus glared at his friend and saw three Werners stand in front of him.

"Wi. Wi. which one is you Werner. I s. I see three of you," Justus drawled drunkenly.

"Take the one in the middle," Werner remarked dryly, "now come lets get you home. No wait, I have a better idea. Lets go to Anita's house. She will sober you up with some good strong coffee." Werner grabbed his friend under his arms and pulled him up from the chair. He flung his cape around Justus' shoulders and steadying his friend with his strong grip by the arm, maneuvered him out of the tavern to the fresh crisp October air outside. With a short whistle, he hailed a public carriage and pushed his friend in. The fresh air began to take its effect and Justus began to feel giddy. Insulting the ears of the poor carriage driver and costing the horse almost to shy up startled, he started to sing at the top of his lungs. Embarrassed, Werner clapped his hands over his friend's mouth.:

"Shhhh Justus, its after ten. You'll wake up the whole city. We don't want the watchman to clap you into the red tower to sober up."

"But, but its my birthday tomorrow. I am celebrating my birthday, Werner," he protested and hiccupped.

'Ah, so that's what is wrong. No one had thought of his friend's birthday and Justus is feeling sorry for himself,' Werner thought. 'I just don't remember Justus telling us, when his birthday was', he mused, while the carriage rumbled in front of Anita's house. Since Werner had left the card games early that night, there was still light in the house and luckily, Franz was still there. Together, they brought Justus into the house and Anita started a big pot of coffee. As they sat in the spacious kitchen, Werner tried to explain Justus' behavior with a good-natured chuckle,

"I think out dear Justus was singing the blues tonight, since no one remembered his birthday is tomorrow."

Anita and Franz looked at each other in surprise and Franz stated,

"We didn't even know it would be his birthday, which by the way is today now. It is shortly after midnight."

Their glances went in question toward Justus and all three young people caught their breath. Justus sat on the chair and big tears rolled into his mustache and beard. They all would remember the look of anguish and raw pain in the young man's face as long as they lived. Anita's heart went out to him and her hand touched his gently. He pulled his hand away, as if she had touched him with an open flame and seeing her surprised and hurt look, an unearthly sound of hurt and torture escaped his chest. Perplexed, the three friends sat motionless looking from one to another, not knowing what to do or what to say. Werner was the first to recover from his shock and asked as gentle as he could,

"Justus, please, you are scaring us here. Tell us what is wrong. No one gets this upset over a birthday, which we didn't even know would be tomorrow. Something else is bothering you. We are your friends and like to help. We can't do nothing, if we don't know what is going on. Please tell us," he emphasized and placed a heavy hand on his friend's shoulder, gently shaking him. Justus placed his hand over his friend's, padded it in appreciation and whispered thickly under tears,

"I can't. You would never understand. I don't even understand myself."

"Try me." Werner attempted a smile and looked straight into his friend's pain stricken face. Justus shook his head and again heavy tears poured from his eyes. Resolutely, Anita stood up from her chair and said,

"I think Justus should get some sleep. Sleep is the best medicine. Please take him to the guestroom Franz. The sheets are fresh and there is some wood in the fireplace." She knew, that Justus was suffering from an incredible shock and was in terrible pain. Whatever it was, that tortured his mind, perhaps in time she would find out. She realized that it must have something to do with a woman. He had pulled his hand away from hers, but not from Werner's touch. Justus stood up from his chair to follow Franz and as if he could read her thoughts, turned and said quietly,

"Thank you, Anita, for understanding. I didn't mean to be rude before."

"Don't worry, Justus, I didn't take it personally," she smiled friendly and turned to clear the table.

"What was that all about?" Werner whispered as Justus had followed Franz from the kitchen.

"Oh, you men are such idiots at times. Can't you see, that it has something to do with a woman. He didn't flinch, as you touched his shoulder. As I touched his hand, he pulled his away like a snake had bitten him. Use your head Werner." She clapped her hand against his forehead to emphasize her point. A slow smile formed on Werner's lips as he remembered the rumor he had heard from another acquaintance, that Justus had moved from the little inn into a woman's house. Why, the little devil. He had never mentioned anything, but it couldn't hurt, to find out. As he thought on it a little more, he realized, that Justus had never really told them anything about his personal life. However, he had been happy as he told his friends, that he found work at a carpenter's shop somewhere in Gablenz. Perhaps it was time, he would pay this carpenter a visit, to find out a little more about his friend. He would not tell Anita or Franz however, until he knew more about their mutual friend.

Knowing, that Justus was safely at Anita's house and did not work on Sundays, Werner went early in the morning in direction Gablenz. He found the carpenter's shop and knocked on the door. Grumbling something about pesky costumers, who couldn't leave him alone even on a Sunday, Emil answered the door. Werner smiled his friendliest smile and greeted the old man with introducing himself,

"Hello, my name is Werner Richter. Is this the shop, where my friend Justus works?" Upon hearing Justus' name, the old man's features softened and he answered,

"Yes, Justus works here with me," suddenly concerned, his face wrinkled and worried he asked, "is something wrong with him?"

"That is what I wanted to ask you. Could I talk with you please. I am indeed worried about my friend," Werner said honestly and the concern was written plainly on his face. Emil noticed and quickly said,

415

"Of course, please come in. It is cold out here."

Werner followed Emil into the comfortably warm kitchen and Emil poured him a freshly brewed cup of coffee, which his wife had made before she went to church.

"Now please tell me what is going on with Justus. Understand, that I like the boy and would like to help if he is in trouble," Emil said with feeling.

"Well, let me start at the beginning. By chance, I went with an acquaintance to the Ratskeller last night and saw Justus sitting there, like I had never seen him before. As I saw him, he was already on his fourth bottle of wine and drunk as a sailor. I took him to a friend's house, who would sober him up with coffee, when he suddenly started crying like a child. I will never forget the pain and anguish in my friend's face. At first we thought, that Justus felt sorry for himself, because no one remembered his birthday. However, we concluded that his sadness must have some deeper roots and I thought you could help me to find out what it is."

"Ah, that's right, his birthday is today. I remember last year, as he surprised his mother on his birthday," Emil chuckled and looked surprised at Werner, who sat openmouthed staring at him. Finding his speech again, Werner asked incredulous,

"Say what, my good man? His mother? I thought, his family is still in Spain."

"Oh no, his mother moved here a long time ago. She is living in the little red brick house next door. He came here to surprise her. He moved into her house a year ago."

So, that rumor was true. He had moved into a woman's house, which turned out to be his mother. As Werner opened his mouth to ask another question, the door opened and Alma walked in. She was in a very good mood. The pastor had told her, that even the angels would stand in line for her heavenly cake. Emil quickly introduced Werner to his wife and told her the purpose of his visit. Her look darkened and she seemed to remember something.

"I was sweeping out front last evening, as I saw Justus storming out of his mother's house. He didn't even see me. He seemed very upset and ran by me as if the devil was behind him. I guessed, that he had a fight with his mother. She is a bit strange if you ask me. Justus is such a nice young man," she finished with an motherly tone. She loved the boy. Ever since he started working with Emil, her husband's eyes lit up, when he told her of the young man's progress and how talented he was. He was happy to pass his knowledge on to someone like Justus. A frantic knocking startled all three people out of their own thoughts. Alma flew to the door and said with surprise in her voice,

"Frau Klein, I have not seen you here for a long time. What's wrong?"

"Please, Frau Fassbinder, its my friend Margaret. She needs a doctor. Oh it is terrible," Gretchen Klein cried.

"Dear heavens, Frau Klein, what is wrong with Frau Ziegler?" Alma said with alarm in her voice.

"She cut her wrists and there is blood everywhere," Gretchen exclaimed.

"Oh no, this is terrible. I'll come with you and my husband will fetch the doctor," Alma said quickly and grabbed for her cape. The two men had listened and jumped up from their seats.

"There is no need, I do have medical training, Frau Fassbinder. I am a doctor," Werner said into the commotion. He never used to introduce himself by his title since he found it somewhat snobbish. Emil was the first to recover from yet another shock.

"Then why are you standing here. Lets go and help." All four people ran toward the little red brick house. The scene that greeted them, was terrible. A trail of blood led from the kitchen table with the bloody knife still lying on it, to the little living room, where Margaret was in the chair. Her skin was pale, almost transparent and her lips had a hue of blue to it. Quickly, Werner felt for a pulse on the side of her neck.

"She is still alive. Quickly, I need some clean strips of cloth to bind the wounds. She doesn't have much time if she loses any more blood."

Without hesitating, Gretchen pulled one of her underskirts off from under her dress and began to rip it into thin long strips. Thankful, Werner smiled at the woman and taking the strips of cloth, bound them tightly around Margaret's wrists. Dear God, Werner thought, what sort

417

of nightmare did I walk into. Yesterday, he found his friend in total despair and today he found his friend's mother, who tried to commit suicide. How could he tell Justus on his birthday, that he had given his mother medical attention and the circumstances, which had called for his medical skill. It was an impossible situation. Justus' state of mind was fragile at best and he did not know, how much more his poor friend could take. Werner did not know, what he should do. He saw only one way, to find out more about it. Werner would have to talk to his own father, who was a doctor at the psychiatric clinic. Perhaps he could help him.

After wrapping the woman's wrists, Werner sent for the carriage from the mental hospital and delivered the unconscious woman into his father's care. He explained to the old doctor Richter, that the woman was his friend's mother and should be watched carefully. Something terrible must have occurred the evening before, for his friend was on the verge of a nervous breakdown himself. He wanted to find out what had happened, that Justus was driven half insane with pain and his mother tried to take her own life. Before he had taken Margaret from her home to the clinic, Werner had told the Fassbinders as well as Gretchen, that Justus must never find out of his visit. It would destroy him. All three people had sworn, not to breathe a word to the young man. Werner took one more look at the woman, who had been strapped securely into the narrow bed. His father, clapped his hand on Werner's shoulder and said,

"Come, let us go to my office. We will talk there." Nodding his agreement, Werner followed his father to the small office and seating himself, took a small glass of brandy from his father's hand, which the old doctor had poured for his son and himself. Seating himself in the other chair, the old doctor asked,

"Now, my son, tell me the whole story. I can see, that you are upset and are obviously very concerned about your friend, whom you mentioned to be this woman's son. Tell me exactly, what has happened."

Werner told his father about Justus' state of mind the night before and leaving out no detail, he mentioned his friend's reaction to Anita's touch and then the touch of his own hand. He spoke of Anita's suspicion, that it must have something to do with a woman. It had been clear, that a female touch had brought Justus to this almost violent withdrawal of his own hand.

Old doctor Richter wrinkled his brow as if deep in thought and asked if Werner knew more about his friend's personal life. His son answered, that he had just found out something disturbing a few hours back. Justus had told his friends, that his family was living in Spain and he had left, to travel a bit. He had liked Germany and had decided to stay for a while. Naturally, they had assumed, that by telling his friends his family living in Spain, would have included his mother. Werner had been very surprised to learn that his mother had been living here in Germany a long time before Justus came to see her. And even then, he had waited a year to actually visit her, though he knew, where she lived. Which was right next door to his mother's house, where he had started working as a carpenter. He had told the master carpenter, that he wanted to surprise her on his 25th birthday, which he did. Justus had been living in his mother's house ever since, until last night. That was exactly one year to the day, for his friend's birthday was today. Doctor Richter looked even more concerned then before, but kept his thoughts to himself.

"Where is your friend now, Werner?"

"I took him to Anita's house, where he stayed in the guestroom. He is all likelihood waking up with a sore head and might feel terrible today with a grand hangover from drinking four bottles of wine."

Doctor Richter knew Anita and her late husband for a long time. Alarmed he asked,

"Is your friend alone there with Anita?"

"No, father, Franz decided to stay the night also. Why? What do you think would happened if Justus would find himself alone with Anita?"

"I am not certain just yet, my son. It seems, he would feel more secure in the presence of a female, if a male would be there also," Doctor Richter told his son.

"Do you think, my friend's mother will live?"

"She has lost a lot of blood, but I think she will survive, yes. I must get back to my patients now my son. Please keep me informed, if you find out some more about your friend. I will let you know, when the woman wakes up. Then I will have to ask her a few questions." Doctor Richter had a grim line around his lips. Werner left his father with the promise to be back soon.

Justus woke up and his head felt as if a herd of wild horses had stampeded through it. Instantly, he remembered the previous night. Disgusted with himself, he looked at his pocket watch and had to look twice. It was shortly before two in the afternoon. Quickly he jumped out of the bed, which he regretted a second later. His head pounded and his stomach lurched. He splashed some icy water from the little porcelain basin on a little table into his face and rinsed his teeth to get rid of the sour taste in his mouth. It didn't help much. His stomach growled and he felt hungry. Yet as he thought about food his innards threatened to turn inside out. As he pulled on his boots, one of them slipped from his hand and fell to the wooden floor. The sound, the tumbling boot made, reminded him of the noisy fireworks his father had at the house in Spain, to celebrate his children's birthdays. Justus winced and squeezed his eyes shut. There was a short knock on the door and Franz peeked his head in the room.

"So, you are back among the living again huh?" He chuckled as he saw, that Justus pulled his head in between his shoulders at the sound of his voice. Franz himself had had a few hangovers and he knew, how Justus felt.

"Come downstairs into the kitchen, Anita has made some coffee," he told Justus, who looked around the room for a brush to bring some semblance of order to his hair. He pulled open a drawer on the vanity and found, what he was looking for. Quickly, he brushed through his hair and binding it at the nape of his neck with the little black velvet ribbon, he placed the brush back where he had found it. As he walked into the kitchen, he was greeted with friendly smiles from his three friends. Werner had just arrived a few minutes earlier and sipped his coffee. All three friends chorused in perfect unison, "Happy birthday, Justus."

Again his head went in between his shoulders and his friends couldn't help but giggle. Werner had decided not to tell his other two friends about, what he found out and what had transpired earlier in the morning. He knew, that Anita had a soft heart and would be, saddened by the news, give his secret away. Anita had managed to bake a small cake and placed it in front of Justus with a small candle on top, which she lit.

"Many happy and healthy returns, Justus." She smiled and Justus managed a rueful smile and a barely audible, "Thank you, you three. You are truly the best friends a man could have."

"I do have another present for you, Justus," Anita said and placed a small package on the table in front of Justus, "I hope you like them. I know you will need them soon. It is getting cold," she twinkled and dimpled prettily.

Surprised, Justus opened the little package and pulled out a pair of leather gloves lined in fur. For a moment, Justus blinked as if something had come into his eyes. He sat and seemed to fight with something inside of himself. He wanted to thank this sweet woman, who was kind, loving generous and honest. Gingerly, he took her hand in his and squeezing with the slightest pressure as if he would hold a little bird, saying, "Thank you, Anita."

Answering his handshake with just the same amount of pressure, Anita smiled friendly into his face, "You are welcome. Now let us have some cake." She would never tell him, that she had bought these gloves for her late husband and had kept them wrapped in her closet. Fascinated, Werner had watched Justus as he took Anita's hand. He knew, that he had been fighting with his emotions, to touch her hand. However, he seemed to have to come to the conclusion, that Anita was not the enemy and he had taken her hand. Then who in the devil's name was responsible for his friend's outburst the night before. He would have to tell his father of his observation.

Justus finally told his friends, that he had taken a room at some house near his place of work and could not go back there. He had had a terrible fight with the owner of the house the previous night. He wanted to move back into the little inn nearby. Anita and her brother

Franz believed his half-true story and assumed, that this must have been the reason for his behavior.

Anita offered Justus, to stay in her guestroom as long as he had not found a different place to live. Werner kept quiet and had his own thoughts.

Werner went back to the mental hospital the next day. He told his father, of his observation, upon which the old doctor shook his head and scratched his beard. The woman had indeed survived and was drifting in and out of consciousness at the present time. She had to be given heavy doses of sedatives, for she started screaming and thrashing in her bed as she had woken up the first time and found out, that she was still alive and in the hospital. She had whimpered, that she wanted to die, she could not live with the shame. Insistently, the doctor asked her about the shame she was talking about. She had stared at him with unseeing eyes, as if she would look through him. A blank expression on her face to start screaming the next minute until she was finally sedated and had been kept that way ever since. The woman was most definitely insane and would have to stay. She was foremost a danger to herself and who knows, what she would do, if released.

Werner knew, what he had to do. However, he needed the help of the carpenter and his wife. He knew, that Justus was working there this day and he waited until he was certain, that Justus had left the workshop. It was dark already, as he knocked on the carpenter's door and was greeted with great respect. The Fassbinders knew, that the young doctor had saved their neighbor's life. Werner told them, that Justus' mother was very ill in her mind and would have to stay in the mental hospital for a long time. It was likely, that she would have to stay there forever. The house next door would have to be cleaned and Justus would have to be told, that his mother had suddenly moved. This way, Justus could move back into the little house and would be near his place of work. He must never find out, that his mother was in the insane asylum. Gretchen Klein would have to be informed also, to never tell Justus, that she knew where to find Margaret.

Both old people agreed, that it would be the best solution to their problems. At once, Frau Fassbinder went with her mop and cleaned the little red brick house. She worked half the night and Werner took the blood soaked chair with the help of Emil to strip it down to the wood and burn the bloody fabric and the sea grass cushions. The next morning, Emil Fassbinder told Justus, that he had seen his mother move away the previous night and had not said anything to where she was moving. She had merely said 'good buy' and she would not return. Justus said nothing and seemed to breathe a sigh of relieve. Telling Anita, that he had found a place to live and was renting a little house near the place where he worked, he moved back into the little red brick house.

It was a few months later on a cold day in January, as Justus received a letter from Sofia. The innkeeper from the little inn he had been staying at before had sent it to the little red brick house. His father had passed away. The strain of everything had weakened his heart and the doctor had not been able to save him. He had suddenly clutched his chest the night before Justus' birthday in the evening and had collapsed, never regaining consciousness. His last words before his collapse had been 'Justus, my son, I should have killed her'. Perhaps Justus knew the meaning of these strange words of the dying man. His father died after midnight on October the 14th. Hammed and Elizabeth had moved back to England together with Laura, to be near her aging parents. Leonardo, his younger half-brother had finally married and had a darling little daughter, Giovanna. Leonora had refused as he knew, to get married and had finally decided to join a convent.

Justus remembered, that the night before his birthday on October the 13th, he had stormed out of the house after his mother's indecent advance around seven in the evening. It had been shortly after midnight as he sat in the kitchen at Anita's house and was suddenly enveloped in an icy feeling of loss, that he had started to cry. For the strangest reason, he had been thinking and wishing to be home in Spain with his father. It was the last straw. Again, Justus went to the tavern and wanted to get himself gloriously drunk. As he entered the tavern, two older gentlemen invited the young man to a friendly card game. They needed the third man to play the game of Skat. He played cards with the older gentlemen and won a great deal of money. Grinning, Justus scooped the money from the table and decided to tell his good fortune to his friends. The card games at Anita's house had never been for any wagers and he decided to change that. The thirty minute walk in the cold air sobered him up enough and his friends did not notice that he had been drinking. Both Werner and Franz agreed indulgingly to play with Justus for small amounts of money and Justus won again. Anita laughingly refused to participate. Since it was late and it began to snow again, Justus was offered the guestroom and he remained the night at Anita's house.

Time went by and another year passed. Justus had started to enjoy the card table at the tavern more and more. Sometimes he won, other times he lost and his hard earned money went into the pockets of his opponents.

It became customary, that the four friends met every Saturday evening at Anita's house. Though Anita had started going out occasionally with her brother and the two other men to concerts and the opera, she preferred the quite home life. Werner, as well as Franz got married and seemed to have less and less time to be with Justus and Anita. Still, Justus went every Saturday to visit her and on one of these occasions, Justus and Anita kissed for the first time in the summer of 1800. He had won at the card table and felt giddy as a school boy. Showing Anita his loot, he swung her around the room and laughing had put her down again, as her arms were still around his neck. She looked deeply into his eyes and her face was close to his. His lips suddenly were on hers and she melted into his arms. Though a healthy young man of almost 28 years of age, Justus had never made love to a woman. Anita had no experience at 26, safe her terrible wedding night with her unfortunate late husband.

Shyly and shaking, they explored each other's bodies all night with much giggling and found out caressing and kissing, what kept Franz and Werner at home with their own wives. They had become lovers. Justus and Anita remained lovers for many years and Anita had occasionally paid Justus' gambling debts. Upon winning, Justus celebrated with wine. Upon losing, he drowned his sorrows away. Frustrated, that his efforts became less and less successful in Anita's arms, he began to blame her and called her an old undesirable woman, who was merely worth something in the kitchen. Anita loved him and said nothing. It was a cold November night in the year 1812. Justus had gambled heavily and lost. His debtor insisted on being paid at once and Justus went drunk and angry to Anita's house. He demanded the money from her to pay of his debts. She refused as she could not afford it any longer.

The small fortune, her late husband had left her, had dwindled down to a small amount of money, which would allow her to live out her days comfortably if she was careful. Angry at her refusal, he threw a vase at her, which she ducked. The vase shattered on the mantle of the fireplace, where she stood. Frightened and angry herself, she grabbed the poker from the fireplace and tried to attack him with it, so he would leave. Seeing her intend, his eyes flashed enraged and he noticed, that the poker in her hand had gotten hung up under the mantle. He was at her with a few long steps and placed his hands around her throat. He squeezed hard and she made gurgling sounds, clawing with her nails at him. Her eyes bulged out and her face turned blue. Her lifeless body crumbled from his hands to the floor, her eyes sightless. Anita was dead.

Suddenly sober and terrified of his deed, Justus realized, what he had done. He would end up in the red tower of the city and would be hung. His life was over one way or the other. He was forty years old. Slowly, he walked from the house like a sleepwalker. He did not feel the cold and walked toward the river with the same name as the city, Chemnitz. It had been bitter cold for a few days and the river was high and partially frozen on a few spots already. Justus found himself on a bridge and stared into the dark murky water rushing beneath him and he took a deep breath. He climbed up the low stonewall and stood for a few seconds, watching a few pieces of ice floating in the raging water. He had never been a strong swimmer and knew, if he would not drown, the cold would kill him in minutes. He saw no other way out and bent over to jump...

CHAPTER 33

Day of Reckoning

"Hesitating only for one more moment, I knew that the life I had led was over one way or the other and I jumped. Hitting the surface of the icy water of the Chemnitz, my head struck the edge from a floating large piece of ice and the force of it broke my neck. There was a moment of darkness and I felt nothing. How long I had been unconscious, I don't know. It must have been no more then mere seconds. As I came too, it became obvious to me that I was unable to move. I had no feelings in my legs or arms. Though I struggled desperately for air, to keep my shocked and panic-stricken body afloat, I submerged more and more into the river and my lungs filled with water. It is one thing, to try and commit suicide, but being unable to breathe, the body's reflexes and life force is suddenly hard at work to survive at all costs. In only a few moments, which seemed like eternity to me, everything was dark and still around me. I knew, I was floating in the icy river, and yet suddenly, somehow I felt in a strange way warm and conscious. As if I was alive and breathing effortlessly.

How much time had passed, I did not know. I had the sensation of total weightlessness and was floating suspended over the river, looking down on a body that was now floating facedown in the dark waters. Only after noticing that the body in the river was wearing the same shirt and trousers and boots as I had worn, became it clear to me, that it was my own body. It was inconceivable to me, that I was alive and seemingly uninjured, if this was I down there, lifeless in the river. It didn't make any sense to me at first and then something extraordinary happened. I felt like being propelled at acute speed through a long and endless void or tunnel. In the far distance I saw a light. Apparently, without my own doing or any effort on my behalf, I was pulled to this light. This light is brighter than a thousand suns but did in no way hurt my eyes. Upon entering this sphere of terrific brilliance I became aware, that someone was speaking to me from this light, a living being. He made his presence known to my mind. The method in which he would communicate, I could not fathom at the time.

Suddenly I was taking inventory of my past life. Three-dimensional images developed in front and somehow all about me as I watched my own life play in precise detail right before my eyes. I was an observer in the middle of it all. Not only could I see and hear everything, that was done and spoken, I also was very vivid aware of the feelings inside the other persons, whom I had contact with in my review. I felt the other's feelings inside my own being possibly a hundred-fold more fierce as the one's, I had hurt. And I had hurt a number of people very deeply. The unimaginable pain inside of myself instantly made me aware of undeniable facts. As soon as I became an adult, I was responsible for my own actions. My hatred and frustration should not have led to escapism through alcohol and violence, rather to a more constructively seeking a life of my own. Instead I knowingly and willfully destroyed other lives by giving in to my own weaknesses, and evil doings. The result was, that I was not able to control myself anymore and feeling only self-pity and rage, I took another persons life. Not to mention, that I took my own life, because I was not man enough, to face a just punishment for my actions.

The review of my life was played out to the minutest detail and yet seemed to speed by like a movie at the fast forward mode. It ended with the same picture, which I saw seemingly only moments ago. It was my body floating in the water. I felt the panic and the struggle I had gone through to survive. At the same moment I realized, that there was no way out of this terrible situation and my whole being began to panic once more. I wanted desperately to awaken from this nightmare. However, there was no waking up. This nightmare would not go away, try as I might. I could no more change the outcome in my mind, as it had been in fact my life and was grim reality. At the realization to what had actually been my life set in, the feelings of terrible fear and panic overcame me. It would everlastingly be the same reality, as I found myself in now. In uncountable repetitions my whole life would play in front of me without the slightest alteration to the horrible end. The light that had surrounded me at first seemed to become dimmer and darker and I found myself cast into darkness and horrendous pain. It felt as if thousands of claws and teeth were ripping my inside apart.

I began to fear my own self and I felt that my own being was about to self-destruct. Then, at the point of deepest despair the nightmare started from the beginning, starting with my childhood. There was no escape from it and I was trapped in a hell of my own making. Totally terrified and appalled by the being I was observing as my own self, I began to judge myself more harshly every time, as my vision came to the scene of killing another person. I had to endure *her* feelings of terror and fear magnified a thousand times inside my own being. Upon seeing my body floating in the river I began to beg my own self, *my soul*, for forgiveness. On my knees I began to beg the everlasting core inside me, to forgive the frightful deeds I had so viciously allowed this willful mind of mine to do. Knowingly I had sanctioned the mind of Justus to become evil, though I had the authority and the comprehension, to know better. I had done nothing to stop my evil ways and was responsible for everything, I had let the living person, Justus, do. And now I realized, I was the same individual still and seemingly nothing could ever be done to safe myself, from myself. I had become my own most relentless judge. My own self had become what I hated, despised and feared most.

I somehow began to concentrate more and more on the innocence of the child I had observed in my reviews and caught myself calming at the sight of little Justus saying his prayers at night. To this day I think of Natty and Patty, my childhood nurses, with gratitude. Raging and judging my own self-destructive ways, I had forgotten God. I started to pray.

I prayed with my whole being and the innocence of a child, for

428

forgiveness from God. I prayed for the souls of all the people that had, however major or insignificant roles played in my life. I prayed for my mother. I repented every unkindness and the crimes I had committed, in earnest. I realized I knelt in a sea of my own tears, which were reflecting the light surrounding me. I prayed again, thanking God for every day of my life and the choice he had given me. My tears became tears of joy at the immense realization of his everlasting love had cleansed my soul and I was still in existence. Up to this point I had never seen myself as a still whole being. I had prayed instinctively with my mind and soul. Though I had seen myself kneeling and I had seen my tears, it had not registered in my mind, that I still and by the greatest miracle of all had a body. The first thing my eyes conceived were my hands, folded in prayer. Begging God's forgiveness again for interrupting my heartfelt prayers, I began to touch myself. I felt my face, wet with tears. I felt my arms, my legs, my torso, I marveled at the discovery, that I was able to wiggle my toes. I was filled with joy. I wanted to shout and share my happiness.

It was then that I slowly became aware of something, another presence. This presence had not helped me to see myself as I had been the past, but rather to realize myself for the being I had become. I was conscious of the presence, which had stirred my own thinking to exactly the instant, where I had come to a breaking point in my personality metamorphosis. Comparable to a person awakening from a stupor. It was then, that I came in contact for the first time consciously with another human being. In all this time, he had been with me and watched me slowly sensing and realizing my own soul and betterment by making efforts on my own. I had no idea, how much time had passed, for I had no conception of time passing. I was dumbfounded to say the least. It had taken my spirit 127 years to emerge from my own mind-made hell. The dimension, which I had left so forcefully in 1812, was now writing the year 1945 on the calendars.

What followed, were countless sessions with the elders to restore my spirit and to teach me how to except what had happened. I was given a second chance of redeeming my soul and see life from a different perspective. I was schooled to become a guide for a living person. I was instructed that at no time in this human's life was I sanctioned, to interfere in the order of her fate. Only using my own sound judgment in case of eminent danger of premature death to my charge, I would be allowed to intervene in such a way that it would not be known by the person as a intervention. These lessons took five years.

It was in the spring of the year 1950, that I eagerly awaited the assignment as a spirit-guide for a tiny little girl. Her name was Ruby, and on April the 14th, I saw her entering the physical world. Little did I suspect, that the elders had known exactly, who this person really was, which they would entrust to me. It was my other half. My soul mate, which I had not found in my lifetime, was my charge. And then one day, after leading me through an emotional roller coaster of thirty years, this charming little charge of mine decided to frolic with the very dangerous thing, which she should not have touched in the first place. It's called 'Ouija board', and there she was trying to contact the spirit world.

Not knowing how very dangerous it could be, and we on our side know only to well; I had to intervene, after quickly consulting with one of my trusted elders. She left me not much of a choice, as to answer her before someone else could from my side, satisfy her curious mind, and let her doubting spirit know that I am indeed as real and alive, as she herself. Only did I find out much later to my own chagrin and our elder's delight that I had fallen deeply in love with her, and *I* began to learn from her the immense power of love. Even though I was guiding and guarding her, I could not forget everything that had happened in my own lifetime. I still felt haunted by it. As insignificant as she might consider herself, she has done what the elders couldn't accomplish. She freed my soul with her loving spirit, and healed my own spirit entirely. And for the first time, in my whole existence I felt capable of giving my own self in total and first experience of true love. My soul has joint it's other half and is at peace. With that, the poem I felt in my soul was given to the only one, worthy of it.

"From the pits of hell you lifted me
Like a giant beam of sunlight, you walk before me
Following you, I can see myself now,
Casting the dark shadows behind that follow me.
I shall not look back,
For I see only the light of your love.
Ruby, my love, my life, now and forever."

Ruby had listened to Justus in astonishment and visibly horrified at times, her hand clutched to her chest. At no time did she dare to interrupt him. Foremost, because her throat was constricted by her tears, and felt as if she was not able to breathe at times. Shuddering shaking her head, she was asking herself over and over, how much a human being could endure. She had no idea, that the level of endurance could be carried to such heights.

Here she had felt sorry for herself at times when things did not quite go her way. But attending Justus's story she was made to realize, that nothing she had gone through so far could be compared with the pain he had felt in all his life.

"What can I say right now," Ruby said sadly, "to even remotely express, what and how I feel. In my life there was always something, that went wrong and many times, I asked myself, why I was so unlucky. Do you know, that I consider myself fortunate, that I never had to experience anything like that? That a parent could do THAT to their own child, is too far and totally beyond my comprehension." Ruby shuddered.

"Yes, I know it only to well. But even in your society is it still a fact, that children and young people are abused and used in the same way, as I was and worse. Though I was in my twenties already, I felt shamed and guilty, that my mother would even consider something as sick as this. Very few young people ever come forward, and seek help from a source outside the home. Many do not, because they feel ashamed and even think it's their own fault, just as I did. But it is not, and therefore, the children and teens should go to an adult they can trust. Encourage your children to please, TELL. A TEACHER, a SCHOOL

COUNSELOR or a CLERGY from their CHURCH, not to mention LAW ENFORCEMENT MUST be notified if someone has touched them inappropriately. Many kids do not tell anyone, because it is someone they know and supposed to be an adult they should trust. Like members of their own family or friends. No innocent child in this world should ever have to go through, what I had to feel. It is not only, that a person carries the scars of abuse and sexual confusion and frustration until the day they die. The misery and anger stay's with a person far beyond, as I should know. How sad and frustrated our kind elders are in my dimension, is hard to describe. It takes them a long time to convince a grown person that they are worthy of love and respect and that it was not their doing. Even if they have been abused and kept silent about it to hide their shame. It is even more horrifying, that some of the young people think about suicide, because they know no other way out. They feel, that they cannot trust anyone, especially not any adult. Their life is not worth living anymore and hopeless and desperately, these kids decide to end all the pain and silent suffering by ending their life. Believe me dear Ruby; this is not the end of all troubles. It's only the terrible beginning.

Nothing in this world, and I say it again, absolutely and definitely nothing in the physical life could be as horrifying and unimaginably painful as the sudden realization that there is no way back anymore. The worst nightmare is a walk in the park compared to what awaits a suicide over on my side. At least from a nightmare, a waking up will follow. But once a person finds himself in my dimension, it is too late. There is never a waking up and the pain is so intense, for one feels the sorrow and helplessness of the ones, who are left behind. Nobody will hear the cries of anguish from the one in the astral world. There is burning pain of loneliness and despair, and that is hell. A vicious realm of darkness of the mind, where it takes a spirit a very long time to emerge from again if there is ever hope. I was one of the lucky ones. I was taught to pray and the memory of my innocent childhood prayers saved me.

Please believe me, I am speaking from my own experience. If there are people out here in your world, going through very trying times, seek help. Suicide is not the answer. Reimbursement for it is unimaginable torture in my world. Our elders are saddened and sick and tired of it. Ending a life means, throwing the precious gift of God right back in his face and is punished severely. The equivalent goes for taking another persons life. No one has the right to take another's life for material or financial gain. However particular and trying a persons life may be, it is meant to live, not to be thrown away. How many parents lost a teen to the senselessness of suicide, and feel helpless and hopeless. I must tell you that their own life guide is just as helpless for a long time. The male or female guide is not able to get through to this sad spirit, who took his or her own life, unless he or she has powerful help. And that's the help of the family, left behind. Prayer from the whole family and their loving thoughts sent over into my dimension is a good way to start. Remember that thoughts are waves of electromagnetic energy and are well received and understood by a spirit. If that is upheld, it is of utmost importance and is immeasurable help to our elders and the person's guide, to bring a spirit back from the darkness of his mind. And believe it or not, the peace and serenity of a healed spirit can be felt by the loving family, if they only would try. No one was there to pray for me. That's why it took my spirit such immense time to emerge from my own hell. Love is a very powerful travel insurance to the light as I told you once before. Nobody in the world is able to measure the depth of love, from a parent to a child, but we can. Remember, that no soul should ever feel as alone and isolated from love and kindness, as I was and many still are. How many mothers in this world would be happy and willing to take their child into her arms and tell them, that they love them and will always be there for them. It is not to late. Right now, take the spirit of your loved one in my world and cradle him or her with all the love you have inside. Be there and pray for them, *not even*, but especially now. Assure them in your prayers, that God and his angels are watching. All our elders would be grateful, and do the rest with skillful compassion and their own love for humanity."

"Oh, Justus, it's wonderful to know that there is help, even for a desperate and lonely soul on your side," Ruby said, while she wiped the tears from her face, "but tell me, what about the spirits, who were killed in a brutal way and lost their life at another persons hand. Are they not angry with the one, who took their life and do they not seek somehow revenge? After all, I as well as others could understand, that a spirit who had his life taken out of the physical body, must feel very furious and cheated for not being able to complete what they had planned in their life. I know, that I wouldn't forgive a person who'd destroy me and keeping me away from my family to put them through the unspeakable pain of loss and separation. Not only that, but I would also hate this person, who had done such terrible deed."

"This is precisely, what happens too many times, Ruby," Justus responded, "that feelings of revenge and hatred actually keep a spirit trapped in between dimensions. The difficulty lies in straightening out the damages that obviously have deep roots. Sometimes, a spirit does not even realize, that he or she has left the physical and is earthbound and bewildered for a very long time. Another reason for staying in the earthbound dimension is indeed feelings of anger and hatred and the seeking of revenge, as you said. Unfortunately those spirits do not realize, that their reactions absorb their positive energy to make them in turn the actual thing, they set out to destroy. Which is malignancy incarnate. Not only do they frighten innocent folks half out of their mind with their antics and harassments. They correspondingly pull their own soul deeper and deeper into darkness, to find that there is no escape. That's why there are many houses, castles, and scenes of crime and even battlegrounds of war, are haunted by trapped spirits who found a definite agitated departure from the physical body. Then there are the countless and senseless additions of spirits, who should not be here in the first place. I mean all those people who have died because of an unnecessary accident. Their number likewise increases at alarming rates. Due to advanced modern technology, we get car-, train-, plane…and other various PDV's all the time. Sorry, I think I owe you an explanation on the PDV's. It means Premature Death Victims. We know that accidents can happen at any given moment, but why for the love of creation aren't persons a little bit more cautious and careful with this precious gift from God. In the wink of an eye someone's life can come to a sudden end on your side, because of carelessness and even senseless thrill seeking. Driving under the influence of alcohol or drugs is another reason for people getting killed senselessly. I have seen our elders many times shake their heads at the utter disregard for life. Another example is mountain climbing without any safety gear or walking a tightrope without a safety net. I could give you many examples, where safety precautions are disregarded and the result is always the same. Terrible accidents in which a person gets either horribly injured or killed before their time. The feelings of accomplishments and high achievements should be acquired by doing something worthwhile and constructive for the advantage of humanity, not for singular recognition and admiration from a very few.

We know, that every human spirit seeks to impress and does want individual praise, however, it should not be done at high risk and by placing their lives or others in grave danger. Besides that we also know, that catastrophe can strike at any moment and take away loved ones by force. Like earthquakes, hurricanes, volcano eruptions and any other natural catastrophe you can think of. But they are well taken care of on my side and feel at peace, surrounded by loving relatives and friends, which have passed one before them. Like I mentioned before, our world is not too much different from the physical. We have numerous libraries, schools as well as other learning centers, which I might state are staffed with the most loving and caring teachers of all times. Learning does not stop and there is no certain time limit. There are parks forests and many other places for rest, solitude and recreation. This is a place, where the need for self expression and respectability by any willing and able individual is as encouraged, assured and supported likewise and more so as in the physical world."

"I might like to think about this school business for a while," Ruby said and wrinkling her forehead. "I do like the idea of reading a lot, though. Tell me, how for instance will someone who is interested in studying music, get his or her hands on an instrument? Where does the material come from, if your dimension is astral, and mine physical?"

"Good question, Ruby, you will recall that I told you about the molecular structure of everything in your world? Whatever has been formed, created and built in your world, an astral replica in my dimension exists from it, and therefore it is just as real to us, as a 'Steinway', 'Stradivarius', or Fender to you. The same goes for books. Every book that has ever been written has its double in our Libraries and though such works have been destroyed on your side, the astral copy is still in existence. Scholars, who were devastated about the many books and scrolls destroyed in fires, like the 'Great Library in Alexandria' are delighted to find out that they are still in existence in our world. You will not believe this, but we do have computers a lot longer than you would think. They are instruments of learning and storing information just like in your world."

"Wait a minute here," Ruby interrupted, "didn't you say that whatever has been build or written, has a replica in your world. How is it possible, that you have computers over there then, if they are in existence only a relative short time in my world? Are you trying to put one over on me?" Ruby laughed.

"Oh no, Ruby, I would not even try to lie to you. You have to remember the old Chinese proverb; 'You can go through the whole world with one lie, but you'll never go the same way back.' Some day, many years from now you will see this side also. If you would find out that I have not been telling you the truth, you would be very angry indeed and kick my butt. I can and will not risk that my dear. I know your temper," Justus finished with a wink.

"Well then explain this to me. I can't figure this one out on my own," Ruby demanded, sipping some more of her coffee.

"Ouch, this is not going to be easy, Ruby. Think about the universe. How many planets and life sustaining suns are out there. And I am talking right now only about this one universe. There are billions and uncountable universes beyond this one. All just as big if not bigger and endless as this one. Would our creator really waste all this space only for one intelligent species? I think not. The earth is only one of countless planets in this one universe alone that are inhabited by intelligent life. Others far away are in existence for a much longer time than this planet. They each have gone through the same or similar prehistoric times and trials and tribulations as earth had to undergo. Including wars. However, they are far more advanced than the earth is in science and technology. This is going on eternally. Time is eternal. There is no beginning and there is no end. Nevertheless, the laws of physics and chemistry are in all the universes the same. You can see now what I am getting at. Since there were always planets with intelligent beings in all universes, we have computers forever already. It is hard to imagine for a living human being. Your five senses are making a supreme effort to fooling you into believing that there is a beginning and an end to everything. Since your own physical body is born at the beginning and at the end dies and decays, it is illogical for your mind to comprehend eternity. A healthy human being has these five senses to live in the physical world."

"Well, some have only four or even only three of these senses," Ruby grumbled.

"However sad and frustrating it may be for the individual, it is interesting to observe a blind or deaf person. Other senses are keener and are trained to substitute for the sense that is impaired," Justus said.

"Do you think that this is fair to be born blind or deaf? Why can't our bodies be perfect and function until we die? Wouldn't it be a much better place to live if everybody would be healthy and not going senile and suffer from Alzheimer's disease, as many older people have to experience," Ruby interrupted once again.

"The human physical body was not meant to be perfect. Since you are in this body for only a relatively short period of time, it is faulty and clumsy. The human body is meant for reproduction and a stepping stone for the spirit to get used to and being aware of it's own existence. Therefore it is not meant to exist forever. Of course it would be nice if everybody would be born healthy. As hard as it may be to understand, Ruby, being impaired has its good sides also. Let me try and explain, how we see it over on my side. People who are born impaired require care and help in many situations in their life. They are your teachers and are helping you to develop your spirit to learn compassion and love. I could give you many examples. But that list would be as endless as time itself. You can set your mind at rest. People are only impaired in the physical body. Once they are over on the other side they are in a perfect body. They are jubilant, once they find out what great purpose and impact their own physical existence had on all the people they came in contact with. Not one of them is angry or sad that their physical body's were far from perfect in the physical," Justus explained.

"Am I to understand then, that people who have lost extremities, are getting them back?" Ruby was incredulous.

"Oh, Ruby, you are such a child sometimes," he laughed softly, "of course these people will get their arms and legs back. Can you imagine going through eternity with missing limbs. God is Love and Mercy, not some sick puppy."

Ruby yawned delicately and Justus noticed.

"I think you should seek your bed for tonight, Ruby. We will talk some more tomorrow." Ruby gladly agreed.

CHAPTER 34

The Truth of it All

Once again, Ruby sat with Justus in her living room on the couch and this question had been burning in her mind all morning.

"You had said just yesterday, that there are other planets with intelligent life. So, you mean to tell me that there is something to the myth of space aliens after all? I myself have never seen one. There are many other people who claim to have had encounters. What I don't understand is how they can get here to our planet. No human could travel at the speed of light. That is what they would have to do if they are really here to visit us. How do they do it?" Ruby questioned.

"I was afraid of that question. my dear. I am not sure if I should tell you. You might not like the answer. Or you might think I'm making this up." Justus smiled amused.

"Oh well, it can't get any more crazy than me speaking to you," Ruby laughed, "come on now, you made me curious. I really would like to know." Ruby wiggled on the couch.

"Very well then, I will try to explain this one also. I have told you about the human spirit leaving the body at the moment of death. As you experienced in your mother's house it can also occur while you are sleeping. This happens sometimes without your doing. However, it can also be done at will. Don't laugh, there are indeed people they practice this form of astral travel and do enjoy them self greatly. Nevertheless, those are only a very few. In other worlds it is not only a few. There, people are trained from an early age on to leave their body at will, with the aid of certain drugs. Those people are so far advanced in their technology that they were able to construct a bio chemical suit almost like a body that is nearly human, including inner organs. This suit is able to withstand the rigors of space travel at the speed of light. At space training centers they are trained to leave their body and inhabit this bio chemical space suit and how to make it move. Conversation is strictly done by mental telepathy. That's why they don't have any or hardly any mouth opening. Once inside the suit, they don't need to eat either since it does not require any nourishment other than certain drugs to keep the organs functioning. You see what I am getting at now?" Justus asked.

"Yes I think I do understand. What about their bodies at home? Do they die if the rightful owner is gone for a too long a time?" Ruby asked concerned.

"I was getting to that, Ruby. They are in a drug-induced suspended animation and are well taken care of while the people travel through space. That is still not all. Since some other worlds are as far advanced with their technology, as this planet will be in a few thousand years, they have done space travel for millions of years already. So they have space stations all throughout the universes with the little suits inside, waiting for an owner. You will ask me now how do they get there? Here is another thing that will be hard to believe. At the moment they fall asleep at the care center, their spirit travels through space at the speed of thought. Arriving just about momentarily at the station in space, which over time has been also developed and modernized, they just 'slip' into the bio chemical suit and off they go for a visit to another planet, including earth. That's the whole secret to their space travel. Remember throughout history fine scientists and scholars always came up with new discoveries and inventions. Most of those inventions were developed and are now super jets, helicopters, televisions, fridges and the list goes on and on. Think of what it might have sounded like to people two thousand years ago. They would have laughed and call anyone out of their mind if they would have been told that we will some day travel in cars, planes and now in space shuttles. You see, everything has to come and develop in it's own good time. The beginnings are already in the making. There are many scientists in this world today who are taking a very close look at the human psyche. They know and realize that there is more to the brain then what meets the eye," Justus pointed out.

"You expect me to believe that? That sounds a little too far fetched even for me. I mean, I realize that it is possible to leave the body while sleeping. That does not mean that I would do it willingly. It scared the daylights out of me the first time around when I thought I had died. Are those people not scared like I was?" Ruby asked.

"Like I said before, they are trained and it is considered a perfectly normal thing to do. They are not only welcoming the freedom to travel like this, they enjoy this within the circle of the whole family. They can visit other far away planets and observe life there without being seen. They do not interfere and are punished severely if they would try. So you see, earthlings can rest in peace and have nothing to fear from them," Justus explained.

"That's not what I heard. There are a number of people out there who claim to have been kidnapped and all sorts of experiments have been performed on their bodies. So don't tell me there is nothing to fear. What and who gives them the right to do that. We earthlings are not lab rats for them to do with us what they think and want. We are still humans with a spirit and a mind of our own, thank you," Ruby said tartly and slightly angry.

"So you think they are bad? Not quite so, Ruby. They are actually trying to do something good for the human race, like they have been doing for thousands of years already. Let me explain that a little better. Just as a planet is born, it will also cool down and eventually die, so that no life is possible. In a few million years, life as we know it will not be possible on earth anymore. Therefore we have to find a different planet to live on. I know, it may seem like a fairy tale. However as sad as it appears to be, the sun will not be a sun forever. It also seems like a long way off. Nevertheless the course of nature cannot be stopped. That is where our little green men come in. They are taking samples from human bodies to find the right environment to be our next planet to exist and live upon. It would be senseless and hopeless for the human race to inhabit a planet where life is possible but the reproductive organs would cease to function after a few years or after a few decades and longer. Some of the planets can sustain life. However, certain bodily functions become impaired or cease to function all together due to certain radiations from the planet itself. This is not what we want and this is not what they want. I told you a few moments ago that they are far more advanced in science and technology than we are. They are also far more advanced in spiritual matters. Since they leave their body at will, they know about the after life. They know about the creative force we call God. They know about cause and effect. If they do not follow the teachings of love and compassion, they are not worthy of an eternal afterlife in peace and harmony. Just remember, that all intelligent life is created in the image of God. Think that they live millions of galaxies and miles from this planet. Nevertheless, they are just as curious about life on this planet as you are curious about them. After all, they are not much different in spirit.

Knowing the human race however and having had nasty encounters in the past themselves, they try not to get too close. They know that people over here shoot first and ask questions later. We are not even trying to understand. Whatever doesn't fit into our concept and is strange, we kill. What a shame. All they are trying to do is prepare the human race to be transferred some day in the distant future to another planet. They have done this with other planets and their inhabitants and some day in a few million years the earthlings will be just like those space travelers helping other dying planets. Then the earthlings will be considered little green men, who, by then are living on a different planet already. You know the saying, 'History has a way of repeating itself'. Just that it not only happens on this planet. It happens throughout all universes. I think you understand now that everything that is happening here on this planet, has happened in some form and to a certain degree on countless other planets already. They had wars and any other disaster you can think of on earth. Floods, Quakes, Volcano eruptions, storms and similar weather conditions and seasons.

Unfortunately, on most planets that are chosen, because they have atmosphere and plenty of water, there are still creatures alive that would see humans only as prey. So they will have to go first. In the case of this planet it was huge creatures we called dinosaurs. Only after they had perished was the human race introduced to this planet. Now you see that we can also explain why there are people with different colored skin and other variations of appearance are living right here on this planet. Once upon a time they all lived on different planets. However, as you can see even to this day, they all have the same organs and extremities. That gives us proof enough that life on other planets will always take on the same forms and shapes as right here on this one."

"You are getting me in really hot water here. No religious leader in this world would believe a word of that. They will call this hogwash and other names that cannot be found in dictionaries. They will still like to stick to the Adam and Eve story. And scientists will stick to the theory of evolution. So, which is true?" Ruby interrupted concerned, wrinkling her brow.

"In a way it's a little bit of both. Adam and Eve could have very well been the first couple living in a certain area, where they had been dropped off. However, when you read the bible carefully, they had sons. And those sons got married to girls from Ur. Where did the people from Ur come from? Do you think that God was in a really good mood and he just formed a few more people out of clay and put them down in Ur? Remember, the bible was written by men of faith not by men of science. It was their interpretation of life coming into existence here on this planet. As for the theory of evolution, there is evidence that animals and birds as well as insects have evolved over millions of years. Many of them have become domesticated, others are extinct. They had to adopt to the environment and to the intelligent race called humans. As for the early cavemen, who actually did evolve as science is telling us, they were not so lucky. Most of them perished due to the harsh climate and environments they had inhabited. The wild animals still roaming the country site killed others. Humans spreading rapidly and increasing in numbers killed many more. Only a very few survived. They went into hiding and don't have anything to do with the intelligent human race. Due to the harsh conditions they have to live by, their bodies have become bigger and stronger with each generation and their skin is covered with a lot of hair. They are very shy and can only be seen by coincidence. There are indeed not many left. Today you call them Bigfoot. Even though their intellect did not develop much, they adapted to the environment. So think Ruby, if man evolved from apes, then why are still apes living in this world. It doesn't make any sense. Why didn't they evolve and develop into humans. God has a great sense of humor about all of this. He knows only too well, that people are a curious bunch and will try to figure everything out. Try as they may, they can only theorize. People really never change. Thirsty for knowledge and new things. However, when someone comes along and is trying to shed some light on the subject, they scream bloody murder. Denial and accusations are the first reaction. Then comes defense. Whatever they have believed so far would have to change. That means they would have to change their way of thinking. To change their way of thinking, they would have to admit that they were wrong. Well, human nature is not that far yet. John the Baptist was right. Pride comes before the fall. Sad story. It happened before and it will happen again," Justus said with a sigh.

"Now wait a minute here. I have changed my mind and I am glad I did so. I believe in the human race. In time they'll come around. As you said yourself, everything has its own time. There are still a million questions I want to ask you. Now I don't know where to start. I think I'll start at the very beginning. I am not an astrologer, however this question is bothering me for a long time already. How did this universe come into existence?" Ruby asked.

"I knew you would give me something difficult to answer," Justus sighed again and continued, "I'll try the best I can. So bear with me on this one. Think of the human body. It is made of millions of cells. They die up and renew them self. Now imagine each cell being a universe. They die up and renew themselves also. It is said that this universe came into existence by a big bang. However, this universe only renewed itself just like a cell in your body. So do all the other universes. This is going on eternally. It's hard to understand, I know. It goes further yet. You are only one person with millions of cells. There are about six billion people in this world. Each person with millions of cells. Add all those people together, and then add their cells. This is a number that nobody could imagine. The zeroes that this number would have would reach around the equator endless times, if you add all the other intelligent beings in this universe alone. That's how many universes there are. It goes on infinite. It has been going on forever and it will go on forever. I told you just a little while ago, that this planet and the sun will not be here forever. It takes billions and billions of years for planets and galaxies to die. To God this is only another day at the office. Only a moment ago his spirit created another new universe. To us in our time it is billions of years. Every universe is a cell on and in God's body. Continuously and eternally renewing themselves. Only God does not have a body, which will die. He is pure spirit. Spirit does not die. Spirit has no beginning and no end," Just finished.

"Wow, my head is spinning. This is immense and hard to comprehend. Each universe being a cell of God's body? This makes me feel like an ant in front of Mount Everest, trying to climb the sucker. What I don't get is, if there are countless universes, why are we the only ones where a Christ was born?" Ruby scratched her head.

"What makes you think that? Every planet with intelligent life realizes and sooner or later comes to recognize the *spirit* of the Christ. They may not call him Jesus. Nevertheless, they do get to know him. Our society was introduced to this pure and wonderful spirit two thousand years ago, inhabiting the body of a man named Jesus. The man was indeed anointed with the spirit of the Christ, which is in turn God himself incarnate in a human body. Therefore, he did not fear death as the end of life and tried to make it clear during his lifetime and after the crucifixion as he came back to prove, that life was everlasting. Others on different planets know him a lot longer and yet others will get to know him later when they are ready. Like I said before, everything in it's own good time. God is not in the hurry. Nobody can take the second step before the first one. You know that God gave us a good hint how everything is happening. Look at each planet. They are all round. Start walking around the equator and if you are gone around once, you end up at the same point where you started out. You might meet different people and see different animals. The landscape however will be the same. So it is with the circle of life for all things. Around and around we go. Continuously and endless like a wedding ring," Justus explained.

'"Tell me about it;" Ruby laughed, "I feel like I'm going in circles. Are you willing to answer me another one of the difficult questions? Since we were talking about circles, is it true then that our soul is also recycled in a new body? I am not sure I want to come back here. Once is quite enough for me," she huffed.

"Just as I had suspected," Justus grinned, "you would want to know about that too. Reincarnation is a very ancient belief. People in all corners of the world tried to make themselves believe, that being poor or sick must have deep roots somewhere in the past. They were asking what they had done to deserve this sort of unkind treatment. Since they didn't do wrong in this life, they must have been doing something wrong, way before. Perhaps the next time around is therefore going to be better. God does not recycle souls. Going through the harshness of physical life is enough for a soul to realize its existence," Justus pointed out.

"Then how come, there are so many people who claim to remember past lives. Are they just delusional or is it wishful thinking?" she wondered.

"Neither, Ruby, they just can't explain why they are having those experiences. Very well, I'll try and explain this one also. Remember what I told you about the brain. It sends out electro magnetic impulses on a certain frequency. It is receiving information on the same frequency and acts as well as reacts upon information and stimuli. No two people send or receive on the same frequency. It is possible however, that in a state of deep relaxation a person can by accident tab into another persons frequency. Here, another explanation is necessary. At the point of physical death, a persons life experiences and emotions are not simply going away or vanish into nothingness. Feelings and emotions caused by interaction with others and even toward material things are still in the air, so-to-speak. Now, if a living person is sleeping or hypnotized, they can see and hear and even feel portions of another's experiences. Only because their frequency is nearly the same as the person who is long dead. However, they will see, feel and experience only small portions of significant events that have occurred in the 'dead' persons life. Mostly feelings of great joy or great despair and fright are responsible, which in turn are felt and experienced like the sleeping person's own. Since time and places are different from their current life, the only logical explanation would therefore be a previous life.

Now here is another astounding fact. It also happens with identical twins. Their frequency is very similar. Often they feel each others pain if one gets hurt. Many mothers also have the same connection to their own children. They suddenly feel panic and just know, that their child has been hurt. They are either woken up out of a deep sleep or they just drop the dishes in the sink, which they were about to wash and clutch their heart. They just know that something awful has happened to their child," he explained.

"I remember seeing stories like that on TV," Ruby clapped her hands exited, "especially on 'Unsolved Mysteries'. Now it makes sense to me. There is however another mystery that I would love to understand. What you just explained are things that already have happened. How about people who have a premonition. They can see an event that is about to occur. Or they dream about it. Can you shed some light on this one also please?"

"I certainly can, Ruby. Several months ago I told you that everybody alive has a spirit guide, weather they believe in it or not. Nevertheless the guide is with them from the moment they are born until the moment they die. I also told you that a spirit guide is not allowed to interfere unless there is danger of terrible injury or even premature death to their charge. They can warn about an event in a dream or agitate a person to the point of sudden panic that something is about to happen. Some people will act upon this warning and will keep them self or a loved one out of danger. Unfortunately, many do not listen to the little warning voice inside," Justus said.

"Why is that? Are their sprit guides not as good as others who get through to their charges? Or are they not as nice?" Ruby worried.

"No, Ruby, all spirit guides are indeed nice, efficient and well trained. It is their living charge that is unfortunately not open to a warning. Many are so busy with their daily lives and worries about making money and succeed in their career, that they have closed their mind to their own sixth sense. That is the frequency they keep willingly dormant. They rely only on their five senses. Many accidents and even murders could be avoided if people only would listen. So, if someone is about to board an airplane or train or get into the car and is suddenly overcome by a sudden feeling of panic, heed the warning. Not always is it a warning of physical danger however. It could also be a warning that there is a nasty person on the ride, who would be a nuisance later on. In case of a car, check the brakes and all other vital parts whose malfunction could lead to disaster. Just listen to the little voice inside. It's there for a reason. We are not there to hurt, we are there to help and avoid danger. It doesn't only take the sixth sense. Sometimes it's just common sense. Millions of people in this country and worldwide believe in God. Why is it, that they won't give him the benefit of a doubt to actually give each soul individual care and protection from danger? Whatever they want to call it, may it be Angels or Guides. It does not make any difference. They are there to stay," Justus said.

"I hope you are not getting mad at me right now. You must have been one of the people who did not listen to the little inner voice then. Otherwise your life would perhaps been a lot different and you might have died much later," Ruby said.

"You are absolutely correct, Ruby. I was one of the arrogant self-centered people who did ignore and totally disregard warnings I received. Believe me, I had plenty of warnings all the time from my trusted friend, Robert. I somehow knew that it was wrong as soon I went out to drink and gamble. I knew all of it. Yet I did not listen to the little voice inside that was telling me, that sooner or later I would have to take responsibility for my actions. Sooner or later there would be an accounting. Little did I know that I would have to pay the ultimate price. Little did I know that my death was only the beginning of the payment. Now I can see, that even my wretched life can bring some good. Through telling my story, I can perhaps prevent someone from making the same mistake. By the way, I am not mad at you. You were merely pointing out the truth. Even if the truth hurts sometimes. It doesn't change facts," he smiled.

"Oh I know that the truth hurts sometimes. It's just, that people don't like to have their nose rubbed in it all the time," Ruby admitted, "but there is another thing that I am afraid of, Justus. People, reading this, might think that if the after-life really exists, then they might want to get there earlier if it is really so nice there and death is nothing to fear."

"Haven't you heard a word I said, Ruby? Nothing will be nice, if someone is forcefully and purposely ending their physical existence. As I said before, the punishment for suicide is severe," Justus admonished gently.

"You can say whatever you want, even with all I know now, I still fear death. Why is that?"

"Because the process of dying and propelling the astral out of the physical into the other sphere of life is in many cases associated with pain and suffering. No one likes the idea of that. You are no exception, Ruby."

"That's correct, Justus, I don't like the idea of that. As I told you before, I would like the idea of reading, once I am in your world. But I also like to take a drive in my car. You wouldn't happen to know a good mechanic over there, who could fix my window?" Ruby giggled.

"I think, I mentioned this before, Ruby, that we have everything here, except things we do not need over here in my dimension, which is cars and trains and airplanes. We do totally nicely without, since we journey just a little faster. We do, what many people sometimes would love, to be capable of doing. We travel by the speed of thought. As daft as it may sound to you, but we transport our bodies of sheer compressed energy with one thought to a distant destination in the fraction of a second. Sound's fun right? But it's true. As everything else I have told you is true, Ruby. So now that you know, just about all there is to know, I would ask you, to do my friends and me a big favor. Formulate everything in your notes into a manuscript, and keep it safe. The time will come, that you must speak for us. I will let you know, when that moment comes. Right now it is time for you to rest. It has been another long night. Good night, Ruby. I'll always be with you and keep you safe."

"Good night, Justus," Ruby said, "I promise to keep the folders with my notes always safe. I do as you asked."

Nodding thoughtfully, Ruby slowly closed her notebook and placed it with the many others, which she had jam-packed with her observations already.

CHAPTER 35

The Time Is Right

Ruby waited many years, and now she was told that the time was right. Praising modern technology and the Lord, for giving the people such ingenious minds, Ruby sat on her chair that stood by the computer and began to write. Carefully and patiently instructed by her friend, teacher and loving companion in spirit world, Justus. She began to recall her timid beginnings, when she had her first encounters with this spirit world. Still, Ruby had questions to ask and said to Justus,

"If I am to write this all down, will there be at least some people who believe me? I know what I might have told a person 23 years ago, had they told me a story like that. It does have something to do with a certain jacket, and a padded room. On the other hand, I also know, that there are many people out there, who have had similar experiences and, fearing ridicule, are not even telling their family or best friends. How am I going to approach people with the subject, without sounding wild and crazy, Justus, I really could use some advice here."

"First of all," Justus started laughing, "it is not many years ago anymore, and millions of folks are open minded about the spiritual world. Think of the shows on television that are trying to take a serious and investigative approach to this topic. I can mention only the few, but you should remember them as well. There is 'Sightings', The Extraordinary', 'The Other Side' and 'Unsolved Mysteries', which confronted the topic frequently. How much more enhanced convincing do people need to realize that there is a definite interest to this mystery indeed. You understand that this is a period when people need to know a little more about us, whence faith alone is seemingly not enough anymore. In a world where people kill each other for, so it seems the pleasure of it, and have no regard for human life we must step in and come forward to issue specific factual indications that we are totally undeniable, and we really exist. In my sphere we have come to recognize, that religious beliefs alone are not sufficient any longer. The only way we can make people understand, is by disclosing exactly in detail what we are, and why there is life after physical death. I think that I gave you more than enough explanations not only to be able to believe, but to know beyond the shadow of a doubt that you can come forward and open people's minds to our world. So many scientists have tried and failed because they did not get the details from the source, which you are very familiar with, which is the beyond. Even if there are some people who do not believe, what have you got to lose? Bear in mind that they will find out all on their own that you were right?"

"Yes I know, that they will find that out some day, but in the meantime there are other people who might think that I am one of the mediums who can get them in touch with their loved ones on the other side. How am I going to clarify that this is, first of all, unethical to the people who have lost a loved one. Secondly, I think, it is totally unnecessary, for a third and absolutely strange party, to get involved in something so very personal," Ruby said, somewhat concerned.

"As I had told you once before, we are not a circus and do not perform any hocus pocus either. Performances are better left to professional actors. We wish for serious consideration, not to enlarge doubt with so-called psychic powers, and blow wind into skeptic's sails. Know that the only thing some 'Psychics' are interested in is how to 'enlighten' people's wallets, not their spiritual minds. Our elders, and other decent human beings over here are enraged at this and do understand that there is a number of people who want to know if their loved ones are well. Let me assure them that they are as aware and alive and as well off as I am. I also told you what to do, in case of suicide, or murder or accident. Pray for your loved ones, and send them loving thoughts. It will help them to go on in my world and heals their spirit. We are very sympathetic of church groups and families who make it their first priority to pray for a beloved one regularly. In turn, it also helps family and friends who are in a state of grief and sorrow, to soothe their broken hearts, and find inner harmony in a surprisingly short period of time. The only things that should not given into, are feelings of hatred, anger and self-pity. We have seen to much of it and know what kind of damage it can do," Justus said sadly.

"Now I know, that I might tread on very thin ice here, but answer me one other question, Justus," Ruby asked, "there is only one God, why are there so many religious denominations and which one is right?"

"Oh, Ruby, this is a tricky argument indeed. Just think of people with different cultural backgrounds all over, as well as their past history. Greeks, Romans, Egyptians, Vikings, and many others did believe in many gods and goddesses for just about every occasion. Even the princes of darkness were called upon for power and guidance in their daily lives. Those people were just as mankind is today, aware of a higher power, but did not have the specific facts, as to how to appeal to this immense and powerful creature. Therefore, only a very few who had some spiritual insight were seated into leadership of the mind and called priests and priestesses, they became the mediators between the higher powers and simple people. Many of those priests, however, were fearful of loosing their power over people, and the only way of keeping the slaves in line, was to put fright into their hearts and minds.

They were well aware of the fact that every coin had two sides and where there is good, there is also the opposite, which is evil. It only had to have a name and address. The rest you can figure out for yourself. However, they forgot to mention that every character is born with the potential for evil and has the freedom of choice to either fight his own demons or let evil have its way. Even to this day it is not uncommon for some people to claim 'the devil made me do it'. It is just a bit to easy, to let something or someone else take the responsibility for his or her own weaknesses and doings. The evil lurks in people's minds, not 'out there' somewhere. Now we also know that people actually could become possessed by something, which is evil. Those are spirits who are earthbound, and have not yet found the way to the light. They are still as weak and evil as when they were in the body of the physical world. Somehow, they found a way into a living persons mind and never let go again.

That is why I am seriously advising against the use of any mind altering drugs such as alcohol or any other drug for a reason that is all to obvious. Many times does it happen that a person, who is friendly and kind when sober suddenly changes into a completely unrecognizable and different personality when under the influence. They become vicious and destructive and do not care whatever happens to their loved ones. It is then that you can see that they are seemingly possessed by a complete strange being and do not even know about it. Believe me it will become worse and worse all the time, until the earthbound spirit has taken over the body entirely and has succeeded in pushing the actual and rightful owner into a feeling of almost nonexistence. Now as to your question regarding which religion is the right one, I can answer you, that all of them are right.

As long as they are praying to one Supreme Being, there should be no argument as to what they call it. It's as simple as that. Rituals and ceremonies are performed differently, but those are choices of the individual mind and should not be a reason for saying, 'I am right and the others are wrong'. It doesn't make the slightest difference how a person believes, as long as their mind is filled with love and respect for this higher being and their fellowmen. Fact is, intolerance, ignorance, and stubbornness has led to misery and human suffering over the centuries and will still cost dearly if people do not change their thinking. I know, what you will say again, that it's going to take a few more centuries, or even eons, before people understand that. It doesn't have to be like that. I can't say it any simpler than that. It is definite that there are millions of people who will feel in their hearts and minds, that we have a very good point to come forward at this time."

"You mean to tell me, that we are actually trying to get through to people's minds, though in the past scientists and religious leaders have done their best to do the same and to what result. People are still too preoccupied and busy with their own problems to listen to what I have to say. To be honest, I feel not too positive about succeeding. You know, as well as I, that I am a realist and do not believe in miracles," Ruby said resigning and shrugging her shoulders.

"Ruby, have I not given you enough material for argument to the truth. I explained to you many things, which were not known ever before and should therefore be reason to at least get people to give us the benefit of doubt. And with what you know now, you do have a responsibility and owe it to anyone who will listen. I know, there are many waiting to be informed to what is really going on in your world and mine. I know you are thinking—'why me',—and I ask you, why NOT you. Remember that in all human history every person is born to accomplish something worthwhile, and to use their mind to the best of their ability. Success is not measured by how large and famous your name is, but rather by what you have added to another individual's life. You should have given them a reason to go on with joy in their heart.

The trash collector who will go home after a hard day's work to his family, and makes his wife and children feel happy and loved, is as successful as the doctors and nurses, who saved a life during their shift. Also the lady cleaning an office on her shift, who is making her family happy, is no less successful than the famous people in the entertainment industry who bring laughter and bliss into the peoples' hearts and minds. If you make a difference for the better in one other human life, you are successful indeed. It is a miracle in itself if only one person out there will stop and start to think for one moment that perhaps you might have a point. I know that there are more then one, and we can do quite a bit of convincing. Even though there are skeptics, and doubting Thomas' in this world, they will in no way be able to argue with a fact, which can be recognized and proven by way of the science of physics and modern technology. We know that every event in this life has a physical law.

Nature cannot act against her own established course of law and a part of nature is our mystery-enshrouded creation in the dimension beyond the five physical senses. It could be too easily argued that artificially produced energy is only ALIVE in the wire to any machinery and having reached it's destination to serve it's purpose, then will cease to exist and is simply gone. That is factual for energy that is produced by humans, but not for the 'bundle of energy', which possesses unlike artificial energy, life force and intellect. Our bodies over here do not in any way defy the law of physics. We don't expect the science of mankind to change, but rather to accept that there are merely a few more possibilities to be considered. Believe me, we are not expecting miracles either, save hope that a few serious minded researchers will assign the given information a thorough investigation and consideration.

This head-in-the-sand ignorance and contradiction displayed by skeptics over numerous years will eventually have to logically rationalize the existence, expansion, and the continuum of intellect into higher vibration spheres. We are a rather stubborn bunch over on my side too, and delight in people who are embracing the other dimension as a beautiful reality of creation. Until now, my world was mostly hoped for and believed in by a whole lot of people of every religious denomination. Replacing faith with facts is not the intension. Our aim, to strengthen faith and hope by giving the facts, proposes to benefit existing mankind and countless future generations to an immeasurable degree. Facts can be proven, by anyone who will listen to logic," Justus said.

"Justus, I understand that we are taking a very big dip here, but I do not wish to be considered a new tutor of the 'New Age' movement. There are too many of them, however well meaning, already and some of them are genuinely interested in an improved world. Unfortunately, some others are merely interested in fame and fortune, and at the point of disclosure of their terrible misleading of masses of people, have led to disappointment, as well as disillusionment. There are also numerous books and articles on this subject with opinions and theories, which defy reason, logic and nature itself. How can I come into all of this, with this new breakthrough, and still be considered a normal person. What assurance can you give me that I will be believed and successful," Ruby asked.

"As all those who are serious about investigating our world, you have the truth and indisputable facts on your side, and nothing and nobody can ever change that. The method of the ostrich will not work for always, and sooner or later scientists will have to, however grudgingly, admit that the world is not flat, why pardon me, wasn't that a fact formerly discovered? Only a few hundred years ago, this verity needed breakthrough into the logic of science and the rational intellect as existing fact. A few centuries back one could not have claimed that the time would come when human beings will be able to step into a big machine that would lift them into the air and carry them to a different part of the world. Today nobody thinks twice of purchasing airline tickets to visit relatives in Europe or other parts of the world. Everything has its time for discovery and to be proven as an existing fact. My dimension is an existing certainty that needs to be proven beyond the shadow of a doubt. We have come to realize that, and are willing to give a few answers as to why we cannot be seen, heard, or felt by the physical world. I have given you all the answers to those questions to the best of my own understanding, and can only pray, that there are a number of people in your world who will listen and can certify the truth of the matter."

"I can only presume," Ruby said thoughtful, "how much comfort it could be to many families in this world who have lost a loved one and do not know for sure what it is like in your dimension. I realize that many books have been written on the subject, but more or less were speculative and theoretical and couldn't even be considered as facts. Yes, Justus, I am positive that we have more than sufficient evidence to get people thinking in the right direction. With the help of modern technology it will not be too difficult to prove once and for all that your world is as real as mine."

"Wonderful, Ruby, just think of how many hopeless people there are in this world who see no way out but to end their own life. We must stop this madness at all costs. There is not one day that we do not receive a sorrowful soul over here whose troubles have not ceased, but are only just beginning. If we can make them think twice, before doing the unthinkable, we've succeeded to an immeasurable degree. Now I believe you also realize the reason, why I would be chosen for the task. I took my own life and know first hand what unspeakable agony is awaiting the disembodied spirit over here. They suddenly must realize that there is no way back and nobody will be capable of hearing their cries for help. One good example would be to visualize oneself in a dark cave where the entrance is suddenly blocked, and nobody is around to help to free the poor soul inside. At first there is panic, and then fear and hopelessness. So begins the vicious cycle of torture, which only the one inside will understand. Sinking deeper and deeper into despair, the soul inside the cave finally faces death. On my side there is no merciful death, the feelings of fear panic and hopelessness are increased, perhaps a thousand times stronger then the poor one in the cave will ever experience. Love is the only cure to help a suicide victim. We also know that there are many fine institutions in the world, which are willing to help a person who is thinking about the unthinkable. If they feel, that there is no hope and no sense in going on, please contact a help-center at any time and at once. Our elders on my side dedicate a lot of time and effort to help, but they are plainly at their wits end and now need help themselves. Please, Ruby, help."

"Yes, Justus, I will do the best I can, but tell me, who are the elders on your side? People might want to know if the elders are the angels we have heard from in the past many stories."

"No they are not angles, the elders are people like you and me who have lived a normal life and are spiritually advanced to such a stage that they are motivated by their love for human beings to bring another soul to a higher understanding of oneself. Angels are beings who never have lived in a physical body, and are pure BUNDLES OF ENERGY with a celestial body, which consists of a much higher density of energy structure than our astral body. Therefore they radiate with a brilliance of light to which I cannot compare anything remotely in the physical world. The only thing that comes to mind would be the sunlight, which hurts your eyes, but the celestial light doesn't, it illuminates our dimension eternally without darkness. Sound's far fetched right, but that's why people in this dimension have no concept of time's passing and can truly feel that they were here for a longer period of time, even though only a few moments passed by or the other way around. Many people have left their body and had a glimpse of our dimension, which they've described to doctors, nurses and family members, who would mostly shake their heads in disbelief and even doubt the sanity of the person who had the experience.

Thanks to modern medicine and technology today it has become possible to bring a physical body back to life by using the tool a soul does respond to. And that is ENERGY. Shocks of electric charges to the body will pull the bundle of energy back to its physical structure. Not only a pair of paddles in a hospital will cause this, but also a person who is performing CPR can pull back a person's spirit. By being in a highly emotional state, they throw out their own shock waves of energy at increased frequency and it is received by the spirit. Provided doctors and nurses measured their own rising level of energy while frantic efforts are made to save a life, they would know what I am trying to say. Thoughts are strength and energy of ethereal structure, and like attracts like. What we also know is that every life can't be saved and sustained if a physical body is damaged to such an extent that it has become impossible for a spirit to re-enter. Unfortunately, the brain cannot receive commands from this life force, 'bundle of energy', if left without oxygen for too long. That is why the other organs sometimes can be sustained and can function with a machine. However, the real persons are not present in the physical body anymore.

Doctors know from experience that a brain-dead person is not coming back. They know that eventually other vital organs will cease to function as well because the life force is no longer present to stimulate the part of the brain, which is responsible for proper reception, and interpretations of the subconscious commands from the actual person. We know how hard and heart breaking it is for a family to take a person off of life-support. However a loved one here is well aware of their feelings and does indeed understand that the motivation for a decision as harsh as this is love and respect for their past loved one. Disregarding this let me also point out that in the event of any indication that there is the slightest activity in the brain, it is possible for a spirit to re-route certain ordinance to the body. There have been more than one case in which patients seemingly miraculously recovered, baffling scientists and medical experts alike."

"I can recall a few of such cases myself from watching TV," Ruby said smiling, "but don't you think that this is a tricky situation where some families, and also doctors find themselves in at times. I can conceive, that people would rather cling to a ray of hope than to think of pulling the plug. I know that I myself could not make such a difficult choice as that, and then live with the knowledge for the rest of my life, who came to this decision. When do you know for sure that it is ethical and morally appropriate to stop another life, even with the good intention to free them from suffering. You are getting me into hot water here. I would like for you tell me that if life is that precious, do we have the right to take it at that point?"

"As I said before, Ruby, it is entirely in the individuals hands when making that decision. If it can be justified from a medical point of view that there is no life inside the physical body, lest it is sustained altogether artificially and organs don't function on their own, it is time to consult the doctor, the clergy and their own conscience for help. Let their own love for the person be their guide. That is the best advice we can give, and assure some peace of mind that their loved ones are surrounded by loving and caring relatives, who are helping the newcomer adjust to this new state of being in existence. Since spirits over here instantly realize that life goes on, they don't get to suffer separation anxiety and sorrow, for they know that they will be reunited with the ones left behind in time. Therefore they can reconcile with the current situation quickly and joyously. There are, otherwise, a few amusing surprises if a newcomer finds that his lost leg or arm is restored and functions quite well without pain.

Many people who have lost an extremity feel sometimes strange phantom pain in their missing parts and cannot explain why they still feel, as if the arm or leg is so vividly present, even though they are not. It's very simple and natural, the three-dimensional so-to-say SNAPSHOT which is the astral, is subconsciously trying to imitate this missing physical extremity without being able to lower its vibrations down to the physical level. Confused by the five physical senses, the astral is present and can be felt, but cannot be properly used. You see now that everything in this world has some rational explanation. But, are people willing to heed? That is an entirely different matter. Even our capabilities are limited to a certain extent and our bodies are bound to the laws of nature. There are still fields that have not been explored yet, and the possibilities for confirmation are always open for investigation. The human mind must just look in the right direction, which in itself holds most of the secrets to discovery and is the key to universal laws.

Require the conscious mind to investigate the inner self, and you will tap into a world far beyond your wildest dreams. You will determine the truth and justification of a being in existence, which is living inside a human body and cannot deny it's own existence and awareness of being. Life can be beautiful Ruby. Do not embrace it with only your arms but with your entire self. Too many people have fallen into the trap of their five senses and are cheating themselves out of a whole universe of treasures. 'Seek and you shall find' was not an intended hint to help you look for your lost house key. Mark my words that praying for the numbers in the lottery is not a prayer that is likely to be answered. We see them as a somewhat humorous addition to some people's foolish wishes, as long as they do not become an obsession. Remember that I know about gambling, and recognized that the winning streak is enduring only, as long as you can hold on to your winnings. The treasures in your soul, however, are there to stay and nobody is able to take them away from you once they are found."

"I understand, Justus, it's equal to the knowledge I did acquire from school. Nobody can take that away either. If only kids today would get the importance of a good education into their minds. I am sure you remember what my grandmother used to say, that stealing is allowed, as long as it is done with eyes and ears and not by hand. Good advice if I have to say so myself. It's a shame that so many people are dishonest and take other people's property without thinking, how hard it is these days to make the money. I feel bad for the millions of people who have come to the sad conclusion, that they can't trust anybody anymore. Honest people have to lock themselves inside their house and the criminals are having a field day on the streets. Tell me, Justus, was it always that bad in the world?"

"Oh yes, Ruby, there were always dishonest people in this world, and unfortunately this is not going to change overnight. We are well aware of it on our side and are only too happy, if one of the corrupt persons suddenly makes a complete turn and changes on his or her own. Even though it was as hard for them as it was for the famous Mister Scrooge. Nevertheless, should everyone keep the phrase in mind, 'what good is it for a man to gain a whole kingdom and lose his soul', which was true thousands of years ago and is still true today. Let me put it another way, perhaps the phrase 'the last shirt doesn't have pockets' will say a little of what there is to be expected. You will take all your wisdom and knowledge into the next life but not your material possessions. There are many who came to realize too late what was meant by it, and are saddened by the greedy relatives who are in a big hurry to get their hands on the inheritance from the dead. We know, as well as you, that money is essential in the physical world. Save to pay the bills and put food on the table. However, charity and compassion toward the less fortunate should always be kept in mind. Believe me, Ruby; there is enough for everybody, and more riches yet to come. No money in the world could ever replace the unimaginable joy of someone discovering his or her own potential for kindness and compassion. Correct, Ruby, how much credit would you deserve if you only love the ones close to you. It's just as easy to be good, as it is to be bad, except in the end it's more rewarding. I had to learn the hard way what that meant."

"Wouldn't it be wonderful if some people would just stop and listen for a moment. However, I know, that there are still many who will stubbornly insist, that their way is the right way and all the others are wrong."

"Ha ha, Ruby, this reminds me of a man who was just as stubborn. Let me tell you about him. Many years ago, this man was a member of the church. Only he did not believe in the 'afterlife' and found himself suddenly in our dimension. Not only did he want to wake up from his 'dream', he outright refused to believe, what had happened to him. Guess what he is doing today? He is one of the elders, and his first priority is to take newcomers under his wing who did not believe at all in the 'hereafter'. He is the kindest and warmest spirit one could find. Well loved and highly respected by all of us. There you can see that it is never too late to change. Even more so, I must agree with a wise man, which had said that more wisdom could be acquired by listening than speaking. It does no good to anyone, to be full of self-importance and insisting that their way is the only right way."

"Tell me, Justus, isn't this communication between us some form of channeling? I have heard of other people who are supposedly in contact with your world and I am afraid, to even think of the possibility to be confused with any of them."

"Ruby, those people claim to be in contact with beings whose earthly existence could not be proven for two very simple reasons. Either they are supposedly exalted beings that never have lived in a physical body, or they have lived thousands of years ago where their existence cannot be proven and there are no records. Perhaps this can be avoided in our case. Anyone interested can check for himself or herself that I was born and lived in your world. My given name, as you know, was Justus Ziegler. Here is a hint, Church records and perhaps even the INTERNET. That should be enough even for the most stubborn skeptics to verify my not too long ago earthly existence. What we are doing is not directly channeling, for the simple reason that we are speaking to each other and I am not speaking through you to others. Some of the things I have told you are nothing but common sense and are how most decent people feel in this world. It does not take a genius or an exalted spirit to figure that out. Furthermore, you don't go into a trance and no other circus is required to talk to me. We have explained in plain and simple enough words why we can, in fact, talk to each other and how it works. There are a number of people out there who are practicing the same form of communication with their own spirit guide and will be thrilled to find out what you know. Believe me, Ruby, we are not the only couple in the world who are in con-tact, but we might be one of the few lucky ones to shed some light on this still mysterious fact. Let me just sum it all up once more for a quick overview to what we have been talking about:

1. How does mental telepathy work?

Answer: The mind is actually this 'bundle of energy', the real you, which is sending and receiving like a radio station on an individual frequency; and, can be consciously trained to receive and send from and to another frequency, which is another person in the astral world.

2. Why does mental telepathy work?

Answer: Thoughts are ethereal waves of energy, and are propelled by electromagnetic impulses to their destination either consciously or subconsciously throughout the physical body or willingly into the ether toward another recipient with intellect in the astral world.

3. Where exactly is the other dimension?

Answer: All around you and throughout the universe at a higher vibration level.

4. Why can't we see into the other dimension?

Answer: The physical eyes can only perceive molecular structures, which vibrate at the same level as the physical body.

5. Why is there another dimension?

Answer: To ensure intelligent conduct by the human spirit after the relatively brief time in the physical world.

6. What is the astral body?

Answer: The exact three-dimensional replica of the physical body, to live and conduct yourself in, while in the astral dimension.

7. What is the astral body made of?

Answer: It consists of an ethereal structure of energy, similar to molecular structure. It is the identical three-dimensional snapshot of the physical body taken by the core of the subconscious part of the intelligence, which is responsible for breathing, heartbeat etc. and is also responsible for infinite continuum of life.

8. How are spirits able to materialize in the physical world?

Answer: By consciously lowering their astral vibrations to the physical level, therefore equaling their ethereal structure vibrations to that of the molecular structure of their former body and vibrations of the physical world.

9. How does the brain work?

Answer: By receiving energy in form of electromagnetic impulses from the intelligence inhabiting the physical body, and operating on one unique frequency to direct the human form.

10. From where does the brain get the energy to function?

Answer: From the intelligent 'bundle of energy', the core of intellect. It is aware of it's own sense of being, which would not be able to function without a vessel we call body in the physical as well as the astral world.

11. What is a soul or spirit?

Answer: The soul is the part of creation sensitized to experience feelings and emotions. The spirit is the conscious awareness, acting intelligently on the soul's behalf.

12. From where do souls and spirits originate?

Answer: They are tiny separate particles of a whole super intelligence, which is responsible for all creation, and continuation of life in all dimensions.

13. What is the sixth sense?

Answer: The sixth sense is a part of the spirit, which is connected to its base of origin; therefore often times can be felt as the intuitive or precognitive sense of the human mind.

14. Does everybody have a guardian?

Answer: Most definitely yes.

15. What is the tunnel-experience?

Answer: The slipping in of spirit and soul to the astral body and transformation of the newly acquired form to a higher dimensional frequency.

16. What are soul mates?

Answer: Two separate halves of one particle, one male and one female, who are temporarily separated due to the inhabitants of two separate physical bodies, but not necessarily during the same time-span.

17. Will we ever be re-united with our soul mate?

Answer: Sooner or later, but definitely yes.

18. Is 'physical' contact still possible in the astral dimension?

Answer: Due to the fact that the astral body is a ethereal structure of energy and is needed to manifest and conduct oneself in the astral world, it feels entirely the same as the former physical. Therefore contact by touch is also not only possible, but just as welcome to show affection and love.

That should be the final answer for now, Ruby, and I can only pray that I have done my job well. Let me tell you that I am happy and proud of the trust the elders have bestowed on me. However without the help of a living person in the physical dimension it would not have been possible. Thank you from all of us over here on my side. Now let's put it to paper and tell a few more people what we know."

"You don't have to thank me, Justus," Ruby replied with a smile, "I only hope that people will listen. But I do have something for you, which I'd like to share with all my friends and which comes from the bottom of my soul."

Ruby's Answer

I did not lift you, you did ascent
Out of the shadow, from under the tree of life
You are not following me; you let me go in front
And what you see is merely the reflection of your love for me. The
brilliance of our love is enveloping us both
Bathing our souls in eternal light
Our love knows no end, we are blessed

Epilogue

Once more and one last time, many years have past. It is the year of our Lord…ah well, we let the Lord decide. Ruby is cleaning the table and placing the dishes in the dishwasher. Bending, a strand of white hair is falling into her face. Impatiently, she wipes the misbehaving hair out of her face and turns the knob to set the dishwasher in motion. As much as she loves her three daughters and grandchildren, she is glad to be alone again. She is looking forward to reading a love story, which she bought at the supermarket earlier. She did not mention anything to either one of her daughters, but she was not feeling too well. Her left arm somehow seems to hurt. The pain was radiating and even the ribs on her left side are being affected. Perhaps she pulled something while making a wrong move. Knowing all three of her persnickety daughters, they would have been dragging her to the nearest doctor. Ruby chuckles softly. Where had time gone? It seems just yesterday, that she changed her daughters' diapers. Now they have children of their own, some of them are starting college soon. Her oldest granddaughter plans to get married. Making herself a cup of tea, Ruby curls up on the couch and in great anticipation, she opens the book. Reading a few pages, her eyes are getting heavy and she pulls the little blanket over her feet. She decides to rest her eyes a bit and places her reading glasses on the little table. Ruby closes her eyes and drifts off into sleep.

How long she had been napping, she did not know. Suddenly a sharp pain throughout her whole left side takes her breath away. She can't breathe. She struggles only for moments to stay conscious. But the pain is overpowering her senses and she seems to fall into darkness. Her eyes are still closed and everything is still around her. She becomes vividly aware of the stillness and opens her eyes. 'Funny, the terrible pain in my left side is gone', Ruby thought. Swinging her legs about, Ruby gets slowly up from the couch. Ah, one of her grandchildren must have left the light on in the room down the hallway. Strange, this light is brighter than usual. Slowly, Ruby walks toward the hallway and feels suddenly, that the hallway is getting longer and wider. The light seems more distant for some strange reason. Puzzled, Ruby turns around and faces the couch. It had been many years, since she had had the experience, but she had never forgotten even a detail. She remembers, how frightened she had been, as she woke up in her late mother's house and saw her own body lying there on the bed.

Once again, Ruby is seeing her own body and this time, she is not frightened. Instead, a calm and wonderful feeling goes throughout her whole being. A soft smile is curling around her lips as she is looking at the body on the couch for one last time. Turning, she feels herself entering this long hallway, which seems suddenly to be all around her. With incredible pull she is now drawn toward this light. She can feel familiar presences around her but she cannot see them. Her eyes and her mind are focused toward the light. She seems to move at acute speed now and finds herself entering this sphere of light. Ruby looks down and feels cool soft grass on her naked feet. She notices and marvels, that her hands and feet look and feel like that of a young girl. Slowly, her glance goes up and she finds herself standing in the middle of a meadow surrounded by majestic mountains, streams and beautiful trees at the distance. She becomes acutely aware of a presence, which is familiar only to her. Ruby remembers and her whole being is enveloped in unspeakable joy, as she sees him standing there.

What seems to start out as a run turns into flight, for Ruby's feet don't touch the ground, as she moves toward him. He opens his arms and with a cry of joy she is melting into his arms and into his safe embrace. Slowly, her face turns up, she looks into his eyes and she takes his face in both of her hands,

"I love you Justus"

Justus smiles and is pointing with his eyes behind Ruby. She looks into the smiling faces of her mother, her grandmother, her aunts and uncles and some of her relatives, which she had never met in her lifetime. Strangely, she knows them as well. Her mother Martha is chuckling softly as she opens her arms to greet her daughter. Neither Ruby's mother nor her grandmother look a day over thirty of age. Ruby is not surprised and a giggle is trying to escape her chest. She remembers Justus' remark many years back.

"We don't need plastic surgeons. Nobody got wrinkles where I live. Our bodies are perfect."

She knew it all along that he was being truthful. Turning back, she once more moves into Justus' arms and with the light of eternal love in her eyes, she whispers with her lips against his,

"I am yours for all eternity."

"I know my love," he whispers back.

"We've got a wedding to plan. You know, I already invited my best friend Kat," she adds with a twinkle.

"Welcome home, Ruby," Justus kisses her and gently turns her around by her shoulders, "first things first my love," he whispers in her ear. Suddenly there is a bright light. A being that seems to be love personified moves toward them. Justus puts his arm around Ruby's shoulder and smiles encouragingly. The being of light points to a scene in a hospital.

A nurse wipes the sweat from Martha's brow. Martha just gave birth to a healthy beautiful little girl. Unseen by the doctors and nurses, a young man is standing in the corner and a tear is running down his handsome face. He just witnessed a miracle. The miracle of life eternal as this little girl will find out some day, many years from now. Her name is Ruby. It will be Ruby, now and forever, his eternal soul mate.

THE END

Printed in the United Kingdom
by Lightning Source UK Ltd.
126063UK00001BA/2/A